BEACH THRILLER

ALSO BY JAMIE DAY

The Lake Escape

One Big Happy Family

The Block Party

BEACH THRILLER

JAMIE DAY

ST. MARTIN'S PRESS
NEW YORK

This is a work of fiction. All of the names, characters, organizations, places, and events portrayed in this novel are either products of the author's imagination or used fictitiously.

First published in the United States by St. Martin's Press, an imprint of St. Martin's Publishing Group

EU Representative: Macmillan Publishers Ireland Ltd, 1st Floor, The Liffey Trust Centre, 117–126 Sheriff Street Upper, Dublin 1, D01 YC43

For information, address St. Martin's Publishing Group, 120 Broadway, New York, NY 10271.

www.stmartins.com

Designed by Donna Sinisgalli Noetzel

The Library of Congress Cataloging-in-Publication Data is available upon request.

ISBN 978-1-250-35823-3 (hardcover)
ISBN 978-1-250-35824-0 (ebook)

First Edition: 2026

10 9 8 7 6 5 4 3 2 1

For Sue and Harry,

with love and gratitude

BEACH THRILLER

Chapter 1

The Watcher

Everyone has secrets. In this town, I know them all. I'm always watching, waiting, learning. It pays to understand people's weaknesses. Knowledge can be leverage. But first, you need to learn how to observe. Watch how someone walks. Is their pace quickened? Or are they at ease, body relaxed during a casual stroll? Notice how they hold their shoulders, move their eyes, and use their hands. If you want to understand someone's inner world, don't listen to what they say, watch what they do.

But sometimes you have to look even deeper. On the surface, Beauport appears to be a charming, peaceful setting—perfect for people watching. But peer into the shadows, and you may uncover lies, betrayals, and conspiracies that span generations. These stories are mine too. I'm deeply connected to it all.

As I wander the streets—unseen, unheard—I collect people's secrets. I gather their misdeeds the way a banker accumulates cash. Information is my currency. And this town could make me rich.

So who am I?

I could be anyone—the shopkeeper who pockets a hundred dollars from the cash register, thinking no one is looking; the tourist who does the same with a pair of earrings she can't afford. Maybe I'm the busker outside a coffee shop, singing for tips. Or perhaps I'm the cop down the street—big and brawny, waving to kids zipping past on their bikes, unaware that the blue uniform hides a darker side.

Or I could even be the wealthiest woman in town. Her money and status afford her plenty of time to hide and observe. Though she's old enough to need orthopedic sandals, hers are gold Guccis, softening the indignity. Cartier sunglasses conceal not only her eyes but also her lies.

Then there's the handsome younger man walking behind her. We could be one and the same. He ducks into a pub to meet someone for happy hour. Is it his lady of the moment or a business associate with whom he's conspiring to close a big deal? Whatever he orders off the menu, his true desire is something neither romance nor money can satisfy.

This town is full of people who harbor hidden truths—and I could be any of them. But I can't be you, Holly. You are special. *You* are the one I'm most interested in. I know you've come to Beauport for a reason. You seek answers, and you believe you'll find them here. But some questions are too dangerous to ask.

You see, everyone has secrets, including me. And I'll do anything to safeguard mine.

Anything.

Chapter 2

Holly

The visitor's guide read: *Welcome to paradise! Beauport, Massachusetts, is the perfect seaside getaway and a must-see destination only an hour outside Boston. Here, glorious sunshine glistens off whitecapped waves, sandy beaches stretch for miles, and salt air rejuvenates the senses and soul in equal measure.*

Enjoy picture-worthy sunsets, languid days on the beach, shopping along the bustling boardwalk, and restaurants galore. Step back in time to simpler days and quieter pleasures.

Oh, give me a break, thought Holly Sinclair, who had picked up the marketing brochure at a rest stop on her way into town.

She wasn't just a visitor. Holly was among the fortunate few who owned an ocean-facing beach cottage in this highly sought-after tourist town, where real estate was expensive and hard to come by.

It was a desirable destination for many, but for Holly, it was the *last* place she wanted to be.

As she cruised along the shoreline on a beautiful summer day in late June—windows down, music blaring—Holly realized she missed New York and the anonymity it provided. There, she could blend into the crowds, but here, there was no escaping her past, no matter how many beachgoers flocked to town.

Bright side, Holly, bright side, she told herself. She'd always loved the ocean and did her best writing with her feet buried in the sand, a legal pad on her lap, pen in hand, scrawling out that brutal first draft, trying not to outthink herself.

She felt a flash of optimism. Maybe she'd go to the beach and get started on the book that was supposed to revitalize her career. There were still several hours of sunlight left in the day. Too bad she had no idea what she wanted to write.

Holly was relieved she had pushed through her exhaustion to arrive before dark. The house would be dreary enough in the daylight after years of neglect. She had also ignored her body—too many hours in the car and an ill-advised decision to fill up on gas station snacks. At least the ocean breeze pouring through her car windows lifted her spirits, if only a little. This truly was a piece of paradise. The past couldn't fully tarnish that reality.

She marveled at how, even after all this time, the scenery remained as familiar to her as the tune playing on the radio: "Landslide" by Fleetwood Mac, a song about the inevitability of change. She sang along, grateful that her only companion was Chester, her cat, curled up in his crate in the back seat. He wouldn't judge her singing voice.

The tune was apropos. There'd been so much change in Holly's life lately—too much, too fast.

She turned forty the day her eviction notice arrived. It felt like a lifetime ago, even though it had only been a few months. Holly was talking to her best friend and former college roommate, Shae, over FaceTime. They were discussing Shae's birthday gift for Holly—a copy of the book *Meow Mindfulness*. Good lord, that title alone! It was the hottest self-help book on the market, with over a million copies sold, all thanks to a rehomed cat named King Fluff.

Holly tried not to envy the author's success, especially because she wrote so passionately about how King Fluff pulled her out of a depression spiral. Still, it was the literary equivalent of the Snuggie or Crocs—an idea so absurd on the surface that few would expect it to have any commercial appeal.

"I'm not going to write cat books, if that's what you're thinking," Holly had said.

"I didn't get it for you to copy someone else's success. I got it because I think you need some help, love."

"From a Buddhist cat? Hell no, I don't," Holly said, though a voice inside her head screamed, *Hell yes, you do.*

"I'd call it more of a 'self-help' cat. And you're deathly unhappy—I know it, you know it, and this cat knows it."

Shae was right, of course. Holly wrote about people like herself—those on a seemingly endless quest for self-acceptance and self-love—which should have been cathartic, but instead kept her trapped in a cycle of rehashing the same issues over and over and over.

Holly might not love the book, but Shae would forever be in her heart. They didn't see each other nearly as much as both wanted. Shae had moved to California eons ago, became a fraud detection specialist for a major bank, and married a guy who sold medical devices. They had a couple of gorgeous, sun-kissed California kids.

Meanwhile, Holly had fucked up and become a writer. If she had realized how hard it was to make money as a novelist, she might have followed in her mother's footsteps and become a nurse.

But to this day, she believed she possessed no other marketable skills. Writing was her livelihood, and she would *have* to write here. Beauport was now her home, and not just for the summer, as it had been when she and her sister, Anna, were children, spending the season with their mother and grandfather in the beach cottage.

Now she'd be completely alone with no end date to her stay. Carol Sinclair's funeral had taken place not long before Holly was evicted from her Brooklyn studio apartment. What would her mother say if she knew her prodigal daughter had returned? Some cryptic remark, she guessed, that reflected her beliefs in the supernatural. *I knew the ghosts would lure you back.*

Holly continued to sing along with Stevie Nicks, mildly off-key, as she drove past the famed beachside boardwalk in her trusty Kia Soul. According to the salesman, the Kia was the cheapest, most reliable vehicle on the lot. For once, a man had been honest with her.

She had bought the car shortly after her novel *Radiant Sun* got long-listed for the Women's Prize for Fiction. It was a massive honor, but she was often long-listed. She was never the winner.

It was no surprise to see the boardwalk jammed with tourists bopping in and out of the charming shops, numerous galleries, and popular restaurants, all just a short walk from Holly's family home. But there would be no shopping for her today.

At half past three, Holly pulled into the driveway of 6 Sea View Lane. Tufts of beach grass lining the road swayed in the wind as if saying hello. Her house stood directly across from a steep embankment that descended to a sandy shoreline. Crescent Beach got its name from the curve of the cove that mimicked the waxing moon. It was one of the longest beaches in Massachusetts, extending from her home all the way to the barnacle-crusted pier jutting out from the busy boardwalk.

Today the seas were calm, the skies bright and clear, but Holly's inner barometer remained dark and turbulent. She had arrived carrying the same guilt and shame she'd left town with eighteen years ago.

One look at the house brought it all back—the good, the bad, and the downright tragic. It was a kaleidoscope of memories, a rainbow prism of glorious nostalgia twisted into something too painful to face: beach days, boardwalk ambles, ice-cream bellyaches, bike rides, and bonfires that had turned into police sirens, screams, heartbreak, and a lifetime of regret.

She pushed a strand of light brown, wavy hair off her face, reflecting on how much she had changed over the years as well. She still had a small frame, kept her hair long, and had eyes that matched her sister's—hazel with flecks of gold—and of course the dramatic cheekbones that were a Sinclair signature. But inside, she was tougher, more guarded, no longer the same girl who had walked these sandy shores.

Holly pulled herself out of the past to take in the sorry state of her home. She had to give credit to the caretaker, who had made good on his promise: The boards that had once covered the windows, protecting them from the elements, had come down. Several stacks of plywood lay neatly on the front lawn, ready for disposal.

Thanks to those boards, the windows were in decent condition, but the rest of the house looked dreadful. A combination of sea spray, rain, and wind had stripped the front of the house bare, bleaching the once-sturdy gray shingles into a sickly pale, weather-beaten facade. Some spots were bare where shingles had been blown off entirely and rot had set in.

Not only was the exterior weathered and worn, but some local kids had taken advantage of her family's absence and spray-painted graffiti beneath the first-floor windows. Holly was glad that Joey loved Emily, but she certainly didn't need his devotion immortalized next to her front steps.

She'd find someone to take care of that soon, along with what appeared to be a lot of other repairs. How she'd pay for those was another matter. A lawyer in town had access to a trust her grandfather had set up to care for the cottage; Holly would certainly follow up soon.

She also needed to contact a landscaper. The lawn would have been in perfect condition if it had been Halloween. Craggy bushes encroached on the windows and vines climbed to gutters that overflowed with debris. Weeds and crabgrass were everywhere she looked, except in the spots where nothing could grow in the rocky soil. No wonder she'd been getting hate mail from her neighbors. With the boards up, the house must have looked like a crack den.

Most people would have been embarrassed, but Holly simply felt sad for herself and her poor little house. It had suffered so much in her absence. She had wanted to sell the place her grandfather willed to her mother, but Carol refused. How many disagreements did they endure over it? Too many to count. But now, Holly felt grateful that her mother's stubbornness was providing her with a roof over her head when she needed it most—assuming, of course, that the roof didn't come crashing down on her in the middle of the night.

"I'm back, Mom." Holly spoke to the heavens, a weightiness pressing on her chest. "I hope you and Anna are watching over me. And if you know anybody who can fix the place up, please send them my way."

She steepled her fingers, even though she didn't pray. It felt like the appropriate thing to do.

Despite the warm day, a chill sank into Holly's bones.

Walk right in. It's just a house. It's not going to bite, she thought. *But it will whisper. It will tell me things I want to forget. Every room will be a reminder of the past. Every creak will feel like a ghost welcoming me back.*

Carol had thought the place was haunted, which was understandable. Ghosts were said to appear after traumatic deaths. And Anna hadn't died of natural causes.

No, Holly's sister was murdered, right here in Beauport. And all these years later, Holly still blamed herself.

Chapter 3

Holly

Before Holly had a chance to slip her key into the front lock, a gleaming silver Acura, sleek as a fox, pulled into the driveway behind her no-frills Kia. A vaguely familiar woman emerged, but Holly couldn't place her face. Chester meowed an alert from his carrier on the front stoop.

The unexpected visitor had shoulder-length, wavy, bleach-blond hair and dazzling white teeth, which she flashed in a smile that was more like a bite. Over her right shoulder hung a fluorescent pink purse that screamed young, hip, and now, despite belonging to a woman decidedly in the middle of her middle age. She'd applied her makeup with a moderate lack of discernment. It was evident to Holly, even from a distance, that this woman's bronzed complexion wasn't from sun exposure.

"Holly Sinclair," she called, voice shrill, practically running with a hand extended, her apple-red nails reaching for Holly like claws.

Holly took the woman's hand because her only other option was to flee. Up close, the air thickened with a floral perfume, reminiscent of air freshener.

"I'm Gail Provost, from Beauport Realty—I heard you were coming to town. I was hoping to catch up."

Holly realized why she looked familiar. This was the same woman who'd been hounding her for years. Gail Provost sent personalized, hand-addressed letters to Holly's Brooklyn apartment with the regularity of a supermarket circular—her smiling face stamped on the upper left corner of every correspondence.

> *Dear Holly:*
> *I'm writing to let you know that the value of your home has increased . . .*

How did this woman know when Holly would arrive? *The caretaker,* she guessed. He had known when she was coming to town and could have easily tipped Gail off. Everyone in Beauport who wasn't a tourist was in each other's business, something Holly knew from experience. She hadn't even stepped into her house, and already she felt the walls closing in.

"I'm so glad to finally meet you in person," cooed Gail.

Holly acknowledged her with barely a smile.

"Come, I'll take your little friend inside." Before Holly could protest, Gail lifted Chester's carrier, jostling it and causing the cat to let out a strangled cry. Holly unlocked the front door.

"Oh my goodness, how stunning," said Gail, trailing Holly into an empty foyer.

Stunning? Holly didn't know what Gail was seeing. To her, the house looked like the setting of a B-grade horror movie.

The furniture—the tables and chairs, the TV console, a few lamps, all relics from Holly's youth—was draped in white sheets, like bodies at a crime scene. The curtains had yellowed to a dull mustard color. Ideally, the trust would cover the cost of cleaners, but it would be up to Holly to clear out the cobwebs and dust, making it livable in the meantime.

"It's only a two-bed, right?" asked Gail, who had plenty of info on a house she'd never set foot inside.

"Yes, but my grandfather slept on the screened-in porch, so it didn't feel small."

Holly pulled a sheet off the couch, her breath catching at the sight of the familiar floral pattern. How many afternoons had she and Anna lounged on this ratty old thing? How many meals did they share in front of the TV, exhausted from a day at the beach?

Instinctively, Holly touched her claddagh ring. The sisters had picked out matching rings at a shop on the boardwalk many summers ago, spending all their babysitting money on what felt like an extravagant purchase. Anna had worn her ring every day. Holly still kept hers on in tribute—a reminder that they'd always be connected, if only in memory.

Gail set Chester down in the living room, heading off to inspect the kitchen.

Holly opened the front of the carrier, apologizing for the woman's brusque handling. Chester was not ready to emerge, his fuzzy gray form cowering inside his crate. Green eyes flashed with reproach. Chester hadn't asked for any of this.

"The stove still works," Gail called from the other room. "Only one burner is out."

Better than the one at my old apartment, thought Holly. She might not have an idea for her next book, but she was going to work in a sadistic, greedy landlord—modeled after the one who evicted her—who dies a grisly death.

She had lived in a rent-stabilized apartment, and he claimed to have made major upgrades to the building as an excuse to justify the obscene (and unaffordable) rent increase. It was bullshit.

She couldn't pay, even if she had wanted to. Her complaints to the Department of Homes and Community Renewal went unanswered long enough for her to accumulate massive back rent. When an inspector finally arrived, he sided with her landlord, who happened to be his cousin. *Unbelievable.*

Holly couldn't believe Gail Provost, either. She ventured into the kitchen and found her plugging in the refrigerator.

"This still works, too," said Gail, patting the sturdy appliance as if it might appreciate the praise. "They don't make things like they used to. I have to replace my modern fridge every five years."

Holly could confidently say there was nothing modern in *this* kitchen. The linoleum floor was the color of coffee-stained teeth, the old wood cabinets were clinging to the walls like desperate mountain climbers, and the round table where she had consumed countless bowls of Cocoa Puffs was scratched and covered in dust. The appliances were all aged white metal with chrome accents. But they still worked, including the refrigerator, which hummed as though it had been roused from a long nap.

Chester finally mustered the courage to abandon his crate. He darted into the kitchen, displaying impressive dexterity despite having only three legs. Holly had known from the moment she laid eyes on him at the shelter, hobbled from a car accident that would have killed him if not for his nine lives, that he would be hers forever—or at least twelve to eighteen years, depending on how things went. She was hoping for as long as possible.

Using the kitchen table as a springboard, Chester climbed onto the windowsill and took in a view of the unappealing backyard. He jumped down, brushing up against Gail's legs.

"Oh my, what an absolute cutie," said Gail, barely paying Chester any mind. Chances were she only paid close attention to things she could sell. "What's her name?"

"*His* name is Chester," Holly replied.

Chester was thirsty. The smarty-pants cat made his way to the sink. But what came out of the faucet was brown and didn't clear, even as Holly let the water run. She shut it off, noticing the countertop around the sink had bubbled.

"I need a handyman," Holly said. "Do you have any recommendations?"

Gail's face lit up like Christmas had come early. "So you're fixing the place up to sell? Oh, let me help." She clapped her hands with delight. "A vacation rental investor would snap this up in no time."

"I have a lot of legal issues to look into before I can consider selling. But I need someone to do repairs so I can live here, at least for now."

Gail smiled, unfazed. "I know just the handyman for the job. Mind if I look around upstairs?" The Realtor was on the move before Holly gave her blessing.

"Be my guest," Holly said to Gail's back. She followed her up to the second-floor bedroom she had once shared with Anna.

The sisters had stayed here every year, from the moment school ended through Labor Day weekend, soaking up summer until it gave its first pre-fall yawn. The bedroom walls were still a vibrant robin's-egg blue, but the dresser with an attached mirror needed a good cleaning.

Two twin beds, their mattresses encased in plastic, lay like prone sentries keeping watch all these years. Everything was as Holly remembered, and it all hurt. She felt as though she'd stepped into a photo album, except everyone Holly loved, all the people who made this place special, were gone.

Gail peered out the bedroom window, marveling at the view, commenting on Holly's good fortune.

The Realtor didn't realize Holly's so-called luck had come at a steep cost: losing her father when she was only a year old, then her grandfather when she and Anna were still in their teens. But the loss of her sister was the most gut-wrenching of all. It happened unexpectedly the year Holly turned twenty-two. Anna was just two years older. Soon after, her mother began experiencing depression-induced dementia. Now Mom was gone, and this house was all Holly had to remember them by.

Some luck there.

Holly stood next to Gail by the window, catching another whiff of her perfume—*Eau d'Argent,* she dubbed it—French for money. Below them, the sea spread out like a vast dark carpet sprinkled with flickering drops of sunlight. Colorful umbrellas dotted the nearby shoreline. As Holly struggled to lift the window, Gail helped pry it open, letting in a blast of ocean air.

Gail sighed, then muttered to herself, "A unique residential property that offers the fortunate buyer an incredible opportunity for seaside living."

Holly's mouth dropped open. "Are you writing the listing in your head?" By this point, Holly found Gail more amusing than detestable. This woman certainly put the *g* in gall.

"I can't help it," said Gail. "The listing writes itself. Stunning, panoramic ocean views, footsteps from one of the best beaches in the

Northeast, and just a stone's throw from a dizzying array of restaurants, galleries, and shops."

Gail certainly took her always-be-closing mantra literally. Holly sniffed the air. "Is that black mold?"

Gail took a whiff, but if she smelled anything, she wasn't dissuaded. "Could be, but nothing a dehumidifier can't take care of."

Eventually, Gail had seen enough. Placing several flyers and business cards on the fireplace mantel, she departed, promising to find Holly a handyman. Chester emerged from the kitchen when he heard the real estate agent drive off. Holly figured he was glad to see her go. But she knew Gail would be back.

At least she wasn't living in the boonies. All the major conveniences were just a walk or a phone click away—including DoorDash.

Holly ate her dinner, a fried haddock sandwich, while sitting in her grandfather's rocking chair, admiring a watercolor her mother had painted years ago. It was a scene of the beach, looking down from their front lawn. The two tiny figures playing in the sand—one in a yellow T-shirt, the other in a pink beach dress—represented Anna and Holly.

Holly didn't have any memories of her father, and her mother never found anybody else after he died. It was always Mom and Grandpa here. His ubiquitous pipe still graced the mantel above the fireplace, next to Gail's flyers.

After dinner, Holly had just enough energy to retrieve her suitcase from the car and undo the plastic on the queen-sized bed in her mother's room, which she planned to make her own. She left a window open, inviting the sea air to wash over her. She had only one blanket, which was more than enough for her and Chester, who lay curled at her feet, keeping them warm.

Holly always had supremely cold appendages. Max Egan, her college sweetheart and first true love, would hold her hand and ask, "When did you pass?" He'd wink, then press a kiss to her chilly cheek.

Max was the kindest, most sensitive man she had ever known. While other boys were swilling beers at frat parties, Max preferred going to the indie cinema or discovering cool bands in underground clubs. He was a connoisseur of ramen noodles, a fan of art openings, and amazing in bed. She would have married him—but trauma had other plans. Through no fault of his own, Max was forever associated with the worst day of Holly's life. Now another woman shared Max's bed and his children, and Holly suspected she had been searching for him (and writing about him) ever since.

Holly drifted off to sleep, bittersweet memories pulling her into a world of chaotic dreams. Eventually she fell into a deeper void, where all thoughts, troubles, and emotions dropped away, her mind finally finding much-needed rest.

She awoke with a jolt. Her eyes sprang open, adrenaline coursing through her, shocking her back to consciousness. Had she heard something overhead? There it was again—a thump or a bump, certainly too loud to be a mouse.

She held her breath, her heart pounding. This was why she hadn't wanted to come back. It wasn't just memories haunting her, it was *entities.*

This wasn't the first strange occurrence Holly had encountered in the cottage. In the initial weeks after Anna had died, she would sometimes hear unexplained noises and see flashes of things that shouldn't have been there. She'd told herself it was grief playing tricks on her mind.

Carol, however, thought otherwise—and for that reason, refused to rent or sell the house out from under her dead daughter's spirit. Of course, this came from a woman who later developed dementia with bouts of psychosis.

"Are you there, Anna?" Holly said into the dark.

No answer, not even a thump.

Great. Now Holly had a new worry to add to her long list of troubles: *going crazy, just like her mother.*

Chapter 4

Holly

The glaring sun woke Holly with the grace of a bagpipe band. She squeezed her eyes shut, pulling the blanket up over her head. Reminder: Install shades as soon as possible.

Holly was up and at 'em at first light, even though she had only slept a few hours. Still, it was a relief not to hear sirens and horns—sounds of the city—blaring outside her window.

It wasn't until Holly went downstairs, Chester padding alongside, that she realized her mistake. She hadn't packed coffee, tea, or any caffeinated beverage. After feeding her cat and calling the exterminator (it *had* been an animal in the attic, she assured herself), but before dealing with anything as mundane as unpacking or cleaning, Holly made her way toward the boardwalk on foot, wondering whether her favorite coffee shop would still be in business.

She took the beach path, following the shoreline. Through the summer haze, the shops and restaurants were visible in the distance. It was a picture-perfect day—just like that brochure described. Boats of all kinds bobbed across the choppy water. The ocean and sky met at the limit of Holly's vision, a seamless connection between sea and air. The clouds were sparse, but the seagulls were not.

She paused at the water's edge, then waded out slowly, rolling up her pant legs as the ocean swallowed her ankles. This was one thing her Brooklyn neighborhood couldn't provide. The ocean had always been a balm for Holly's soul. Yet even with the wind and waves, the sounds of children at play, she couldn't entirely shake a nagging sense of foreboding.

Refreshing as the water was, it was no substitute for caffeine. Holly trudged across the dry sand to a long pier that protruded out into the ocean. At low tide, she and Anna used to explore beneath the pier's sturdy pilings, careful to avoid any rusty nails sticking out of the wood, while pretending the structure was the remnants of a shipwreck. It was amazing how the smell of the ocean infused into the wood could conjure up such sharp, vivid memories.

Holly ascended the sturdy wooden staircase at the base of the pier that carried her all the way up to the boardwalk. Although it was early in the season, throngs of people slipped in and out of stores, many of which Holly recognized from her youth. Her life had changed, but this place had not.

The shops had no shortage of T-shirts for sale, or sunglasses, sunblock, and other beachy accoutrements. The coffee shop that Holly had her heart set on—assuming it was still open—was halfway down the walkway, where cars were prohibited from driving over the sun-worn wooden planks.

She did a little window-shopping, browsing the beautiful paintings displayed in the galleries that gave Beauport its reputation as an artists' community. Soon there'd be long lines at the two ice cream stores, the homemade fudgery, and the Lobster Shack. Tourists visiting Beauport literally put their money where their mouths were.

As Holly passed by the old-timey General Store, which still sold penny candy in glass jars, a woman in a blue shirt crossed her path.

Holly's heart went still. It was Anna—she had no doubt about it. The woman was young and beautiful, with a curtain of wavy auburn hair framing her heart-shaped face, full lips, and hazel eyes that were almost the same shade as Holly's.

Holly's breath caught and the ground beneath her seemed to give way. She took hold of her sister's arm but couldn't manage to speak.

"May I help you?" asked an unfamiliar voice. The woman pulled back, freeing her arm from Holly's grasp.

Holly blinked, coming to her senses. Anna would be over forty now. This woman looked like her, but from many years ago. As the sunlight struck her face, Holly realized this person's features were sharper, more angular, and not much like Anna's after all.

"I'm sorry, I mistook you for someone else," said Holly in a quiet voice.

The woman in the blue shirt shrugged it off. "It happens to me all the time," she said. "I guess I have one of those faces."

Holly gave the woman a half smile. She realized she hadn't fully processed her loss, but did not expect to hallucinate seeing her sister after only five minutes on the boardwalk. But what troubled her even more was the possibility of running into her sister's killer without realizing it. The police files had been gathering dust for years. They weren't investigating anymore.

Anna's death certificate listed her manner of death as "undetermined," a designation used when there was no clear resolution as to whether the death was an accident, a suicide, or a homicide.

But Holly knew better. Houses don't often spontaneously combust.

Anna had died in a fire on the property of the richest family in town. Holly's writing instincts told her there was more to the story. But accidents do happen—as the police had said—and the gas stove that had started the blaze was old and perhaps defective. But cover-ups happen as well.

Clearing her mind, Holly returned to her mission—searching for the coffee shop—but to her dismay, a clothing retailer had replaced it. Good news: There was another not too far away, a savory-smelling establishment cutely named the Bean There Café.

A busker was stationed in front of the coffee shop, nearly blocking the front steps. He wore a gray scally cap and a white button-down shirt with visible sweat stains under his arms. He looked a bit like a singing rat, with pinched features, a pointy nose, and a face weathered by the elements. Dirty scruff covered his sallow cheeks and chin, adding to his unwashed appearance.

Even though she was counting dimes, Holly dug out her wallet to give the man a couple of bucks. He was a creative type, and she always had a soft spot for those, even if he sang off-key and strummed the guitar like he was plucking feathers off a goose.

"Thanks," he said gruffly when she added her bills to the meager sum lining his red velvet guitar case. She had caught the tail end of his rendition of "Sweet Caroline," but when he segued into the next song, "Take It Easy" by the Eagles, it sounded remarkably similar to the previous tune.

Entering the coffee shop, Holly could still hear him crooning. Evidently, so could the employees, who grimaced as if subjected to some form of black-ops CIA torture.

"You didn't feed him, did you?" asked a young man with thick eyebrows and a nose ring, who waited to take Holly's order. "That just encourages him."

The busker switched to a Simon & Garfunkel song that sounded just like the other two songs.

These poor people, thought Holly, suspecting she'd inadvertently involved herself in a local feud. "Does he do this every day?"

The young man's coworker, a petite blonde with the fresh face of a high schooler, lowered her head in defeat. "Every. Single. Day."

Holly grimaced in solidarity. "At least you have a lovely view," she offered, pointing to the bank of windows that overlooked the ocean. Her eyes traveled back to the busker. She watched him clear out his guitar case, shoving crumpled bills into the pockets of his grimy, ripped jeans before strategically placing a single crisp dollar into the case that practically screamed, *Poor me.* Not only was he annoying the baristas with his shoddy renditions of popular songs, it appeared he was a scammer to boot.

On her way out, latte in hand, Holly nearly bumped into an older gray-haired woman. The woman's billowy, bohemian-style skirt caught a breeze as she moved quickly, with surprising grace and fluidity for someone her age, avoiding a direct collision. The bangles encasing her arms—a throwback to the eighties—clinked together from the sudden change in direction, sounding musical. She wore a casual loose-fitting jersey—a look suited to someone who was never in a hurry. Except today, when she'd come barreling into the coffee shop in a rush.

She paused to assess Holly, removing her sunglasses and squinting as though Holly's face was familiar. Her gray eyes matched her hair. They were mesmerizing, like looking into moonstones.

It was rare for Holly to be recognized—she was a self-proclaimed D-list celebrity (a quip she often made at book talks that always got a good laugh). Writers, even the famous ones, were generally known for their words, not their appearance.

"You can't be her," the woman said, her voice hitched.

Holly suddenly understood. Even though Anna was two years her senior, the sisters had often been mistaken for each other.

It clicked for the woman as soon as it did for Holly. "Oh my god, of course, you're Holly."

"Serena?" said Holly, almost at the same time.

The two women shared a quick embrace. Holly was careful not to spill her drink.

"I haven't seen you in ages," Serena said with delight. She pointed to Holly's beverage. "I'm grabbing a coffee, too, but I need to get back to the shop. I left the door unlocked—should be fine in this town, but you never know. Do you have time to sit and catch up?"

Why not? thought Holly. Who better to ask about her ghostly encounter than the local psychic?

Chapter 5

Holly

She hadn't been inside Serena's Psychic Studio since she went with her mother for a reading shortly after Anna's death. Serena was Beauport's most famous medium; everyone who sought answers from the beyond went to see her, Holly's mother included.

Holly didn't *actually* believe in all that psychic mumbo jumbo. You lived, you died, and then you got sent into the great nothingness. But she wanted to have her coffee away from the annoying busker, who was bad enough to make Tom Petty's spirit show up with a cease-and-desist order.

The shop was as Holly remembered. It was inviting, with soft light emanating from an assortment of glass lamps, reflecting off colorful crystals, gems, and pendants likely meant to provide protection to the wearer. Tapestries covered the walls, lending additional warmth to the atmosphere. Holly sat on a plush red chair intended for readings, and Serena took the bridge chair opposite her.

Earthy-smelling incense, strangely enticing, relaxed Holly, like a smoky drug. Wooden shelves stocked full of glittering crystals, various occult oddities, including a deck of gilded tarot cards, as well as books about astrology and the esoteric, competed for Holly's attention. Scattered throughout were statues of Buddha and other deities whom Holly couldn't identify, let alone worship. She felt like she was floating in a spiritual bath connecting her to other realms, realities visible only to those with special sight. Holly's special sight was limited to the reading glasses she purchased at the drugstore.

"You look well," Serena began. "I've been following your career success."

Holly suppressed the urge to blurt out the truth. When it came to publishing, people didn't want to know about the struggle—the reviewers who crafted cruelty with twisted glee; the large chain bookstores that carried two copies of a recent release, if that, thinking they were doing you a favor; the salespeople who looked at Holly like she was a vandal anytime she offered to sign their paltry stock.

Once, Holly would have given a book talk to an empty room if it weren't for two people looking for a place to knit and a homeless woman who stumbled in to get warm. After the talk, Holly tried to give the woman some money, but she took off before having the chance.

"Yes, it's all going quite well—a dream come true." Holly grimaced inwardly at the lie.

"I'm so glad," said Serena. "And how's your mother? Is she here with you?"

Holly felt a sharp stab of grief. She flashed back to the last time she'd seen her mother at the memory care facility.

Her mom looked so fragile; she was thin everywhere, skin clinging to the bone, veins visible. Her hair, coarse and thinning, had been cut short, as though marking how much time she had left. Gone were the blue eyes of her youth, replaced by a milky haze.

Her doctors diagnosed it as pseudodementia, probably caused by depression. According to her MRIs, Holly's mother shouldn't have experienced such a significant cognitive decline. The initial symptoms were mild—fading memory, malaise, loss of appetite. As anyone familiar with the unpredictable effects of grief would expect, they appeared shortly after Anna's death. However, her condition worsened rapidly, resulting in poor recall, insomnia, and grim hallucinations.

The nurses were very attentive. Carol developed a close bond with one caregiver in particular and sometimes seemed to remember her better than her own daughter. The staff treated her mother like family, which made sense because Carol Sinclair had spent much of her career working as a traveling nurse. Sadly, by the time she was under their care, she could barely change a Band-Aid.

Holly had taken her mother's frail hand in hers.

"Mom, maybe we should sell the beach cottage. We could afford better care for you. You could live with me, and I could hire some help." Tears had sprung to her eyes. She didn't want her mother trapped in this gray, depressing room that smelled of bodily fluids mixed with disinfectant.

"Anna is there," her mother answered in a raspy, tired voice.

"No, Mom . . . Anna is gone. It's just me, Holly. Your living daughter."

"She's always there," her mother had said, her voice bolder, firmer this time.

Holly snapped back to the present, returning to Serena, almost forgetting the question about her mother. "No, it's only me, I'm alone. My mom—she passed away recently." Holly felt the familiar lump form in her throat. She cleared it with a hard swallow. "I'm going to live here for a while, fix up the cottage . . ."

Serena's hand reached for Holly's. "I am so sorry to hear that," she said, her eyes brimming with sympathy. "I wish I had known. I would have come for the services. Carol was such a dear friend for many years."

Holly remembered Serena's visits from her younger days. She and Anna would titter at the silly predictions the young psychic gave their mother over coffee or dinner at the cottage. Their grandfather thought it was all nonsense as well. But Serena had been a kind, steady presence in her mother's life, and for that they were all grateful. Carol carried a deep loneliness after the loss of her husband, and Serena's friendship had been a healing salve during their summers in Beauport.

Serena gave Holly's hand a reassuring squeeze. "She's here with us in spirit. I hope you believe that."

Holly returned a forced smile—she did *not* believe it. "Thank you. You meant a lot to my mother. I miss her every day, and I sometimes wonder if she's watching over me, the way she believed Anna did." Holly paused, hoping to escape the flood of emotions that threatened to overwhelm her. She looked out the window at the sparkling ocean in the distance and changed the subject as smoothly as she could. "So how's business? I've come to Beauport hoping it'll be a good place to work—get some inspiration for a new novel."

"Oh, there's no shortage of inspiration in this beautiful town," Serena said. "What are you working on?"

Holly's reluctance to share the dire turn her career had taken clashed with a compelling urge to tell someone—anyone—about her recent conversation with her agent, Dan Bishop.

She'd given Dan her first draft of *The Ashford Orchard Chronicles*. The book wasn't where she wanted it to be. The grandmother's character needed fleshing out; her backstory about the affair with the itinerant apple picker wasn't quite working. And the conflict with the middle daughter, trapped between a desire to appease her mother by staying at the farm and a wish to follow her dreams to the West Coast, could be weightier. But she liked how the characters leapt off the page, how the sisterly bond felt real, with pieces of it pulled from Holly's experiences with Anna. She'd hoped Dan would be able to rush a deal with her publisher, knowing full well that speed went with publishing like patience did a toddler.

Unfortunately, Dan's reaction was worse than Holly had anticipated. Her publisher wasn't serious about re-upping *at all.*

"It's not the book, Holly—it's the sales record," Dan had said over the phone. "They don't want to insult you with an offer that doesn't match your acclaim."

"My acclaim?" Holly was aghast. "Have you ever tried to eat acclaim, Dan? It's deficient in almost every macronutrient. What the hell were they offering?"

Holly heard the number and gasped. "Holy hell, I'm dead."

"There's not a writing career out there that's traveled in a straight line," Dan assured her.

"King. Grisham. Roberts. Their lines seem to always go up."

"You can reinvent," he said.

That was agent code for writing something with murders or bodice-ripping protagonists, which had never been Holly's cup of tea. She didn't need to reinvent—she needed a backer with deep pockets, someone who believed in her talent. Too bad that someone wasn't her publisher.

"Dan, please, last year I was Patron of Letters for the Virginia Literary Awards—that's a big honor. And I got long-listed for a PEN

American Center award only a few years ago. That should be worth *something*."

"It would be if you'd won."

Ouch. That hurt, but Holly worked with Dan for his honesty, not his tact. He had a point. People loved winners, and Holly was always an "almost" when it came to the big awards. She'd been long-listed also for a Massachusetts Book Award and an Andrew Carnegie Medal for Excellence, none of which she'd won. She could call herself Holly Long-List, like a pirate.

"What can we do, Dan?" Holly had asked. "I need money—*stat.*"

"Try writing something that sells," suggested Dan, which had sent Holly's blood pressure skyrocketing.

"I do that with every book," she said. "I wouldn't want my name on the cover of something I didn't think was worth purchasing."

"Holly, I'm not talking about your skill," said Dan. "I'm talking about your approach. Maybe it's time you told a more . . . I dunno, *universal* story. Something geared toward the masses."

"How about a book about learning mindfulness from a cat?" suggested Holly.

Dan's voice brightened. "Yeah, that, but it's already been done. *Meow Mindfulness*—it's flying off the shelves. Have you read it?"

"Fuck, Dan. I know all about it. Hell, I own a copy. I was joking. And besides, it's not really fiction, even though it *is* fiction."

"Right—yeah," Dan stuttered. "Well, at least it's selling. Look, Holly, you're a brilliant writer. But if it's money you need, you may want to broaden your horizons. Next summer, imagine everyone reading Holly Sinclair's first-ever romance or mystery or thriller. Those sell like hotcakes . . . not that I've ever actually bought a hotcake, but the point stands. It could be your ticket out of trouble."

Holly winced as she recalled her first attempt at writing a novel like that, a book she'd started the summer she turned twenty-two. It had all the ingredients Dan told her to include—love, betrayal, revenge, and deadly secrets. She couldn't think of anything more cringe-inducing than rereading those words from her younger days. But even worse was facing the real reason she had stopped writing that story in the first place.

Holly inhaled the incense that filled the room, returning to the moment and to Serena's question: *What are you working on?* Like Holly had never heard that one before. The only inquiry more common at a book talk was: *Where do you get your ideas?* Yawn.

"Maybe I should write about hearing ghosts," Holly said, sheepishly sharing her wake-up call the night before. Although she was certain that the source of the noise she'd heard had a pulse, it was a good segue out of the writing business.

Serena's eyes brightened. "It's probably Anna. Let me come over. I'll do a reading. No charge at all." She was practically begging. "Consider it a welcome-back-to-the-neighborhood gift."

Free *anything* was Holly's catnip, and her pragmatic side kicked in like a reflex. The exterminator she'd called would charge 150 bucks, regardless of whether they found a critter. Holly feared encountering something up there with sharp teeth and beady red eyes. Having Serena beside her would make exploring the attic a little less frightening. Besides, it would be nice to have company.

She accepted the offer with gratitude.

"Wonderful," Serena said. "I'll see you tonight at eight. And you can tell me all about your exciting life as a published author!"

Chapter 6

The Watcher

I've been following you for hours. I saw you as you walked the beach and strolled the boardwalk. Why are you back here after all this time?

Honestly, I can't believe you dared return. Brave, brave girl. But how brave are you? Are you daring enough to dig up the past? Is that what you've come here to do? If so, you might be bold, but you're also foolish.

I watch you take it all in, exploring your old stomping grounds, a place that's seeped into your soul the way the tide fills the salt marsh. You act like a kid at a carnival, awed by the deluge of colors, all the sights and smells, a symphony of sounds that lulls you into a false sense of security.

This place—so familiar—must also feel foreign. How long has it been? I suppose that's not as important as what brought you here. Perhaps it was inevitable. Like a moth drawn to a flame, you've been lured back to where it all started—or ended, depending on whose perspective you take.

But what do you actually know? That's what troubles me the most. This town may be small, but it holds many dark secrets. And I am one of them. I'm invisible to you, just one in the crowd. I'm everywhere and nowhere. I could be hiding in plain sight or lurking in the shadows. Wherever you are, I'll be there, around each corner, down every street, outside your house at night while you're sleeping. You won't know where I am. You won't realize how much danger you're in.

I watch you linger by the shops on the boardwalk. You seem so uncertain—your hands are fidgety, your steps tentative. Are you scared? You should be.

It's my mission to prevent you from discovering things you shouldn't. You are a writer, after all. Have you come here chasing a story, or will one fall into your lap?

Either way, be careful what you wish for.

Chapter 7

Holly

Serena was punctual, knocking on Holly's front door at precisely eight o'clock. She carried a black bag that reminded Holly of a doctor making house calls. Hopefully, her guest wasn't hungry. Holly had gone to the store for some provisions—coffee, cream, a little fruit, some greens, and a few frozen dinners, which were a lot cheaper than DoorDash, but the contents of her fridge still looked sparse. She had checked her bank balance, and the annoying busker certainly wouldn't be getting any more of her dollars. It was a good thing Serena insisted on providing her services free of charge.

Holly wasn't sure how to dress for the occasion. Was there special attire for connecting with the supernatural? Maybe feathers, beads, or a headscarf? She thought about flowing silk wraps or a fringed shawl—something that felt spiritual—but opted for the tried-and-true: jeans and a lightweight sweater.

Serena wore leggings and an oversize linen button-down top. She presented Holly with a bottle of wine and a gracious smile. "I used to buy plants as housewarming gifts, but then people felt guilty if they died. Hope you like cabernet."

Holly seldom drank, but when she did, she preferred something red. "It's perfect, thank you. Would you like a glass?"

"No thanks. I actually don't drink. Messes with my tool kit." Serena pointed to her head. Her hair was wavy and wild.

Holly felt a twinge of jealousy at this woman's free-spirited nature.

By comparison, she was so tightly wound that if she were a watch, her springs would snap.

Chester approached to assess their second visitor in as many days.

Serena scooped him up, no hesitation, as though he were her familiar. "Who is this delightful fur baby? And so quick on three legs. Cats can teach us a lot about resiliency."

Holly made the introductions as she set the wine bottle on a nearby table. "Can you connect with deceased animals as well?" she asked. It was a ridiculous question—cats couldn't speak on Earth, so how could they start talking to us from another realm? Yet Holly found the idea of staying connected to Chester comforting.

Serena set Chester down on a chair, from which he leapt to the floor with his usual grace. "Of course. I can connect with anything that has a soul," she replied.

Holly found her confidence reassuring.

"Many people believe only what they can see with their own eyes," Serena continued. "But there's deep wisdom in the natural world that goes beyond what we perceive with our five senses."

"I'd like to use my five senses as a starting point," Holly said. "Why don't we go to the attic and take a look around?" Her voice held a note of trepidation as she envisioned rabid squirrels attacking her from all sides.

"No, no, that won't be necessary," Serena said. "The energy of this spirit fills your home. I felt it the moment I stepped inside."

Holly shuddered. Her eyes darted around, but she saw only peeling wallpaper, old furniture, and curtained windows blocking the gathering darkness.

Something drew her attention. She thought the rocking chair, where her grandfather had spent hours with a newspaper, had moved, tilting slightly. But when she looked again, the chair remained still. Just another trick of her mind, like the woman in the blue shirt.

"How do we do this, then?" Holly inquired. "Do we light candles, spread crystals, say a prayer? Most of what I know about communing with spirits I learned from *Ghostbusters*."

Serena's warm laugh filled the room. "I promise, I didn't bring an ectoplasmic vacuum cleaner. I wouldn't want to do that to Anna, anyway."

Did Serena truly believe her sister's ghost was here? With them at this very moment? The chill in her bones deepened, but with it came a sense of . . . *hope*? To connect with Anna one more time, perhaps to apologize, to express all the love she had in her heart, would be an amazing gift. But she certainly didn't want Anna tied to this lonely, abandoned building, unable to move beyond her tragedy.

Holly rearranged a couple of chairs around the old card table where her grandfather had taught her to play pinochle.

Serena draped the table with a purple cloth she'd retrieved from her black bag. She kept unpacking: a small quartz crystal ball she placed on a sturdy wooden stand, a candle in a glass holder, a brass bowl, and a clear pouch with a bundle of dried herbs.

Holly sat in a chair across from Serena, as instructed.

"We'll begin by stating our intention and focusing our energy," Serena explained. She struck a match and closed her eyes, revealing a dusting of light blue eye shadow. Tilting her head skyward, she declared, "I am here with good intentions and an open heart. I ask our spirit guides to protect us from harm. If there are benevolent spirits in this house who wish to communicate, I call you forward. Reveal yourselves to us now."

She lit the candle and ignited the sage bundle, which released an earthy, slightly sweet aroma. She placed the smoldering herbs into the brass bowl and set it on the mantel beside Holly's grandfather's pipe, creating the illusion that he was smoking it once more.

Holly silently sent her intention into the universe. If Anna was lingering in the house, Holly needed to know and wanted to help. But a voice in her head told her that only justice would bring her sister peace.

Am I as fanciful as my mom, believing in ghosts? Holly wondered. *What's next? Forgetting to pay my bills? Wearing mismatched summer clothes in a snowstorm?* Holly had watched her mother unravel, with each lost memory and poor judgment call signaling her gradual decline.

She shook off the fear. Lots of people consulted psychics, and they couldn't all be crazy. Besides, she was just humoring Serena before addressing whatever rodent had taken up residency in her attic.

Serena returned to her seat and clasped Holly's hands. The flickering candle reflected in her intense gray eyes.

"Focus on the flame," Serena murmured. "Relax your mind—you might receive messages through the light. I feel a powerful presence." Her voice trailed off.

The candle wavered, though no windows were open, and the curtains hung still.

Holly couldn't deny she felt something. A gentle brush against her leg made her flinch. Looking down, she saw it was only Chester, curious as ever. He pressed against Serena's legs before curling up on the floor and resting his head on her foot. This was unusually friendly for him. Holly thought it might be a sign, but she wasn't sure of what.

Across from her, Serena appeared to slip into a trance. Her head lolled side to side, her expression one of rapture. She muttered words so low that, even leaning close, Holly couldn't discern them. Was it English? Or something else?

"Do you feel that?" Serena asked, squeezing Holly's hand.

All Holly felt was Serena's perspiration.

"Um, maybe . . . No? Not sure—"

"The energy is so strong," Serena said.

And so is your grip, thought Holly, pulling her hands free. She felt torn between skepticism and the eerie gravity of the moment.

"I'm not sure I'm picking up anything—"

"Try harder," Serena insisted. "Calm your thoughts and concentrate."

That felt like a contradiction, but Holly didn't object. She squeezed her eyes shut, trying to feel something with all her might. But the only thing her tight squeezing and concentrating did was give her the decidedly familiar sensation of being constipated.

Her friend wheezed a strangled gasp. Holly's jaw clenched. Would she have to perform CPR? *Shit.* She had done the course, but that was ages ago.

Serena lifted her gaze to the ceiling—or heavens, Holly couldn't say which.

"You have a message from Anna," Serena whispered.

Fear rippled through Holly. She gaped at Serena, who sat motionless, her once-vibrant eyes now dull as stone.

Serena raised an arm and pointed at Holly with deliberate care.

"Anna is here . . . she's always here," said Serena—or not Serena—her voice now a deeper, slower cadence.

Holly's body trembled.

Serena clutched her chest. Was it a heart attack—or heartache? Had Anna revealed her killer's name?

"You shouldn't have come back," Serena said.

Holly's breath hitched. Serena's voice had an unsettling similarity to Anna's, making it seem like her sister was speaking through her.

"You're not safe in Beauport."

Chapter 8

Holly

Please keep in touch," Serena said. She opened the front door slowly, hesitant to leave. Holly felt the ocean breeze pick up. Was a storm coming or had one already arrived? She read the subtext in Serena's strained expression: *Heed the advice from the other side—get away from here and never return.*

Alone again, Holly felt adrift. What would she do now? Pack up what little she owned to escape an unknown threat? And go where? This *was* her plan B.

What type of danger did she face? And from whom? Who would care that she'd come back to Beauport?

Anna's killer. Houses don't spontaneously combust, chimed a voice in Holly's head.

Holly thought a glass of wine might dampen the spiritual chatter. Fortunately, the bottle Serena had brought was a screw top, since she had no opener.

She settled into her grandfather's rocking chair, her glass of wine on a nearby table and a pad of paper and pen in her lap—her sword and armor. It was time to go to battle. No wallowing in self-pity or pondering the occult. As Dan suggested, she could pivot and write a bestselling thriller or mystery novel. Why not? *It's not what you write, it's how you write it!* So what if she'd never written a grisly murder or steamy sex scene? Writing is writing, so she would roll up her sleeves and get cracking on some riveting, pacy prose.

On paper, Holly jotted down *Step One: What am I going to write about?*

She laughed at herself—that standard book-talk question rearing its head once more. *Where do you get your ideas?*

Holly stared at the empty page. Hell if she knew. Nothing was quite as frightening as a pure white, completely blank space to fill. She took a deep breath, summoning her favorite writing mantra: *Be fearless!*

She cleared her mind and jotted down her first idea: *Woman found dead on a train with six other passengers aboard, a conductor, and nobody else.*

Hello, originality! Next . . .

Mismatched couple lost in the jungle after a plane crash, with mysterious cargo on board that someone is willing to kill for.

Sounded like an action-adventure novel and not something Holly wanted to write. (Nor would she write it well.)

She tried again: *Philandering husband meets the end he deserved.*

Yawn. Done a million times. She crossed it out.

Chester approached. Holly looked down at him and wrote: *A woman finds her rescue cat is an alien. He's also a gifted storyteller. In return for her kindness, he gives her the perfect story.*

"So, Chester," she said, gazing into his furry face, "let's have it. What should I write that will sell a lot of copies?"

Chester meowed, presumably because he was hungry. But before Holly could feed him, she heard an unmistakable thud, something heavy falling overhead, like a body dropping.

"What the—?"

A shock wave ran up her spine. She jumped to her feet, scaring Chester, who scampered away—his meal could wait. Some guard cat he turned out to be.

Holly paused to listen but heard only her thumping heart. She stood motionless, waiting for another noise, but all remained ominously silent.

Ghosts don't thump. Do they?

Either way, she'd done enough guessing. She was stuck in this house—and she wasn't going to pay an exterminator unless she saw a creature with her own eyes. If it were a ghost, it wouldn't be corporeal, so she had nothing to worry about. It would be spooky, strange, weird—maybe even inspiration for this impossible book of hers. But if she couldn't touch it, it couldn't touch her. Now, a rabid animal—*that* was a different story.

Holly headed upstairs holding her pen, which wasn't a wise choice for armament—definitely not mightier than the sword. But it was too late now. If she retreated to the kitchen for a knife, she'd lose her nerve to investigate.

First, she checked the upstairs bedrooms. They were quiet and vacant, thank goodness. Now it was on to the hard part—the attic. Access was through a pull-down ladder in the ceiling, and Holly had seldom gone up there, even when she was young. It was dark and creepy, with nothing to see except boxes of memories she'd rather ignore.

The ladder lowered with the creak of old hinges. Holly peered into the dark. Shadows leaked out, vanishing into the hallway light, but the space above loomed like a black maw waiting to swallow her whole.

Up she went, her breath sputtering as she felt around for a pull chain, fearing an animal might pounce at any moment. Eventually she found it and was surprised when the bulb worked. She couldn't say when the light had been changed last. She needed a moment for her vision to adjust, rejoicing in the good news that nothing had bitten her face.

She began searching for signs of animal activity: droppings, nests made of old newspaper or insulation, claw marks on the floor. While she didn't see any rodents, possums, or raccoons there were plenty of markers of her personal history: boxes galore, accompanied by furniture that was too old and beat-up to use, but as familiar to her as yesterday. She would need to clear this space out at some point.

The floor consisted of plywood boards resting on two-by-fours that ran north to south. She could move with ease, but had to watch out for the uncovered areas with pink insulation or else she'd risk putting her foot through the ceiling.

The wall facing Holly had a portal window covered in grime. The space smelled like an old barn filled with heated hay and wood chips. It was certainly an inviting place for an animal to take refuge. But where was the creature hiding? In front of her stood a tall, wide bookcase stocked with dusty books. One book was on the floor nearby, its cover facing the ceiling. *Had it somehow fallen?* Holly wondered.

Even in the hazy light, Holly could read the spines. The bookcase held all the mysteries she loved from her childhood—the Nancy Drews, the Baby-Sitters Club, and most of the Goosebumps series. Could this cunning critter have knocked a book off the shelf?

Holly moved across the room, holding her pen in front of her like a dagger. The space between the bookcase and the wall was large enough to hide a Rodent of Unusual Size. (*Thank you,* Princess Bride.) Her eyes fell on an old broom propped up in a corner. She snatched it, a far better weapon than a writing utensil.

She advanced, holding the broom handle in front of her like a lance. A distinct rustling behind the bookcase stopped her dead. A tense shiver rippled through her. *Got you,* she thought, sure she had pinpointed the location of the invading species.

But before she could peer behind the shelves, another noise stopped her. Holly froze. Her chest constricted, her fingers and toes went numb. It wasn't a scrape, a scurry, or a hiss that she heard.

It was a *sneeze.*

Ghosts didn't sneeze, and it was way too loud for a mouse. She ran through the possibilities—a thief, a drug addict, a rapist, or a killer? A scream erupted from her throat, raw and untamed, full of pure terror. Her instinct was to run—fast—but before she could retreat, a figure scrambled out from behind the bookcase.

She clutched the broom in her trembling hands. *Fuck. Why couldn't it have been a squirrel?*

Chapter 9

Jade

What can I say? I have a dust allergy. I was pretty impressed with myself for staying hidden as long as I did, but you drop one book, and it's game over. Ironically, the title of the novel that made a racket was *Silent Treatment* by Michael Palmer, whoever that is.

I guess I shouldn't have been surprised when the woman screamed. I'm sure I startled her, but she's acting like I'm some kind of intruder—which I realize I am, but I'm not *that* kind of intruder. I admit I have a weapon—a seven-inch buck knife concealed in my backpack. But I'm not going to use it on her, or anybody for that matter, unless I'm forced to. It's for emergency protection only, but this lady doesn't know all that, and she's too hysterical for me to explain.

To my dismay, she also has a weapon—a broomstick tucked under her arm that she flips around so the bristles point at my face. It's not the most lethal choice for self-defense, but it annoys the shit out of me. She lunges forward like an Olympic fencer and swats at me as though I'm a fly. Thick straw bristles rake across my cheek, and it genuinely hurts.

"Ouch! Stop it!" I yell, using my hands to thwart her advances, but she's not cooperating. She's primal, revved up like a modded Honda Civic. (I know a lot about cars, and I'll smack anyone who qualifies that by adding, "for a girl.")

I'll give her credit: She's quick on her feet. But if our roles were reversed, I'd be a hell of a lot more effective with that broom. Too bad I wasn't more careful with the books.

I'm trying to explain myself, but my attacker's not listening to a word I say. She's got her mind made up that I'm dangerous. She's not the first to think that. Just one glance at my dirty jeans, green army jacket, and dyed black hair suggests I'm a deadbeat and maybe even a violent drug user. My dark eyeliner and studded jewelry seal the deal.

But I'm no threat. I'm simply misunderstood, and okay—maybe a *little* dangerous.

"Who are you? What do you want? Get out of my house. Get out!" she yells.

She comes at me again with those bristles. While it doesn't really hurt, she could still poke my eye out. Since my attacker is hell-bent on keeping up the fight, all I can do is shield my face with my hands, but I quickly tire of being her punching bag.

With one quick upward motion, I grab the bristled end of the broom like it's the hair of a girl in lockup.

I yank my arms back, pulling the weapon from Broom-Hilda's grasp. Once it's safely in my possession, I flip it around so that the bristles point straight at my adversary. She raises her hands and steps back, like the broom's a loaded gun.

"Come on, I'm not going to hurt you," I say, inching out from my hiding spot behind the bookcase.

My assurances don't have the desired effect. Broom-Hilda's nostrils flare as she casts a worried glance over my shoulder, maybe fearing that I have an accomplice.

I wish I hadn't made this poor woman tremble.

"I'm not going to hurt you," I repeat, dropping the broom.

Standing in the light, she can now see that I'm not a creepy dude who's been lurking in her home. She is genuinely surprised, and relieved, to see that I'm a girl. Her eyes have softened—most of her fear has ebbed, but she's still on guard.

She holds her ground, eyeing me warily.

"Who are you? What do you want?" She still has her hands up, even though I'm not pointing anything at her.

"My name is Jade Jensen," I say in a calm tone, "and I am truly sorry that I broke into your house, but I had no choice."

Her eyes narrow, assessing me in a way I know all too well.

"How long have you been hiding here?" she asks.

"Um—" I'm not exactly sure. "Hard to say," I tell her, grimacing. "A week and a half, maybe two? When you squat in an empty house, time kind of gets away from you." I laugh, attempting to lighten the mood.

"You've been living in this house for that long? And while I've been here?" She looks both horrified and amazed.

I offer a shameful smile. "Guilty as charged," I reply. "I stayed downstairs at first, but when the boards came down, I moved up to the attic. I figured somebody might show up, and I was right.

"I was sure I was going to get busted the way that nosy blond bitch was snooping around. How pushy was *she*? Lucky for me, the attic isn't a selling point."

"I didn't see any sign of forced entry. How'd you get in here?"

I clear my throat to make way for my confession. "I cut up a plastic Coke bottle, slid the shim between the doorjamb and the metal latch, and voilà, I was in. If you get the lock changed, remind the locksmith to push in the deadlocking plunger." I shrug sheepishly. The lady doesn't look impressed.

"Where on earth did you learn that?"

I'm not about to tell her the truth, so I blurt out the first lie that comes to me. "The internet."

"Right." She shakes her head in dismay. "How could I have no idea that you were here?" she asks, bewildered. "I thought you were a family of squirrels or something."

"You also thought I was a ghost—and that psychic . . . hope you didn't pay her much."

Sadness fills her eyes. "I didn't see a trace of you anywhere. And where have you been peeing? The water wasn't even on."

"It's easy to sneak into the YMCA to use the bathroom. And they have showers. Also, I'm pretty good at covering my tracks." I stand taller, a little proud of myself. "Slept on the couch most of the time until I moved up here. Kept my bag packed in case I had to make a run for it."

"And food?"

"Let's just say it's a good thing there *weren't* squirrels living up here, or, well—you know, desperate times, desperate measures."

She looks sorry for me. I hope that means she's not going to rush to call the cops.

"And it's only you? There's nobody else up here?" Her voice wavers.

"I swear—it's just me."

I think she believes my story, even though she's still jittery.

"Look, let me explain a little more," I say. "It's not what you think. I'm not going to rob you or hurt you or anything like that. I just needed a place to crash, somewhere warm, dry, and safe. I really didn't think anyone lived here. I kind of thought I'd struck gold."

She appraises me anew, cocking her head to one side like she's now more perplexed than frightened.

"Where are you from?"

"Pennsylvania," I tell her. "Outside of Philly."

"Philadelphia?" she repeats. "You're far from home."

"Not far enough," I mutter.

A pale clamminess crawls across my skin. I need a place to stay, and right now I'm not getting generous vibes from my host.

"My parents died." My voice chokes with emotion. When I think of them, it's still raw. Everything that happened, it's all too painful. "They were in a car accident on I-95 about two miles from our house in Bristol—a drunk driver going the wrong way. They were coming back from dinner with friends. It was instant, that's what the police told me, but almost every night, I still have dreams about it. I saw photos of the wreckage . . ."

Tears well in the corners of my eyes. "I wasn't the easiest kid," I admit. "I caused a lot of trouble and put them through a lot. Spent some time in juvenile detention—" I pause because I feel I need to come clean about my earlier lie. "That's actually where I learned how to pick locks with a Coke bottle—in juvie."

"Juvenile detention taught you how to get into more trouble?"

"Ironic, I know."

She raises an eyebrow. "A criminal who can properly use irony. Impressive."

But she's not impressed. Her arms are folded across her chest; her foot tapping a swift beat against the floor.

"We were putting all that behind us when—when the accident happened."

Even though I shut my eyes tight, a salty tear leaks out.

"I am so sorry," the woman says, braving a step toward me. This person, who was ready to wallop me with her broom moments ago, looks like she wants to pull me into a hug.

I take a step back, and she gets the message.

"I don't understand—why did you run away? If your parents are both gone, who did you run from?"

"I'm not eighteen," I tell her. "So I had to go live with my aunt. She's a tyrant—emotionally and verbally abusive. She has three kids, and they're all messed up, just as mean as she is."

She nods, compassion in her eyes. "My name is Holly," she says, extending her hand. "Holly Sinclair."

My face lights up. "Are you the writer?"

Holly does a double take. "You've read my books?" She sounds astonished.

"Oh, you have more than one? I only read what I found up here in loose pages."

The color vanishes from her cheeks. Her hand flies to her mouth. "Are you telling me that you've read—?"

I finish the thought. "Yeah, I read *Beach Thriller*, by Holly Sinclair. I found it in a box in the corner. It looked interesting, and I had nothing better to do. I love to read. It's a really good book. Like, it felt super realistic, even though the title makes it sound like a mystery."

Something tells me I've struck a nerve.

"It's pure fiction." Holly's tone is brusque. "Just a story I made up when I was young and didn't have much writing experience."

"Did you ever finish it? I want to know what happens to Anna. And does Conrad leave that nasty ho, Elizabeth, for her? I feel like Anna's getting herself into a lot of trouble. Am I right? It's so good, but—"

I see daggers in Holly's eyes.

"But what?" Holly wants to know. "Are you a squatter *and* a book critic?"

I clear my throat. "It's just that you're a character in your own novel . . . and it doesn't quite read like fiction. And I read *a lot* of fiction. These characters feel too real—like autobiographical, or a memoir."

A curtain comes down over Holly's face, veiling her emotions. I can't tell if I've given her a great compliment or majorly pissed her off.

"Could I see the book, please?" she asks in a low voice.

I go to the little nest I've constructed out of old clothes and some ratty, yellowing pillows. I dig around and find the dilapidated box holding the book.

"Here you go," I say. "I just want to know how it ends."

"Me too," says Holly, her voice distant and sad. "Why don't you come downstairs? You can take a shower. I'll make you something to eat."

Chapter 10

Holly

Dinner for Jade would be boxed mac and cheese along with an apple, sourced from Holly's meager food stash. It wasn't the most well-rounded meal, but as Holly's mother would say to her picky-eater daughters back in the day, *You get what you get, and you don't get upset.*

The old-fashioned metal teakettle whistled on the stovetop. Bottled water (until the tap got fixed) bubbled inside. Underneath it, the oven groaned, making alarming noises as it heated up their late-night meal. It was sad that Holly's big dream had been reduced from literary glory to one day owning a stove that wasn't teetering on the edge of extinction. But *you get what you get . . .*

As Jade showered, Holly focused on the sound of hot water flowing through the old, jangly pipes. She found the noise oddly comforting. It was a sign that someone else was in the house, a reminder of the old days when her family was ever-present, the shower always ran, and the sounds of daily life filled the air like the low buzz of a white-noise machine, noticeable only in its absence.

The house felt *alive* again—all thanks to a stranger, a troubled kid whose safety and well-being Holly couldn't guarantee, especially when she could barely take care of herself. Besides, could she even trust this girl? Holly had read enough novels with unreliable narrators to question Jade's telling of events. But whatever the story, the girl's painful emotions felt sincere, and she seemed to have nowhere else to go.

Was she really going to let her bleeding heart get her into even more difficulties? Jade might have been in lockup, but Holly didn't feel threatened by her presence. She was five-two at most, barely over a hundred pounds, and was a bedraggled, rumpled mess—like a dirty shirt pulled from the bottom of the hamper.

Jade's alluring onyx eyes had managed to turn a shade darker when Holly shared her intention to call the police—not to press charges, but to get the girl some help.

"You can't do that," Jade pleaded. "They'll get in touch with my aunt. I can't go back. I—I have to stay here." Her voice was sharp, even panicky.

"And why here?" Holly asked.

"Like I told you, there weren't a lot of abandoned houses to choose from." Jade punctuated the obvious with a crooked smile.

"No, I mean why come to Beauport at all?" Holly clarified. "It's a long way from Pennsylvania."

Jade hesitated long enough for Holly to wonder if she was crafting a lie. "I love the ocean," she said, her voice softening. "Always have. I wanted to hide at the beach until I turn eighteen in a couple of months. Then my aunt won't be able to control me anymore. After that, I'll figure out what I'm going to do with the rest of my life."

Holly didn't need to be a seasoned detective to know Jade wasn't telling the whole story. But for now she had a decision to make. Was she really going to let this drifter—an intruder and a minor, no less—spend the night?

Her conscience told her to help. The girl was vulnerable and in need of guidance. Besides, it was getting late. Where would she go if Holly turned her away?

Maybe call Shae? Holly mulled over what she would say. *"Hey, love, found a lost girl in my attic. A runaway. She's unarmed, a squatter, been in juvenile detention—but she's orphaned, poor thing, with an abusive aunt. It's basically a modern Dickens story. Should I let her stay?"*

Holly could already hear Shae's response: *"Are you f'ing crazy? You're going to let a stranger from juvie live in your house? Is the sea air affecting your common sense? Let the police sort this out. Her problems aren't yours to solve."*

Right. They weren't, Holly reminded herself. Who was she to decide what was in this young woman's best interest?

As her thoughts tumbled, Holly reached for the box of loose pages she had brought down from the attic. Jade's enthusiasm stirred something inside her. Maybe she should take a peek at what she had written all those years ago . . . but as soon as the thought surfaced, a warning followed: *You stopped writing it for a reason. You don't want to revisit that story. Not now. Not ever.*

And then Dan's voice echoed in her head: *Write something that sells.*

Could *Beach Thriller* be it? Was she meant to finish this book? Was this a sign from Anna?

Jade had been so excited about the characters and the story—and young readers *sell* books these days. What a story for TikTok! Runaway finds a lost manuscript and inspires a broken writer to tell the story she couldn't bring herself to finish years ago. It becomes a bestseller, Netflix catches wind, and soon Nicole Kidman is attached to the project.

Holly's hands trembled as she lifted the lid on the old corrugated box. It felt as if she had cracked open a tomb. The title page leered at her like a taunt.

She braced herself for what she had to do. How could she expect to live in Beauport and face the ghost of her sister if she couldn't even revisit a novella she had written ages ago?

With a deep breath, Holly reached for page 1, unsure of what she would find.

Beach Thriller

i

Will they all live happily ever after?

That's the fairy-tale ending we all dream about. True love's kiss. Rags to riches. Discovering we're a lost queen.

What a load of crap.

In real life, the frog doesn't turn into a prince. He becomes a cheating scoundrel who breaks your heart after he steals your money. The wolf *always* eats the girl. The young woman, trapped in servitude, remains forever impoverished and despairing.

Which brings us to young, dedicated Anna. She's beautiful; of course she is. You can't have a fairy tale without a captivating princess. But Anna isn't royalty—she's humble, kindhearted, and has a simple dream of becoming a teacher. Hopefully, her fairy godmother will grant her a reasonable cost-of-living increase.

But tonight, money surrounds Anna. It's summertime by the ocean, early June, a lovely night for a party. Floodlights slice through the dark, illuminating a turreted stone manor nestled behind a thick wrought-iron gate. The home is perched on a tall, craggy cliff overlooking the awe-inspiring Atlantic Ocean. The properties in this part of town are all high-end homes, but none compare to the one called Miramar. The Spanish name, prominently displayed on a plaque bored into a gatepost, translates poetically to "Watcher of the Sea."

The roof is steeply pitched and dotted with tall chimneys that from a distance look like stone fingers reaching up to scrape the sky. The windows carved into the stone facade give the impression of dark eyes keeping watch over the meticulously manicured grounds.

In the center of the circular driveway, a resplendent fountain bubbles. Bronze figures of a man and woman in flowing robes tilt pitchers, pouring water into a pool that is as clear as a mountain stream.

Fairy lights twinkle in the ancient trees surrounding the path to the beach, forming a magical canopy, guiding guests to the shoreline below.

The partygoers are dressed in bright summer fabrics: a mix of floral-patterned midi and maxi dresses for the women, creating a bouquet of color under the party tent. The men must have received a similar dress code. They're wearing madras shorts and button-down linen tops, looking very casual cool.

The entire party is an ode to the ocean—at least that's what the hostess would like everyone to believe—but in reality, the guests are paying homage to her. And there's a twist. Instead of the ankle-breaking heels and Italian leather shoes expected at most high-end parties, the crowd is dancing barefoot on the white sands of Maeve Carmichael's private beach. In place of a coat check, Maeve offers a shoe check, which ensures the mandatory *No Footwear Allowed* rule is followed by all.

The Barefoot Beach Ball (play on words intended) is the event of the season in Beauport. The sublime sandy soiree is famed not only for its splendor but also for the murmured complaints of the local staff, who have to trudge everything to the beach.

Partygoers descend the illuminated stone steps carved into the cliff, leading from the lush lawn at the top of the bluff to the white party tent just beyond the reach of the lapping ocean waves. A row of burning tiki torches lights up the darkness, their flickering flames casting alluring shadows.

Some walk along the warm sand, their drinks topped with fancy umbrellas, while others sway to the sounds of a nine-piece jazz band, melodic notes pulsing through the night air. Guests dance in a whirlwind of movement as caterers navigate through the crowd, ensuring drinks and appetizers are served before people even realize they want more.

Maeve, with her status and prestige, doesn't think much about the woes of the exhausted staff, who are working for a promised bonus while also enduring a grueling workout going up and down the stairs to the beach. Lines of electric cords attached to generators high above dangle against the bluff like climbing ropes from gym class.

And the sand. . . it's everywhere, except on the long tables draped in white cloth that are covered with an array of seasonal, light, and visually stunning dishes. It's a savory feast for the sophisticated palate—no hot dogs or hamburgers at this beach cookout.

Sea air filling your lungs and sand between your toes can lift anyone's mood. Even the most serious bankers can't help but feel like children playing on the shoreline. For these select few guests, the night feels magical, embodying perfection. For Anna, it's as if she'd been granted her greatest wish—except for one minor flaw. She wasn't invited to the party; she's working it. And she wears shoes that are killing her feet, since staff aren't allowed to go barefoot. In Maeve Carmichael's social hierarchy, shoes reveal your lower-class status.

Anna's job is straightforward: Serve food and drinks to the barefoot guests without making a mess. Everything has to be flawless, and for good reason. Historically, Maeve's Barefoot Beach Ball has been a major fundraiser for various causes. But tonight, the elite of Beauport have gathered to celebrate her son's engagement to a member of the prominent Ward family. Maeve wants all the influential attendees to raise their champagne flutes and toast to the bright future of Prince Charming and his lovely bride-to-be.

Anna lugged her silver tray full of hors d'oeuvres across the spongy sand. Who knew crab and goat cheese palmiers could weigh so much?

Thank God Holly was working alongside her. Anna's sister was two years her junior, but if you asked Holly, she would claim to be three years wiser.

"Hey, your eleven lines are showing," Holly warned. "You're not getting a Pap smear—you're serving food to rich assholes. Try smiling more, and maybe we'll get a few tips out of this gig."

Funny how the tables had turned. It was Anna's idea to apply for the job. She was the one with serving experience—even if it was scooping ice cream for screaming kids at the Dairy Dip.

"I'd smile more if I didn't have beach sand in every crevice of my body," she told Holly in a hushed whisper. "Besides, I've had a sinking feeling in my stomach since we started working. It's like I *know* something terrible is going to happen tonight."

As if on cue, Maeve Carmichael approached. The wolf had arrived. Fear prickled the back of Anna's neck. The hostess looked stunning in her light blue, plunging-neckline dress that flowed as if ocean waves were enveloping her. Not a single grain of sand marred her expensive pedicure. She had shaped her platinum hair into a gravity-defying style that resembled the topiaries out front. Anna straightened, trying to stand taller. Maeve's burning gaze locked on her, allowing Holly to sneak off.

"Where is the caviar?" Maeve snapped.

"I'm sorry, they gave me the crab to serve," Anna said, eyes drooping.

Maeve curled her upper lip. "I told you and your sister to serve the caviar with the Dom Pérignon, which has been circulating for twenty minutes. This is my son's engagement party, and everything needs to be perfect."

"I'll take care of it immediately," Anna stammered, enduring a crush of embarrassment.

"Hurry," Maeve barked. "I knew I shouldn't have trusted a pair of townie mutts to do this job. But I listened to my son, who urged me to give the locals a chance." She turned her nose up at the word *locals,* equating Anna with trash.

Ah, the damsel in distress and the wicked witch. What could go wrong?

Maeve's dismissive wave sent Anna scurrying after Holly. *What a terrible, horrible, awful woman,* thought Anna on her way up the steep staircase and back to the kitchen. Her stomach was in knots, her palms sweaty. As unpleasant as her encounter with Maeve had been, Anna feared something far, far worse was yet to come.

Up and down she went, tray after tray of fancy foods, until finally break time arrived. Thank goodness for small miracles.

At last, Anna had a moment to herself. She was far enough from the beach that the jazz band sounded like a muffled melody. Perched on the edge of the fountain in front of the stone house called Miramar, she drank water from a plastic bottle. Her feet felt like two melons stuffed into tiny black shoes.

Out of habit, she pulled a penny from her pocket. With her eyes closed, she made a wish. The penny flew from her hand and landed with a soft splash. It sank to the bottom, resting on heads.

She checked the time. Fifteen minutes had never gone so fast. Anna got up to leave, turning quickly—she'd been gone too long. In her rush, she nearly bumped into a handsome man who had appeared out of nowhere. He stepped back with the grace of a dancer.

"You startled me," she breathed, putting a hand to her chest.

"I'm sorry," he answered sincerely. "I didn't mean to frighten you. I needed a break from the party and saw you by the fountain. What did you wish for?"

As he stepped closer, moonlight lit his face. Anna had never swooned before, but there was a first for everything. This guy wasn't just good-looking—he was a work of art. Dark hair, like the night sky, framed a boyish yet rugged face. He had a strong jawline and lips made for kissing. He shot Anna a stunning smile. His dark eyes sparkled, causing her knees to buckle. His button-down shirt fit his broad shoulders and slim torso perfectly. Khaki shorts showed off his muscular legs. It didn't hurt that he also smelled like cinnamon.

"Oh, it was nothing—just what people do with fountains, right?" Anna offered a nervous laugh.

Somehow, this stranger amplified the charm of his to-die-for smile. "Well, sure," he said, "but maybe not *this* particular fountain."

Anna traced his finger to the glowing water. There, in the middle of a clean, coinless pool, was her lone copper penny.

"Oh my god, no," she muttered, horrified. She reached to retrieve the coin, but the young man placed his hand softly on her shoulder before she could dive in.

"Leave it," he said. "I don't want you to lose your wish." His voice soothed her like a smooth-talking DJ. "Tell me what you asked for. I don't think that will keep it from coming true."

Anna's gaze lingered on the penny, feeling the weight of her foolishness. She wanted to shrink to the size of a goldfish and disappear into the water.

"It's so ridiculous," she said, shuffling her feet. "I wished that I'd be an invited guest next time, not staff." She gestured to her uniform, shame rippling through her. It sounded so much better in her head. The last time she felt this idiotic was, well, *never.*

"Parties like this—even barefoot in the sand—are just a chance for people to show off. I don't think you're missing much." Was it Anna's imagination, or did a dark cloud pass over his chiseled features?

She smiled, blushing. "Well, I'm about to get fired for taking too long."

"The boss is on you, huh?"

Anna returned an emphatic nod. "She's a little . . . um, strict." She stole a glance over her shoulder, half expecting to see Maeve storming her way. "She called me a mutt because I didn't serve the caviar on time."

His eyebrows shot up. "A mutt? That's awful." She assumed he was trying to be sympathetic, but his voice carried an edge of amusement.

Anna became bolder. "What a raging bitch, right?" She hoped he would agree. He seemed like an ally, but his expression remained impervious.

"Oh yeah, I know better than most," he said, his dimpled smile widening. "She's my mother." He extended his hand toward her. Anna went stock-still. "I'm Conrad Carmichael. It's a pleasure to meet you."

Anna warily took his hand. His touch sent a rush through her body, a strong jolt that wiped away her crushing embarrassment. A profound realization took hold—this was a rare connection, like a gift from the stars.

But alarm bells went off, too. *Was this the terrible event she had feared all night?* She wasn't sure. All Anna knew was that, for better or worse, this man was her destiny.

. . . .

Holly returned the pages to the box, feeling an odd mix of apprehension and excitement. She hadn't thought about this story in years. And to her surprise, the book *did* sing. It wasn't great literature—not by any stretch. It was youthful and unrefined, but not unfixable. And

Jade believed readers would feel curious after the first chapter: What happens next? Does Anna's terrible premonition come true? Who is Conrad's betrothed? Do Conrad and Anna have an affair? Does she get fired?

In hindsight it was naive to use real names for her story, but back then, Holly thought it would help her get the characters right—ground her narrative in verisimilitude. Or maybe it was just therapy. Either way, she had planned to change the names later, until later became *never*.

Holly sighed. She had more pressing matters to deal with than what to do with an old manuscript that held ghosts pressed between its pages. Jade. She had a difficult choice to make. She didn't know what was best for Jade, and it wasn't her decision to make.

Resigned, Holly looked up the number for the Beauport Police Department and hit the call button—always there when you need them, twenty-four hours a day, seven days a week: handing out tickets, arresting vandals, stopping drunk drivers, calming angry vacationers, and leaving only one cause and manner of death as "undetermined."

Chapter 11

Jade

Hot water from the antique showerhead cascades over my body and into the cast-iron tub. Dirt slides off me like a snake shedding its skin. It's the longest, warmest, most life-affirming shower I've ever taken. This sure beats the gross public bathrooms at the Y.

While I'm grateful for small miracles, my hostess remains an enigma. Who keeps a house like this boarded up? She acts like it's a travesty to be here when it would be a shame *not* to live in this amazing town with the ocean as your front yard.

I couldn't believe my luck when I found this place. I don't usually catch many breaks, and I definitely don't believe in guardian angels—unless you count that guard named Big Sally, who always had my back in lockup. But shortly after I rolled into Beauport—a tourist town at the beginning of its summer season—I found this abandoned house across from the beach. It was like the *perfect* hiding spot fell into my lap.

One day, I'll figure out how to make amends for all my crimes—stealing, break-ins, and that one joyride in a stolen car that got me sent away. But these days, I only break the law when it's necessary for survival.

You're always causing problems, Jade.

I hear my mother's voice whisper in the back of my mind, putting me in my place. I can't seem to turn it off, and she disparages me at the worst times. I can run from Philly, but I can't escape all the darkness I've carried with me.

The hot water turns lukewarm, but I don't want to get out. My body needs this. Every part of me aches from the nights I spent sleeping on the attic floor. At least I had those books to keep me company. Reading has always been my escape hatch.

I really did enjoy Holly's novel. I want to know what happens next, but she doesn't seem eager to finish her story. Maybe I could persuade her to continue or even offer to help, like an editorial assistant or something. I don't have a college degree—I don't even have a high school diploma—but I've read more books than I can count.

I hope Holly lets me stay. I could use a friend right now, someone I can trust, but not many adults have been honest with me—my parents included.

Maybe Holly will be different. Instead of calling the cops, she's cooking me dinner. I've been living on fast food, convenience store snacks, and dumpster diving long enough to drop five pounds I couldn't afford to lose.

I step out of the shower, reaching for a fluffy blue towel. I dread the thought of putting my dirty clothes back on. Maybe Holly will let me use her washer and dryer. I know there's one in the basement.

As I dry off, the towel catches on my necklace and the clasp comes undone. I manage to catch the silver chain before it drops into the sink.

I look it over. The clasp isn't broken, though the necklace is already badly damaged. I hook it back around my neck, where it's hung ever since I found it in my parents' bedroom. I turn it around, reading the inscription on the back of the silver pendant like I've done a thousand times: *Beauport, MA,* the reason I came here.

I found it in my parents' dresser. I suspected it was meant for me. My mother didn't own much jewelry, and I certainly never saw her wearing this necklace with its inscription and jade pendant—my namesake stone.

When I decided to leave my awful situation, I used the necklace as my compass. I had been directionless, but the inscription became my guide. It gave me purpose.

Unfortunately, now it's broken. The jade stone came off the silver backing and I want it fixed by whoever sold it. I have some questions for them.

I also want to punch the guy who broke it.

I recall the man's face, and in a flash, I'm right back there, not too long ago—at his gas station somewhere in Connecticut, where I thought I'd score something to eat.

I wasn't after a microwave burrito—that's fine dining in my book. My score was some Gatorade, a bag of chips, and a few candy bars. I slipped them into my pockets without anyone noticing, or so I thought.

I left the convenience mart without stopping at the register, already thinking about my next move. It had been a long journey out of Pennsylvania, and it was still quite a distance to Beauport. I had enough money to get halfway there by bus. But hitchhiking? Apparently it's out of style—no one stopped. I walked for hours on a lonesome road, wet from a recent rain, to get to that gas station. My feet ached, and my stomach grumbled the whole way.

Now, at last, I had something to eat. Soon it would be fueling the next leg of my trip north.

But eating would have to wait. The gas station owner burst outside, charging after me as I walked away. At least I assumed he was the owner—who else would care about junk food worth only a few bucks?

He was a snub-nosed Goliath of a man in his fifties, possessing a barrel chest and greasy dark hair plastered to his pockmarked scalp. His grimy white shirt struggled to contain his belly, and his deep-set eyes resembled two pits carved into his thick skull.

One look at his furious face, and I knew I was in trouble.

"Give it back. All of it," he demanded.

Before I could argue, he grabbed my arm above the elbow with an iron grip. I swear I could feel my bones cracking.

"Okay, okay. Let go of me," I pleaded, my voice shaking. I could hold my own in a fight, but this would be like Tinker Bell taking on a rhinoceros. The pain in my arm was blinding. I twisted and turned, but I couldn't break free.

He started dragging me back toward the store. I had been the only customer (and I use that term lightly). As far as I knew, the place was empty. A new fear took hold.

"Let's call the police, and we can straighten this out," I suggested with a lot more bravado than I was feeling.

He laughed. "I'm gonna teach you a lesson you won't forget. Don't need the police for that."

I yanked my arm, slamming my foot into his shin as hard as I could. But he still wouldn't let go. He kept dragging me toward the empty store. I pictured a back office where no one would see us—or hear my screams.

Desperate, I spat at him, hissing like a wild animal. A thick glob of saliva slithered down his ruddy cheek. His fury exploded. His eyes darkened, and then—

Crack.

His open palm struck my face so hard that my skull rattled. My vision blurred, legs buckling, jaw burning.

He grabbed my shirt to keep me upright, readying to strike again. His fat fingers caught the chain around my neck, and the clasp gave way. A flash of silver fell to the dirt-covered pavement.

His gaze followed. He must have guessed that the necklace was important because he stomped on it, grinding it under his boot.

But for a brief moment, he was distracted.

I reached into my pocket. Instead of the food I had put there, my fingers closed around the can of pepper spray I'd bought on my way out of Pennsylvania. I sweet-talked my way out of the age restriction. No safety top, no fumbling required—I pulled it out and squeezed the trigger.

A blast of acrid-smelling spray struck Goliath square in the eyes. He bellowed, stumbling backward, pawing at his face.

At least he let go of me.

I had to make a break for it, but I wasn't leaving without my necklace. In one swift motion, I scooped it off the ground—having to make a second grab for the stone he'd knocked loose—then sprinted away.

His voice roared behind me, calling me every horrible name imaginable. But he didn't matter anymore.

I rounded a corner breathless and wide-eyed, searching for a place to hide when I spotted a run-down auto body shop with a pickup truck parked out front. Without thinking, I dove under the blue tarp covering the truck bed, landing in a pile of construction debris and tools. It wasn't until I got settled that I realized I had dropped my phone in the tumult, but there was no going back for it now.

I hoped to have a moment to catch my breath, but a few minutes later, the driver got in. The engine roared to life. Before I could say, "Let me out," we were on the road.

I curled into the fetal position for warmth, jolted with every bump. We drove for an hour, my teeth chattering the whole time. When I couldn't take it anymore, I banged on the cab window.

The startled driver pulled over. He was older, maybe in his sixties, with quiet, kind eyes. A jeans-and-work-shirt guy. He listened with care as I told him about Goliath.

"You want me to call the cops?"

I shook my head. "I just need to get to Massachusetts," I lied, saying I had a friend there.

He saw right through me. Still, he invited me to sit up front. He bought me dinner at McDonald's, and after, he handed me a hundred bucks. He even purchased a bus ticket to my final destination.

"Be careful," he said. "I'll pray for you."

Then he was gone.

The smell of creamy, gooey mac and cheese wafts up the stairs, pulling me from that awful memory. My stomach rumbles, but thoughts of my savior linger. I never learned that man's name, never got to thank him. I want more than anything to add Holly Sinclair to my short list of helpful souls.

I emerge from the bathroom wearing a stained T-shirt and jeans that I haven't washed in weeks, wondering again about the washing machine in the basement.

When I reach the stairwell, there are blue lights flickering through the windows. *Shit. Cops.* I retreat quickly as something brushes against my leg. I almost scream. Looking down, there's Holly's three-legged cat staring up at me. We've met a few times when I dared come downstairs to use the bathroom while Holly was out.

He speaks to me in a gentle meow. I press a finger to my lips, begging the cat to stay quiet so he doesn't give me away. No cops. Not ever. That's my golden rule.

Sorry, Holly. I wanted this to be different.

I have my bag with me. Luckily, I brought it down from the attic, and I know a safe way out of here.

The cat follows me into the bedroom, still meowing. My pulse races as I slide the window open. Thick, humid air bathes my skin. A sea breeze carries the scent of rain. The thought of getting caught in a storm almost makes me reconsider. Almost.

Before I know it, I'm halfway out the window, testing the trellis. It feels strong enough, but I can't be sure.

One foot. Then the other. I cling to the windowsill, too terrified to look down. With one hand, I steady myself, inching one foot lower. These things are built for plants, not people, but it holds strong. I descend with caution. When my feet touch the ground, the wave of relief almost knocks me over.

The blue police lights flash brighter outside. A pang of regret hits me. For a moment, I thought Holly and I could be friends—that I wouldn't be alone anymore.

But some girls just have to keep running.

Chapter 12

The Watcher

Now, it's getting interesting—and more dangerous. What did you think would happen, Holly? How foolish are you? You're about to start a fire you cannot contain.

I saw it all: how you called the cops, which sent the girl fleeing into the night. That's probably for the best. If she's with you, she isn't safe either.

You don't realize how close you are to the truth. You don't even understand what you're looking for. But you're going to stumble across it at some point. That's what I fear. It's like a curse you can't avoid, a destiny you cannot outrun. The Fates have spoken.

When you discover the girl is gone, you will look for her, won't you? I've watched you long enough to know how you'll react. You can't let this stranger go, but you should. The fire you're starting will surround you, consume you, along with anyone who gets too close.

I'm sure you've been through a lot, Holly, but so have I. You have no idea what the passing years have taken from me—living with my secrets and sins. But now, all I can do is protect those secrets. It's hard enough for me to face what I've become. I refuse to let others know my wickedness. All I can say is that shame burns—it swallows you whole. You can do nothing but bathe in its corrosive acids until you're no longer the person you once knew. You become someone unrecognizable, capable of doing the unthinkable.

It's time for me to take more decisive action. Watching is one thing—but it might not be enough. You need to start getting my message loud and clear.

You don't belong here.

You cannot stay.

Chapter 13

Holly

The cop at Holly's door looked familiar. He had a weather-beaten face and tired eyes, like a man who'd endured long hours on the job for far too many years. Holly had expected a rookie to be stuck with the graveyard shift, but this officer was north of sixty. He filled out his uniform in a way that suggested a fondness for beer, desserts, and a comfy couch. His chin sagged under gravity, and shags of silver hair spilled beneath his blue cap. He wasn't a picture of health but had a strong build and broad shoulders. His thick legs gave him the swagger of a former Marine.

But Holly knew better, because she recognized him at last. This was no military man. It was Officer Tom Walker—or Tommy Boy, as the locals called him back in the day, a nod to Chris Farley's movie character from the nineties. Beauport's version of Tommy Boy patrolled the beach, busting underage drinkers and stomping out illegal bonfires.

Holly wasn't surprised he was still on the force—he'd always presented himself as a lifer—but it didn't look like his career had gone far.

Then again, neither had hers.

"Good evening, Holly. I heard you were back in town," said Tom Walker. He spoke in the low, authoritative voice of someone issuing a speeding ticket.

How had he known? A name popped into Holly's mind—Gail Provost, from Gail Provost Realty. Ah, the trusty Beauport gossip mill working overtime. It was a good reminder that if Holly wanted to keep a secret in this town, she'd have to hide it from herself. But a fugitive minor wasn't something to keep under wraps.

Holly invited Walker inside. Chester approached with caution, little tufts of fur sticking up on his back. If Holly wrote this scene in a book, she was sure she'd receive a few scathing comments for using her cat to foreshadow Walker's questionable character. But she wasn't fabricating Chester's raised fur, and she trusted her cat's instincts. He, too, must have noticed Tommy's cold, flinty eyes.

"I'm not surprised that someone broke in. This place has been empty for a long time," said Walker, his tone scolding.

"It's not like I hung a vacancy sign on the front door, Officer," Holly countered.

"The boards and graffiti advertise well enough."

The smug look on Officer Know-It-All's face sparked her temper. She folded her arms across her chest. Now she understood Jade's reluctance to involve the authorities.

"What brought you back to Beauport after all these years?" Walker asked. "We figured that the house would be swept out to sea before a Sinclair returned to town."

Holly struggled to maintain a measured tone. "This town holds bad memories for us. My sister was murdered here and your police department botched the investigation."

Walker's eyebrows shot up, his whole face coming alive. "Murder? Is that what we're calling accidents these days?"

A bitter taste filled Holly's throat. "My sister went to break up with the guy she was seeing and the guesthouse on his property just happened to explode?"

Holly surprised herself. When she left town, asking questions of the police felt like picking a scab over an infected wound. She had been too traumatized to speak her mind. Maybe that's why she had left out one important detail: She was supposed to have been with Anna the night she died. Were it not for her infatuation with Max and his poorly timed phone call, she would have been.

"Accidents happen all the time, Holly. And if you have the answer to the age-old question of 'Why me?' I'd be eager to hear it."

"Sure they happen," said Holly. "But not usually at the house of the richest, most powerful family in town on the night my sister went there to break off a secret love affair."

Walker didn't have a quick comeback to that one.

As a writer, Holly could imagine the worst—what flames that hot might do to a body—and those images haunted her.

They haunted her mother as well, who had gone to the morgue to identify her daughter and came home looking like a shell-shocked soldier returning from the battlefield. The police kept some items as evidence, with Carol's permission, including Anna's claddagh ring, which matched the one Holly still wore.

Walker sniffed the air. "Late-night meal? Once you feed a stray cat, Holly—"

Holly's pulse spiked. "Jade is not a cat," she said, scooping Chester into her arms. His fur remained on guard. "She's a runaway and an orphan. Her parents died in a car accident, and she's been living with an abusive aunt. She's desperate and frightened, and I hope you'll treat her with kindness. She's been through a lot and doesn't trust the police."

"Most criminals don't." If that was Walker's attempt at levity, his joke came without a trace of a smile.

Holly felt tempted to send him on his way. She didn't believe she was breaking the law by allowing Jade to stay with her. But there was this thing called better judgment.

"I'll go get her. You wait here." Holly's tone was firmer than she had intended. She turned her back, making her way to the stairs.

Walker called after her with the sensitivity of a bullfighter. "I'm sorry about your mom, Holly. Nice lady. She'd been through a lot. Take some friendly advice, will you? Sell the place. You can make a lot of money, go somewhere new—get a fresh start."

Holly paused halfway up the stairs, gripping the railing. She thought about telling Tommy Boy the same story she had told Gail: The house was still in her mother's name, so it wasn't hers to sell. But the words she spoke surprised her.

"A fresh start is a state of mind. You can do that anywhere. This is my home now, like it or not."

Holly called Jade's name. All was silent. *Odd.* She noticed the bedroom door was slightly ajar. She knocked as she called for Jade a second time, pushing the door open when nobody answered.

The room was empty, but there was an unexpected breeze. Holly discovered the source—a partially open window. She didn't think anything of it until she went to close it and saw the trellis. She poked her head outside. Flashes of strobe lights from the police car parked out front lit up the back lawn. *Oh shit.* Jade must have known the police were here, and her instincts took over.

The air felt heavy and damp. Rain was in the forecast, most likely on the way. Guilt squeezed Holly. Had she made a promise? Not in those exact words, but the meal, the shower, and a bedroom suggested a safe haven.

Downstairs, Holly found Walker nosing about, keeping himself occupied. He cased her living room like he was assessing a crime scene.

"The place could use a little updating," he said, hovering near her grandfather's old pipe. "I don't think anything has changed since the last time I was here."

"Including an unsolved murder."

"It's still an active case, but again, it's not a homicide," said Walker, running a hand along the fireplace mantel, checking his fingers for dust. "We need to follow the evidence to make an arrest. Justice doesn't take shortcuts."

"It shouldn't take forever, either," said Holly. She moved to the front door, holding it open for him, all but ordering Walker to leave. Jade would never come out of hiding if she saw her with a cop.

A light rain began to fall. Steady winds whipped up the sea like a cauldron starting to boil.

"The girl is gone," Holly said. "I'm going to go look for her."

"I'll help," offered Walker, pulling up his sagging pants.

"No thanks, I'll go on my own," said Holly, resisting the urge to call him Tommy Boy to his face. "You can look for her if you want, but something tells me this girl knows how to hide from the police."

Holly kept watch for Jade as she drove toward the boardwalk. A gentle rain continued to fall, leaving streaky marks on her front windshield. Streetlights left many dark spots where Jade could hide, making her search nearly impossible, but Holly remained undeterred.

She tried to imagine where Jade would dart off to, but she was having difficulty thinking at all. The last two days had been a whirlwind—returning to the cottage, dealing with the pushy Realtor, the psychic reading, and then finding a squatter in her attic. A ghost would have been easier to handle. What Holly wanted was a cup of tea, a good idea for a book, for her mother to be alive, for the house not to be a shit mess, and for Jade to have picked another landing spot for her antics.

You get what you get . . .

Holly tuned out her internal whining. She had a roof over her head and food in the pantry. Jade had nothing but the clothes on her back, which would soon be drenched by the rain.

To catch a teenager, you have to think like one. Holly imagined a character in a book inspired by Jade—someone tough and resourceful who would rather be cold and hungry than turned over to the authorities.

Where would I go? Holly asked herself. A fast-food place seemed like a logical choice. But the nearest one was miles away and closed at this hour. If nothing changed, the poor girl might end up sleeping outside, even on a night like this—maybe on the beach, with no protection from the rain, which was falling harder now. Where could she find shelter outdoors? The answer came to her almost immediately: *on the beach, under the pier.*

Most likely, no one would notice a curled-up bundle on the sand, wood planks high above acting as a roof, offering some protection from the elements.

Holly had no trouble finding parking. Beauport was a sleepy town at night. She half expected to see Officer Tom Walker on patrol, but more likely, he had gone home or returned to the police station. He hadn't shown much interest in Jade. In fact, Holly had the distinct impression that Walker had used the call as a pretext to check on *her*. But why? He had made it clear he'd love nothing more than for Holly to leave town. Was Walker worried she'd cause him trouble—ask questions about Anna's death that he preferred not to answer?

Holly walked carefully across the wet planks of the boardwalk toward the wooden staircase by the pier. She descended the stairs to the beach, calling out to Jade. Rain had turned the soft sand unyielding, while clouds obscured the moon. The ocean stretched out before her like an endless black carpet. The rumble of stones tumbling under the churning water reminded her she was alone in a gathering storm, exposed and vulnerable.

Sips of light from the streetlamps on the boardwalk allowed Holly to see the outline of the sturdy pilings that held up the pier, casting deep shadows beneath.

She stepped under the towering structure, the tangy smell of the sea growing stronger, brine mixed with some kind of decay, life and death sharing space. She took out her phone; her flashlight's faint illumination told her the bulky shapes in the sand were nothing but clumps of seaweed.

Discouraged, she readied herself to leave, rethink her plan. She shut off her phone light, and that's when she saw it: a tall, narrow shadow in the sand looming behind her. The shadow moved, coming closer. She spun around, almost losing her balance as her feet sank into the sand. For the second time that day, Holly felt the urge to scream, but her voice abandoned her.

A lanky silhouette, decidedly male, inched toward Holly like a cat stalking its prey. Holly stood rooted to the spot. Fear filled her lungs.

He was right there, a few feet in front of her—no longer a shadow, but a man with a recognizable face. Her eyes opened in alarm. It was the busker. His thin frame and pinched features were as unmistakable as the scally cap he wore. He even had his guitar case slung over his shoulder.

"Didn't think I'd see anyone else on the beach in this weather," he said in a nasal voice.

A wave crashed hard, like a thunderclap.

"I know who you are," he continued. Even in the half-light, Holly could see his eyes narrow. "You shouldn't have come back."

Holly retreated a step. "I'm looking for someone, a girl," she said, her voice faltering. "She's about seventeen. Have you seen her?"

The busker closed in. "All I see is you—and I'm telling you, you're not welcome here."

Holly bristled. "I have no idea what you're talking about, but I'll call the police if you come any closer." Her high-pitched voice betrayed her panic. She had good reason to be afraid. She was under the pier, out of sight, and far from everyone.

The busker's eyes darted to the cell phone in Holly's hand. "You can call the police if you want, but you can't trust them. You can't trust *anyone* in this town—including me."

Holly tried to unlock her phone, but the rain rendered her screen unusable. She wiped the screen against her jeans in a frantic effort to dry it off.

The busker continued his approach.

Holly turned to run, but her feet lost traction on the slippery sand—and down she went. She threw out her hands to catch herself, only to land hard on a rock. Pain shot up her wrists. Her phone skittered away. She scrambled after it, gritty sand filling her mouth.

Behind her, the busker laughed contemptuously, sounding like he was right in her ear. She braced for something terrible, then felt hands on her shoulders, gripping her hard and pulling her to her feet.

"Back off, motherfucker. That's my friend you're messing with."

The voice was as familiar as it was shocking. The last thing Holly expected to see was a soaking-wet girl, weighing about a hundred pounds, holding a glinting knife. But there was Jade, who had lifted Holly up and now stood beside her, confronting the busker. The crazed look in her eyes said it all: She was a small dog with a big bite.

The busker threw up his hands in surrender, backing away. "Hey,

hey, I didn't do anything wrong," he squeaked before scurrying off into the dark.

Holly turned and wrapped Jade in an embrace, not caring that she was coating her in wet sand.

"Thank you, thank you," she said, breathing hard. "Come back to the house. Your mac and cheese is getting cold."

Chapter 14

Jade

I would have stayed out all night like an alley cat, scrounging for food and shelter, but Holly assured me there'd be no more cops. It's hard enough running without also being chased. I came all the way here on a mission. I'm not going to abandon it now.

Once my stomach is full for the first time in ages, and we're settled in the living room, I decide to show Holly the inscription on the back of my pendant. "I wasn't exactly honest with you about why I picked Beauport," I say. Holly doesn't act like that's breaking news.

"I found this in my parents' dresser. I never saw my mom wear it, but it was packed away in a special box, so it must have meant something to her. I took it as a sign that I should come here. I want to find the store that sold it and see if they can tell me anything about it."

That's mostly true, I rationalize.

"And here, look." I hand Holly the stone that I've kept in my pocket since it was broken off. "I need to get it fixed, and I'm hoping the store that sold it can also do the repair."

Holly makes the connection. "It's a jade."

"Exactly. I'm guessing it was meant for me—a gift my parents were never able to give me themselves. I don't know—they aren't around to ask. But it's weird, right? This was in their drawer, never worn. The box was faded, so I figured it wasn't a recent purchase. It comes from Beauport, which I'd never even heard of, and the stone has the same name as mine. Maybe it's nothing, but it feels meaningful."

Holly looks sad. "My mother died a few months ago—more like

three months and seventeen days, not that I'm counting." She offers a faint smile. "It's not the same as what you're going through, but I understand what it's like to lose someone close to you."

She hugs me. It's a little awkward, but also . . . kind of nice. Hugs were a scarce commodity in my house.

Holly doesn't know any stores that sell a necklace like mine. I head upstairs to change into the pajamas she gives me, neatly folded and smelling freshly washed.

When I come back down, Holly does a double take, like she's seeing a ghost instead of a scrawny seventeen-year-old in pink floral jammies. They're definitely not my style, but I don't think they look shockingly bad on me.

"Those belonged to my sister," she explains. "She passed away as well, but a long time ago."

I want to know more. Was she sick? Was there an accident? But Holly doesn't offer, and I get the sense she doesn't want me to pry.

The next morning, Holly is down in the basement doing laundry while I sip coffee in the living room with Chester on my lap. I'm surprised to feel so at home. Last night, I slept like the dead.

Something tells me that Holly is grateful I'm around. I'm like a remedy for loneliness, a diversion from her troubles. I don't know exactly what troubles she has, but she's got them. There's a weightiness about her, one I can relate to. Either way, I don't think she'll be kicking me onto the street anytime soon, so I can relax a little.

Holly is still downstairs in the basement, but she left the door open. I can't help but overhear as she takes a phone call.

"Really, Dan? I can't even afford my shampoo," she says.

Who's Dan? There's a pause. "Sorry, but I like good-quality shampoo—you know, the organic kind, cruelty-free and vegan." Another pause. "Well, I'm fucking delighted Head and Shoulders works for you, but that's not really my point, is it?" Pause again, then Holly huffs in exasperation. "No, I haven't started a thriller yet."

I light up. I love thrillers. I imagine us turning a corner of the living room into an office. Holly types away while I edit her work. Then, voilà! We become the authors of next summer's biggest read! Okay, she's the author . . . but the point stands.

Holly trudges upstairs, laundry basket in hand, to find me with Chester, curled up in her comfy chair, reading a book I found lying around.

"I need to ask you something, Jade," she says. Her tone is officious.

Uh-oh. "Shoot," I say.

"Are you being honest with me? About your parents, your aunt, why you came to Beauport, all of it? I need to know the truth if you're going to stay here."

I take a deep breath, centering myself. I fix her with the most pointed, unwavering, convincing stare I can muster.

"I swear," I say, my voice as steady as a steel beam. "Unfortunately, it's all true."

A few hours later, I head toward the boardwalk, happy it's within walking distance. I hit the local pharmacy with a goal in mind. It's a typical chain and not too crowded. Most shoppers are families with sick kids or beachgoers who forgot their sunscreen.

I wonder if Holly and I will enjoy a day at the beach together—that could be fun. I can count on one hand the number of beach trips I took with my parents. There's nothing like living by the ocean, inhaling the salty air, and feeling the sea breeze in my hair. It's a dream come true.

For a moment, I dare to believe that anything is possible. I've always wanted to be a writer, and how wild is it that I'm staying with a published author? We even shared some laughs over breakfast. No doubt, we've come a long way since the broomstick incident. I was surprised how smoothly our conversation flowed. It's as if we've known each other our whole lives.

I'm so grateful she's letting me stay with her, which is why I can't ask for money as well. But I have super painful cramps, and I'm in desperate need of Advil. I could offer to work around the house for some cash, but based on the call I overheard, Holly can't even afford quality shampoo. Nope, I'm on my own—as usual—so I have to be resourceful.

When another cramp hits, my guilty conscience creeps into the back seat. I prepare to do what has to be done—steal.

Shoplifting isn't exactly rocket science. I don't need a degree in criminal behavior to get what I want. I just need guts, determination, and very fast fingers—all of which I have in abundance. I give myself the usual justifications: The system is unfair to people like me. Inflation makes it hard to afford the basics. Corporations, like the pharmacy chain I'm stealing from, exploit workers. They also fuel the opioid crisis and overcharge insurance companies. Sorry, not sorry.

My old therapist would label this type of thinking rationalization, but it tamps down my guilt, though not my anxiety. That's a good thing. A little case of the jitters before breaking the law keeps you on your toes. The cocky criminals are the careless ones, and I can't afford to make mistakes.

I march down the cold and flu aisle, trying my best not to draw attention to myself. Go figure, the dusty carpeting makes me want to sneeze. A familiar tickling overwhelms me, but I manage to stifle the urge.

I scan the aisle. The colorful medicines stand in a row like tiny obedient soldiers. On one side are the orange and green bottles of NyQuil and Delsym. On the other side, I find the blue and red bottles of Advil and Tylenol.

Rule one of shoplifting: Don't hesitate. In one swift, seamless motion, I snag what I'm after—a box of ibuprofen, eight bucks for a fifty-count.

Even though this isn't my first rodeo, an uneasy sensation slides down my spine. I feel like someone is watching me. But when I look around, I only see an eighty-year-old woman, and she can't see much at all.

I slip the pills into my hoodie pocket with the deftness of a skilled magician, then check over my shoulder to ensure no one noticed. So far, so good. I'm equally confident security cameras haven't recorded me in the act. Yet, I can't shake the feeling that someone has been watching me.

I let the thought go. Rule two kicks in like a reflex: Don't linger. I got what I came for. Time to disappear. But as I make my way for the exit, the shampoo aisle catches my eye. I know I should leave, especially with this sense of unease, but Holly has been so generous, and I'm compelled to return the favor. The bottle will simply appear in the shower. Holly doesn't need to know the details.

Marching down the fragrant aisle, I scout out a good-quality shampoo. I have no idea what brand she uses; all I remember is her mentioning "cruelty-free." Of course, that means I have to look at the fine print. What the hell am I thinking?

I scan the shelves for the most expensive product that comes in a small enough bottle to fit in the waistband of my pants. I grab one and glance at the back, pleased to see the little bunny symbol that verifies the company does not do animal testing. Score. I slip the container under my hoodie and head toward the door.

At last, the tightness in my throat begins to ease. The stabbing fear in my chest recedes. The door is right there; daylight is streaming through it. I hold my breath as I move closer to the exit. But the anxiety returns, washing over me like a tidal wave. Something is off, I can feel it.

I quicken my pace, breaking rule number three: Don't panic.

As soon as I pass through the screener, I hear it—an alarm so loud and repetitive that I'm sure the blaring sound reaches Holly's cottage. Shit. The expensive shampoo. I bet it's tagged. I start to run, hoping to make a break for it, but someone grabs the hood of my sweatshirt, pulling me back.

"What the fuck!" I yell, whirling to face a burly man whose tight grip on my hood starts strangling me. I size him up in an instant. He's got the red vest of an employee, and it's tight-fitting across his stocky frame. He's around forty with wispy strands of dark hair and beady brown eyes that bore into me from behind a pair of silver wire-frame glasses. He might not be a hulking monster like Gas Station Man, but he's no pushover. I can't take him on without one of us ending up bloody—and most likely, it will be me.

My only hope is to talk my way out of this. "Isn't this like . . . assault?" I wheeze.

He has my hoodie twisted around in front of me, so the fabric is legit constricting my windpipe. At last the clerk releases his hold. He latches his hands to his hips, puffing himself up to look more intimidating.

I stand tall in response, acting a lot braver than I feel. It's not good that I already have a record.

"I don't know about that. But I do know it's illegal to take merchandise without paying for it. It's called *stealing*." He says the last word slowly, like I'm not very bright.

I glare at him with defiance and try to deny it, to defend myself, but the words catch in my throat.

"I—ah—umm . . ." Maybe I'm not so bright after all. My face is burning, my palms are slimy, and I seem to have forgotten the English language.

"Excuse me, is there a problem?" says a suave voice, calling me to my senses. I look over to see a handsome older man, tall with dark, neatly styled hair. He's dressed nice enough for a fancy luncheon, no swim trunks and sunscreen for this guy. He's holding a pharmacy shopping bag and still has his wallet in his hand from paying at the counter.

"Yeah, there's a problem," the clerk snaps. "This punk just stole shit from the store."

"I believe there's been a misunderstanding. She's with me," the attractive stranger says with authority. "Perhaps the cashier forgot to ring up a few items? I asked her to pick up Advil and shampoo and told her I'd pay for them at the counter."

I perk up. I knew it! Someone was watching. He saw exactly what I took.

He looks at me, his gaze conveying a clear message: *Play along*. Taking out his receipt, he hands it to the manager, who examines it with care. "You see, it does appear a couple of things were forgotten. I'll pay for the rest before we leave." My nameless savior gives the man his credit card, along with a warning look.

One thing's for sure—this guy has pull. The clerk grumbles, likely happy to receive payment but disappointed not to be playing the hero.

I silently follow this tall, dark stranger to the register. I offer no explanation as I pull the stolen items from their respective hiding places and set both on the counter.

A few moments later, I'm outside in the bright sunshine, afraid of what this guy might expect in return for his generosity. He's going to be sorely disappointed.

"Hey, thanks," I mumble, looking at my feet. I sneak a glance at him, and he seems clean-cut, but if there's one thing I've learned in my travels, it's that looks can be deceiving. "Why did you help me?" I want to know.

He shrugs. "It seemed like you needed it. Advil and shampoo aren't exactly luxury items." He pauses. "Are you new in town?" he asks.

Now I'm the one who shrugs. "Kind of passing through . . . maybe. Not sure yet."

"Are you here with your family? Do you have a safe place to stay?"

"Yeah, yeah, I'm crashing with a friend. I just don't have any money. Things have been . . . rough."

"Well, I'm glad you have a friend in town. And if you need a little work while you're here, I might be able to help you." He hands me a business card. It reads: *Conrad Carmichael.* The name is familiar, then it hits me: *He's a character in Holly's book.* The card has his email and phone number in very small font, but there's no actual business referenced, so I have no idea what kind of work he's offering.

He notices my quizzical expression. "My mother's health isn't what it used to be. She often needs help with simple tasks around the house. Nothing major and no pressure. Just beats stealing and getting in trouble with the cops."

His smile is so warm, I almost believe him.

Chapter 15

Holly

By midafternoon, Jade hadn't returned from her trip to town. Holly tried not to worry. Why should she? Jade wasn't her child. She was practically an adult. They hadn't set any ground rules. That was probably a mistake. She gave herself a pass, having never parented anything with two legs before.

Holly couldn't have contacted her even if she wanted to—she didn't have Jade's number. *Did she even have a phone?* She must. Then again, people used phones to stay connected, and Jade seemed alone in the world.

Except me. Now she has me, and I don't know where she is, Holly lamented.

She released her semi-inexplicable, though not unjustified, worry. Jade would return to the house at some point—she was more resourceful than a fox. And foxes needed to eat, which reminded Holly that she should have extra food in the fridge, and probably fresh sheets on the bed, and clean towels, and . . . *What the hell?* The night before, she had been desperate to rid herself of the urchin in the attic. Now she was acting like her caretaker. Maybe she felt as alone as Jade must.

As Holly searched for her car keys to make a run to the grocery store, a silver Acura arrived in her driveway. A large blue pickup truck pulled in right behind it.

Gail Provost emerged from the Acura, her plastered-on smile tailor-made for a highway billboard. The driver of the pickup appeared from his vehicle shortly afterward. Holly's gaze settled on a man in worn jeans, a plain white T-shirt, and heavy work boots. He carried a toolbox in his right hand and a coffee thermos in his left.

He wasn't flashy—broad-shouldered, yes, but more lean than bulky, his frame shaped by real work, not gym vanity. His dark hair was wavy and a little unruly, like he'd already had a full workday. Something about him felt quiet and decent. Holly had the impression there was a softness beneath his calluses, perhaps a poet's soul trapped inside a builder's frame. A kind smile confirmed her suspicion. He didn't look her over, didn't flinch at the graffiti-scrawled siding or the sorry state of her home. No judgment—just calm focus on the task at hand.

Holly couldn't pull her eyes away. As a writer, she was always inventing stories about people. In this man's wistful gaze, she saw someone who had faced his share of ups and downs. It seemed likely he carried more tales than tools in his toolbox.

"Holly, this is the handyman I promised you, Ethan Greene. Ethan, meet Holly Sinclair, Beauport's most famous author. She's also the homeowner—for now." Gail shot Holly a telling look. Ethan noticed, suppressing a smile. He seemed to understand how Gail operated.

Holly tried to act casual as intrusive images flashed through her mind. It wasn't her fault that his T-shirt was almost transparent and it was easy to picture him without it. Ethan, shirtless, replacing the shingles on the house, fixing the kitchen sink, then taking a nice cool shower . . . *Okay, okay, that's enough.* She didn't write romance novels. Wouldn't she need a romantic life first? Her imagination was good, but it wasn't *that* good. Even so, at the moment, the handyman fantasy was vivid enough to make her blush.

In her defense, she'd had such a long dry spell that her body likely qualified as a desert ecosystem.

"Seems like you've got a bit of work to do," said Ethan, still smiling as he stepped back to survey the graffiti, a broken window, and an obvious area of rot.

Meanwhile, Holly surveyed Ethan. She noticed his eyes were caramel-colored, like Max's, the boy she once pined for—and he was strangely familiar, too, but only in the vaguest sense.

When he came to stand beside her, Holly felt a spark. Her mind clicked into thesaurus mode, as a writer's brain is wont to do. Intrigue? Allure? Desire? Her palms turned clammy, and her cheeks flushed. A wave of lightheadedness hit her hard, as if she might topple over.

But this wasn't swooning—no, something was *wrong*. She was genuinely not feeling well. A flash of light blinded her, and when it started to clear, little stars danced before her eyes. A tingling sensation, like a prickling of a limb falling asleep, traveled up and down her hands. But it was the ethereal light show that she found most unsettling.

Holly clutched the railing by the front steps, bracing herself. She had no idea what was happening or why, but the sense of unreality, as if she'd entered a dream, only intensified.

"Hey? Are you all right?"

Ethan's voice sounded like it was bubbling up from the bottom of a well. Holly latched onto it, using the sound to pull her back from whatever abyss she was teetering on. At last she felt her feet on the ground, her fingers tight against the railing. Her vision cleared, and she was back to reality, away from that strange, murky dreamland. *What the hell was that?*

"Yeah, yeah," she managed. "I'm okay." She shook her head, still uncertain. "I think the heat and the stress are getting to me. It's been a little . . . overwhelming."

Ethan nodded. "I hear you, but don't worry," he said. "I've seen houses in much worse shape. A little sanding, a little paint, and it'll be as good as new. Right, Gail?"

But Gail didn't answer. She had slipped inside the house unnoticed during Holly's episode. Holly heard her puttering about, likely taking measurements for the Zillow listing.

Ethan chuckled, and she felt woozy all over again.

"Gail's rather . . . *industrious,* which makes her great for referrals," he said.

Good-looking and tactful, Holly observed, maintaining her composure despite feeling a little out of it.

"I'm sure I can help with whatever projects you have. Come on, let's take a look inside and get out of the sun for a few."

Taking her by the arm, Ethan led Holly into the house. They found

Gail muttering to herself in the kitchen. "Maybe just a breakfast bar or a new window . . . let in more natural light . . . ooh, or a sliding glass door to an outdoor patio."

"Gail!" Holly called out. "Will you please stop redesigning my house for resale value? I'm on a budget. Let's fix the plumbing before doing major excavation work."

Gail glanced over, hardly registering Holly's plea. Her eyes went immediately to Ethan's hand on Holly's forearm.

"Uh-oh, careful, honey. Don't fall for this guy—you'll be competing with every woman in Beauport." She tossed her a wink, raking her eyes over Ethan's physique.

Ethan dropped his hand with an apologetic laugh. "Don't listen to her, Holly. Gail loves small-town gossip."

"Don't try to shift the focus. Every sad country song is written about a guy like you."

"Oh, I'm so sorry," said Holly emphatically.

"For what?" asked Ethan.

"Well, you must have lost your girl, your dog, and your truck all in one day."

Ethan chuckled. "Yeah, it's been rough. That's a rental." He thumbed out the window to his pickup truck. "No, really, it is. My truck just died. I swear, I'm not making that up."

They all burst out laughing, but soon got down to business.

Holly showed Ethan around the house, pointing out areas that needed repair. All in all, it was a *very* long list.

"I should be able to get the work done in about six weeks. I can give you a full estimate by morning."

"Hopefully, I can get the money—I have to see a lawyer about that."

"Allen Spellman?" Gail guessed.

"How did you know?" Holly asked.

"Small town, few options, and Allen is the local go-to for estate work. Same as Ethan is a town favorite for home repairs . . . among other things." Gail looked mischievous.

Ethan cleared his throat. "If you're worried about my ability as a handyman, I could send you some references. Or better yet, I've done a lot of work at the Carmichael estate. They're regular clients. That place is so old, there's always more to do. If you're up for it, we could take a drive over, and I'll show you some of my skills." Ethan flushed. "What I mean is, uh—"

"I know what you mean," said Holly, who had seen boiled lobster less red. Her kind smile saved him from further embarrassment, and she hoped it left a door open to other possibilities. It rained in the Sahara, if seldom.

The light of gossip sparked in Gail's eyes. "Oh, you're going to take her on a tour of the Addams Family house?"

Holly didn't need a tour. She knew plenty about the Carmichael estate, and had no interest in ever going there again.

Besides, she wasn't a fan of stone houses. She found them cold and a little creepy—a touch too gothic for her taste. The Addams Family reference was appropriate. But Gail's tone suggested it was the residents that reminded her of the monster show, not the building itself. Holly agreed.

Gail would love nothing more than dirt on the Carmichaels, and Holly could give her a truckload. But that would mean opening up about her connection to that family, which she was reluctant to do. She was, however, curious what had happened to them over the years. Holly had long ago lost track of the Carmichael clan and their staff, who came and went like the seasons. If anybody knew their recent history, it would be Gail.

"Are the Carmichaels as influential in town as ever?" Holly inquired.

Gail shrugged. "They've faded into the background a bit these days. You could say their heyday has turned to mostly hay." She laughed at her own joke.

"That's too bad," said Holly, masking her insincerity. "They used to be pillars of the community, big into their charitable causes."

"Not anymore, they tend to keep to themselves," said Gail. "Even summer people like you, Holly, probably remember the soirees they used to throw. The Barefoot Beach Ball? Over the top, or so I heard. I didn't come to town until after that era had ended."

Of course, Holly knew all about those parties, but she played dumb.

"I can't count how many buildings in Beauport are named after them," Gail went on. "It's like Pottersville from that movie . . ."

"*It's a Wonderful Life,*" said Ethan. "We watch it every year. It's our favorite holiday flick."

Holly felt a stab of disappointment. *We. Our. His girlfriend, or worse, his wife.* She sighed on the inside. *Oh well, easy come, easy go.*

Gail brightened. "That's it—the Carmichaels were the Potters of Beauport," she said. "Only Geoffrey Carmichael, the patriarch, wasn't so smart with his money."

"Geoffrey died a long time ago," Ethan said for Holly's benefit, though she already knew.

Gail added to the history lesson. "He was quite the gambler. When he passed, the family was in financial ruin. Conrad was in college, so he wasn't bringing in the bucks. I guess the situation was dire—but leave it to the matriarch, Maeve Carmichael. She plays matchmaker, marries her son off to Elizabeth Ward, daughter of Baxter Ward, founder of Ward Pharmaceuticals, and *voilà*—the family finances are miraculously saved.

"And then, wouldn't you know it, Maeve and Baxter—both widowed—take up with each other." Gail's eyes brightened. "I've heard coffee shop chatter before, but this was other level. No surprise Maeve put an end to the Barefoot Beach Balls—she was no fan of the whispered talk."

Holly cringed. "Wait . . . Doesn't that make—"

"Conrad's wife also his stepsister? Yes, it does. Hello, Pornhub," said Gail gleefully.

"Maeve and Baxter must have been head over heels for each other to spend that much social capital on a marriage," Holly said.

Gail shrugged. "I always took Baxter Ward for an opportunist—a dead one now. Heart attack or something, not that long ago. If you ask me, I'd say his marriage to Maeve was one of convenience. She was a fixture on the planning board, and wouldn't you know it, after the wedding, the town approved permits for a new Ward Pharmaceuticals plant to be built on environmentally sensitive land on the outskirts of town.

That raised some eyebrows." She gave Holly a knowing look. "And that wasn't the *only* scandal surrounding that family."

This time, it was Ethan who seemed uncomfortable. "I'm sure Holly doesn't need to be bombarded with tall tales from Beauport."

Holly was more than ready to end the conversation. Though her curiosity was piqued, talk of the Carmichaels was starting to give her a headache. "Honestly, I don't need to inspect their home. I trust Gail's judgment. She wouldn't recommend a shoddy handyman to fix a house she's hoping to list soon. I have a small deposit I can give you to get started. I just hope Allen Spellman is able to get the rest of the funds from the trust quickly, or I'm not going to be able to do much of anything."

"I've given Allen a lot of business," said Gail confidently. "If he's not responsive, let me know, and I'll nudge him along." Her smile was conspiratorial.

By the time they left, Holly's headache had become much more intense. Her skull felt like a cracking dam, ready to give way to a torrent of pain.

Serena had been trying to warn her away from Beauport. Now it felt like her body was doing the same.

She searched the house, and, wouldn't you know, she had no Advil. Holly was about to go to the store, worried she might be unable to make the drive, when Jade strolled in.

"I got a job," she announced, brimming with excitement.

Holly bristled. *For fuck's sake, are we roommates now?* She'd never wanted to live with anybody long term other than Chester. A job felt like Jade was putting down roots.

"That's great news!" said Holly, who meant it, despite her reservations. All the while, the little drumbeat on her skull kept on thump, thump, thumping.

Chapter 16

Jade

I'm all smiles and sunshine, but Holly looks like someone's rained on her parade. I know what will cheer her up: "I'll basically be working with the cast from your novel."

"My novel?" Holly flinches like I've thrown a punch.

"Yeah, I'll be helping Maeve Carmichael around the house. She lives in this ridiculous mansion up on the hill. Anyway, I met her son, Conrad, in town and we got to talking, and he offered me a job. Oh, and the house is called Miramar, just like in your book, so I'll let you know if you did a good job describing it. I start tomorrow."

I could read the concern in her furrowed brow.

"You'll be working for Maeve and Conrad Carmichael? I can't believe it." Her voice carries a shock wave.

"Isn't it amazing? I can't wait. Apparently, they have a real-life butler—and he *lives* in the house. There are, like, seven bedrooms or something like that." I'm hoping Holly joins in my excitement, but she still hasn't climbed aboard the enthusiasm barge. She looks mildly seasick, actually.

"You can't work there," she declares, surprising me. "I won't allow it."

I pull back. "Um, yeah, *Mom*, I can," I say, really laying on the sarcasm. "What's your problem? Conrad seems cool and rich, and I need money."

"You don't know that family like I do. It's not safe."

Holly folds her arms across her chest like that's the final word.

I scrunch my forehead. "I know the Carmichaels were pretty sketchy in *Beach Thriller*, but didn't you say your book is fiction?"

"It was . . . it is," Holly stammers.

"So what's your problem with them? Did you ever work for them, like you wrote in the book?"

Her hands go to her hips. "No, I didn't. But just because the story is fiction, it doesn't mean they're good people. I don't know them well, but I know . . . things."

I squint at her. "Didn't you just say that I don't know the family like you do?"

Holly's words get stuck. "Yes, I did, but, it's hard to explain—"

I straighten, emboldened. "Okay, soooo, you don't know them well, but you know enough that I shouldn't work there, is that right?"

Holly is realizing how persistent I can be, especially when challenged. But I get the sense she's trying to protect me, so points for caring.

"How about you just trust me?" says Holly, her expression grim.

"Are you going to hire me instead?"

"I don't have any money to pay you."

I smile, victorious. "Then unless they're serial killers hiding bodies in a wine cellar, I'm taking the job. Good talk." I pat Holly on the arm and head upstairs before her useless objections turn into our first fight.

Holly calls up to me, her voice defeated. "I need to go to town to get something for my headache. I was going to pick up dinner, too."

I turn around on the stairs and smile. Reaching into my pocket, I take out the bottle of Advil and toss it to Holly. She catches it, confused.

"Thanks, but I'm not hungry," I say. "Conrad bought me a sandwich."

Chapter 17

Holly

It was clear this young lady was as easy to redirect as an ocean liner. And now Conrad Carmichael was casting himself as Jean Valjean from *Les Misérables*—the redeemed hero? Please. Holly knew better.

She went upstairs, took three Advil, and lay on the bed. She'd had migraines on and off since Anna's death, but she'd never experienced an aura before. That was likely what her strange experience had been when she was talking to Ethan. She would have to look it up on WebMD, though she always regretted going there—it was full of worst-case scenarios. For now, she needed rest.

In her room, she cracked open the window, closed the curtains, and lifted Chester onto the bed. Resting her head on the pillow and pulling the blanket over her shoulders felt incredible. But as she closed her eyes, the pain only intensified. Flashes of something like the aura struck her again, but these were different. Even with her eyes shut, she felt blinded by a bright orange light. No, not light—it was . . . flames. She could feel the heat scorching her skin.

Holly's mind conjured the smell of burning wood and the chaos of police and fire crews shouting orders. People rushed around, trying to help. Sirens blared. Holly pressed a pillow to her ears, hoping to block out the noise, trying to escape it.

A familiar figure emerged from this netherworld, engulfed in flames. She bolted upright.

No, she told herself. *Enough.*

Rubbing her eyes, the images finally cleared, but her anxiety did not.

Thankfully, the medication was beginning to work, although her heart kept racing. She had hoped the comforting surroundings of her mother's bedroom would calm her. Instead, her gaze fell to her old manuscript on the bureau: *Beach Thriller*—where it all began.

She couldn't help herself. It was masochistic, but maybe it was exactly what she needed to do: face her past. She picked up the pages and continued to read from where she'd left off.

Beach Thriller

ii

Our intrepid princess returned to the party with newfound excitement. Moments ago, Anna had glimpsed her fate, or so she believed. The raw, unbridled energy coursing through her was unlike anything she had ever experienced. Somehow, some way, she was meant to be with Conrad Carmichael. She knew it in her soul. The when and how were details to sort out later.

Anna caught herself and laughed. What an idiot she was being. This was the man's engagement party—he was going to be married soon. And she'd had a sense of foreboding all evening. How could she suddenly feel elated? Yet she couldn't shake the visceral conviction that her life was meant to intertwine with Conrad's. What on earth could explain this connection after only a few minutes of idle conversation?

The answer made her feel worse. Anna had grown up on a steady diet of romance novels, rom-coms, and glossy magazines. She was a natural-born dreamer who couldn't resist visiting any psychic's studio she passed, hoping for a quick glimpse into her future. What would the psychic foretell if she followed her childish heart? She could guess. *Buckle up, sweetheart. It's going to be a bumpy ride.*

Anna filled her tray with more beverages—tall champagne flutes for the grand finale, the big toast of the night: cheers to the future bride and groom. At least she'd found her smile; Holly should be happy about that.

The setting could not have been more perfect—or more romantic, Anna lamented. The scent of salty ocean air mingled with fancy perfumes. Gentle waves lapped at the shore, a rhythmic lullaby beneath the cheerful notes of the jazz band. The tiki torches flickered in the breeze, bathing the beach in an air of mystery. To make the toast more festive, the staff handed out flowered Hawaiian leis to all the guests, their bare feet dusted with sand, turning the Barefoot Ball into a moonlit luau.

Meanwhile, Anna passed out the champagne, daydreams filling her head. *Mrs. Anna Carmichael.* She had to admit, it had a nice ring to it. The fantasy pulled her deeper. Suddenly it was *her* wedding day. Bells ringing, bubbles and confetti filling the air. She and Conrad rushing down the broad stone stairs of the big white church (how many movies had that scene?), their arms linked in a symbol of togetherness. They looked like a glorious pair—cute as a couple of cake toppers. They climbed into the waiting limo decorated with colorful signs and washable paint. Time to honeymoon, but first, they had to make the wedding official under the sheets.

Love at first sight *was* a real thing. Anna always wanted to believe it was true, and now she was convinced. Judging by the way Conrad's eyes tracked her every move, he might be a believer as well. However, she felt another gaze burn even hotter—Elizabeth's. Conrad's perfectly perky blond fiancée didn't appreciate the attention her betrothed lavished upon the help.

Anna navigated through clusters of the town's best-looking and best-dressed people, her feet sinking into the sand, careful with her steps like someone crossing a minefield. The ornate champagne flutes clinked together on her tray in a delicate, chiming melody.

She soon ran into Baxter Ward, father of the bride-to-be, who had silver hair the color of a glittery fish and the red eyes of a drunken sailor.

Anna carefully balanced the tray while Baxter took a drink he didn't need. He placed his free hand on her hip, his fingers pressing into her flesh. She wanted to scream or stomp on his bare toes, but any retaliation would risk alienating her from Conrad.

"Where have you been all night, beautiful?" he slurred. He took his hand off her hip only to reach into his pocket for a business card, which he slid onto her tray. "That has my private number. Call me any time you need . . . *work*."

Anna managed a smile, even as her skin crawled, then slunk away before he could pinch her ass—or worse.

Thank God her shift was nearly over. She needed to find Holly and spill every tantalizing detail of her conversation with Conrad at the fountain. But first, she had to get these drinks handed out—and avoid Elizabeth (and her creepy dad) at all costs.

Funny enough, Elizabeth—who had been aloof all night, her focus laser-locked on the party VIPs instead of her betrothed—now clung to Conrad as if she were his cologne. Wherever Anna turned, there he was—Conrad, standing next to the stunning Elizabeth, whose curves were made for a race car.

She fawned over him in a sickening way. Anna could hardly bear it. Elizabeth threw him doe-eyed looks, laughing like he was the funniest man alive, her head tossed back for emphasis. Her fingers ran up and down his strong arms. Maybe it was the alcohol. She looked a little wobbly on her feet.

But she wasn't so drunk that she failed to recognize Anna as a serious threat. The blaze in Elizabeth's eyes implied Anna had wandered into the wrong den.

Baxter Ward, eager for another glass of champagne (not that he needed it), waved Anna over—right near where Conrad and Elizabeth stood. She made her way toward him cautiously, her steps steady.

It happened in a flash. Despite her focus, something caught her foot, and Anna lost control. Her body lurched forward, the tray slipping from her grasp. Six crystal champagne flutes filled with sparkling bubbly flew through the air. They soaked Baxter's shirt like he'd gone for a swim, before cratering into the sand. A few glasses shattered into sharp pieces as they struck one another. Anna fell with them, landing hard, her hands pressing into broken glass, slicing her delicate skin.

The beach erupted into a collective gasp. Anna's thoughts blurred, dulling what should have been stabbing pain in her palms.

Baxter let out an uproarious laugh. "You're not getting paid to make sandcastles. Get up!"

Before she could process it all—the shocked faces and her embarrassment—Anna felt someone lift her to her feet. Then a loud voice called out over the crowd.

"Oh, my fault, my fault." It was Conrad, his voice booming. "I am so sorry. I must have bumped into you. Here, let me help you get cleaned up."

Bumped? No. Someone had tripped her. Anna was sure of it.

She looked around at the mess she'd made, horrified. She caught sight of Maeve, eyes piercing, and Baxter, who grinned down at her, while Elizabeth looked . . . triumphant.

Chapter 18

Jade

I've clearly entered a ritzier part of town. The houses on this hill are all mansions of one type or another, each perched precariously close to the steep drop-off as if jockeying for the best view. The higher I ascend, the more impressive the homes become, but none match the grandeur of the Carmichael estate, which stands proudly at the top of the hill.

I arrive at a tall wrought-iron gate that resembles a prop for a movie about a school for magical children. Set into the gatepost is a weathered plaque engraved with the name MIRAMAR. It's just like Holly wrote in her fictionalized tale of the family I now work for.

To my left, I have a stunning view of the Atlantic. The sea changes colors daily as though declaring its mood. Today it seems happy, light, and inviting, with countless drops of sunshine reflecting off its smooth surface.

If my mother could see me now . . . *Girls like you don't belong in a place like this.* I can hear her words as though she were right next to me. And I know she's right. My dyed hair, piercings, and scars—both inside and out—are like a black mark on this estate. But I don't need to fit in. I need to take the money they pay me and run.

I push a button on the intercom and hear a click, followed by a crackling, disembodied male voice.

"Welcome to Miramar. If you're selling anything, believe me, we have it."

"Um, it's me, Jade, excited to start work today," I say enthusiastically, trying to sound like the motivated go-getter Conrad believes he's hired.

"I'm sorry," says the voice, though I'm not sure if he's apologizing for misidentifying me as a salesperson or advancing sympathy for what I'm about to endure.

A buzz sounds as the gate swings open. It groans on tired hinges, suggesting visitors are infrequent. I traipse along a driveway as wide as a road, leading toward a sprawling stone estate that's like something out of a fairy tale. The gardens lining my path are full of colorful, lively new blooms, leafy trees of all varieties, and shrubs sculpted into perfect angles.

Miramar is everything I imagined and more. It's stately and noble, with towering chimneys and elongated arched windows set deeply into rough-cut stone walls that are weathered and veined like old bones. In the center of a large circular driveway stands an ornate fountain featuring a bronze sculpture of a man and a woman holding a jug of cascading water.

The "castle meets country club" elegance is stunning, enhanced by the ocean backdrop, which takes my breath away. To my right is a manicured lawn that looks like it's been tended with the precision of nail clippers.

The front of the home is grand and inviting, featuring three columned archways fit for a king or queen. But what catches my eye is the stone tower attached to the building, rising like a vigilant sentinel until it reaches the domed copper crown. It extends at least fifty feet into the sky.

A seagull has perched itself on one of the many gables adorning the steeply pitched roof, its beady black eyes watching as I approach the front stairs.

Part of me thinks it's issuing some kind of warning, a message from Holly. *Keep away . . .*

Perhaps I should listen, but it's too late—I'm already at the front door.

I reach for the doorbell, but don't have to press it.

I should have realized someone would be ready to greet me. After all, I was buzzed in at the gate. The door opens, revealing a tall, angular man who looks as though he were present when the first stones of Miramar were set into the ground. He's dressed in a black suit so crisply pressed I have the impression it's never been worn, though it hangs a touch too loosely on his lean frame.

His thinning silver hair is carefully brushed back, suggesting age won't overtake him without a fight. His heavy-lidded, inscrutable eyes flick over me with practiced efficiency. If he's sizing me up, he keeps his conclusions carefully hidden. I can only imagine what this sharply dressed man thinks of my hoodie and worn-out Converse shoes.

He says nothing while peering down his long aristocratic nose. Not unkind, but shrewd.

"Hi, I, uh . . . I'm here for Mr. Carmichael." I hate the shake in my voice.

"Welcome to the jungle," says the old man, gesturing for me to enter. I guess he's joking, trying to connect with a young person by using a Guns N' Roses reference that's ancient history to me. But at least I know the song—my mom used to blast the tune on repeat. She was a big eighties hair band fan.

"We've been expecting you."

I'm led into a grand foyer, with a ceiling so smooth and arched it feels like walking beneath a wave. Although there's undeniable elegance to the space, the interior echoes its former glory more than its current state, as if the house recalls its best days—sunset cocktail parties, linen suits, elegant swimwear, and glamorous dinners—all relegated to the past.

Stone walls in the entryway show their age, their mortar cracked and discolored. The furniture is the sort you'd expect to see roped off in a museum—old and uncomfortable, with faded upholstery and uninviting cushions. The wood throughout is sun-bleached and weathered, as if it made its way through ocean currents before washing up on the shoreline. The banister lining the grand, curving staircase is worn to a dull sheen by generations of hands. Area rugs that might have once added bright splashes of color are now faded and threadbare.

Large oil paintings in gilded frames fail to lift the mood. The nature scenes, even those with green hills, are painted in drab colors. Perhaps dust has settled on the canvases. If there's a house cleaner here, they're being overpaid. My allergies threaten again.

"My name is Sidney," says the old man. "I'm the butler of Miramar." He doesn't extend his hand, so we don't shake, but I notice that he keeps his nails impeccably clean and neat.

"Does the name mean 'watcher of the sea'? I read that somewhere." I don't drop Holly's name.

Sid's eyebrows lift. "You've done your research. And yes, it does. Maeve Carmichael, whom you'll meet momentarily, is obsessed with the ocean. She takes a swim every afternoon, often in weather I wouldn't advise, but you'll soon find out that she does as she pleases."

I gulp, recognizing a warning when I hear one.

"If you have any questions about the house, its history, or how we do—or don't do—things around here, please ask. It's my duty to ensure you feel like one of the staff—which is to say, rarely seen and often blamed."

I can't say this is the best pep talk I've ever had, but at least I've got a job. Not long ago, I was hiding in the attic of a stranger's home, and now I have the run of a castle. Life sure does throw curveballs.

"Mr. Carmichael is waiting for you in his private study."

Old Sid gestures to a large door to my left. I follow his loping strides into a gorgeously appointed office. The ambiance is rich and warm, with an ornate area rug set in the center of a massive, airy room. Mahogany bookshelves line the walls, filled with hardback books whose spines suggest antiquity. I want to take down each volume, flip through the pages (gloves on, of course; I'm not a savage), and immerse myself in olden times and fantastical lands.

But I have to shelve that desire because my new boss is here, sitting at his spacious, decorative desk and sipping a steaming mug of coffee. Light floods the room through a tall bank of windows behind his chair. I imagine, during winter, logs in the large hearth will burn brightly, fighting the cold stone for warmth.

Conrad stands to greet me, his smile just as friendly as when he first offered me the chance at gainful employment.

"Jade," he says, coming around from behind his desk to shake my hand. "So glad you're here. Any trouble finding the place?"

He smiles as if it's a joke he's told hundreds of times, and it's never been funny, but I give him an obligatory chuckle.

"Yeah, it kind of stands out," I say.

"And has a good view, too." Conrad points out the window to where the lawn drops off and the sea rises to meet it, creating a stunning ocean panorama. I hope he wants me working in this room, surrounded by all these books and looking out over the water. I take a peek out the window, and that's when I notice a framed drawing of Miramar hanging on the adjacent wall. It's remarkably well done and captures both the grandeur and creepiness of this place. The signature says Conrad Carmichael.

"Wow, that's really great." I point to the drawing. "You did this?"

He looks wistful. "Yes, a very long time ago," he says. "I don't think I could find my pencils if I wanted to."

Sid clears his throat. "Mr. Carmichael, Miss Jade . . . um," he trails off, looking mildly abashed. "I'm afraid I don't know your last name."

Conrad laughs. "I don't know it either," he admits. "Sometimes I make rash decisions, but I usually get my employee's full name. My apologies."

"It's Jensen," I say brusquely. "Jade Jensen." I leave it at that, hoping he doesn't inquire about my long, sad history.

"Shall I go get your mother?" Sid asks Conrad.

He nods, and Sid departs to retrieve Maeve. I'm offered a seat in the cushy chair across from Conrad's desk. Sunlight and comfortable furniture—I make myself at home.

I notice Conrad tugging at the sleeves of his shirt, and I catch a glimpse of an expensive-looking watch and his polished gold cuff links, which bear his initials, *CC.* I wouldn't be surprised if someone had stitched his name into his underwear with gold thread.

"So, Jade, I went over the plan with Mother and managed to get her approval," he says, settling into his leather chair. "Her husband, Baxter Ward, passed away several months ago after an extended illness—"

I interrupt, my impulse control failing once again. "Oh, does your mother go by Maeve Ward now? I don't want to call her the wrong name."

"No, she kept the Carmichael name even after her second marriage. Legacy is important to my mother. She wanted to have the same name as her son and grandchildren, not that there are any . . ." His voice fades, leaving me with the impression he's got his own sad story to tell, but he doesn't elaborate.

"As I was saying, my stepfather passed away, and unfortunately, my mother's health has also declined. Don't get me wrong, she's still a very strong woman at seventy-eight, but she needs to take it easier these days. She's not up for going through his belongings and clearing everything out. Of course she believes she is. It's hard for her to admit that she can't do everything she used to, but the work involves some heavy lifting—nothing too intense. I think someone young like yourself would be better suited to the job. My mother can give you instructions on what to do with specific items. Any questions?"

Yeah, like a million. I knew I'd be helping around the house. But a strong-willed, reluctant widow overseeing a punk kid going through her dead husband's belongings? Sounds like a recipe for disaster.

Before I can say, "Second thoughts," Maeve appears in the doorway with Sidney. She's tall, but only comes up to Sid's shoulders, and although she's thin, her arms look strong. Her posture is near perfect, head held high. I'm certain she could sift through Baxter's things without a problem, although I can't picture a woman this fashionable getting her hands dirty. Her makeup softens her strong features. She styles her shoulder-length white hair with care. The ivory blazer and long skirt are crisp and crease-free.

She greets me with a tight downturned smile, as if the world always disappoints her. Her stony, gray-blue eyes pierce me like a javelin. *Great.* Two minutes on the job and I can tell the lady I'm hired to help doesn't want me around. *This should be fun.*

From across the room, she says, "Jade, it's a pleasure to meet you." Her tone is so clipped and self-important that she might as well have said, "What do you think you're doing in my house?"

As she crosses the rug to shake my hand (or slap me, can't say which), I'm reminded again of *Beach Thriller*. Old Sid might not have made it into Holly's book, but I've no doubt Holly didn't stray far from fact when she wrote Maeve Carmichael onto the page. Though something tells me the real-life Maeve is even icier.

She takes my hand and, as expected, her skin is cold and clammy. But then, without warning, I see her teeter on her feet. Her color turns gray. Her eyes widen as her knees buckle. I don't have time to think—I extend my arms as she falls into them. Christ, she smells like potpourri. I strain to support her, my tiny frame overwhelmed by this woman's stature, but somehow I manage to keep us both upright.

Conrad rushes to my side. "Mother!" he exclaims, taking her from me and guiding her with care to a nearby sofa.

Maeve's head rolls back. She groans but doesn't speak.

"Sidney, call the doctor immediately," Conrad orders.

I grab a pillow to support Maeve, trying to make myself useful. Conrad's hands tremble as he loosens her shirt collar to ensure her airflow isn't obstructed. I check her breathing and elevate her feet.

It's crazy how thirty seconds can feel like an eternity during a crisis. As full panic sets in, I hear Maeve speak. I can't understand her, but I'm flooded with relief.

Thank God I haven't inadvertently killed my employer on my first day at the job.

Chapter 19

Holly

Ethan returned in the morning with his tools and know-how. Holly wasn't staring, she told herself, she was just . . . noticing. Maybe for a beat too long . . .

But she crash-landed. He had used the pronoun "we," and although she didn't see a ring, he must be spoken for. Some lucky girl would get to watch *It's a Wonderful Life* with this hunky handyman, and it wouldn't be her. If nothing else, it was amusing fodder for a book: *Captivating carpenter stirs inner turmoil.*

She had to focus on money over personal pursuits, anyway. To that end, she had a meeting with the lawyer, Allen Spellman, scheduled in thirty minutes. Still, there was no harm in appreciating Ethan's aesthetics. And if she couldn't get money right away, this might be the last time she'd lay eyes on him.

He approached with a smile that could melt ice. Why did he seem so familiar to her? Why did little alarm bells go off in her head as he neared? He wasn't even her type. Almost all of Holly's past boyfriends were artists of some sort. There was the sculptor with the alcohol problem, the fellow writer with the bank account problem, the musician with the honesty problem, and the actor with every problem in the book.

The only notable exception was Max Egan, the boy with a mop of brown hair and caramel-colored eyes that swam with depth and sincerity. Did Ethan remind her of Max? Was that the source of her strange reaction?

"I have my pressure washer and solvent in the truck to remove the graffiti," Ethan said. "I believe it's high time Joey and Emily's love affair gets washed away. My gut tells me their relationship ended a long time ago." He smiled. It was adorable.

"That's great, Ethan. Do you mind if I write you a check just for today's work? Hopefully, my meeting with the lawyer will go well, and I'll be able to pay for everything in your estimate . . . but in my line of work, I've learned not to count any chickens until they're hatched."

He held up his hands, objecting to the prepayment, but Holly thrust a check at him anyway. He glanced at it, eyes widening. *Oh no,* Holly worried. *Do I owe him even more?*

"How cool! I might make a copy of this and paste it into my book," he joked.

Holly didn't get what he meant at first, but then remembered that Gail introduced her as a local author. But did that mean . . . ?

"I own a copy of *Beyond Horizons.* Didn't want to be presumptuous and bring it with me to get it signed. I don't know how that works—you're the only published author I've met."

Holly was in shock. "I'd be happy to sign your book. But—you actually *read* it?"

Ethan nodded. "Read it and loved it," he said. "Wait, I'm trying to remember—it was Dove, right? And what was the name of the shopkeeper?"

"Emma Lou," Holly said, awestruck.

It was one of her early works, placing Ethan among a highly exclusive group of twelve or so people Holly knew for certain had read it. *Wait, is he sensitive* and *hot? Or is this a tactic he uses to get girls to fall for him?* Either way, he'd scored points with Holly, which upped his dangerousness.

"I'll be back in a few hours," Holly said, wrapping up their mini book club before she was head over heels. Her dry spell had been long, her bed was cozy, and her repairman fantasy was quite vivid.

It was time to go.

. . .

The law office of Allen Spellman wasn't much to look at. Neither was Allen Spellman. He was short, squat, and balding, but appeared industrious. The sleeves of his button-down shirt were rolled up, his navy-blue tie hung askew, and his sport coat was draped over the back of his black leather chair.

She had no trouble finding his office. He worked on the second floor of a small brick building that had received historical designation from the town of Beauport, a label the committee handed out like candy on Halloween. Everything in Beauport was historic, even dull, boxy buildings like this one.

Spellman's workplace was as bland as the man seated at his desk. There was no ocean view. The walls were painted gray, the windows covered with vinyl mini-blinds, and a few black metal filing cabinets lined a back wall over which hung a single framed seascape. Holly scanned the books on the shelves of the built-in bookcase, seeing a collection of legal publications, which meant nothing to her beyond offering assurances that she was in capable hands.

She was nervous as she took a seat across from him.

This will go better than expected, she told herself as she shook Allen's hand.

"Holly, Holly Sinclair," he said brightly. "It's nice to finally put a face to the voice."

Holly's spirits lifted. He wouldn't be Mr. Chipper if he were about to share doomy, gloomy news.

"I was so sorry to hear about your mother's passing," he began. "We didn't know each other well—I took over the firm after she had set up her will. But she gave me power of attorney over the account used to maintain the beach cottage, and as you know, I'm also the executor of her will. I've been busy working through all the probate issues before the remaining funds pass to you."

Holly added her own narration: *You are a lazy daughter who should have been more involved in your mother's finances, but you left it all to an expensive stranger.*

Shit. She really wasn't the best daughter. But her mother had checked out of life after Anna's death, so neither of them deserved the Family Member of the Year award.

It took a moment for Allen's words to click: *Probate issues . . . double shit. That doesn't sound good.*

"I know money was tight for your mom," Allen continued, "and I want you to know I did a lot of the work for a reduced fee."

"I appreciate that," Holly said, omitting that she, too, was in desperate straits. "The house needs some serious attention, especially now that I'll be living there full time."

Allen's face lit up. "Oh, you're going to be a local again. That's great—welcome back!"

Holly managed a strained smile. "Thanks, I, uh . . . I really need to fix up the cottage to make it livable. Publishing is a fickle business, and money is a little tight. This probate thing won't take long, will it?"

Allen coddled her with his eyes like she was a naive child. "The good news is you can live in the house even while it's in probate, and you can legally make the necessary repairs. You've lived there in the past and there are no remaining relatives to contest the will. But unfortunately, I can't legally distribute assets until the statutory period for creditors to make a claim has expired, which is one year in Massachusetts. Since the assets weren't in a trust, I'm afraid that's the law."

Holly's face fell. She thought there *had* been a trust. She heard the voice again—loud, clear, and quite cutting: *Why weren't you on top of things, Hol? Why did you neglect your mother's affairs? You've been so self-involved—obsessed over words and characters that nobody cares about, lamenting over reviews and paltry sales. Now it's come back to bite you in the ass like a cartoon dog.*

Holly's heart began palpitating. "Allen, I'm really short on cash. I've got a handyman ready to do the work, and I can't pay him in tuna casseroles, not that I'm much of a cook. Can't I get some money for repairs? I could use a little for myself, too, until my ship comes in." *Or sinks to the bottom of the sea.*

Again, Allen cleared his throat in that "sucks to be you" way. "Holly, I'm sorry. The law is the law. When your mother was alive, we could distribute funds for home maintenance. Now that she's gone, those funds are frozen."

Holly's blink-and-make-it-all-better trick didn't work. "Wait, you're telling me that I can't get any money—not a dime—until a *year* from now?"

"Well, less," said Allen. "More like eight months. It's been some time since your mother passed."

Holly hadn't thought to check on the will because her mother had no money or assets other than the house and the fund established to pay for it. She thought her mother had put the money into a trust, but she never followed through. How careless she had been.

Holly tried to avoid clichés in her writing, but sometimes they said it best: She was up shit creek without a paddle.

"The good news is you have plenty of money in the account to take care of the property. Here, I'll show you."

A moment later, Holly was scanning a printout of several months' worth of statements. Indeed, there was enough money to do the repairs and more, but she noticed something else. There were regular monthly transfers to unknown recipients—not utilities, taxes, or legal expenses—and always for the same amounts.

She pointed them out to Spellman. "What are these?" Holly sifted through the pile, confirming that, as she suspected, the transfers went back years.

Allen studied them for a moment. "Honestly, I'm not sure. Those were in place before I began managing the accounts. I recall asking your mother about them. Her explanation was vague, but she was adamant that they be kept in place. And that's my job—to see that things are handled according to your mother's wishes."

Holly nodded. The transfers hadn't drained the account, and now those were likely frozen as well. "Is there any way I can draw money for a short period—you know, like take out a loan against myself?" She imagined the cold of October when temperatures plummeted and winds tore off the ocean.

"Holly, I wish I could help you, I really do. But there's no way around this probate stipulation. I do understand your conundrum . . ." His voice trailed off, and he leaned his head on his hand. A smile spread across his face.

"Let me write you a check from my account. Think of it as a personal loan. Just a little something to tide you over, and you can pay me back when the courts release the funds. I've worked with your family for years now. I'm sure I can trust you."

Holly felt elated and pathetic at the same time. She wasn't holding a paper cup and a cardboard sign at the entrance to a highway, but she wasn't that far off. "Would you? I'm sorry to take you up on that, but I'm in a tough spot, and no bank will give me a loan when I'm out of contract."

"Don't give it another thought," said Spellman, who pulled his checkbook from a drawer. "I'm happy that the cottage will be loved and cared for."

She beamed when she saw the amount. It was a loan, so she tried not to feel too guilty. But it was odd that there were literally no strings attached—no paperwork, no agreement to sign, no formal commitment to repay it. Then the adage of not looking a gift horse in the mouth came to mind.

"I can't thank you enough. I missed Beauport, but it's been hard not to dwell on the past. This will help me focus more on the future," she said.

A dark cloud passed across Allen's face. "Yes . . . your sister. I'm sorry about that as well. Terrible accident."

"Or not," said Holly, almost as an aside.

Allen perked up. "Do you think—?"

Holly's brief silence filled in the blanks. "I didn't want to come back. Too many awful memories and not enough closure."

Allen looked sympathetic. "Being here must be like reopening the wound. But what are you suggesting?"

Holly leaned forward, pressing her elbows against his desk. "You're this town's only lawyer."

Allen brushed off the observation like it was a compliment. "There are three of us, to be precise, but I might be the most well-known."

"Then you must know the police in town. You've probably heard things." Holly's voice dipped a degree lower. "I don't think Anna's death was an accident," she said. "And for some reason, the cops gave it the brush-off."

Allen straightened. "Th-that's a pretty big claim," he stuttered. "Do you have any evidence?"

"Call it a gut feeling," Holly said, her voice subdued. "In my opinion, there were suspects who weren't properly investigated—powerful people in Beauport."

The look on Allen's face all but named those people without saying a word. It was a small town.

"But why would anyone want to harm your sister?" he asked.

Holly decided less was more. "Tom Walker was one of the officers on the case, and I don't think they were thorough—there were leads they should have followed. They never even learned how the fire started. I saw him the other day and picked up on the not-so-subtle message I'm not welcome in town. Why would that be? I'm guessing Walker thinks I've come back to start trouble."

Allen's expression softened. "Look, consider me a friend of your family after all this time. I know Tom Walker—and yeah, I've heard things. In fact, he's come under fire recently. I don't know much about your sister's death, but I do know Walker is bad news. The details have been kept hush-hush, but his wife left him recently, and I think it's related to his troubles on the force. I'll try to get some info for you without being overt.

"But, Holly, believe me when I say the cops in Beauport like to let things lie, if you know what I'm saying. You need to tread very lightly."

Holly left Allen's office feeling much more optimistic. His check would keep Ethan around and Chester fed. Jade, too. The girl was part of her life now. Not only that—talking with Allen had been a big step in confronting her past. And Allen had validated her concerns. Tommy Boy was a crooked cop, and people were catching on.

She knew what she had to do next—go to the police station and ask to look at Anna's old case file. She needed to see the hard evidence.

Holly marched along the boardwalk with purpose. She'd spent enough time being passive, ignoring the family finances and burying old trauma. She was forty years old, and it was time to get a handle on it all.

As Holly approached the police station, she passed the Bean There Café. The busker was planted outside, singing his sad songs in his horrid off-key tone. He looked up at Holly and stopped mid-chorus.

Keeping his eyes locked on hers, he slowed down his strumming and switched to a different song. She recognized the tune immediately, even if his rendition was sorely lacking. She could feel his cold eyes on her as he began to sing "Every Breath You Take" by the Police. She rushed past as fast as she could, his words trailing behind her: "I'll be watching you . . ."

Chapter 20

The Watcher

What are you up to, Holly? My guess is no good.

I've been keeping an eye on you, and I don't like what I see. I've noticed a newfound determination in your stride. You're a woman on a mission, that much is obvious.

You didn't notice that I followed you to the lawyer's office. I'm assuming you have to make financial arrangements for the house, which looks dreadful. But not for long, right? That handyman will fix it up for you. You could stay there for a long time . . . unless you keep putting your nose where it doesn't belong. Then all bets are off.

I didn't stay for your whole meeting. I had other things to do. But now I'm back on your trail, watching . . .

I see you despite the crowd of tourists. You're certainly in a hurry—no window-shopping today, no time for a shot of caffeine. Given the path you're taking, I believe I know where you're headed.

It's a bad idea, Holly. A very bad idea.

Remember, you're a professional writer, not a trained investigator. You should keep your head down, typing away. I know you won't outline your next story. You never do. You call yourself a pantser, as in flying by the seat of your pants. I've learned that about you from the privacy of my computer.

That's just another way I watch.

Here's what else I know: You're working on your fifteenth book. As a teen, you loved reading and devoured classics like *Jane Eyre*, *Sense and Sensibility*, and—of course—anything by Shakespeare. When you began writing, you focused on crafting stories about human emotions and meaningful relationships. You pride yourself on telling a good tale that doesn't need a dead body to move the plot along.

But that's the old you. You're changing, Holly. It's happening right before my eyes. This new you might decide to try writing about a murder, one that actually took place, maybe even one close to home. I'm here to tell you: You shouldn't. You think you're finally making progress, but you have no idea the danger you're stumbling into.

So I do what I do best—I follow you. Just another face in the crowd, seen but unseen. I am a phantom. I am your ghost. I'm right behind you when you march into the police station.

There's danger there—danger all around. I reach into my pocket. I feel the sturdy cold steel beneath my palm. It's right there, waiting for me, in case I need it.

Don't push it, Holly.

Chapter 21

Jade

Good news: Maeve isn't going to die.

She's resting on the couch in Conrad's office. The doctor is here. His name is Dr. Vernon Hill, but I'm told everyone calls him Vern.

Dr. Hill isn't what I expected. He doesn't look like a typical doctor with his fedora, Hawaiian shirt, and old-fashioned wire-rimmed glasses (back in the day, they would have been called spectacles). He's almost the same height as Conrad and moves like a much younger person. But his gray hair, bushy mustache, and wiry eyebrows suggest he's in his sixties. He looks strong for his age—one of those guys who still thinks he's twenty when he's at the gym.

The doctor does all the doctor things: gives Maeve pills, checks her blood pressure and temperature, listens to her heart and lungs, applies a cold compress to her forehead, and checks her reflexes.

"Stop it! Stop fussing over me," Maeve says, swatting at Dr. Hill as she pulls herself into a sitting position. "It was nothing."

Conrad's voice is heavy with concern. "It's your third fainting spell in as many weeks. You should go to the hospital, get some blood drawn, and run more tests. And no more swimming. It's not safe for you to be out in the ocean—especially alone."

"Nonsense," Maeve insists, her spine straightening. "I got a bit dizzy, that's all. I'm perfectly fine." She shifts her gaze to me. "You there, girl."

Even though she's pointing at me, I look around as if a person named Girl might be standing nearby. "Get me some iced tea, five ice cubes, two sprigs of mint, and a teaspoon of sugar. Be quick. I need an energy boost."

I pull back, stunned. *Um, no, I think you need some manners.* But I keep that thought to myself as I head off to fulfill Maeve's request, unsure how to find the kitchen.

Conrad takes my arm, holding me back. "Mother, this is Jade," he says as if speaking to a woman with dementia. "I've hired her to help you sort through Baxter's belongings. Remember? You agreed to this. She's not the housekeeper." He pulls out his phone and sends a text. "I've sent a message to Rose. She'll bring your tea."

The mention of Rose's name is enough to make Maeve's ghostly pallor turn red.

"That woman is useless," she says. Her rouged lips pucker in disgust.

"If you hadn't fired most of the staff, we'd have other options. Unfortunately, you've gone through all the available help in town, so I've hired Jade to assist with some additional tasks that need to be done."

He presents me like an offering. Where do they keep the altar for human sacrifices? Now I understand why he hired a shoplifting pierced rebel—no other options.

The doctor shines a penlight into Maeve's eyes. She flinches as if he's poked her.

"Enough, Vern," she snaps, turning her head. "I'm fine. I told you that. What I need is some breathing room."

"Dr. Hill, can you please talk sense into her?" Conrad asks.

Dr. Hill grimaces like a cowboy tasked with breaking a wild stallion. "Maeve, Conrad is right. You've been having fainting spells far too often. You really should have more tests done."

A woman appears outside the office. She hovers in the doorway. Nobody is blocking her way, but she refuses to enter. Instead, she holds out a tall, dew-drenched glass of iced tea, which Conrad takes like a relay baton. I examine the drink in his hand, and sure enough—five ice cubes and two mint sprigs float in the amber liquid.

"Thank you, Rose," Conrad says, bringing the glass to his mother.

Rose—short, round, and in her fifties, with jet-black hair pulled into a tight bun atop her head and eyes dark with animosity—departs without a word.

"Rose and Mother don't exactly get along, but I pay her well enough that she hasn't quit—yet," Conrad whispers to me while giving his mother a frustrated side-eye.

Maeve drinks her tea in a ladylike fashion, pinky extended, offering no comment about Rose. They're like feuding neighbors, trapped together and resigned to resenting each other. If Maeve tries to turn me into her punching bag, I'll be out of here faster than a bullet. There must be a pawnshop somewhere nearby, and there are plenty of gilded goodies I can slip into my pockets on my way out the door.

Half of Maeve's tea is gone when she sets down her glass with a thud. She quietly gets up, without assistance, shifting her weight from one foot to the other to test the strength of her legs, then smooths her skirt with her palms as if that alone can restore her dignity.

Dr. Hill readies himself to catch her should she topple again.

"Conrad, see to it this young woman has something productive to do—and keep her out of my hair. I'm going upstairs to work on the fundraising gala for the Beauport Art Association. This party has to be perfect. It's the first one we've had in years, and it could be my last."

Conrad squints, rubbing his chin. "Mother, I think hosting a party is too much for you right now. Can't we postpone?"

Maeve's smile comes off as a sneer. "I'm not getting any younger, and you're not giving me any grandchildren. I need to create some sort of legacy before I'm gone. The Barefoot Beach Ball is going to make a grand resurgence."

I'm reminded of Holly's novel as Maeve heads out the door, breezing past like I don't exist. Dr. Hill follows closely behind, his eyes wide with worry.

She might be dead at any moment. It's hard to imagine that many people would mourn the loss.

Conrad invites me on a tour of the grounds. I follow him along a narrow dirt path parallel to the sea. The massive stone house with its imposing tower stands like a scar against the sky. I know about homes like this only from books: opulent estates with a maze of rooms, lush manicured gardens—an oasis for birds and butterflies.

"This place is amazing," I say, marveling at a graceful willow tree, its loping branches forming a shady canopy under which stands the cutest wooden bench, perfect for reading. "Is it historic or something?" *What I really want to ask is: Is it haunted?*

"It's registered with the Beauport Historical Society, and I've given them most of the archives for posterity."

He doesn't ask if I know what posterity means.

"Are you a history buff?" he inquires.

"Not really," I admit. "But I like castles and romantasy novels."

I catch his slightly raised eyebrows. I must sound like a child.

"It's a portmanteau," I explain. "Romance and fantasy combined, like brunch—which is breakfast and lunch."

He laughs. "I know the word. I just didn't realize you're a big reader. I thought kids your age were more into their devices than the written word. I'm impressed."

I blush.

"Maybe, you'd be interested in the history of the house?"

"Of course," I say, hoping it'll be brief.

Conrad clears his throat. "Miramar is designed in the High Victorian Gothic style, inspired in part by Henry Vaughan, who likely trained under British architect George Frederick Bodley—a leading figure in the Gothic Revival movement."

Oh God. I'm suddenly on a field trip. A yawn rises up, almost impossible to fight off, but I asked for this, so I listen.

"My great-great-grandfather was an industrialist and successful banker. After visiting the Washington National Cathedral, he was inspired to build a home that echoed its design. Fortunately for him, granite mining was booming here in the late 1800s and early 1900s. Most of the stone was quarried locally, though some of the rocks came from ruined castles and abbeys. Those were embedded into the walls."

I nod like I've never been more fascinated, but dread creeps in. I felt uneasy inside the house as if something more than old stones were buried in the walls. Tragedy. Sorrow. The air practically hums with it. Why is the outside kept pristine while the interior seems to have been neglected? Maybe it's a metaphor for the family, or perhaps I've simply read too many novels.

"Do you have a gardener as well as a housekeeper?"

"We *had* a gardener, but he quit. Now I hire a landscaping company for a lot more money. My mother is good at driving people away."

I could see that after my first five minutes in Maeve's company. At least Maeve is planning some kind of fundraiser, though I strongly suspect it's more about showing off than a sudden flare of altruism.

Why did Conrad lure me into this job when he knows how his mother treats the staff? Is he that desperate? Or is he playing some kind of game? Rich people have twisted ways of getting their jollies when there's nothing left in life to conquer.

"I'm not expecting you to be any different," he says. "Don't hang around and suffer her abuse on my account. I'm not trying to sugarcoat it, Jade, though I should have warned you up front. I'm happy to pay you for your time today—maybe two hundred? And you can move on if this isn't the right opportunity."

"Opportunity? Is that what they're calling verbal abuse these days?" I laugh, making sure Conrad knows I'm kidding. Luckily he joins in. The warmth of his laugh puts me at ease. What could I get for a bonus if I last through the summer? Considering how much he'll pay me to leave after a few hours on the job, I'd bet a lot. Keeping Mom out of Conrad's hair has got to be worth a hefty payday. *Challenge accepted.*

"All I'm saying is, I'd understand if you decide this isn't for you."

"No, no, it's fine," I say. "I'm looking forward to it." I almost believe myself. "So what's that over there?" I point to some sort of ruin. This is the only part of the grounds they haven't kept pristine.

The path is overgrown, with clusters of weeds sprouting around the remains of a stone structure. The rocks look blackened, which could be from exposure to the elements—or something else more destructive. It's a lonesome, sad sight for such a beautiful location, that's for sure. Any building that stands here would offer breathtaking views of the sea, and I'm surprised someone hasn't put the land to better use.

"What happened there?" I ask, pointing but keeping my distance. This spot feels sacred, as though we've stumbled upon an archaeological find that we must not desecrate.

Conrad goes completely still, almost spellbound, as though he can peer into the past. I look, too, imagining the building that once occupied this land—one made of stone, with a big bay window overlooking the sea.

His chest caves, his shoulders curling around him. Conrad's eyes glisten from unshed tears, though I could be imagining that. He inhales a deep breath of salty sea air, which works as a reset. The very next instant, he is Conrad of yore—stoic, good-natured, and buttoned-up.

"That was our guesthouse," he says in a heavy tone. "It was destroyed years ago, and I didn't have the heart to rebuild it. So here it lies, a ruin on our castle grounds."

He turns his back on the abandoned site and moves along the path, his hands clasped behind his back, a gentle cadence to his steps. I hurry to catch up.

The tower looms before us. "So cool you have an actual tower. I'd love to see what's up there." My tone is cheerful, but the moment the words exit my mouth, I regret them.

Something flashes in Conrad's eyes. Rage? Fear? Either way, his glowering look gives me the feeling that the tower holds secrets he'd rather keep locked up.

We stop in the middle of the path. We're all alone. The wind rustles the tall grass bordering what's left of the guesthouse. Far below, ocean waves crash against the jagged rocks.

"Jade," he says in a calm voice, his focus unwavering. His dark eyes have taken on a cold, menacing quality. "There are three rules for employment. They are non-negotiable. The job will pay you well—very well, I assure you. But you must never violate these three caveats." He pauses, allowing his words to land.

My gut twists. This feels like an initiation into some cult. A wiser, less desperate person might have explained the gig wasn't for them and hightailed it out of here, but I can't walk away. I have no money and no other prospects, so my options are limited. If we were playing poker, Conrad would be holding the far better hand.

"Sure. Ah, what are they?"

"One." Conrad holds up a finger. "The tower is off-limits, *always*. No exceptions. Is that clear?"

I nod.

"Two." He adds a second finger. "You are never, and I repeat, *never*, allowed on the grounds of this property before seven o'clock in the morning, nor are you permitted to be here after seven at night. This rule applies whether you're employed here or not."

"Fine by me. I'm not an early bird anyway." My laugh is shaky.

The darkness in Conrad's eyes only deepens. "What's the third rule?" I gulp.

"Don't steal," he says in all seriousness. "Not one item, no matter how insignificant it may seem. Don't even think about it. The old you—the thief—that girl no longer exists."

His words land like a slap. *That girl.* He says it like I'm dead and buried, but I'm still here. Still me. And still wondering why I'm not running away.

"Are these rules clear?"

I nod again but don't utter a word because I'm too afraid of saying the wrong thing. However, a little voice inside my head warns me: When it comes to Conrad and the Carmichael estate, any infraction, big or small, will result in serious consequences.

Chapter 22

Holly

After what felt like an interminable wait, a loud buzzer sounded near an imposing metal door. Tom Walker entered the waiting area of the Beauport Police Department and shot Holly a cold, reptilian stare.

"Holly Sinclair . . . let me guess, you found the girl, brought her back for a nice meal, and she walked off with your purse." He gave her an unkind smile.

"No," Holly said, crossing her arms. "I'm here to look at the evidence box from the investigation into my sister's death."

The words alone were enough to transport Holly back in time. The years between then and now folded in an instant. The sick flush of shame she'd carried out of Beauport filled her anew, as though she'd never left.

Anna shouldn't have been alone that night. I should have been with her. Her death is my fault.

Walker would have growled if he could. "You called me out here for that?" Then he laughed, a grating sound that made her blood pressure surge.

She straightened, her resolve hardening. "Yes, *Tom*," she said, purposely forgoing any formalities. "I need to take a look for myself."

"And what exactly are you looking for?" Walker latched his hands to his hips, inches from his gun.

Holly noticed his chest swell as he tried to appear more intimidating. She'd expected pushback and had come prepared. "I won't know what I'm looking for until I see it."

"Are you implying that we didn't do our job—that *I* didn't do mine?" Heat radiated off him.

"I'm not implying anything, Officer Walker," said Holly in a measured tone. "I'm simply asking for information about my family."

Walker leaned back on his heels. His broad frame continued to block the entrance to the inner sanctum. He cleared his throat.

"I'm afraid that's not possible, Holly," he said. "Technically, the case is still open. I'm sure you wouldn't want to do anything to violate the integrity of the evidence. If there's a development and something got mishandled, it could impede our ability to make an arrest."

Holly eyed him with disgust. "This case is close to twenty years old. Is anyone actively working on it?"

Walker cocked an eyebrow. "Any open case is always an active investigation. And besides, the evidence box isn't even here. We keep older case files in an off-site storage area. I couldn't get to it even if I wanted to. We'd need to contact the DA's office first. There's paperwork to file—bureaucracy, you know how that is—and there are no guarantees you'll even get permission. You're better off letting bygones be bygones."

But Holly didn't let it go. "Why is her death listed as *undetermined*? That alone means there's more to investigate."

Walker shrugged. "All that means—and I apologize for being tactless—is that your sister's body wasn't in good enough condition for the ME to determine what exactly killed her. But let's be honest, we all know it was the fire. And there's no evidence the fire was anything other than a tragic accident. When you hear hoofbeats, think horses, not zebras. Know what I mean?"

Holly craned her neck to meet Tommy Boy's hard stare. "To my ears, you sound like a man with something to hide."

Walker grinned as if he enjoyed being challenged. "I'm just doing my job and following protocol. You have an overactive writer's imagination, Holly. Don't let it get you into trouble." The message rang loud and clear, a veiled threat from a shoddy small-town cop.

Holly turned to go. Tommy Boy wasn't worth any more of her time. She'd find a way to work around him.

As she marched out of the station, her writer's brain kicked into high gear. She composed a list of "Unusual Ways to Die" in her head, with Tommy at the center of every mishap—shark attack, fall from a cliff, an incident with a hot frying pan. Better still: an accidental firearm discharge into a very sensitive part of the male anatomy.

Chapter 23

Jade

Back at Miramar, the stone walls of the manor feel colder, and the space has grown darker. I don't see Dr. Hill or Maeve, but Sid is milling about, and I've received the first task of my new position. I'm sorting jewelry that belonged to Baxter's first wife. I'm not sure what her name was, but I guess she died young—and he kept way too many of her belongings. I wonder how Maeve felt about that.

I'm seated in a velvet chair at a large, kingly table with a mirror-like polish in a spacious dining room. A massive crystal chandelier hangs overhead. My task is to detangle all the necklaces and arrange the rings and brooches in some semblance of order.

When I open the lid of the massive walnut jewelry box, I feel like a pirate. I've never seen such a collection of glittering jewels, splashes of gold and silver intermixed. Is Conrad testing me? Even though the necklaces are tangled, it's possible that he has inventoried every last piece and plans to check afterward to account for all items.

"I have to go into town for business," he says. "Mother is still resting, so when you're finished organizing the jewelry, you can head home for the day. Come back tomorrow, and we'll get you started sorting through my stepfather's old closet. Nine AM?"

"Sounds great," I reply, wondering what happens before seven. But I know all three rules, and he can count every piece of jewelry when he returns. It will all be here—except for the piece hanging around my neck.

I peer at the inscription etched on the back of my pendant—Beauport, MA.

The detached stone is in my pocket. I almost showed it to Conrad so he knows it's mine, but then I'd have to explain too much. I could ask him about local jewelers. He might be able to help me figure out where it came from. But I bet he only knows the super-high-end shops, and my piece—though I love it—is hardly Carmichael caliber.

The detangling work is mind-numbingly tedious but oddly satisfying. It's very quiet. The home has the weighty silence of an empty church.

A sound outside the dining room catches me by surprise. I take a break to investigate. If anyone asks, I'll say I'm stretching my stiff legs.

I peek into the great hall, expecting to see Sid wandering around, but instead, it's Rose. She casts anxious, fleeting glances around her, not noticing me as she fishes through her apron pocket and pulls out a large brass key. She slips the key into the lock of a door, which I suspect leads to the top of the tower. I hear the click as the lock disengages, the creak as the door slides open, and then another click as Rose locks the door from the inside.

Only when I'm sure no one is coming do I dare approach. The wooden door is tall and impressive, made from smooth, weathered teak. A polished, antique doorknob shaped like a seashell shines like it doesn't get turned often.

My intuition tells me to walk away. But something about this door beckons me, daring me closer—a challenge it knows I will accept.

Pressing my ear to the brass keyhole, I listen.

Someone is talking in a low voice, muffled and indistinct. Then I hear something else—a sad, lonesome moan. It's eerie and quiet, like the faint cry of an owl in a deep, dark wood.

Another noise bounces down the stairs—this time, a piano plinking. I'm not sure if it's a recording or if someone is playing. But I'm certain I've heard the song before. It's a famous lullaby. It's beautiful.

The moaning stops as the music begins. The melody wraps around me, sweet and sad, like a memory I can't grasp. But that moan . . . that wasn't singing. That was something else, more like a trapped animal, not entirely human.

Great. Wouldn't it be my luck to get caught up in a werewolf saga?

I'm lost in the music when a loud thwack strikes right above my head. I jump. My heart rockets to my throat. For a second, I can't breathe.

It's Conrad, his palm planted flat against the wood about three inches above my head. He hovers over me like a tall shadow.

I turn slowly to face him, trying to control my breathing. I can barely meet his eyes.

"I forgot something," he says in a deliberately cool, calm voice. "And it appears you forgot something as well: Rule one, Jade. The tower is off-limits. *Always.*"

Chapter 24

Holly

Making dinner for two was a foreign concept for Holly, but she was getting the hang of it. The green beans were a little soggy, the chicken and rice a little dry, but overall, the risk of food poisoning was pretty low, so that was a win.

Before diving into the meal, Jade put her hands together in a prayer position.

"I didn't know you were religious," said Holly, who didn't know much about Jade at all, though, oddly, dinner together felt normal—familiar, even. *Good lord.* If a runaway helped Holly feel grounded, how woefully out of balance was her life?

"I'm not religious," Jade said. "I just feel like Joey and Emily need all the help they can get now that their love is gone."

It took Holly a second, but then she laughed. Oh yes—Ethan had cleaned off the graffiti. He'd made good progress on the other work, too. And thanks to Allen Spellman, Holly could pay for his time and materials.

She raised her glass of water. Jade reached for her Dr Pepper, a beverage choice Holly had never understood. It wasn't her place to patrol the girl's nutrition, yet she had the urge to get her a glass of milk instead.

"To Joey and Emily," said Jade in solemn reverence. "May their love continue, or may they find true happiness elsewhere."

"If Joey loved with all the powers of his puny being, he couldn't love as much in eighty years as I could in a day."

Jade's eyes grew wide. "Whoa, that's beautiful," she said with complete sincerity.

"Yeah, it is," said Holly. "Wish I had written it. It's Emily Brontë, *Wuthering Heights*. But I added the Joey part."

"Heathcliff," said Jade, surprising Holly.

"You know the book?"

Jade made a *pshaw* sound. "It's a classic, but it's not a love story, in my opinion. Catherine and Heathcliff had a super toxic dynamic. Way too obsessive to be healthy. If spray paint had existed in the late eighteenth century, I bet Heathcliff would've tagged Catherine's name all over the moors."

Holly laughed so hard she spit out her rice. For that brief moment, she felt downright at home.

"Speaking of the graffiti, how's that handyman?" Jade asked, narrowing her gaze. "I caught a glimpse of him on his way out yesterday—he's a total DILF."

Holly didn't get the reference at first, but then realized it was the male version of MILF.

"Any sparks?" Jade teased. "Seems to me you could use a little excitement in your life."

"Taking in a runaway is enough excitement for me. Besides, I think he's got a girlfriend." Holly was surprised to hear obvious disappointment in her voice.

"So? You're way better. I don't even need to meet that woman to know she's trash. He should dump whoever she is and go out with you."

Jade finished everything on her plate, so Holly got up to grab her seconds, along with a glass of milk.

"I'm not looking for a relationship. I have too much on my mind and too much to do to let a man distract me," she said.

"Like the book you have to write," said Jade, drinking the milk without prodding.

"Yes, exactly. I have to focus. Writing is an extremely disciplined profession."

Jade set her elbows on the table and leaned over her plate, a hungry look in her eyes. "Can you teach me your process? I'd love to learn."

Holly didn't hesitate. "Step one: Come up with a good idea. You do know why people finish books, don't you?"

"To find out what happens," Jade said, as if the answer were obvious.

"They read because they care about the characters," Holly explained. "Not all readers will connect with your characters the same way. That's why writing a book that everyone loves is impossible. But you, as the author, have to love the people you create on the page. You have to care about what happens to them. If you can do that for yourself, others will come along for the ride—and enjoy it."

"But not everyone," Jade said.

"You can't please the world, Jade." Holly set her knife and fork down on her plate. "Speaking of pleasing people, how did it go at the Carmichaels'?" She couldn't hide the trepidation in her voice.

Jade slid another bite of food into her mouth, chewing with care. "They seem pretty normal to me," she said. "It should be an easy job and good money."

"I'm glad to hear it," Holly said, though Jade's words didn't exactly sound convincing. "But let me know if you run into problems. I'm concerned about you up there in that big house, with that family . . . which reminds me, don't you think you should call your aunt Alice? She's probably very worried about you."

Jade's face fell flat. "She doesn't care what happens to me. She isn't rooting for my character in her story."

"Touché." Holly gave her a tender smile. "But please, let her know you're alive, will you?"

"I can't get into it tonight. I'll deal with it tomorrow, okay?"

Holly wasn't going to argue. "Give her my number if she wants to talk. You don't have to go back there if you don't want to. You can stay here—at least I'll know you're safe. But she should know that, too."

Holly couldn't believe her own words. Had she just invited Jade to live with her for an undetermined period of time?

Jade's relieved expression said it was an offer she was more than happy to accept.

Tom Walker appeared to be right about one thing: *Once you feed them, they don't want to leave.*

Beach Thriller

iii

It was a picture-perfect beach day—low humidity, temperatures in the mid-seventies, and a gentle ocean breeze wafting over the sunbathers. Bright sunshine warmed Anna and Holly as they lounged on beach blankets. They covered themselves in tanning lotion, the fresh coconut scent filling the air. Waves crashed rhythmically on the shoreline, lulling the sisters into a peaceful, dreamlike state.

Anna stretched her legs long, burying her toes in the dry sand. They had the whole day to themselves. Thank God. The embarrassment of the catering catastrophe wasn't a fresh wound, but for Anna, the shame still lingered. She hoped it would disappear completely when the cut on her palm finally healed. Meanwhile, all Holly could do was offer words of support.

"Nobody cares," she repeatedly assured her sister. "Those people aren't thinking about us. We're nothing to them."

That much was true. Anna hadn't known any of them beforehand, including Conrad—whom she couldn't get out of her head—and it seemed doubtful they'd ever cross paths again. But as soon as the thought entered her mind, Anna noticed none other than the dark-haired Adonis she'd been obsessing over strolling up to their spot at the beach.

"Hey, you two," Conrad said cheerfully. He wore red trunks and an unbuttoned shirt revealing his taut, tanned torso. "Fancy running into you two here."

Holly looked about, confused. "Where? The beach?" She laughed. "I'm sure you've run into us plenty of times and never noticed."

But Conrad was noticing now. He couldn't avert his eyes from Anna, who was nervously playing with her auburn locks.

"Have you summered here for a long time?" he asked.

"Only our entire lives," Holly said, grabbing a book from her beach bag, implying she had better things to do than have this conversation. "But I suppose we travel in *very* different circles."

Conrad cleared his throat. "I missed a couple of summers in Beaufort. There was boarding school, then college—after a gap year in Europe . . . Guess I'm out of the summer scene. My loss."

Anna gawked at him, wondering if he had a clue how privileged he sounded, but he prattled on. *Nope, no clue.*

"I apologize again. That was quite a night." Finally he appeared a little chastened. "Anna, I hope you're feeling all right—no lingering injuries?"

She shook her head, recoiling not only at the memory of her embarrassing fall, but also Baxter Ward's octopus arms. Conrad continued: "Look, can I buy you both ice cream? Help make it up to you?"

Holly started to speak, but Anna cut her off. "Sure, but make mine a hot fudge sundae, extra whipped cream." She popped up from her beach towel, grabbing her oversize tee and pulling on her short shorts. She couldn't help herself. Conrad may be pretentious and self-involved, but he was also alluring. *Besides, it's only ice cream,* she told herself. *What could go wrong?*

The local hot spot on the boardwalk—the Dairy Dip—had a long line, but that wasn't unusual for this time of year. It was one reason Anna was grateful to no longer work there. The other reason was Conrad. If she'd kept the Dairy Dip gig, there'd have been no party, no fountain, and no destiny.

"Best place in town for a sugar fix." Conrad flashed a wide smile. "I'm getting my usual—a soft-serve twist. I probably won't even have to order; they know what I want here."

He was fishing for his wallet when they heard an unctuous, high-pitched voice behind them.

"Oh, there you are, sweetheart! I've been looking all over for you."

Anna turned and laid eyes on Elizabeth, who looked like she had just stepped out of a *Sports Illustrated* photo shoot in her blue string bikini and white gauze cover-up, which didn't cover up much of anything.

"I was just talking about you!" she chirped, slipping one arm around her fiancé and extending the other toward Anna to show off her dazzling diamond ring. "Isn't it amazing? I knew I could trust Conrad to find the perfect piece!"

Anna and Holly barely acknowledged the audacious rock on her finger. They turned their attention to the menu board instead, even though they knew it by heart.

Elizabeth scoffed. "Love, don't waste time here. We have plans, and I don't want to be late. Remember? We're meeting my girlfriends for cocktails before the concert."

"Oh, right, what time?" Conrad pulled at the roots of his hair like he could extract the memory.

"Soon. We really need to go shower and get ready." Elizabeth traced her finger down his chest, her intense, seductive gaze fixed on his eyes. Anna had a vision of them in the shower together, their soap-lathered bodies pressed against each other. Her stomach flipped, and she immediately shoved the thought away.

Conrad perked up. "Oh, okay . . . Anna, Holly, instead of ice cream, how about joining us tonight? There's a whole group heading to a concert—it's an amazing lineup."

"Conrad, honey," Elizabeth interrupted. "Don't embarrass them." She glanced over at Anna. "The tickets cost a lot, and I'm sure they can't afford to go."

Anna's face flushed hot. *How dare she?*

Conrad shifted his weight from one foot to the other. Anna thought he always knew what to say, but this time, he seemed at a loss for words. That didn't last long. "Hey, sorry, um . . . let's take a rain check on ice cream. And look, I know you both have a cool catering gig this summer, but if money is tight, my mom is looking for help at the house. Come by anytime; I'll put in a good word for you."

"Thanks, but no thanks," Holly grumbled, but it was unclear if Conrad heard her.

"I'll come by tomorrow," Anna blurted.

Elizabeth beamed. "Oh, how sweet," she said, her voice layered with contempt. "You'll look cute with a duster."

Conrad offered an awkward smile while Elizabeth guided him away, their arms entwined. As they exited the Dairy Dip, Elizabeth tossed a Cheshire-cat grin over her shoulder, leaving Anna without a drop of ice cream or a shred of dignity.

Chapter 25

Jade

The heavy door knocker falls with a thud. A moment later, Sid ushers me inside. He's dressed impeccably once more—a dapper dark suit, not a speck of lint.

"Jade Jensen. Back for day number two. And to think they say your generation lacks grit and common sense. I guess one out of two isn't bad."

I offer an uneasy laugh as Sid steps aside to let me in. I sort of agree with him. Part of me can't believe I'm back. Conrad's explosive behavior should have warned me away like alarm bells, smoke signals, and a crack of thunder all rolled into one. But what can I say? I like money. And I might like a good mystery even more.

Miramar has me under its spell.

I keep hearing that familiar piano melody from the tower, and it's struck a chord. I can't believe, after my long journey, that I find myself in a gothic seaside setting—like Manderley in *Rebecca*—a place full of secrets, tinged with darkness, and rife with closed-off areas that beg to be explored.

The grounds even have an honest-to-goodness ruin. Holly should be the one working here, gathering inspiration for her novel, though it's obvious she's done that already. Holly might claim the book is all fiction, but the Miramar in *Beach Thriller* is pretty true to life. Now I wonder if I could help her finish her story.

As I walk through the vast foyer that echoes with traces of yesteryear, the eyes of stoic figures in massive portraits appear to follow my every move. The high-vaulted ceiling amplifies my footsteps, drawing attention to the loneliness of the space. Miramar is enormous, which might be why it feels so desolate. A house like this should be bustling with staff and guests. Is that why Maeve is reviving the Barefoot Beach Ball? Can she no longer stand the isolation?

Even the threadbare rug stretched across the center of the cold flagstone floor adds little cheer. The air feels damp; the curtains are drawn, keeping the sun out and the moisture in. Is joy not allowed in this house? It's no wonder Rose is so miserable.

It seems Old Sid, who leads me up a wide staircase to Maeve's second-floor bedroom, his steps so tentative that he uses my arm as a second railing, may be too close to death to care.

The sight of Maeve Carmichael's bedroom takes my breath away. It's large enough to be two—maybe three—rooms. It's more like her "chambers." Contrary to her demeanor, it's also the warmest and most inviting room I've seen yet. Wall-to-wall carpeting, the color of faded rose petals, feels springy under my feet. I still have my shoes on, and that seems wrong. Sid doesn't tell me to remove them, but I take them off by her door.

Rich antique furniture fills the space. A sitting area includes an ornate desk with intricate carvings. Velvet-upholstered chairs are scattered about, and the glossy mahogany dressers boast brass handles polished to a shine.

At the far end of the room stands a majestic canopy bed, the likes of which I've never seen before. An elephant could stretch out and still have plenty of space. Lush burgundy bedding covers a plush mattress that begs you to get lost in its satin underworld. Luxurious draperies frame the windows, cascading in rich folds over sheer curtains in a delicate cream color. The ivory wallpaper boasts an intricate design I could imagine adorning the robes of royalty.

Maeve sits at her vanity, applying makeup. Again, she's dressed for success in a tailored silk blouse the color of champagne. A cashmere shawl in a delicate blush tone falls over her shoulders. Her wide-leg trousers match the blouse. Although her clothes are elegant, they convey no warmth.

She glances at her gold watch, speckled with diamonds. "You're early," she says, without a pleasant smile or cheerful hello.

Two seconds into our first full day together, and on a scale of 1 to 10, I put the Suck Factor at a solid 4. Judging by Maeve's deep frown and knitted eyebrows, I'm confident that we will exceed that by the end of the day.

"This is such a terrible idea," she mutters, loud enough to ensure that I hear.

"Good morning, Mrs. Carmichael. In case you forgot, my name is Jade," I say.

Her gaze narrows. "Yes, I remember," she frowns. "I have a heart condition, not dementia."

"Right." I avert my eyes. I need to watch my words, or they'll cost me my job. A smart girl would have already applied to scoop ice cream in town.

Sid turns to Maeve. "It's almost time for tea. Would you like it brought to your room?" His voice is fuzzy and buzzy, the way it sounds over the intercom.

"I'll have it in the drawing room today. Thank you, Sidney."

"Oh, cool, you have a drawing room?" I blurt. "Just like in a Victorian novel. I'd love to see it."

Old Sid winces. Maeve's eyes fill with contempt.

In his quiet, raspy voice, Sid clarifies: "You saw it on your tour. The drawing room is what you would think of as a living room."

"Oh yeah, I remember, that room is sweet," I say—and I mean it. It's actually bright and cheery—no dark furniture in sight. Everything's been refinished in soft, sun-bleached tones, like pieces of driftwood. The stained-glass windows reminded me of looking through sea glass. Instead of tapestries, the walls are adorned with large-scale coastal landscapes. The whole room smells faintly of salt and citrus.

"I like the telescope that's in there," I say. "I thought I saw a whale, but it was just a rock. I didn't see any paper and pencils, though." I'm expecting everyone to laugh, but I'm the only one who does. Maeve looks confused. Sid skews more toward horrified.

"You know, drawing room . . . pencils . . ." I explain, my voice soft and uncertain. Still no smile from Maeve.

Sid clears his throat. "Jade, around here, we view humor like a weapon. Wield it carefully," he advises.

At last Maeve finds her grin. "Leave us be, Sidney. I'll be down in a minute. I want to get Jade started on her *big* job." She doesn't roll her eyes, but the implication is clear: She thinks I don't belong here.

In my head, I hear an imaginary train conductor: *Next stop, Condescensionville.*

Sid bows slightly before turning to go. An uncountable number of shuffling steps carry him out the door.

Once he's beyond earshot (which doesn't need to be far), Maeve explains my duties for today.

"We have two closets." She directs my attention to the large oak doors, each positioned on either side of the massive canopy bed. "The one on the left is mine, and the other is Baxter's."

I'm expecting Maeve to show some emotion when she utters his name—a window opening to her soul, if only a crack. She's talking about her dead husband's belongings. It's only been a few months since his passing. But her eyes are as lifeless as his.

I don't know much about Baxter Ward, but going through his personal belongings will tell me a lot more than an online obituary.

Meanwhile, Maeve projects the sorrow of a wax figure. Perhaps her upbringing demands that she repress her deeper feelings. I'm determined to coax them out of her. I have the crazy notion that Maeve and I could possibly connect on a meaningful—dare I say, life-altering—level.

Throughout this emotional journey, as we sort through item after item and layer after layer of Baxter's life, we'll simultaneously discover things about each other. Together, our bond will strengthen, helping us rise above our challenges and overcome petty differences to become better people. I see a future book about our experience: *In Baxter's Closet*, or *The Closet Connection*, or maybe simply *The Closet*. It'll be a *New York Times* bestseller.

Shit, I hope Holly won't be jealous.

Maeve interrupts my fantasy. "Conrad told me you're a thief. If you steal anything, I'll cut off your fingers—just like in *Victorian* times. Do I make myself clear?"

Her smile is chilling.

So much for my book idea.

Maeve escorts me to Baxter's closet. She opens the door, beckoning me to follow.

I step inside, shocked by what I see. The closet is bigger than any bedroom I've ever had. Jesus, it might be bigger than the apartment I lived in with my parents—well, not really, but it's not far off.

It actually has its own chandelier—no shit—and a walnut floor with a patterned area rug. The walls are lined with built-in shelves and dresser units. There are hanging garments galore and shoe racks aplenty. But what I notice most is the mind-numbingly audacious amount of *crap*. There are boxes atop boxes, overfilled bags, and every corner is crammed with stuff, stuff, and more stuff.

Talk about job security.

Maeve's eyes spark like she's excited for the torture to begin.

"To start, you'll bag up all of Baxter's clothes and shoes and bring them downstairs. There are extra garment bags on the back shelf that you can use. I have a number for you to call to arrange pickup from a high-end consignment store."

Is high-end consignment an oxymoron?

"His other personal items will have to be weeded through more slowly. Since Conrad refuses to do it and feels I'm too frail to manage on my own, I'll have you bring each box to me in my sitting area by the window. We'll go through every item together, and I'll decide what will be saved and what will go. Is that understood?"

I nod as though I'm a small child on the first day of school. Maeve might be physically frail, but she's no pushover.

"I expect you to take your time and be thorough. I've already given several items to Dr. Hill, who is obsessed with vintage fashion. While you're busy bagging up the clothes and shoes, I'll enjoy my tea elsewhere, and perhaps take a swim. I also have a party to plan, and the last thing I need is an uncultured teenage girl interrupting my fundraiser arrangements."

With that, Maeve turns on her heels and heads out the door.

I roll up my sleeves. Time to get to work.

Several hours later, having sweated out gallons of water traipsing up and down the stairs carrying an excessive amount of expensive apparel, I plop down on the closet floor, iced tea in hand.

I've hardly made a dent. And it's past lunchtime. Where is Maeve?

Without question, Baxter had a pathological obsession with *things*. I found multiple shirts with the same pattern, several gold watches, and more matching cuff links than a person could ever need. I guess when Baxter found something he liked, he stuck with it.

And the worst is still ahead of me. The piles of boxes seem endless. The plan is to go through them with Maeve, but she's too busy right now. Am I supposed to sit and do nothing while I wait?

I peek out the door. No one is around. I take the lid off one of the larger boxes. I figure I can poke around and start mentally organizing the stuff. I'm getting paid too well to waste time, right?

The first box is full of books. Oh no, will I need to carry these down the winding staircase as well? They're all business books. The titles alone bore me. I quickly move on.

The next box is smaller and, thankfully, much lighter. It contains some random paperwork in folders and a few manila envelopes. I look through them but don't linger. I don't know what I expected, but spreadsheets weren't on the list. My imagination keeps picturing an old man who harbored secrets, but so far, Baxter appears as bland as melba toast.

I drop a folder while returning the stack to the box. Papers spill out, littering the walnut floor.

Shit.

I scramble to retrieve the fallen items. A few photos are mixed in with the paperwork. One of them is a black-and-white image. It's not old, but it's meant to be artistic. I take a closer look, and yes—it's an elegant wedding photo. The groom is Conrad, much younger, dressed in a classic tux, holding the hand of a woman who must be his bride. The woman has long, flowing hair but keeps her face turned away from the camera. Her dress, however, is the focal point. It reminds me of *Gone With the Wind*, with its undulating folds of lace and satin—or is it silk? Either way, no expense was spared on this gown.

It shouldn't surprise me that Conrad got married—he was engaged in Holly's fictionalized account of Miramar—but I'm a little perplexed that no one has mentioned it. Maybe there was a volatile divorce, and now it's a taboo topic.

I'm restacking boxes and starting to wonder if I should drag Maeve away from her party planning so I can get back to work. Out of the corner of my eye, I notice a pair of shoes stashed on a shelf that I had missed. They're old and worn and likely made of Italian leather. I need to put them in one of the bags downstairs. I'll bring them down and use them as an excuse to check in with Maeve.

I grab the shoes, and when I do, I hear an odd jangling noise from within. Strange.

I tip the shoes upside down, and an old ring of brass keys falls into the palm of my hand. My heart skips a beat. I've stumbled onto something important; I know it.

I slip the key ring into my pocket.

The thief in me can't resist.

I'm about to descend the stairs when I hear Maeve returning from her swim. Peeking over the banister, I see her wrapped in a plush white robe, towel-drying her hair.

Conrad emerges from his office, greeting her with a frown. "Mother, I told you to come get me before going for a swim. It's not safe, especially by yourself. I should at least be on the shoreline."

Maeve waves off his concern. "I can think of no better way to die than being swallowed by the sea. I don't need you playing *Baywatch* on my behalf. And I prefer to be alone. It's meditative for me, and I have a moment's peace away from that barnacle you stuck me with."

I can guess who she's referring to and take that as my cue to get back into the closet where I belong. Before I go, I hear Conrad defend me. "She's a good kid, Mother, and she wants to help. Give her a chance, will you please?"

"I don't know where your altruistic streak came from, but you didn't get it from me. Fine, I'll give her a chance, but not today. I have more important things to attend to. Tell the girl to take the rest of the afternoon off. We'll start up again tomorrow."

The girl. Could be a lot worse, I suppose.

Chapter 26

Holly

Holly took a deep breath, inhaling the ocean air. She had set up her al fresco office on the shoreline of Crescent Beach, where she watched the seagulls patrol the skies in search of an unattended bag of chips.

A pang of longing sank into her chest. All her favorite memories were here, from building sandcastles to boy-watching with Anna. The chair on which she sat was the same one she'd used to read the first two volumes of the Sookie Stackhouse series.

She had everything she needed for a productive workday: an umbrella for shade, a cooler full of seltzer water, and a legal pad and pen.

What she didn't have were any good ideas.

She dug her toes into the sand, the grit pressing into her flesh like a pleasing foot massage. She sipped her drink and gazed out over the water at a scattering of white sails and the occasional frothy wake of a passing motorboat. If she couldn't find inspiration here, perhaps she would never find it.

She came full circle, back to *Beach Thriller*. Jade's enthusiasm continued to tug at her. Perhaps she *could* finish the story she stopped writing when Anna died. The tricky part was getting started again. Watching the looping circles of the sailboats wasn't going to butter her bread.

After an hour of false starts and dead ends, she balled up the new pages and tossed them into the cooler, destined for the trash. Then the doubt set in: What if she'd thrown away something good—words she'd never get back? When she went to fetch them, one of the crumpled pages started taunting her like the damn thing could talk, a deep fold in the paper shaped like a mouth that moved up and down like a paper puppet.

Had she overdosed on sunscreen? Her imagination was certainly running wild.

You don't know exactly what happened the night Anna died. Find the answers. Clear your conscience. Finish your story.

"Fuck off," Holly said, closing the lid on the cooler with authority, silencing the puppet.

But she hadn't silenced her phone, which rang, shocking her out of her reverie. Holly contemplated letting Dan's call go to voicemail. She had no progress to report. Her agent wanted to talk? Fine. He could know the sorry state of her existence.

"Holly, it's Dan," he said in a cheerful but officious manner. Didn't he know that all incoming calls had caller ID? She let it go.

"Dan, how nice to hear from you," she lied.

"Look, I wanted to apologize if I was pushy on the phone the other day. I'm never that way with my clients, and I don't know what came over me."

Holly thanked him for his concern, assured him it was fine, but she understood the real reason for his call.

"No flashes of inspiration yet. But you'll be the first to know when the muse strikes."

Holly swore she could hear her paper puppet calling out from the cooler in a sibilant, evil little voice. *Find the answers . . . finish your novel . . .*

"I still think you should try your hand at a romance—those are perennially popular. Maybe pick up a summer fling for yourself so you have real-life material to work with."

Holly groaned. How sad that even Dan knew it had been way too long.

"Look, Dan, I have to go," said Holly. "Jade will be home from work soon, and I have to get dinner ready."

"Jade?" Dan asked. "Who is Jade?"

"Long story."

"Can you write it?"

Holly almost laughed. "I promise I'll call when I have pages to share, okay? I'm going to get there."

"I believe in you. You can do anything you set your mind to."

God, she hated when he used the "pep talk" voice.

No sooner had Dan ended the call than her phone trilled again. It was a FaceTime request from Shae. How the hell was she supposed to get any writing done? Holly braced herself for the conversation. Shae had a way of seeing through her masks.

One tap, and there she was, her smiley, life-is-perfect, *I-love-California* face, filling the screen.

"Haven't heard a peep from you, and that makes me worried." Shae raised an eyebrow.

Her friend could be a worrywart, and Holly was in no mood for life advice. She had to say something that wouldn't raise Shae's other eyebrow.

"I'm at the beach working—what could be better?" She turned her phone around to give Shae a view of the beachgoers frolicking in the water.

"Wish I could be there with you. How's everything else?"

"Things are good. Just getting settled. The house is in rough shape, but I have a handyman helping me out."

Shit. Holly had tried for a neutral tone, but she had put a little too much emphasis on a certain word.

"Oh, a *handy*man . . . is he hand*sy* too?"

Jeez, Shae was perceptive. Her kids were never going to get away with anything.

"He's gorgeous and taken," said Holly. "But that's for the best," she added, reading the disappointment in Shae's eyes. "I'm busy trying to get this place together and write my book." *And doing all that while looking after a teen refugee,* she added silently.

"I can't talk long anyway. I just wanted to see your face and know that you're well."

"Oh, my god. I'm so well. I'm like—extra well. Thank God for *Meow Mindfulness* because I'd be a disaster without it. That cat is a lifesaver."

Shae's warm laugh was like comfort food. "I hope you're actually reading it because I really think it can help. I'm worried you're lonely. Tell me you're not lonely."

"I'm not lonely," said Holly more emphatically. "And I have enough money," she added. "I know if I say otherwise, you'll try to force a handout on me, and I don't need handouts. I'm genuinely okay." For once, she wasn't lying. Allen Spellman had bailed her out. She should do something nice for him. Maybe bring him a signed book—though he'd most likely get more out of *Meow Mindfulness*, like the rest of the world.

Holly ended the call, promising to check in more often, then packed her things to go. It was only a short walk along a sandy path lined with beach grass to her house. It should fill her with gratitude, but instead, it just made her miss her family and the good times they once shared.

When she cleared the embankment, Holly was surprised to see Serena standing on her doorstep, holding a casserole dish covered in tinfoil.

Holly called to her, waving as she crossed the street. She set the beach stuff down against the side of the house. They greeted each other with a couple of cheek kisses.

"My psychic powers told me you hadn't made dinner yet," Serena said.

"You have the gift," said Holly, and they shared a laugh.

Serena's billowy skirt flowed behind her as she trailed Holly inside. She headed straight for the kitchen. Holly appreciated that she seemed right at home. It gave her a feeling of community.

"It's eggplant Parmesan. My grandmother's recipe is so delicious, you won't believe it." Serena set the dish next to the stovetop before turning on the oven. "I thought you could use a home-cooked meal and a little company."

Holly was sure it was the smell of food and not Serena's jangly bracelets that summoned Chester. He jumped up on a chair, meowed for a morsel, but received a scratch behind the ears instead. That seemed to please him.

"It's nice of you to do this," said Holly, who set the table for three.

When Serena saw the place settings, she eyed Holly slyly. "I knew it," she said. "I just knew it."

Holly finished setting out the silverware. "Knew what?"

"That you were going to have a visitor," said Serena. "I felt it strongly: someone joining you. This person is important in your life and will change *everything*, but in ways you can't begin to imagine. It's all happening, Holly. It's substantial. Seismic, even. There's a *lot* of energy surrounding you."

Holly blanched. "A lot of energy? Like, is that good or bad?" She feared the answer. Though this important person was likely Jade, what if it was a more threatening presence—such as an intimidating cop, angered by her questions? Or even—?

"Hey, do you know the creepy busker who parks himself outside the Bean There Café?"

"Of course," said Serena. "He's a scourge around these parts, and one of those conspiracy theorist types. What about him?"

"I'm worried he might be following me."

Serena's lips parted slightly, her brow furrowing. "Hmm. You need to listen to those feelings. My guides keep telling me that you have to be extremely cautious right now. It's that big energy around you. Maybe we should do a reading."

Holly declined. What if the cards told her to stop asking questions? She didn't want to be scared off her path.

"I need a trivet for the casserole dish," Serena said as she started digging through the cabinets. All she found was a small stack of paper plates. Holly barely had enough silverware for three.

The front door opened and closed quickly. Jade appeared in the kitchen doorway holding a box, about to say something to Holly, but turned her attention to Serena instead.

Serena's eyes went wide as two saucers. "Oh, it's you. *You're* what I was picking up."

Jade looked perplexed. "I'm sorry, who are you?"

Holly introduced everyone. Since Serena saw things that most people couldn't, Holly chose honesty over a concocted story. "This is Jade. I found her squatting in the cottage, so I gave her a place to stay for a little while."

Jade spoke up. "And I just got a job, working for Maeve Carmichael, helping to sort through her dead husband's belongings."

Serena took it all in stride. "It was meant to be. You two are together for a reason."

Holly heard the puppet voice again: *Find the answers . . . finish your novel . . .* Maybe Serena could ask the spirits if she was going insane.

Jade set the box she was carrying on the table. "I found this outside. It's addressed to you."

The small parcel, about the size of a shoebox, was wrapped in brown paper and addressed to Holly, but had no return address or postage.

Holly set it aside for later. "How was work?" she asked Jade. The question struck her as funny only because it was so perfectly ordinary—as if they'd had this arrangement for years, not days.

"Maeve is a menace," Jade said. "But there's so much stuff to sort through that I'll definitely be busy. I'm not sure I can get it all done before the big party she's planning."

"What party?" asked Holly, feeling a slight squeeze in her heart.

"She's hosting a benefit for the Beauport Art Association. Oh, and you're invited, by the way." Jade handed Holly a gilded-edge, ivory vellum envelope with her name and address penned in a neat hand. "I saw it in the pile—saved them a stamp. There's a donation form inside, but the invitation gets you in."

Holly was shocked and revulsed to be included. "Did they invite me because you're living here?"

"I haven't told them," Jade said. "They don't seem too interested in my life. Conrad forgot to ask for my last name."

Holly wasn't surprised. If this town gave out superlatives, the Carmichaels surely would win Most Self-Involved. She'd be sure to be busy *that* night—rearranging her sock drawer or playing a game of Parcheesi against Chester.

Jade added, "I think Maeve needs to feel important because she's old and dying and freaked out about being forgotten."

"You can tell Maeve she has nothing to worry about," Serena said. "Death is merely a change of address."

"Really?" Jade pursed her lips in uncertainty. "That doesn't make me feel any better."

Holly drew back slightly. "Jade's, uh, been through a lot, Serena. She's lost her parents. That's a tough topic for her."

"Oh, I'm so sorry." Serena looked stricken. "I realize that offers little comfort when you're in the throes of grief. I won't pry, but if you'd ever like a reading—on the house, of course—you let me know." Serena placed a hand gently on Jade's shoulder.

Holly was happy she didn't pull away. Maybe Jade was softening.

"The eggplant should be ready—smells delicious, Serena. Why don't you both take a seat and I'll get the food."

Holly ferried the hot pan from the oven to the table using dish towels as potholders. After helping themselves to generous portions of the savory meal, Serena piped up: "Jade, tell me about yourself. What brought you to Beauport?"

Jade forked some eggplant Parm into her mouth and spoke while chewing. "Well, my parents were both killed in a car accident."

Holly found it strange how detached, almost matter-of-fact she sounded. It was as if that tragedy had happened to someone else. But Holly understood that sometimes grief became your constant companion, so ever-present that it often went unnoticed, like the air we breathe.

"I'm not quite eighteen, so I had to go live with a crappy aunt who's like a total tyrant. I couldn't deal, so I took off and came here."

"You're a runaway?" Serena's eyebrows arched. "Why did you choose Beauport?"

Jade shrugged. "After my parents died, I had to clean out their stuff and found a necklace in their bedroom. I guess it was meant for me, because it had a jade stone attached to it. It has Beauport, Massachusetts, engraved on the back and I really want to find the store it came from. I can't explain why, but it's important to me." Jade removed her necklace and handed it to Serena.

When it fell into her palm, Serena went stock-still. She stared unblinking at the piece.

"Do you recognize it?" Holly's gears churned, trying to puzzle out Serena's strong reaction.

"I, um—no. No, I don't. I thought I did, but I'm mistaken." Serena handed the piece back to Jade, who clasped it around her neck. "What about the package?" Jade asked Holly, who had forgotten all about it.

Holly never cared much for mail because it seldom brought good news. But this was a curiosity—no return address, no stamps. Someone had personally dropped it off. Maybe it was a scented candle from Gail for staging her home. She grabbed the parcel and a knife from the kitchen and slit the tape, careful not to cut too deep.

"Christmas in July," she said with cheer as she opened the lid. She reached her hands into the box. "Ah, it's a book." A touch of uncertainty seeped into her voice. Something didn't feel right.

As she hoisted the book to eye level, small bits of burnt paper descended onto the table like black confetti. Someone had taken a torch or lighter to it. The edges of the book were charred and uneven. Some of the singed pages curled up like blackened rose petals. The title on the cover was left intact—intentionally, it seemed.

When Holly realized what she was holding, she gasped and dropped the book as though it were still on fire and burning her fingers. The whole thing landed in the center of the casserole dish with a splash, right on top of what remained of the eggplant Parmesan. Bits of marinara sauce stained the cover like blood spatter while thoroughly soaking the charcoal pages in red.

Serena and Jade leaned over the table to get a better look, their jaws hanging open.

Even with splotches of marinara sauce on the cover, Holly could make out her name and the title: *Beyond Horizons*. It was the same book Ethan had said he'd read and enjoyed. Evidently, someone didn't feel the same way. The burnt edges weren't a coincidence. This was a message—more like a warning. What happened to Anna could happen to her.

Jade fished the desecrated novel out of the casserole dish. She flipped open the cover, sauce oozing down its charred edges like it was hemorrhaging.

"Holly, look at this," Jade whispered. She showed Holly the title page, which appeared to be the only one left uncharred.

At a glance, Holly understood why. If the burnt pages weren't enough, the inscription in big block lettering, every word capitalized like a scream, made the sender's intentions abundantly clear: LEAVE TOWN OR I'LL DESTROY YOU.

Chapter 27

Jade

Maeve might be super annoying, but this job definitely has its perks. No way would I get tea and scones, served on a sterling silver tray by a real-life butler, if I was scooping ice cream downtown. That gig probably wouldn't even offer me a meal break.

I'm in the sitting area of Maeve's chambers, perched on a velvet window seat. Across from me, Maeve lounges on a chaise, enjoying the warm morning sunlight streaming through the dormered windows. She's wearing a moss-colored blouse decorated with pearl buttons, silky trousers, and satin slippers—exceptionally well-dressed for a day at the house, and I doubt she's expecting visitors. Aside from me and Dr. Hill, it seems no one else comes to this place, not even the mail carrier.

Which makes me wonder who delivered the package to Holly's house—or is it our house now? The thought makes me smile, which is ridiculous. I know this is a temporary situation. Holly feels bad for me and is letting me stay, but it won't last. Good things never do.

And God knows what kind of mess Holly has gotten herself into. She brushed off the threatening delivery, but what if the danger is real? Nobody bought my theory that it came from the superslick real estate agent, Gail Provost. What better way to score a prime property than to spook the owner into hightailing it out of town? But, if it wasn't Gail, maybe it was someone with a more dangerous agenda.

While I still have a job and a place to live, I need to make the most of my circumstances, but Maeve is meeting my smiles with scowls.

Rather than be discouraged, I'm resolved to win her over by the end of the afternoon. The key to success is to be a good conversationalist.

Big Sallie, the guard from juvie who saved me from being throttled on more than one occasion, gave me that tip.

"You don't mean shit in here. Not even the 'shit on the bottom of your shoe' kinda shit," Sallie preached. "You wanna make friends? Ask about other people. Everyone *loves* to talk about themselves. Ask more questions than you answer and you might not get your ass beaten daily."

It was solid advice and easily applied to this situation. I'll feign interest in all things Maeve, stroke her ego, and eventually break open that hard exoskeleton.

After lunch, Maeve snaps at me to bring her some boxes. I jump like a nervous dog. Following orders, I head to the closet, pondering how to initiate Operation: Win Over Maeve. Perhaps I should ask about Conrad. The mystery reader in me must follow the trail of bread crumbs without being overly intrusive. A marriage no one talks about? A locked tower? An old ruin? I'm compelled to investigate.

I haul the boxes over to Maeve, my muscles straining. Now I get why Conrad worried about his mom. This job might be too much for me.

"Let's get this over with." Maeve sighs, already bored. "This fundraiser is very important, and events of this caliber don't organize themselves." She studies her nails as if they're far more deserving of her attention than I am.

"I'll try to be efficient," I promise, opening the first box. I already know what's in here, but Maeve does not. I hand her some manila folders. She quickly rifles through the paperwork.

"Most of this can be shredded," she says with annoyance. "They're just old business documents—long out-of-date."

"What was Baxter's business?" I plaster on a cheery smile.

"Pharmaceuticals, mainly," Maeve replies, flicking the air to push me onto another topic.

"And what about your first husband? I heard he passed away. He must have been fairly young. I'm so sorry."

"I'm not," Maeve bites back. "He was useless. I try to forget about Geoffrey. He was a gambler—almost lost everything we had. An impressive feat, given our wealth. The Ward family rescued us from financial ruin. I don't consider Baxter to be my second husband. He was my only *real* husband."

Her eyes are sharp, but . . . are they misty? Is there actual emotion leaking out?

"As it happens with most businesses, Baxter's company hit some hard times," Maeve continues, almost talking to herself. "The drug business is not for the faint of heart. It's expensive and competitive, and there are too many government regulations. It's hard to bring any drug to market. But even when he faced obstacles, he was a master at pivoting and switching tactics. That's what a real man does."

Oh, Maeve, your boomer is showing. I let her comment slide, hoping she'll keep sharing.

"Is his company still in business?" I ask.

"No, he sold it some years ago to a larger drugmaker. They eventually shut down—laid off all the employees. It was like Baxter's work had never been." Maeve shakes her head. "Enough with the twenty questions. Just put all this in a pile to shred. Sidney can take care of it."

"What about the photos?" I blurt, even though Maeve hadn't acknowledged those.

"Photos?"

I guess she hadn't noticed. I hand her a few random pictures mixed in with the files. As she examines them, I note the paper quivering slightly in her grasp.

"So long ago," she mutters. "This was our last big party at the house." Maeve points to one of the images.

"Was it a fundraiser?" I ask.

"No, it was Conrad's engagement party."

"Oh, he's married? I didn't know."

"You'll have to ask him about that," she answers cryptically. "Too bad they never had any children. Now I'm left without an heir after my son. What will happen to this place?" She scans the room, as if the walls are vanishing before her eyes.

Then I swear, I hear the click of a lock snapping around her heart. Her gaze hardens. "Shred them."

In my quest to please the queen, I go to toss the pictures into the "shred" pile, but something catches my eye—something, or more accurately, *someone* I hadn't noticed before. I examine the photo more closely, confirming my suspicions. Age doesn't change a person that much. I fold the picture without Maeve noticing, tucking it securely into my pants pocket, right next to the brass keys that I had stolen as well.

Holly lied right to my face when she said she hadn't worked for the Carmichaels. And I'm going to find out why.

Chapter 28

Holly

It was nearly ten o'clock when Holly finally woke. When was the last time she had slept this late? Probably back in college when she and Shae were still partying.

The smell of freshly brewed coffee pulled her out of a black, dreamless void. Maybe there were perks to having a roommate. *Someone gets me*, she thought, calling Jade's name as she padded down the stairs.

Holly had tossed and turned most of the night, images of her burned novel flashing through her mind. What would come next? An armed intruder kidnapping her? Ending up in the trunk of a car—or in a ditch, her corpse charred, just like her book? The questions kept her awake long past midnight, when her body finally gave in to exhaustion.

She entered the kitchen, surprised to find Ethan—not Jade—filling two mugs.

"Hey there," he said, flashing a combustible smile. "You didn't have cream, so I picked some up from the store."

Holly had forgotten she'd run out. She wasn't used to shopping for two and would've kicked herself if she'd had to trudge to the Bean There Café.

"And you needed sugar, so I got that as well," Ethan added, stirring some into her coffee.

He was heavy-handed with the sweetener. How did he know that was her early-morning indulgence?

She took a sip—it was divine. "So you like your coffee light and sweet as well," she observed with a smile.

"To quote the Beastie Boys: I like my sugar with coffee and cream. I noticed you do, too." He laughed, taking a hearty gulp.

"Oh, I love the Beastie Boys!"

"They were my first concert," he said. "I still have the T-shirt I bought at the show. It's ratty, but super comfortable and perfect for yard work."

Something else was extremely comfortable: Ethan. His presence felt strangely natural, his awareness of her needs so precise, so prescient, it was as if he'd moved in while she was sleeping. Honestly, if he had brought over a suitcase, she wouldn't have minded.

But just as the thought occurred to her, an unexpected pulse surged behind her eyes, almost like a strobe light flashing in her brain. She recognized it as the sensation from before—an aura enveloping her, a warning of a painful headache coming on. She felt spacey and slightly off-balance. A shimmering light flickered in front of her, and her face felt tingly. Maybe she needed a couple of Advil with her coffee, but why did she experience this strange, almost otherworldly warning signal whenever Ethan was near?

What was it trying to tell her?

Probably that it was stupid and childish to imagine being with him. What did she really know about this man, besides that he wasn't single and had nice hands (which she admired as he drank his coffee)?

Or was it something more? A burnt book had appeared on her doorstep—the same one Ethan had mentioned a day earlier. Coincidence? Maybe. But good luck trying to find a copy of that novel within a twenty-mile radius, maybe even farther.

She didn't know whether Ethan had lived in Beauport the summer Anna died. Could he know something? Was he involved in some way? He might be playing a game—getting close to her, working on her house to gauge what kind of threat she posed.

The old saying about keeping your friends close and your enemies closer came to mind.

Holly sipped her coffee. For a moment, she entertained the idea that he'd spiked her drink and that, in a few minutes, she'd pass out and wake up barricaded in a dingy basement with blacked-out windows. *Hmm.* Perhaps she *was* a thriller writer after all.

"Where's Jade?" she asked.

"She wasn't here when I showed up. Maybe she went off to work," said Ethan. "And the door was unlocked. Sorry if I was presumptuous letting myself in. But I figured I could get a few things started."

It was then Gail sauntered into the kitchen, her pearl necklace white as her teeth, her hair lacquered in place. She took one look at the morning coffee klatch and smiled.

"Oh, already?" She winked at Ethan, implying he had spent the night. "I warned you, Holly. This one's a real charmer."

"How charming can I be when I'm eating dinner alone most nights?" Ethan chirped back.

He eats alone? Had Mr. Handy (and potentially Mr. Dangerous) recently become Mr. Available? Her common sense kicked in. Mutilated book. Weird aura. Handsome stranger. Unsolved murder. Keep your hands to yourself, Hol.

"Ethan just got here, Gail," Holly said. "Not that it's any of your business," she added under her breath.

"The front of the house looks great," Gail said, on her own trajectory. She grabbed a mug from the cabinet (*How did she know where they were kept?*) and poured herself a cup. *Make yourself at home; everyone else does.*

"I'm starting on the kitchen today," Ethan said.

"Well, you may want to put your toolbox away." Gail's eyes were alight. "We just got an offer on the house."

Holly felt the floor shake, and that odd Ethan aura vanished in the aftershock. "What do you mean, you got an offer?" she asked. "Gail, the house isn't for sale. It's caught up in probate."

""I know . . . I know . . ." Gail's red manicured nails sliced the air, brushing away Holly's concern. "But that doesn't stop people from making offers. And this person wants to remain anonymous, even from me. They sent a letter with a PO box for a return address, no name given, but I can smell the money. They're offering twenty-five percent over market value. That's crazy. Plus, they'll cover all your relocation expenses."

Holly squinted, suspicion flickering. "What's up with this town? I have a lawyer writing me personal checks without paperwork, and an offer on a house that isn't even on the market."

Gail gave a lopsided smile. "Allen does that sort of thing. Don't overthink it. It's the small-town way—people here actually *like* helping their friends and neighbors, and nobody betrays that trust."

"If they're so trusting, why doesn't this mystery buyer tell us who they are?" Holly asked.

Gail shrugged. "Money makes people behave strangely. But they want the house right away, and they're rich enough that you can hold on to the deed until probate clears—they'll settle for a memo of understanding. Twenty-five percent over the market value! That's a *huge* offer."

"If they're interested now, they'll be interested later, when, and *if*, I decide to sell," Holly said firmly. Instead of tallying numbers, Holly's thoughts reeled back to the threat she'd received, which had also been delivered anonymously. Same person? Most likely. But why menace her with one hand and pay her off with the other? The truth had no price tag, and she was here to stay.

One giant obstacle, however, stood in her way: a nasty cop named Tommy Boy. Holly had an idea.

"Gail, let's have our coffee on the screened-in porch so Ethan can get started in the kitchen." She shot the Realtor a look, and Gail followed her to the wicker chairs in the sunroom while Ethan went to retrieve his tools from his truck.

The old furniture creaked as they settled in. Holly cast a glance over her shoulder to make sure they were out of earshot. She assumed Gossipy Gail already knew about her family's tragedy.

"To be honest, there are too many questions around my sister's death for me to leave town. I went to the police station to look at the evidence box from the investigation, and Tom Walker is guarding it like it's the nuclear codes. You know everyone in Beauport. Any suggestions on how I might get around him?"

Gail snorted in disgust. "Tom Walker is a POS, pardon my French. But good news—I know his supervisor. Sold him the cutest three-bed townhouse." Her eyes turned wistful. "Open-concept kitchen, beautiful quartz countertops, and it had this to-die-for walk-in pantry. Such a find."

Holly realized she was dealing with a savant of sorts—someone who not only saw the world not in numbers, but in comps and sellable features. In order to close so many deals, Gail had to be adept at knowing which levers to push and pull to get results.

"I'd really appreciate it if you could help me with this," said Holly.

Gail's devious smile read as quid pro quo: *I scratch your back, and you sell this place to that anonymous buyer.*

"I'll make a call, sweetie—or we could go to the station together," said Gail. "If I can sell a house that's not even on the market, I can certainly help you peek at an old case file."

After Gail left, Holly set out to write at the beach. She settled into her chair at a spot near the shoreline, away from the umbrellas and noisy children. Though the sun hid behind clouds, Holly still lathered on plenty of sunscreen and wore a wide-brimmed hat made of dyed blue straw. Her mother's voice echoed in her mind, reminding her you can still get sunburned on cloudy days.

The steady wind turned the sea frothy and rough. Holly put pen to paper and started to write.

Thirty minutes later, she had nothing but a stiff neck, achy butt, and plenty of scratch marks on the page. At least the ibuprofen was helping with her headache.

When her phone rang, Holly couldn't have been more relieved. She'd take any distraction from her pitiful efforts. The sun's glare made it impossible to see the caller.

She answered and was surprised to hear the voice of her lawyer, Allen Spellman.

"Glad I caught you," he said after exchanging pleasantries. "I've got some news on our local cop."

Holly moved to the edge of her beach chair, pushing it deeper into the sand.

"There are some disturbing allegations against him," Allen continued.

She wrote on her pad: *Dirty cop.* "What kind of allegations?"

Allen cleared his throat. "Tom Walker was briefly suspended after a woman he'd arrested accused him of offering her a free pass in exchange for a little something in return if you know what I mean. The claim went nowhere—he said/she said kind of thing. But where there's smoke, there's usually fire."

Holly cringed. "So there might be other women out there who were let go after being coerced into giving him sexual favors? That's horrifying."

"That's exactly what I'm saying, but they were probably afraid to come forward. And remember how his wife left him? I wonder if she found out what he was up to."

The idea of a corrupt cop abusing his power was hardly new. A cold shiver ran through Holly as she remembered Walker blocking her attempt to access Anna's case file.

"I hate to tell you this," Allen continued, "but, did you know Anna was nearly arrested?"

Holly's throat closed. "Arrested? No . . . I know Maeve Carmichael accused her of stealing when she worked at Miramar—earrings or something, but she didn't do it."

"Well, Maeve did more than accuse. She called the cops and filed charges. The police investigated and spoke to Anna, but those charges were dropped. And the attending officer was none other than . . ."

"Tom Walker," Holly guessed.

"You got it."

"What if . . ." Holly had trouble getting the words out. "What if he made the same deal with my sister, and that's why the charges were dropped?"

She remembered the jewelry incident and was sure someone had framed Anna, probably Elizabeth Ward, Conrad's jealous fiancée. But the thought that it had turned into something so depraved made her stomach roil.

“My source at the PD told me there’s an incident report on file,” Allen continued.

“Can you send me the report?”

Allen’s sigh came through loud and clear. “My source can’t release it—it’s against department protocol. But I’ll see if I can get more details for you.”

The ocean waves grew larger and more menacing, mirroring Holly’s darkening mood. A new revelation took hold: Tom Walker wasn’t just a menace; he might also be a killer. Had Anna threatened to expose his predatory behavior, and that’s how she ended up in a house fire on the Carmichaels’ property?

It made sense to Holly why Anna had kept her in the dark about her near arrest, especially if Walker had done something to her. Shame was a powerful silencer. Or maybe Anna had tried to be brave, not wanting to burden her younger sister with her suffering. That was just like Anna, always there to protect her.

Holly thanked Allen for the insights—and for his generous check. “Really, it couldn’t have come at a better time. I was getting desperate.”

“It’s no problem. You can repay me after the funds clear. And if you need a little more, let me know.”

Holly resisted the urge to tell him she might be knocking on his door again soon.

Back at the cottage, Holly prepared lunch, if an apple and peanut butter counted as such. Ethan was gone for the day, so the house was quiet.

She went back to work, sitting on the couch, staring at her legal pad, full of self-loathing. Chester lay curled atop her copy of *Meow Mindfulness*, mocking her as if he and King Fluff were blood brothers.

Holly ended her pity party, reminding herself that her job was somebody’s dream—which only made her feel worse. So she did what most writers in her situation did: scrolled through social media. Such a mistake.

Two seconds in, Holly was writing a condolence tribute for a lost pet and another for a grandparent who had passed. Then she felt guilty about not donating to a GoFundMe for a boy she didn't know who'd lost his parents in a car accident, a post from a total stranger that somehow wormed its way into her feed. Of course, morbid curiosity made her read the details.

As Holly read, molten heat crept up her neck, spreading to her cheeks until her entire face burned hot. She gripped her phone, knuckles turning white.

There would be no more writing today. Instead, she would spend the rest of the afternoon contemplating exactly what to say to her new roommate, who couldn't return from work fast enough.

The boy on the GoFundMe had a story remarkably similar to the one Jade told Holly when she found her in the attic.

Holly fumed. She'd been lied to before, but never like this.

Chapter 29

Jade

After an exhausting afternoon, I lug the final box of the day down the stairs to the first floor, taking slow, careful steps. My legs burn. My arms feel like they might fall off. I've decided I'm not being overpaid after all.

I leave the box by the front door. That's when I hear Conrad's low voice coming from his office.

Checking my phone, I notice I'm well within my "allowed hours" to be on the premises, so I decide to be polite and say goodbye.

I poke my head inside, catching Conrad's eye as he's putting his phone away.

"Jade, come in, come in. How's it going with Mother?" His tone suggests he fears the worst.

"I'm surviving," I reply, wiping my brow for added emphasis.

This brings a genuine smile to Conrad's face. "Glad to hear it!" he says. "She's a lot to handle. And now that her gala is coming up, I'm afraid she'll become even more—er—let's say, challenging.

"Everything will have to be perfect, which of course isn't possible—so she'll likely take that out on the entire household."

Entire household? Like him and Sid? Or Angry Rose? Or me? It really is a big place for so few people.

"I'll be extra careful not to upset her," I say, which gives me the perfect opening to pry a little more. "Your mother told me there hasn't been a party here since your engagement. I didn't know you were married."

Conrad's face darkens the way a chameleon changes color.

"Jade . . ."—his voice carries a warning tone—"I need you to stop asking personal questions. You're here to do a job—nothing more." His fists clench and unclench as though he's holding a stress ball.

Then Conrad softens a little. "But no, to answer your question, I'm not married. Not really. My wife left me a long time ago."

I stand quietly, unsure how to respond, but Conrad continues, "Look, it's getting late. Time to go. And come back tomorrow—that is, if you can keep your mind on your work and out of my personal affairs."

"Yes, of course. Sorry," I say, backing toward the door. "I'll see you in the morning."

I arrive home (*home* being a misnomer, since I'm technically homeless), my thoughts whirling. I can't wait to show Holly the picture that almost went into the shredder, although I'm nervous about how she'll react. Anything Carmichael-related instantly puts her in a bad mood.

But it seems I'm too late. Holly's already in a mood when I find her in the living room.

She's settled on the sofa with Chester curled up nearby. I don't like the way she's looking at me. My mother had that same expression on her face when I came home after a night carousing with the wrong crowd. I found her waiting for me, along with a few police officers.

You steal one car . . .

Thankfully, they didn't try me as an adult (which had been a real possibility, according to my public defender). But they did send me to the Bucks County Youth Center to wait for a hearing that would determine my future.

I spent a month with kids who were much tougher than me—and not nearly as well-read. Eventually the judge let me go. The courts prefer to rehabilitate juvenile offenders, not punish them. When I stepped outside the barbed-wire fence, the first taste of freedom was a real hallelujah moment.

My probation came with conditions: no alcohol, no drugs, no

skipping school, and definitely no more grand theft auto. But there weren't any stipulations about fighting.

The obnoxious girl, hereafter known only as My Antagonist, should've known when to shut her big mouth. From the moment I got back to school, she harassed me nonstop. *Jailbird. Jade Capone.* She asked about my girlfriends in Baby Jail—a name I liked and adopted.

She kept running her mouth like that, thinking she was funny until her mom got the bill from the dentist.

I ended up in front of the same silver-haired judge as if I had taken a full-circle ride on the courthouse's revolving door.

The next thing I knew, I was back in Baby Jail for at least another month until my disposition hearing, when the court would decide a fitting punishment for a broken nose and two missing teeth.

Baby Jail had a special stench that no disinfectant could kill. To this day, overhead fluorescent lighting makes me twitch. And don't let the "youth center" part fool you—it was a prison for the under-eighteen crowd.

My room was big enough for a toilet and sink, a small metal cot holding a threadbare mattress, and scratchy blankets that the army would reject.

The first rule of Baby Jail is you follow the rules—or you pay a price. To get back into our room, we had to stand in line in front of our cells, hands behind our backs, waiting for the buzzer. I got used to that part. It was the buzz that locked the door behind me that hurt most. For a girl who'd been running her whole life, I had nowhere to go. There was nothing to do but wait for the next buzzer to go off.

As part of my court order, I had to meet with a therapist three times a week. She was so young she could have been my sister, with wavy dark hair and a sweet smile.

At our first session, she asked the most obvious question: "Jade, why are you in here?"

She knew my record. What she wanted was the *real* reason.

I could tell her some of it, but not all.

"My father is an abusive asshole, and my mother is too drunk to care," I said. "So stealing and fighting are my ways of putting a little joy into each day."

"Do you think your behavior is a cry for help?" she asked.

I set my elbows on the metal table separating us, leaned in, and locked eyes with her. "Lady," I said. "Think of it more like a scream."

Now, out of nowhere, it's *Holly* who looks ready to scream—at me, no less. I had planned to thrust the photograph I stole from Maeve into her hands and call out her deception with hard evidence, but Holly slaps her phone into my palm instead.

"I would like you to call your aunt Alice," she says, deadpan like she knows a fuck-ton more than I want her to.

Shit.

I try—and fail—to keep my voice steady. "I told you, Alice is awful . . . but she knows I'm alive. I've texted her. That's good enough."

Holly's face tightens. She either doesn't believe me or doesn't care. "*I'd* like to talk to her," she says.

I hand the phone back to Holly like it's a hot potato. "No thanks," I say.

Her face is inscrutable as she focuses on her phone, searching for something. The next thing I know, the device is back in my hands.

I gulp when I see a GoFundMe page in a browser window.

It's a terrible story about a sixteen-year-old boy from Pennsylvania who became an orphan after a drunk driver killed his parents.

According to the graph, the fundraiser was going gangbusters. Nearly ninety thousand dollars had been raised—well over the goal.

I knew the GoFundMe was making the rounds, but I didn't think it had gone far enough to land in Holly's lap.

Fuck.

Holly recites the highlights from memory—though I also know them verbatim.

"He's from Bristol, same as you," Holly says, sounding sarcastically amazed. "And he has an Aunt Alice as well. Go figure. But this Alice seems quite nice—starting the GoFundMe to raise money to cover funeral costs and education expenses. The boy's parents were killed by a drunk driver on I-95 while returning from dinner with friends, leaving their only child—a teenage son—an orphan. Sound familiar, Jade?

"Accidents happen, but what are the chances that two kids from the same town experienced the same tragedy on or around the same date? I'm no statistician, but I'd say you've got a better chance of being struck by lightning—thrice."

I swallow hard. It's like I've walked into that living room full of cops all over again. Busted. "Look, Holly, I know this looks bad, but I can explain."

Holly folds her arms across her chest. "Oh, please do. I'm all ears."

My mind goes blank. My internal lie machine has shut down at the worst possible moment, leaving me with one terrible option—*the truth.*

Chapter 30

Holly

Holly tapped her foot in a quick rhythm. Sensing trouble, Chester sprang off the couch and padded away. Smart kitty.

"Your parents are alive and well, aren't they, Jade?" said Holly, who suddenly felt solidarity with beleaguered moms and dads of deceptive teens everywhere. She remembered being young and stupid herself. Her mother had her hands full back then—two daughters bubbling with hormones, primed for poor decision-making, and only a grandfather to help keep the peace.

"Are they alive and well?" she pressed. "Did you steal that poor boy's story from the GoFundMe page?"

"Yeah, I did," Jade admitted. "And my parents might be alive, but they're not well. Besides, I don't call Buck *Dad.* He's essentially dead to me—so it's not entirely a lie."

Holly probed Jade's eyes and saw real pain. Although she was irate and dumbfounded, she empathized. Something intense had to have been going on to make her lie, cheat, and steal.

"I went to high school with that kid, so that's how I knew about the accident. He's a grade younger. I thought it was a good cover story."

"It's a brilliant cover," said Holly. "It worked on me, and I'm a fiction writer."

"I'm sorry I wasn't honest with you," said Jade, with an apologetic smile.

"And I'm sorry you and your father are at odds. I feel for you, I do. But I want to talk to your parents *now.* They must be worried sick about you. They need to know you're safe, and I need to apologize for my role in all this." Holly slapped her hand against her forehead. "And then I want you to pack your bags. You need to go home. You've been staying in my house under false pretenses. That's unacceptable."

Jade's face crumpled. "Holly, no, please. Please—you can't."

Sorrow stabbed between Holly's ribs. She felt like she was punishing herself, too. The house felt lonelier, and Jade hadn't even left yet. Something about having her around was comforting. It was sort of like caring for Chester, only she didn't have to change the litter box.

The bottom line was that she liked the girl, despite her lying. Holly found Jade spunky and daring. She was the embodiment of the characters she loved to write about: people hurtling through life on the razor's edge of control, desperate for happiness, willing to put everything on the line to get it.

Maybe that was why Jade's betrayal felt so personal. She admired her and saw qualities in the young woman that she wished to embody. Even though Jade was young and impulsive, Holly had to give her credit for taking fearless action in all her decisions. Meanwhile, what was Holly doing? Had she become a secondary character in her own story? So guilt-ridden over Anna, so afraid and trapped in grief, that she'd run away from her life, exited center stage—to do what? Cocoon herself in New York, writing about other people to avoid looking in the mirror?

That's why writing was more important than sales. She sought an immersive distraction from herself. Her habit of hiding in plain sight bled into every corner of her existence—even her choice of men. Emotionally stunted. Unavailable. Max, meanwhile, she'd hoisted onto a pedestal so high that no one could ever measure up. That way, she had a good excuse for never finding her person. She didn't have to try.

Following Anna's death, Holly had become a hollowed-out version of the woman she aspired to be. She'd transformed into the kind of fictional character even she couldn't relate to. Worse than unlikable—she was forgettable.

When she died, who would care?

Shae, for one . . . and Chester, of course. Dan would be sad, but not for long. There'd be another Holly to pluck out of the slush pile. Serena might mourn. Gail would probably wipe away a few tears while hammering the For Sale sign into the ground. Ethan might lament the lost work.

Was that it? The sum total of all the people in her world? The thought stung. Her funeral would be like one of those movie scenes without the money to hire enough extras.

Somehow, in a strange way, Jade felt like . . . family.

Holly battled back a wave of melancholy. She had practical matters to attend to. "I'm sorry, Jade. But I have a responsibility here."

Jade's lips quivered. The girl was on the verge of a breakdown—anyone could see that. And this wasn't an act.

"You don't know my parents. I can't go back there," she pleaded. "My father's abusive—I can never do anything right. He called me a whore, all because I got my belly button pierced without his permission."

Holly winced as though the insult had been directed at her. She suspected Jade *did* need parental permission, but the reaction was unquestionably abusive, if true. Then again, she had to remind herself that Jade didn't exactly have a love affair with facts.

"He's always pissed at me. I don't clean the house right, I'm not respectful enough, my grades aren't good enough. This from a guy who works for Busy Bee Septic—I mean, he literally sucks shit for a job."

Holly couldn't stifle a laugh. Jade joined in, laughing through her tears. The anger between them dissipated.

"Where's your mother in all this?" Holly asked.

"My mother is afraid of being alone, so she never stands up to him. Makes excuses instead. *Dad's tired. He works hard to provide. He loves us, he just doesn't know how to show it.* It's bullshit. She uses vodka as a lie chaser—helps make her self-deception a little less bitter. And I don't blame her," Jade added. "She knows exactly how he treats me, because he does the same to her. And then, to keep from getting hit, she'll join in. At least that's what I tell myself because I don't want to think my mother is that shitty. But maybe she is."

Jade's whole demeanor shifted. She seemed resigned to her fate. Her shoulders sagged forward. "I'll go pack my things. I'm not going back there, but I'll be out of your way in no time—and thanks, Holly, for everything. I mean it. Being here with you has been the best few days I've had in a long time."

Her face was so downcast that it dragged Holly's heart to the floor. She waited until Jade got halfway up the stairs before calling her name. "Jade—don't. Just . . . let's talk about it."

Jade whirled on the stairs, came back down, standing tall, fixing Holly with a defiant stare. "Give me your phone, I lost mine on my way to Beauport." She held out her hand.

"Got it. No aunt, *and* no phone."

Jade kept her hand open, again asking for Holly's device. "You talk to them, and if you think I'm exaggerating after the conversation, I'll be on the next bus out of town—that is, if you don't mind lending me the bus fare. I don't get paid until next week."

Holly agreed. Jade keyed in a number before handing the phone back to Holly. A moment later, she heard a woman's voice—slurred and surly.

"Yeah? What do you want?"

Holly cleared her throat, unnerved. "Are you Jade Jensen's mother?" she asked.

"What the fuck did she do this time?"

Holly inhaled sharply. "Um, nothing," she said, feeling suddenly off-balance. "I'm just letting you know that she's fine. She's in Beauport, Massachusetts. She made her way here, and she's been staying with me. I'm sorry. I'm Holly Sinclair. I should have introduced myself."

Why was she so nervous? They were just two adults having a chat about a troubled teen. But something was notably off. She'd heard no sigh of relief, no vocal cue to suggest joy or elation. Holly might be conversing with a zombie.

"Huh? Whatta you talkin' about? Jade's with you?" This woman was also blotto. All her words ran together.

In the background, Holly heard a gruff man yell: "Hey—who is it? Is that a telemarketer? Tell 'em to fuck off."

Jade stood to the side. She couldn't hear the conversation, but her expression implied she knew how it was going. Holly heard loud footsteps in the background. Suddenly the man's voice was blaring in her ear.

"Hey, fuck off, all right," he spat. "We don't need whatever shit you're selling."

Holly grimaced. "No, I'm with your daughter, Jade. She's okay. I simply wanted you both to know that, and—"

"Put her on. Put that bitch on."

Holly blinked hard. His harsh words stole her breath. She wanted to reach through the phone, grab this jackass by the neck and wring it until he cried out in pain.

"I'm sorry—what did you just say?" Holly practically spit out the words.

"You heard me. Put that bitch on."

Holly handed Jade the phone, though she second-guessed whether she should.

Jade, bless her heart, put the call on speaker.

"You took two hundred dollars from the dresser. Did you think I wouldn't notice?"

Good lord. Those are the first words out of this horrid man's mouth? How dare he!

"So what if I did?" Jade clapped back.

The man grunted like cattle. "So it's not your fucking money to take, Jade."

"Then I didn't take it."

"You're such a liar."

Holly thought of calling the police to report this abuse, but what would they do? Naturally they'd try to find a safe place for Jade to stay—but she had one already.

Holly had heard enough. She took the phone back. Jade might well have stolen the money, but if she had, whatever she took wasn't nearly enough to cover the damage this monster had inflicted. Holly's tone was fierce when she spoke, her words clipped like shears. "Mr. Jensen, sir," she barked, the term of respect delivered mockingly. "Jade will be staying with me for the foreseeable future. I'll leave it up to her to decide when, and if, she'll contact you again. I thought I should inform you that she's safe and cared for. That's all I have to say. I'll get your address from Jade and send you the two hundred dollars so you have no reason to get in touch. Goodbye."

She ended the call with a tap of her finger, half expecting Buck to call back, but he didn't. *Thank goodness for small miracles.* Maybe he'd use her number to track her down, but Holly doubted he cared enough to bother.

"What a horrible human being," Holly said.

"He's that and more," said Jade, exhaling with relief. "Thanks for sticking up for me, but you don't have to pay him back. I mean, yeah, I took the money—I couldn't have left town without it. That's actually when I found my necklace, going through their stuff looking for cash. But Buck's a total piece of shit who deserves a lot worse than losing a couple hundred dollars."

Holly couldn't agree more. "True, but it's better if we settle the books with him," she said. "And you can stay here as long as you'd like. You might need to chip in a little for food, but not until you start getting paid. Sorry, money is tight here, too. And we do need to get you a new phone. I don't want you at the Carmichaels' with no way to call me if there's an emergency."

Jade beamed with relief. Her joy was so palpable it could have hugged Holly on its own.

"Thank you, thank you—and I'm happy to contribute whatever I can," she said. "But I have one request. Since I came clean, I think you should, too." With a glint in her eye, she produced an old photograph from her pocket and handed it to Holly.

"This was taken at Maeve's last Barefoot Beach Ball, celebrating Conrad's engagement to a woman I didn't even know existed until today. You told me you hadn't worked there, and that *Beach Thriller* was pure fiction. Want to explain?"

Jade pointed to a figure in the background of the photograph, a young woman in a caterer's uniform holding a silver serving tray. "Does she look familiar?"

Holly didn't answer, but the truth was written all over her face.

"That's you," Jade said. "I'm sure of it. And did you know there was also a guesthouse on the property? What a coincidence. Now it's nothing but ruins. It looks like it burned down."

Holly finally found her voice. "Where are you going with all this?"

"You found it strange how my story mirrored that GoFundMe page. Well, I find it odd that you're a caterer in this photo at Conrad's bougie engagement party, just like you wrote in *Beach Thriller*. I suspect there's more truth to your fictional tale than you're letting on."

Holly swallowed hard. She couldn't meet Jade's eyes.

"Okay, you got me. The book is based on some real-life events," she admitted.

Jade flashed a victory smile. "I knew it—and to me that makes the story even better."

Holly shrugged off the encouragement. "Doesn't matter, I can't finish it."

"Writer's block?" Jade tossed out the term like she'd experienced it herself.

"Until I know what happened to my sister on the night she died, that story is dead, too."

Jade's eyes caught fire. "I think I can help with that."

Beach Thriller

iv

When you unpack it, *Cinderella* sends a terrible message. It reinforces the "pretty equals worthy" trope. The beautiful, kind, but passive woman gets the prince, while the objectively less attractive stepsisters deserve nothing. Granted, they're cruel and horrid—but the point still stands. And what's Cinderella doing about her plight? Nada, that's what.

She remains stuck in a toxic environment, taking no steps to improve her lot in life. Yet suddenly she's deserving of a kingdom, all because of a biological quirk that gave her tiny feet? Come on. Talk about conveying the notion that luck and looks matter more than effort and skill.

But don't tell that to Anna. She's essentially living the role. She's dressed for the part, too, wearing what amounts to rags compared to the designer clothes her employers flaunt around the house. They're like walking advertisements for top brands: Couture, Abercrombie, Hilfiger, Lauren, and more.

But look on the bright side, Anna—nothing lasts forever. At least the daily humiliation was funding grad school. And she had already learned a valuable lesson: imagining how the other half lives was much more fun than having it shoved in her face every day.

Today was no exception.

Maeve had gone for a swim while Anna cleared the greasy breakfast dishes from the long mahogany table. She polished the counters until they shined. Conrad and Baxter Ward were holed up in the study, discussing real estate. From what she overheard, Conrad was getting an education on how business was and wasn't done at Ward Pharmaceuticals. He would soon be family, and Baxter was taking Conrad under his wing.

Anna had nearly finished cleaning the kitchen. It looked spotless, like breakfast had never happened. What a pity she was actually skilled at this job. She understood all too well why Conrad had kept the job description vague. Now here she was, down on her hands and knees, scrubbing floors, killing brain cells from the chemical fumes. And she knew why: to be closer to Conrad.

Who is going to be married, screamed a voice in her head. But the heart and mind were often at odds.

When all her tasks were finally finished, Anna went outside for a quick break. She sat in the garden, admiring the ocean view. She told herself, *You don't need money to enjoy this.* The sun sparkling on the ocean always captivated her. Her grandfather likened the view to a million diamonds spread across the water—absolutely priceless. She missed him terribly. He'd been gone several years, but it felt like yesterday. He was the only father she remembered; her own had died the summer she turned three, and her mother had been too grief-stricken to remarry.

"Penny for your thoughts," said a voice behind her. Anna jumped. "Get it—a penny? Like how we met?"

Anna laughed uneasily. "Oh—hi, Conrad," she said, flustered. "You, uh, caught me daydreaming."

"Sorry to interrupt, but I thought you might want this." He offered her one of the two glasses of lemonade he was holding. He'd even thought to garnish it with a sprig of mint.

"Thank you," she said, mildly abashed. "Is it okay that I'm taking a break?"

She sipped the sweet, refreshing drink, savoring the taste that embodied summer.

"Of course." His warm voice coated her like a soothing balm. "My mom might gripe, but that's just how she is. You've already lasted longer than most of the help."

The words stung—*the help. Oh shit. In your place, Anna—back in your place.*

Conrad seemed to realize his mistake. He looked sorry, which softened the impact. He cleared his throat and took a sip of lemonade. She tried to ignore the tangle of hair falling in front of his eyes and those sensuous lips.

"What I'm trying to say is it's like Grand Central Station with the staff. People come and go before I even get a chance to know them. But the pay is good, and hopefully . . . you'll stick around."

Anna read between the lines: *Stick around . . . for me.* Tentatively, he reached for her hand, and a jolt ran through her. His smile was charming—but *nervous? Was there a vulnerable side to this handsome man?*

"Let's take a walk . . . get away from the house so Mother doesn't see you relaxing, God forbid."

They left their glasses on a small garden stand. Anna made a mental note to collect them before Maeve noticed.

They walked in silence until Anna broke the spell.

"How's the real estate business treating you?" she asked, fumbling for words, her heart pounding.

He looked at her keenly, and she worried he was upset that she'd overheard his conversation in the study. But he smiled.

"I dream in square footage," he joked. He took a piece of paper from his pocket, unfolded it, and showed Anna a remarkable hand-drawn picture of a brick building, with the dimensions marked neatly on the sides.

"You drew this?" she asked in amazement.

Conrad nodded. "Art was my first love—drawing, especially—but a career as an illustrator isn't fitting for a Carmichael."

"You're still young—there's always time to change course."

Conrad laughed off the notion. "You don't know my family. Elizabeth just graduated from law school. She did her internship with her father's company and now she's working there full-time. They offered me a position as well, and everyone expects me to take it."

His hand dropped away at the mention of his fiancée. "*Coerced* might be a better word than *offered*. Her dad's huge in pharma, and I'm set to run his real estate division." He paused. "Honestly, I don't want the job." Conrad's eyes drifted to the ocean. "I don't want any of this," he mumbled.

He balled up his drawing and stuffed it back in his pocket.

"*Any* of it?" Anna hoped he would know she wasn't just talking about work.

"I thought I did. Elizabeth and I go way back—we were high school sweethearts. Everyone expected us to get married. But she hasn't been the same since her mom died. It was sudden, really tragic. She was a model, still working in her forties—not the healthiest lifestyle, too thin, a smoker . . . but still, you don't expect that." He left it there, and Anna didn't push.

"I did my best to support her, but after her mother's death, she started drinking heavily. I thought it was just a phase, but it kept getting worse. I don't like to judge. I love having a good time as much as anyone, but not the way she does." His jaw tightened. "I don't know why I'm telling you all this."

Anna almost reached for his arm but pulled back. "It's okay—I'm glad you're sharing. I've been wondering. The engagement party was lovely, but let's just say . . . there were undertones."

Did he understand she meant *him and her*, not Elizabeth?

"If it's as bad as you say—why . . . ?" Her voice faded.

"Why get engaged?" Conrad sighed but looked at her as if she were his lifeline. "I guess I felt trapped. Elizabeth depends on me for emotional support, and now there's family pressure to make it work. But I'm done cleaning up after her drinking. I don't want this fancy job with her father's company. I just want to say *fuck it*—fuck it all."

His face turned gray; his eyes darkened. "My family can go to hell with their expectations."

He bent down, picked up a stick, and snapped it in two with an audible crack, like he was breaking someone's neck. Anna flinched, startled by his sudden outburst. After a few deep breaths, he calmed, color returning to his cheeks.

"I want out. I want a new life, away from all this." He gestured to the large house and lush gardens that would be the envy of most. "But Elizabeth and my family—it's like they've trapped me inside a box."

"It's a pretty box," Anna said gently. "And you have a bright future. Not to mention you've got money. I'll be lucky if I make rent in my first year of teaching."

Conrad looked at her, embarrassed that he hadn't asked about her aspirations. "You want to be a teacher?" He said this as though she were Mother Teresa.

"Yeah, I love kids. I grew up with just my mom and my sister." She told him about her grandfather stepping in after her dad died. "More than anything, I want a big family. Holidays, kids running around the yard, a white picket fence, all that. I studied early childhood education—there's nothing more important than teaching the next generation."

Conrad looked wistful. "I wish I had a sibling. But I don't think my parents liked each other enough to try again. Honestly, it's a miracle I'm here." He laughed mirthlessly. "There's a loneliness to being an only child. And I'm sorry about your father. My dad, Geoffrey, passed away, too. I guess we share that sad story. I miss him every day, but my mom doesn't feel the same way."

Anna's heart constricted. She hardly remembered her father, but Conrad's grief felt raw.

Perhaps Conrad felt he had overshared; he quickly changed the subject. "So, teaching, huh? That's a lot more noble than real estate." His smile returned.

"I like to think it's a calling," Anna said. "But we need buildings to teach in—so your job matters, too."

Conrad's smile widened as he laughed. The rage and sadness she had glimpsed was now as distant as the sun trailing their walk.

"I want a big family, too. Maybe in a house where you don't worry about breaking priceless antiques wherever you turn. The other night, you wished to be invited to the party. But I want to run away from it—go somewhere else, build something new. Does that make sense?"

His eyes were so earnest, she felt a lump form in her throat.

"Does Elizabeth know how you feel?" she asked, stepping over an invisible line.

Conrad seemed sincere, but he had a fiancée. Was he prone to making promises he couldn't keep? Was he only saying what Anna wanted to hear?

"Yeah, she knows. But once she has her heart set on something, there's no stopping her. She's Daddy's girl and she's used to getting what she wants."

They reached the edge of the estate. Ahead stood a sweet cottage with two stories, whitewashed shingles, and a small porch. Unlike the main house, it felt warm and lived in.

Conrad noticed her interest. "That's the guesthouse," he said. "We barely use it. It was my hideout as a kid. Want to see?"

He took her hand and led her up the steps. "The door sticks a little, but it just needs a shove." He bumped it open with his shoulder.

Anna was enchanted. Dust hung in the air, and the place smelled faintly stale, but it was cozy. A woodstove sat in the corner, with a cushioned bench under the window. The kitchen was compact, with a kettle on the stove and a breakfast bar. A spiral staircase curled upward to a second story.

She pictured herself seated by the fire, glass of wine in hand, Conrad beside her. Her face flushed.

"It's perfect," she said softly. "A cottage by the ocean? I can't believe no one uses it."

Conrad's eyes didn't leave her. "I'm enjoying it now." His voice was low. "You're glowing—it's like you belong here."

He stepped forward. She smelled spicy notes of cinnamon on his skin, mixed with the freshness of lemons. Anna felt she should move back, but she always did what was expected of her.

"Why did you take this job?" Conrad asked.

"I need money for school," Anna answered nervously, looking away.

He touched her arm, encouraging her to meet his gaze. "Is that the only reason?" His words came out in a pleading whisper.

Anna was never much of a liar. "Maybe because of the way you're looking at me right now," she said.

The air grew tense. She felt a pull of gravity dragging her where she shouldn't go. Maybe, just this once, she could break the rules.

Now she met his gaze, unwavering.

He leaned in slowly, his warm lips brushing hers, and she melted into his embrace.

Chapter 31

Jade

I'm grateful Holly is letting me stay. I should be able to relax, to let my guard down.

But I know better. Good things never last; opening up leads to hurt, and trust equals pain.

Holly and I have come to an understanding: I'll pitch in with the groceries, split the housework, and I can help with *Beach Thriller—sort of.*

When I told Holly my plan to investigate the Carmichaels' connection to Anna's death, I got serious pushback.

"It's too risky. Too dangerous," she said. "Fine if you want to make money cleaning Maeve's closets, but don't go looking for skeletons. Any writing blocks I have, I'll overcome them on my own. Is that understood, Jade? This is non-negotiable."

What she offered instead was a shit deal to be her first reader. Talk about getting the consolation prize. Here I am, thinking I can help her write the blockbuster of the summer—and essentially, she's tying my hands behind my back. No sleuthing, no writing, nothing glamorous at all. I'm like a furry sidekick in a cozy mystery. Chester has a bigger role than I do. But I'll show her. Since when have I followed the rules? I'll figure the whole thing out, and she'll thank me all the way to the bank.

I don't think Holly realizes how valuable I am. I'm at the scene of the crime every day. Or alleged crime—it's hard to tell fact from fiction, and Holly's explanation raised more questions than answers.

"We were both working as caterers at the Barefoot Beach Ball, which happened to be Conrad's engagement party that year. That's where Anna met Conrad. There was a spark—a big one—and it only grew. Back then, I was a young writer looking for a story, and a classic love triangle fell into my lap. I figured it would be easier to write if I used the characters' real names, but I never intended for anyone to read it that way. I included some secrets my sister told me.

"Anyway, I thought the book was building toward a mystery where the Carmichaels were up to no good, and my protagonist, *Anna*, would get in over her head. But then real tragedy struck."

"What happened to her? How—how did she die?" Tough question, but I had to ask.

"Depends on who you talk to," said Holly, who thought she was going to leave it at that, but my stare demanded otherwise.

"No one knows. Maybe it was a gas leak that started the fire that killed her," she said. "All I know is that Anna went to break up with Conrad, and she was inside the guesthouse on the Carmichaels' property when it exploded."

The ruins. My skin turns clammy. What a horrible way to die. It's right up there with being attacked by a wild animal.

"But Jade, please remember I was writing a fictional story based on some real events. I never imagined there would be an actual death, let alone my sister's. What I do know is that Elizabeth hated my sister, Maeve falsely accused her of stealing and fired her, Baxter was a total creep, and Conrad risked losing everything if his affair came to light. Plus, his ego was probably bruised from being dumped. I don't trust anyone in that family, and I believe someone at Miramar is responsible for Anna's death. But either way, after the fire, I couldn't keep writing the story. It was too much."

Holly may not have all the answers, but I'm determined to help her find them. Then again, this family won't be easy to crack. Maeve is more closed off than the tower I'm banned from entering. And I've already caught glimpses of Conrad's dark side—not to mention his weird hang-ups about sunrise and sunset.

Do his secrets have something to do with the tragedy *Beach Thriller* is "loosely" based on? Could there have been a cover-up within the Carmichael clan? If so, the only logical explanation would be that Anna's death was, in fact, a homicide.

Something tells me I should start by searching the tower—the one place Conrad has forbidden me to go. I form the start of a plan. Gripping the key ring in my pocket, I stroll through downtown Beauport, acting like a girl without a care in the world.

I don't have to be at work until noon, so I take my time poking into every jewelry shop on the strip. I can't find a store that sells my necklace, but the stubborn girl in me can't stop checking. Maybe the inventory turns over? Maybe the salesclerk got it wrong. *Maybe. Maybe. Maybe.*

The first two places I check don't have anything like the piece hanging around my neck, so I slip into a third store with lots of expensive silver and gold jewelry displayed in glass cases. The preppy girl working the register keeps her eye on me. She senses I could be trouble. Smart girl. But I'm on my best behavior today.

As I browse the cases, a burning sensation ripples up the back of my neck. I glance at the register, thinking it's the clerk staring me down, but no—she's focused on another customer. Still, the hairs on my arms stand up—my danger radar pinging. I whirl around to see a figure slip out the door in a hurry. I follow, but by the time I'm outside, he's already halfway down the boardwalk.

He's moving quickly, but not so fast that I don't notice the guitar strapped to his back.

Chapter 32

The Watcher

I see what's happening: You're settling in, finding friends. You're here for the long haul. I watched through your window as you opened the desecrated book. That must have been quite a fright. It looked like it was burnt *and* bleeding after you dropped it in the sauce. That part wasn't even planned, but sometimes the universe just gets it right.

Except it didn't—not exactly.

That special delivery should have sent you packing your bags and hightailing it out of Beauport. But no, it appears you're *very* determined. You're obviously going to make this as difficult as possible, aren't you?

Two can play at that game.

I wait until the house is empty. You've taken the car, and your roommate has gone off to work. I've been watching her, too, and I likely know her schedule as well as you do. She'll be gone for a while, but I can't be certain when you'll return, so I have to use my time wisely.

The good news is, I know what I'm looking for—I just don't know where to find it.

Getting in is a breeze—as easy as having a key. I've been doing this for a while now. I close the door behind me, and it latches with a gentle click. The house feels lonely. The scent of warm, sun-soaked fabric fills the air, reminiscent of a summertime nap.

Your small, three-legged creature immediately greets me. I bend down to say hello. Making friends is in my best interest. The cat lets out a sweet meow—or is it a cry of fright? Cats normally have a wariness around strangers; it's an important survival instinct. But this one isn't hissing. Its ears aren't flattened. It's definitely your cat, Holly—just as unaware of danger as you are.

I make sure the back door is unlocked in case I need to make a quick escape. After that, I give the kitchen a once-over. All I see are dishes in the sink. And you really should turn off your coffeepot when you leave the house, Holly. You, of all people, should be aware of the fire risk.

I find an upside-down legal pad in the living room—possibly the start of your next book? That is what I came to find. What are you considering? What story are you going to share with the world?

My chest tightens as I turn over the pad, and then I breathe easier. You're struggling, I can tell. You have ideas, but nothing is sticking. You don't have the story.

But I stop myself. I'm being too confident. After all, I haven't searched the whole house yet.

It's strange to be in your home, Holly, amidst your belongings. But they're not really yours—they're mostly your mother's. How does it feel to be back in this house, trapped in a time capsule, surrounded by so many ghosts? Do they haunt your dreams?

I've been watching you for so long, but now I feel like I'm walking in your footsteps. I try to think like you. Maybe you can access your deeper thoughts and creative ideas only in private. I know you, Holly. You're an introvert. You close the door, shut out the world, and create one of your own—on paper, in prose. It's safer there. The real world feels unreliable. Threats lurk around every corner.

I should know.

This house has only two bedrooms. It's easy to tell which one the teenager lives in, so I focus on the other. My footsteps are as quiet as your cat's when I slip into your private space. I open a few bureau drawers, but I find nothing but clothes. Then I see a box next to your bed, the lid slightly askew. I peer inside. It's full of loose pages.

The title page jumps out at me. *This*—this is what I'm looking for.

My fingers tingle with anticipation as I lift the stack of paper. I begin to read. My throat tightens on page one.

This is exactly why something needs to be done.

You must be stopped.

I hear car wheels on the gravel drive. Slipping the pages under my arm, I silently descend the stairs. I try to be quiet, but the screen door creaks on its rusty hinges as I push it open.

Somebody should really fix that.

But it's no problem—you didn't hear me. I'm out the back door before you've even parked the car.

I imagine how upset you'll be when you discover your book is gone. But it's safer this way—safer for *me*.

Chapter 33

Holly

Holly met Gail outside the police station, a heavy anxiety weighing her down. Was she wrong to trust her? What other choice did she have? With one call, Gail had accomplished what Holly couldn't—she got the police to cooperate. She'd come down to the station to make sure everything was in order. She didn't even ask for anything in return.

The day was warm and bright. The sweet scent of vanilla drifted from the nearby ice-cream shop.

Gail stood with her hands on her hips, assessing the police station as though prepping to sell it to the highest bidder. She wore well-fitted navy dress slacks with a subtly patterned blouse. An elegant gold watch dangled delicately from her wrist. In contrast, Holly had shown up in jeans and a burnt-orange T-shirt (a women's cut, at least), looking about as put together as an IKEA desk still in its box.

Gail greeted Holly with an air-kiss that said *we're close, but not lips-to-skin close.*

"Okay, I handled all the details," said Gail, breathlessly enthusiastic as always. "Tom Walker's not here, and his supervisor said he's happy to help. You can look through the evidence to your heart's content."

In a blink, Gail's exuberance downshifted from fifth to first. She lowered her sunglasses, allowing Holly to see the regret in her eyes.

"Forgive me. I got so carried away that I forgot *why* you're doing this." She gently squeezed Holly's hand. "Are you all right?"

Holly swallowed hard. Was she okay? She had to be. There was no turning back.

"Yeah, I'm fine. Thank you for helping."

Holly steeled herself for what she needed to do. Why hadn't the Carmichael family and staff been thoroughly investigated? There had been many personal conflicts within the walls of Miramar, yet the police had paid little attention to its residents.

And assuming the blaze was an accident, how did it start? And why was Anna alone in the guesthouse if she'd gone there to meet Conrad? The incident had been treated as a closed case even with all these unanswered questions. She'd never get a straight explanation out of Tom Walker, who was cagier than a zoo—but perhaps the evidence would paint a clearer picture.

"Did you bring the mangled book? It could be related to your investigation."

Holly shook her head. She'd told Gail about the book when they were finalizing their plans for the day. "No, I threw it away. It got a little gooey after its marinara bath. The sauce probably destroyed any useful evidence anyway."

"It was a threat, Holly. At the very least, it warrants police attention."

"I'll think about it. Right now, the police aren't on my most-trusted-partners list—but you've earned a spot there. Thanks again for helping me."

"I'm sorry I can't stay." Gail placed her hand on Holly's arm. "I tried everything to reschedule my showing. It came up at the last minute, and the buyer won't budge on the time."

"No, please, it's fine," Holly said. "It might be better this way. This is something I should do on my own."

Gail gave Holly a reassuring hug. "Call after. Let me know how it goes."

Holly went inside, straight to the dispatch window, letting a young officer know she'd arrived.

The wait felt interminable. Holly suspected this was a fool's errand. Freeing herself from guilt couldn't be as easy as peeking inside a box.

With little to do, her mind drifted back to the last day of Anna's life. The aftermath might have been blurry, but the hours preceding Anna's death were seared into her memory like an iron branding. Her sister remained frozen in time, forever twenty-four. Her hair would always be lustrous and full-bodied. Her hazel eyes would never stop shimmering.

On that fateful day, Anna had slipped into their bedroom at the cottage like a girl with a secret. She moved Holly's copy of *The Time Traveler's Wife* from the edge of the bed and sat down.

She had on the cutest summer dress—it was yellow and strappy and hadn't looked half as good on Holly when she'd tried it on. But her sister's usually radiant smile was dim. Trouble lurked in her eyes. And only then did Holly realize it had been that way for several days.

"I need a favor," Anna said.

Holly sat up straighter. Her big sister hardly ever asked for help. It was always the other way around. When they were small, Holly needed help reaching things high up. Later, Anna taught her how to ride a bike and ice-skate. As they grew, her sister assisted Holly with schoolwork and gave her advice on boys. But suddenly, Anna needed Holly. It was a rite of passage.

Holly closed the lid on her laptop, lest Anna see she was writing a fictionalized account of her sister's summer romance with Conrad Carmichael. She was editing the scene where Elizabeth (Conrad's fiancée) tripped Anna in the middle of a big posh beach party because she was a jealous cow.

Holly shut off her MP3 player, which had been blasting "Hollaback Girl" by Gwen Stefani—so boss.

"What's going on?" she asked, though she already knew. It must have something to do with Conrad. He had taken up the whole summer. Holly understood the attraction. He was dreamy, but in that asshole preppy way that didn't appeal to her in the slightest. After the catering gig, Holly wanted nothing to do with him or his highfalutin family, but Anna had been smitten from the start. Holly didn't like seeing the emotional toll the fling had taken on her sister, but she bit back her *I told you so* and asked what she could do to help.

"I got a note from Conrad. I have to go meet him later. He wants to see me, but he doesn't know I'm breaking up with him . . . I need to do it—tonight. Can you come with me?"

Holly blinked in confusion. "Um, isn't that like a *you* thing? That's kinda personal."

Anna returned a frustrated smile. "Yeah, I know. That's why I need you there. I might get second thoughts or cold feet if I'm alone with him. I can't let that happen. You don't have to do anything. Just be there for me."

Holly shrugged. "When are you doing this? Sorry, when are *we* doing this?" Why was she jittery when it was Anna's love life on the line?

"Just meet me in front of the candy shop at seven thirty, okay? And be discreet. I don't want Mom asking any questions."

Holly agreed. She didn't have plans that night, and she'd have another few hours to write before she had to leave. But then Max called—the beautiful boy who made her heart leap. They talked about everything. Back then, both were obsessed with the TV show *Lost*. Holly shared all her theories, and Max had a few of his own. They both had MySpace pages, and Max bragged about his new cell phone.

Coincidently, they were conversing about *Lost* when Holly realized the time.

Her stomach dropped like it did when she and Anna had ridden the Superman roller coaster at Six Flags. She raced to the candy store on her bike but arrived twenty minutes too late. Anna wasn't there. Holly waited long enough to know she'd missed her.

Holly rode to Miramar, up that big hill, short of breath as she pedaled as hard as her legs could pump. When she arrived, the gate was locked. The fences and surrounding shrubbery were both tall and spiky. No way was she climbing over that. If Anna knew a secret way in, she had never shared it. There were lights on in the main house, but Holly wasn't about to hit the intercom. What could she possibly say to explain her presence? Anna didn't even work there anymore.

She rode home, feeling even worse.

She arrived to an empty house. Her mother had gone for a walk; a note on the kitchen table said that she'd be back soon.

Holly trudged upstairs to her bedroom. It was the first time Anna had asked for her help—and Holly had let her down big-time.

Her mother returned a short while later. She asked about Anna, who hadn't yet come home. Holly said she didn't know her whereabouts. At least it wasn't an outright lie. She assumed her sister had fallen back into Conrad's arms but couldn't say for certain.

Holly tried to read to distract herself from the guilt that wouldn't let go. Eventually she fell into an uneasy sleep.

Her rest didn't last long. Something woke her with a start—a loud explosion powerful enough to shake their cottage.

Holly met her mother in the hallway, both frantic. When they got outside, the sky was burning orange. A plume of smoke rose ominously from the bluff, swirling against the flickering blaze.

Miramar.

Holly had just been there, standing outside a locked gate.

Her mother looked at her with alarm. Did she know more about Anna's romance with Conrad than she'd let on?

"Where did your sister go tonight?" Her voice was stern.

This time, Holly couldn't lie.

They took off, still in their pajamas, running side by side up the hill toward the Carmichael estate. The blaze roared in the distance. Fire trucks and ambulances screamed past them, sirens blaring, as flames swallowed the dark.

Beach Thriller

v

She transitioned from Cinderella to Anna Karenina in about a month. Oops. She and Conrad had been stealing moments together in the guesthouse for weeks, exploring each other on every level. At least Conrad wasn't as cold and bureaucratic as Count Vronsky, but he was engaged and soon to be married . . . so yeah, it was hard to be the heroine of *that* story.

But let's be honest: Fairy tales and romantic comedies deceive us as easily as politicians, selling romantic idealism like it's a narcotic. Let the girl enjoy her fun. Conrad was unhappy with Elizabeth, and Anna was in love. What could possibly go wrong?

Unfortunately, if it can't be happily ever after with a fairy godmother and all that jazz, then their story *must* be a tragedy.

But we get ahead of ourselves, for it wasn't tragic at the moment.

Anna's eyes blinked open. Memories of last night flooded back—all the things they did, the ways he had touched her, the words they'd whispered in the dark. He was hers. She was his. What kind of fool was she to fall in love like this? He belonged to another. But she had always longed for the type of connection she felt with Conrad. It passed through flesh and bone all the way to her soul.

She glanced at the bedside table. There was the pencil drawing he made of her last night. He had worked diligently but efficiently, studying Anna with his artist's eye as he moved the pencil across the page. When he had finished, he showed her the results.

Anna's breath caught.

"It's beautiful." The words were inadequate, but the image was stunning. Not only was Conrad incredibly talented, but Anna also noted a sensitivity in his handling of line and shadow. He had even caught an expression she hoped she'd been hiding—a look of vulnerability. Her hair flowed like a waterfall, her skin appeared smooth and delicate, and her eyes looked as luminous as pearls. Was this how he saw her? Anna blushed.

"Even if I were a thousand times more skilled, I could never truly capture your beauty."

This morning, sunlight streamed through the open window across from her, gauzy cotton curtains gently billowing in the summer breeze. She knew what she had to do. Be smart. Wake up from this fever dream. She had to go.

But she was held in place by an invisible force. Conrad slept soundly beside her. His soft, gentle breathing was hypnotic, luring her back under the sheets.

He was the anchor and she couldn't break free. The guesthouse was her castle, and she, the princess, bound by a magic spell—or was it a curse?

A fragrant cinnamon candle flickered on a nearby nightstand, its flame whispering to her, just as it always did during their interludes high up on the bluff, where she had a dreamy view of the sapphire sea. *Go. Leave him. You're only going to get hurt.*

But she never left, and the candle flickered on, its warning unheeded.

What would her family say? Anna could easily fill in the blanks. Her sister's voice rang loud in her guilty conscience: *Are you crazy? Have you lost your mind? Do you have a death wish?*

No—she had a life wish.

She nestled closer to Conrad, trying to quiet the storm of guilt coursing through her veins. She thought back to their first kiss in the guesthouse. How could something so sweet be so wrong? It was the most natural thing she had done in her life.

She hadn't planned for a kiss to turn into an affair. It amazed her how easily she had fallen into the role of the "other woman." That part took no effort at all. The real challenge was keeping it a secret. The guesthouse offered them a refuge: a place for her and Conrad to be together, away from prying eyes. But she couldn't hide from her own shame.

She pushed on his shoulder, and his eyes fluttered open. He blinked, dazed, still basking in the haze of his afterglow. He had made promises to her when their bodies were entwined, when she was doing things to him that nobody had ever done before. Would he remember? Would he honor his words? Or was he toying with her emotions?

This wasn't a game for her. She wasn't playing around. Love wasn't something to trifle with. He should know that broken hearts had incredibly sharp edges.

"Is it morning already?" he asked languidly.

"I need to know," she replied.

He sat up in bed, and she pressed her body against him. How she loved the feel of his warmth, the way her skin melded with his.

"Need to know what?" he asked, wrapping his arms around her.

Before she responded, Anna allowed herself a moment to envision their life together. She imagined herself as an elementary school teacher, while Conrad gave up real estate to pursue art and philanthropy. They would attend gallery events and support important community causes. At last she would be at the Barefoot Beach Ball *without* shoes, Maeve being inexplicably accepting of their love. They would have children, a big family, and live at this incredible estate.

"Conrad, I need to know that you mean it—that you'll call off the wedding." *God,* Anna chided herself. *Talk about a mood breaker.*

Conrad cleared his throat as if he were about to make a speech—or maybe crush her soul. "I will, but it's . . . delicate."

She cupped her hand over his chest. "Delicate is a flower or a porcelain vase. But I'm a woman, and so is Elizabeth. We deserve to be treated with respect. I know it will be difficult, but you need to confront this . . . unless what you told me isn't true." Anna's chest tightened.

Conrad took her hand, kissing her knuckles. "I promise I'm going to call off the wedding."

She searched his eyes, looking for any hint of deception. Instead, she saw the depth of his love. She could get lost in that gaze, but he had more to say.

"I don't want to marry Elizabeth. But my family won't accept this easily. They'll say I simply have a case of the nerves. I promise I'll take care of it. It just won't happen overnight."

Anna sighed. How could this ever work? His family's refusal to accept his decision meant they wouldn't accept her, either.

She needed to walk away from this, not just for herself, but for Conrad. It was the right thing to do. But he leaned in, lips caressing hers, and she allowed his touch to soothe her. She responded, kissing him fervently. This time, her lips traveled down his neck, his chest. Her fingertips traced his inner thigh. She felt his muscles stiffen and his breath catch. He was brimming with need as she used her lips, her tongue, to bring him pleasure.

Afterward, she lay in his arms, and he pressed his lips against the top of her head, inhaling the honey-tinged scent of her shampoo. "This is what I want, more than anything," he whispered.

Anna basked in the relief that washed over her. They didn't need a castle. All they needed was each other.

But her mind wasn't completely at ease. "I'm worried someone is going to get hurt."

Conrad lifted her chin, looking her in the eyes. "You're right," he said. "*I'll* be hurt—if you leave me. I love you, Anna. From the moment I saw you at the fountain, I knew you were my destiny."

What a line. What a completely, unabashedly shameless line.

And she believed it with all her heart.

Anna wiped her brow, noticing dirt on the back of her hand. What a harsh reality shift. An hour ago, Conrad had held her naked in his arms, the bedsheet twisted between her legs and her body bathed in sweat and sea air. Now she was hauling old furniture up from a dusty storage area in the basement with a new hire named Krystal, who had recently joined Team Carmichael—poor thing. They lugged the furniture into the library like pro movers. Anna's back ached.

Elizabeth was there with her father. Baxter didn't bother to greet the help. They may as well have been invisible. If he wasn't leering at them, he was looking right through them. They existed only to serve him drinks, pleasure, or preferably both.

Baxter slipped away to another room, but Elizabeth stayed behind. Her breath smelled like gasoline. Whatever she drank, it had to be burning a hole in her liver.

"Be careful." Elizabeth's top lip curled as she addressed Anna. "Some of these chairs will be used at the rehearsal dinner. A scratch on one of these antiques could cost more to repair than your combined salaries." At least Anna now knew how underpaid she was.

"And, Anna, when you're done, please clean the downstairs bathrooms. The toilets need a good scrubbing. The wedding planner will be here soon, and we can't have a guest use them in their current condition."

Elizabeth popped a few breath mints and marched out, a confident sway in her hips. She waved over her shoulder, all but saying, "Bye, bitches!" Then she headed to the dining room to join her father and Maeve as they planned the wedding seating.

The work was tedious, scrubbing layers of grime from antiques using vinegar and water. Anna applied a soft toothbrush to the hard-to-reach crevices, thinking horrible thoughts about Elizabeth and lovely ones about Conrad, both of which would make her Catholic grandmother weep.

Elizabeth had wanted to stick Anna with the most menial labor she could devise. But did she know about the affair, or simply suspect? Either way, Anna was in a precarious position and had to be careful.

Krystal, fair-skinned, slender, with sun-streaked hair in a loose braid, was a diligent worker. But she was also a thief. Twice Anna had seen her pocket small items: a gold letter opener and a crystal figurine, value unknown. Yet Anna had no plans to report her. It wasn't in her nature to be a rat, and as the harlot of this story, she couldn't claim moral high ground. At least Krystal took only small, inconsequential things, items Maeve would never miss. She wasn't stealing the heir apparent, like Anna was currently doing.

Krystal all but admitted to pawning the stolen loot to pay rent and help support her ailing mother. Anna sympathized, which was partly why she wouldn't snitch. If Krystal got caught, it would be because of her own carelessness.

Anna left to refill the vinegar bucket, wondering what might be missing when she returned. On her way back, she detoured past the dining room.

She crept quietly across the cold marble floor, lurking outside the doorway. "Oh my gosh, I cannot wait," Elizabeth squealed. "These flower arrangements are perfect. Labor Day can't get here fast enough. *People* magazine will cover it. I have connections."

Anna's heart sank. She understood Conrad hadn't followed through on his promise yet, but the reality of the wedding plans struck a deep chord. Elizabeth was all in on their nuptials, and she was a force to be reckoned with. What if Conrad backed down?

"Elizabeth, darling, the guest list has grown considerably . . . the cost, dear . . ."

"Not to worry, Maeve," Baxter declared with authority. "I have only one daughter, and I won't let cost get in the way."

"Oh, good, Daddy," cooed Elizabeth. "Then you won't mind that I've hired a new wedding planner."

"New?" said Maeve, surprised. "I thought the woman I found was doing an excellent job."

"Excellent?" Elizabeth couldn't have sounded more incredulous if she'd tried. "That woman was dreadful. My god, did you see those tacky napkins she picked out? I would never . . . Anyway, Daddy, I found someone much better. But she's based in New York. You'll fly her out for me, won't you?"

"Of course, Sugar Bear," said Baxter. "Anything you want."

Sugar Bear? Anna suppressed a giggle.

"Good. That settles it," said Elizabeth, with a clap of delight. "Maeve, you need to let that dreadful planner go today. And speaking of firing—" Elizabeth's voice dropped.

Anna leaned in, straining to hear. "That new girl you hired? She has to go, too. I hate to tell you this, but she took something from your jewelry case."

"Are you talking about Krystal? She just started." Maeve huffed in disappointment.

"No, I mean Anna. You can't trust that girl. And besides, I swear I constantly smell liquor on her breath. If I were you, Maeve, I'd inventory your diamond earrings—and then call the cops."

Anna felt rage bubbling inside her. Her face flushed. How dare Elizabeth accuse her of theft and drinking on the job? It was Elizabeth's breath that could have caught fire with a match. And the police?! Panic, then nausea, swept through her. Had Krystal sold her out—used her as a scapegoat—or had Elizabeth concocted the whole story? Either way, Elizabeth had it in for her; it was an argument Anna couldn't win.

Shaking with anger and dread, Anna hurried to the bathroom. She arrived just in time, dropped to her knees, and emptied what she'd had for breakfast into the toilet, wishing she could purge herself of every awful emotion tearing through her.

Chapter 34

Jade

When I arrive for work, I'm surprised to see a sweet vintage car parked in front of the big fountain. It's not a vehicle that I've seen here before. Visitors aren't frequent, so this is curious.

The little beauty in the circular driveway is a cherry-red Alfa Romeo convertible—no clue about the year. It has chrome wheels and a sleek, sporty interior with black leather seats, red piping, and spotless plush carpeting. The old me would be thinking about stripping and twisting the battery and ignition wires to get the engine started. But I'm New Leaf Jade—with an honest job and a side gig as a self-appointed sleuth.

Sid greets me at the door. "Jade, what a lovely surprise. Congratulations, you've already beaten our average attrition rate."

I shrug. "What can I say? I'm a glutton for punishment."

He almost smiles. "I try to limit my gluttony to sweet cream and berries—doesn't always work."

Castle Carmichael is as cold and uninviting as ever, but Sid's a little warmer. Even so, with his long limbs and sallow, wrinkled skin, he reminds me of a smokestack in a dying factory town. I follow him into the foyer. He moves like the Tin Man. I imagine he'd need half a quart of oil just to muster a genuine grin.

"Maeve is on a planning call for her benefit party," he tells me in his low, droll voice. "Word of warning—at the last Barefoot Beach Ball, half the guests were drunk enough to go skinny-dipping. I'm telling you this in case you prefer to duck out early. Some things can't be unseen."

"Appreciate the heads-up," I say.

"Also, Maeve asked me to give you some paperwork to file, but first, Conrad would like a word."

A word? That sounds ominous.

I hear voices coming from Conrad's office. Maybe one belongs to the driver of that old car. Since Conrad is occupied, I decide to mine Sid for information. We're not exactly besties, but in a house where staff come and go like dandelion seeds on the wind, he remains rooted. Who better to ask?

I sidle up to him before he can slip away. "So, uh, Sid—" I say with added cheer. "I have a question for you."

He turns, surveying me with dull gray eyes from high above. "Y-e-s-s-s." He elongates the word like a creaky door.

"I was walking the grounds with Conrad—I'm sorry, *Mr. Carmichael*—and we passed by an old ruin. I guess it was a guesthouse once? Do you know what happened to it?" My voice catches. Not surprising—I've dipped a toe into murky water.

I didn't think it was possible, but Sid gets even stiffer. His jaw tightens ever so slightly, and he squints as he leans toward me. I have a disturbing vision of him keeling over and crushing me under his dead weight. His breath carries something sharp and tangy—booze? Is Old Sid a closet drinker? Honestly, I wouldn't blame him.

"Jade," he says, his voice as joyless as a grave, "I don't ask questions about the Carmichaels' affairs. I keep to myself and do as I'm told. I strongly advise you do the same."

He finally smiles, but it's too wide and too empty, calling to mind a jack-o'-lantern.

Old Sid slinks off, leaving me rattled . . . but as a distraction, I decide to eavesdrop on Conrad's conversation.

He's still in his office. I glance around for Maeve or Rose. The coast is clear. I press myself against the wall beside the door and listen. I hear two people talking: Conrad and a voice I recognize as Dr. Hill, the one who looked after Maeve after she fainted. It sounds like a business meeting—professional tone, no raised voices, very matter-of-fact.

Conrad: "So we should increase the dosage?"

"Absolutely," says Dr. Hill. "Her condition isn't going to improve."

They must be talking about Maeve. Is she really that sick? Is it terminal? Their voices grow somber as they discuss specific medications and her prognosis. I'm not familiar with the drugs, but they sound heavy-duty. Is that why Maeve's throwing this party in such a hurry?

"I'm so sorry it's come to this," Conrad says, his voice tinged with emotion. "Does Mother know?"

"No. Not yet."

"How long does she have?"

Dr. Hill exhales loudly. "It's hard to say. Could be months, but I wouldn't be surprised if it's less."

I cover my mouth. *Poor Maeve.* Now I'm worried the stress of this party might speed things up. I step away from the wall just in time. Conrad and Dr. Hill emerge from the office together.

My heart's pounding, and it's not just the adrenaline from almost getting caught. I'm thinking about Maeve—bitchy as she is—heading for the end. *Why do I even care?* But I do. I feel . . . sad. Like, I want to comfort her.

Come on, Jade, I tell myself. *You don't get paid enough for that.*

Conrad approaches. He gently takes hold of my arm, like he's glad I'm there. "Jade, you remember Dr. Vernon Hill. He was here the day you started working for us."

I laugh, but it's more like a squeak, as if he made a joke—but it's only nervous energy escaping. "Oh yeah, of course. When your mom had her fainting spell." I try to mask my emotions, but worry my eyes are giving me away. Maeve is dying and she doesn't even know it yet. "So, is that your car out front?" I ask Dr. Hill, trying to be conversational. "It's a sweet ride."

Dr. Hill flashes me a smile, his bushy mustache arching. "Ah, you're pretty young to be interested in such old things," he says. "And you have good taste. That's a 1958 Alfa Romeo Giulietta. It's a four-cylinder with four on the floor—a classic roadster."

"Dr. Hill sort of lives in the past," Conrad explains. "He's got antique cars, a vintage motorcycle, and he even restored a 1970s motorboat that's a real beauty now. If it's not old, it's not worth his time."

Dr. Hill chuckles. "Guilty as charged. But at least my medicine is up-to-date."

Conrad smiles warmly. "The doc here has been our family physician since I was a boy. A true pillar of the community."

"The way you're describing me, *I* could be classified as an antique."

They share a laugh, and I feel compelled to join. Vernon's appearance supports his observation. He's wearing a tweed jacket and worn loafers. The black doctor's bag in his right hand is made of aged leather, and in his left, he holds his signature fedora. This guy puts the *folk* in folksy—but I overheard the list of pills he's prescribing Maeve, so I know he's no joke.

"They don't make things like they used to," Dr. Hill says. "Quality clothing lasts, same as those old cars. You just have to know how to take care of things."

"Like this watch," says Conrad, who lifts his shirtsleeve to reveal an elegant timepiece. The face is deep black, shiny as a mirror. Slim gold hands move smoothly past the delicate baton markers indicating each hour, encased in domed crystal as if time itself were captured inside a snow globe. The watchband resembles a gold mesh bracelet, with tightly woven links that can bend like fabric.

"This is an Omega Seamaster De Ville—a true relic of the 1960s," he says, with odd reverence for an era that he didn't actually live through. "It was Baxter's—older than I am, but still works as if it were new."

"Simple yet elegant—the perfect timepiece for the man who appreciates quiet status," says Dr. Hill.

"It looks great," I say. While I'm not really sure how much to gush over a watch, I do know that it's *time* to get back to business. "Um, Sid mentioned you wanted to talk to me?"

Conrad offers a nod goodbye to Dr. Hill, along with a muted thank-you, and sends him on his way. I mean, what do you say to the guy who just told you your mother is going to die?

"Come into my office," Conrad says. "I have news for you."

My muscles tense. Am I getting fired? I mentally prepare my plea to stick around because I *have* to be here—for Holly, for the story. But if I'm forced out, at least I won't have to watch Maeve slowly decline.

Before Conrad has a chance to say anything, I blurt: "Please don't fire me. I really need the money."

Conrad tilts his head. "Fire you? Jade, you're doing a great job. In fact, I spoke to my mother earlier, and apparently you've impressed her quite a bit."

I gulp. "Oh . . . wow, okay. Plot twist."

"You're getting something of a promotion," he says, eyebrows raised as if the news surprises him as well. "I have to say, it's a rare person who receives a compliment from Maeve Carmichael. You should be flattered."

"Sure—yeah, like, super cool," I say, though I'm really just confused. I didn't do anything other than what Sid advised. I did my job and mostly kept my mouth shut. "What's the promotion?" I ask.

"You'll still be clearing out my stepfather's belongings, but now you'll also be helping with some of the last-minute party preparations. Of course, you'll make more per hour with the added responsibilities. Mother can fill you in on the details. I would help, but my planning skills are woefully lacking—I don't even plan my lunch."

There's sadness in his smile. I project that he's thinking about planning a funeral.

"Mother is upstairs resting. I wanted to catch you first, in case you don't want the extra responsibility. This party means a lot to my mother. It's going to be stressful."

"I can handle it," I insist, certain he can detect my hesitation. The last thing in the world I want is Maeve Carmichael riding me like a donkey for her sandy fiesta, but my mission outweighs all my reservations.

Before I can offer additional assurance that I'm the girl for the job, an alert on Conrad's phone distracts him. He sends me off with an apologetic, albeit dismissive, wave. Clearly it's an important call. Private, too, for he shuts his office door as soon as I exit.

I return to the echoing foyer, feeling off-kilter. This family sure knows how to throw me for a loop. I thought Maeve couldn't stand me, and here she is, offering a promotion.

I'm not paying attention to where I'm going when I nearly collide with the housekeeper, Rose, who appears to be rushing for the door. She's wheeling a small suitcase and has a black bag slung over her shoulder. She's dressed in her work outfit—gray pants and a white button-down shirt—but doesn't have her apron on.

"Oh! I'm sorry," I stutter. "Is everything okay? You seem to be in a hurry."

Rose checks her surroundings as if nervous she'll be overheard. "No, everything is *not* okay. Unfortunately, my mother is very sick. I need to fly back home to be with her." Her eyes fill with worry. "I won't be returning."

I recall Conrad's earlier observation that employment here is akin to a carousel—round and round, they come and go. Now Rose is departing.

"Maeve did not take the news well, so be warned—she's in a foul mood."

I grimace, expecting the worst. "Thanks for the heads-up, and I'm so sorry about your mother. Where does she live?"

"In Tennessee. I've missed it. I don't like New England weather, but—well, I have my reasons for coming to Beauport. Just like you, Jade. I've seen you snooping around."

Shit.

Rose adjusts the light sweatshirt draped over her arm. We lock eyes. Her expression is hard to understand—it's part warning, part encouraging.

"No, you've got me all wrong," I say. "I just needed a job, and this fell into my lap."

Rose's smile is telling. "Okay, if you say so. But trust me." She pulls me close. Her grip on my wrist is firm as she puts her lips beside my ear. "If I were you, I'd hurry out the door as well. The money isn't worth it."

I pull back. Her candor surprises me, though not so much I can't push for more. I keep my voice low. "Rose, what's up in the tower—and why doesn't Conrad want me anywhere near this place at sunrise and sunset?"

Rose's expression darkens. "This family guards its secrets carefully. I've been here a long time trying to get answers of my own. If my mother weren't ill, I'd probably stay and suffer more of Maeve's abuse." Her eyes dart about as if the walls have ears. "But if you find out anything, anything at all, will you promise to call me?" She presses a card into my hand.

"Sure," I say, though her request shocks me. Rose and I have barely exchanged three words, and I'm suddenly her lifeline? *Strange.* "What exactly should I be looking for?"

"I wish I knew," she responds cryptically, heading for the door.

An Uber is waiting in the driveway. I help load her luggage into the trunk.

"I can tell you have a good soul," she says, speaking to me through an open window from the back seat. "I don't want you to create more problems on my account. But if you're determined to look in places you shouldn't, be very careful. If this family finds out you're prying into their secrets, there's no telling what they'll do. Trust me, they can make people *disappear.*"

Without further explanation, the car pulls away. Rose waves goodbye. I watch the car head down the drive.

The day is already warm, and yet a fierce chill has sunk into my bones. I shake it off. Rose might have departed under vague circumstances, but I'm still here and feel more determined than ever to get to the bottom of things. If that means sucking up to Maeve Carmichael, my lips are already pursed.

I head back inside, pausing at the door to the tower. I could try one of the keys in my pocket, but I don't dare go snooping, not right now. Rose's words of warning linger.

Standing by the door, I hear a sound from high above. I listen intently, almost daring to put my ear to the keyhole. For a moment, all is silent. This house feels strangely alive, like it's breathing, talking, calling to me, but it won't tell me its secrets. All it gives me are the few notes of that same, vaguely familiar piano melody, set on repeat, drifting down from atop the mysterious tower where I am not permitted to go.

I hear footsteps approaching from the kitchen.

"Maeve is ready for you," says Sid.

But am I ready for her? Doubtful, but at least I have a plan. Checking my phone, I do some simple math: There are about seven more hours until sunset.

Chapter 35

Holly

A cop named Finn McNeil, middle-aged, with a friendly smile, sharp eyes, and an aquiline nose, escorted Holly into a cinder-block room devoid of windows. Inside was a small refrigerator with a coffee maker on top and a round table on which sat a simple card-board evidence box. The room smelled of stale pizza.

"This is our break room and interview room," said Finn. "Sorry we don't have nicer accommodations. We're a small operation, so most spaces are dual-use."

Holly fixated on the box. It was like an urn, but instead of ashes, it held the details of a tragedy.

"I have to stay in the room," said Finn. "Hope you don't mind, but it's protocol." He wrote his name on the evidence tag under the *Chain of Custody* section.

Holly noted the last entry was made over fifteen years ago. This case wasn't just cold—it was downright frigid. The last name written on the tag before Finn's didn't surprise her: Tom Walker.

"Do we need gloves?" asked Holly.

Finn shook his head. "No. Any evidence that needs protection is bagged and tagged. You're free to look to your heart's content."

"And what do I do if I find something useful?"

"You tell the police." Finn's smile suggested the answer was obvious.

But Holly had another question that she kept to herself: *What if I find something that points to the police?*

Her throat tightened as she removed the lid. She leaned her head over the opening as if she were gazing into an abyss. Finn gave her space to investigate. The air grew heavy and oppressive. The walls seemed to close in. She reached inside, her hands trembling as she pulled out a file folder. An inventory sheet, clipped to the top, detailed the contents of the box.

Before she could open the folder, Finn said, "Hey, I reviewed everything beforehand, and just so you know—there are photographs in there you might find, uh, distressing."

Holly nodded gravely. She could peer into the past, but she couldn't look at those pictures. That was where she drew the line.

She paused for a moment, gathering her resolve before commencing the worst trip down memory lane. She reviewed the 911 call logs, imagining the panicked voices summoning help. Beauport had a volunteer fire department, but the blaze was so fierce that police and fire crews from several nearby towns arrived to assist.

"Do you need some water?" Finn asked.

Sure enough, her throat was parched. He retrieved a bottle from the refrigerator.

Holly drank deeply as she skimmed a brief interview with Maeve Carmichael—a woman so desperate to maintain her financial status that she married her son's father-in-law, Baxter Ward. Or maybe it was love. Holly knew only that if humans didn't make questionable choices, she'd be out of her job as a writer.

The interview was dry and factual. Maeve had been at home when the explosion occurred. Nobody was living in the guesthouse at the time. She had no idea whose body the firefighters had wheeled out on a stretcher.

She read a later police report about Maeve, equally brief, this one dated after Anna's body had been identified.

The property owner, Maeve Carmichael, admitted to firing the victim, Anna Sinclair, a week before the explosion. She had filed a complaint accusing the victim of theft. Officer Tom Walker investigated. No arrest was made. Mrs. Carmichael speculates that the victim might have attempted to destroy the guesthouse as retribution for her firing and was accidentally caught in the ensuing explosion.

Holly resisted the urge to crumple that report and toss it away. What a gross insinuation. She had her own theory. Anna had gone to end things with Conrad. What if it turned violent? What if Conrad had killed Anna? Strangled her? Stabbed her? What better way to cover up your crime than to incinerate the evidence?

And what about his jealous fiancée, Elizabeth? Maybe she discovered the love affair and committed a crime of passion. As a Carmichael-to-be, she had been protected as well. Holly made a mental note to learn more about Elizabeth Ward.

The interview with Conrad Carmichael, which Tom Walker also conducted, was cursory at best. And there was one glaring hole in Conrad's story.

I haven't seen Anna since she was fired from her job, he reported.

Holly's blood boiled. That was a blatant lie. Anna had gone to see him that night—at *his* invitation. He had left Anna a note, asking her to meet him. Those two were together every moment they could sneak away.

The note was never recovered. It was probably in Anna's pocket at the time and burned in the fire. Holly told the police about it, but without physical evidence, they didn't seem to care. If they had, Conrad might be behind bars instead of walking free and offering jobs to impressionable young women.

Holly pushed through her mounting anxiety to examine the remaining items in the box—everything except the crime scene photos.

Next was the medical examiner's report. She read it carefully, grimacing at the gory description of the body. In the *Cause and Manner of Death* section, the box for *Undetermined* was checked.

Holly continued searching through the contents. Her sister's claddagh ring was bagged and tagged. She held it up to her eyes. The gold appeared dull, especially when compared to the color of the matching ring she wore in her sister's honor.

"Could I have this back?"

Finn didn't think long before he shrugged. "Don't see why not. Nobody is asking for it. I'll fill out the forms. Go ahead and take it."

She placed the bag holding the ring into her purse as unbidden tears leaked from her eyes.

Reaching into the box, Holly pulled out a clipping of a newspaper article she remembered reading when it was first published. It was a follow-up article, written several weeks after the fire, but held no new information, and was cursory at best. For most people, that might have been enough—short and sweet. But for Holly and her family, the quick overview had felt more like an insult.

She turned the clipping over as she returned it to the file, but something else caught her eye—a familiar face, staring at her from a black-and-white photo on the back of the article. The shock made Holly gasp.

Ethan.

There he was, standing beside an older woman whom Holly didn't recognize. But there were two other figures in the frame she identified immediately: Maeve and Conrad Carmichael. Under the photo was a title and a short blurb:

Carmichael Family Continues Its Philanthropic Tradition

Despite the recent tragedy at the family's estate, the Carmichaels made their annual donation to the Beauport Literary Society this past weekend, though without the usual gala they would have hosted in the past. The Literary Society expresses its deepest thanks to the Carmichael family for the donation that all but sustains them throughout the year.

From left to right: Maeve and Conrad Carmichael, Barbara and Ethan Greene.

Holly was confused. She assumed Barbara was Ethan's mother—they looked enough alike—but Ethan had never mentioned a connection to Conrad, besides doing carpentry work at the estate. Was it just an innocent oversight, or had he purposely withheld that detail when they'd talked about the family? Alarm bells rang in her head—or was it just another headache coming on?

Those questions would have to wait. She had more to examine.

She'd never seen the report from East Coast Gas and Propane, the company that helped the fire department inspect the gas lines after the explosion. The report stated there was no indication of foul play, but Holly noticed something else. She credited her fledgling writing career for catching this detail. When she typed short stories on her grandfather's old Olivetti typewriter, she often used Wite-Out for corrections. That might explain why the bright white patch in the report's conclusion section stood out so sharply.

She'd seen that same unnatural whiteness before—on photocopies of her typed work that she'd made at the library. Not only had someone used Wite-Out on this report, but Holly was beginning to doubt she was even looking at the original.

And something else was off.

"There's an item missing from the box," she said to Finn, who came over to take a look. "It says here you recovered a partially melted prescription bottle for Lypotrel—whatever that is—but the bottle itself isn't in here."

Finn scratched his temple. "That's odd," he said.

Holly kept her suspicions about the gas report to herself. Until she knew who to trust, the less she said, the better.

"Do you mind if I take a picture of this inventory sheet?" she asked, lifting her phone.

Finn nodded permission. She snapped a photo.

This one box held many secrets: a potentially doctored report, a missing prescription bottle, Conrad's blatant lie, and a surprising connection between Ethan and the Carmichaels. On top of that, there was proof Tommy Boy had been a key investigator—*and* the last person to handle the evidence.

Was he behind the threat she received at the cottage? Could he be part of a larger effort to scare her out of Beauport before she uncovered the truth?

Holly's suspect list had just grown: Conrad, Elizabeth Ward, Maeve, the odd busker, Tommy Boy, and—she gulped—Ethan?

For Holly, justice had never felt so close—and yet still so far away.

She left the police station feeling dazed. The bright blue sky dazzled her eyes. She sensed the same strange aura she felt around Ethan, surrounding her like a fog. She pressed her fingers to her temples as she coped with the pounding headache.

At that precise moment, her phone rang. It was Gail.

Holly squinted at the screen, barely able to tap the answer button.

"How'd it go?"

"There are definitely things to look into," Holly said.

"Like what?"

Before Holly could respond, a stab of pain cut through her thoughts. "Sorry," she said, breathing heavily into the phone. "That whole experience gave me a brutal headache."

"Do you get migraines?"

"Usually only when I write," she joked—sort of. She winced as the throbbing intensified. "This one's a doozy."

"Have you seen a doctor? You should get checked out," Gail said. "Go see Dr. Hill—I bet I can get you in right away."

Holly couldn't help but smile. Gail was *clearly* wired into this town.

"I have superpowers in Beauport, if you haven't figured that out," Gail continued. "And so does Dr. Hill. We call him the Candy Man. You won't have any trouble getting a little something for that headache—or your nerves, for that matter."

Holly had to admit something to help her settle didn't sound so bad. And who better to ask about Lypotrel than a doctor?

Chapter 36

Jade

I'm beginning to regret my promotion.

We've been working together for an hour, but somehow it feels like a full day. Maeve's usually organized environment is in disarray. Papers are strewn across her bonheur du jour—that's the proper name, according to Maeve, for her delicate writing desk, which is now cluttered with invitations and notebooks, all part of her party-planning tool kit. She's converted a plush stool into a makeshift workspace for the overflow paperwork.

The work is taking a toll on her—or maybe it's her declining health. By anyone's standards, Maeve looks ready for the opera, but I know better. Her perfectly coiffed hair has a few strands out of place. Her eyes are sunken, like a college student after pulling an all-nighter. A brooch hangs askew on her silky blouse, and her nails no longer have the sheen of a fresh weekly manicure.

It's hard to work knowing my boss's days are numbered, and Rose's warning weighs heavily on me. Meanwhile, I'm toying with a mildly hazardous plan to ignore Conrad's orders. I'm not vying for Employee of the Year, that's for sure.

As for this party, we've already accomplished a lot in a short period. The first task was the menu, which Maeve and I reviewed with the caterer. For the record, if I were the caterer, I'd have quit. Maeve made enough last-minute changes that it felt like starting from scratch—and she did so without even an apology. On top of that, she added twenty more people to the guest list.

I could tell the caterer was fuming. Her tone was clipped as she acquiesced to one change after another until all of Maeve's requests were approved. I'm guessing this is her biggest job of the summer, and she can't afford to say no.

Next, we went over lighting, music (trust me, Maeve and I didn't see eye to eye—all jazz? no dance music? no hip-hop? gimme a break), and lastly, attire. Maeve reviewed the dress code for the Barefoot Beach Ball, which unsurprisingly insisted upon no shoes. It's bright dresses, festive colors, upscale beachy. *Don't show up in your ratty old bathing suit,* she warned.

"This party is my ode to the ocean," Maeve explains. She walks to the window, where she gazes at the vast expanse of water stretching out before her, like a sea captain's wife keeping watch for her husband's return.

With her back to me, Maeve whispers, "*Finis* . . ."

She's talking to herself, but I speak up, "Finis? What does that mean?"

Maeve turns around, narrowing her eyes. "It's Latin, often used at the end of a play or a film. People these days are so unsophisticated. Google it, you might learn something."

Ouch. For a second, I thought Maeve and I were having a moment, but I'm quickly grounded back in the reality of her hierarchy.

"Also, we need to work on your outfit. You can't look like you shop at Goodwill," she quips. I don't bother telling her that I've actually *stolen* from Goodwill. "What sort of dresses do you own?"

Shame washes over me, then a rush of sadness. My mother was too busy drinking to take me shopping. Besides, appearances aren't so important when you're focused on survival.

"I don't actually own a dress," I confess, assessing my jeans and Converse sneakers, feeling woefully inadequate.

Maeve shakes her head with the judgment of a Catholic school nun. "I figured as much," she grumbles.

From her closet, she removes a garment bag. "I found this when I was going through some old things. I know, I'm supposed to leave that job up to you, but I get bored spending my days convalescing." She gestures to the bag. "Open it. I'm pretty sure it will fit. I have an eye for these things. Of course, you don't have to wear it, but you certainly can't come to the party in that." Her side-eye is harsh, but I swear she follows it with a half smile.

Maeve Carmichael, you might just like me.

"Th-thank you," I stutter, unzipping the bag. "If it fits, I would love to wear it." And that's not a lie. Just because I like dark eyeliner and studded jewelry doesn't mean I can't appreciate pretty clothing. It's a sleeveless shift dress by Lilly Pulitzer in a vibrant blue, decorated with an intricate swirling paisley pattern in shades of teal and white. The light fabric and above-the-knee hemline make it breezy and summery.

I thank Maeve for the dress, which is perfect and has a neckline that would show off my necklace if it hadn't been trampled on. Which reminds me . . . "Mrs. Carmichael . . . I don't suppose you've seen a necklace like this around town?" I take the silver chain out from under my tee and show her the jade stone that's always in my pocket. "I know it's not your caliber of jewelry, but I want to get it repaired at the same place that sold it. It's definitely from around here—I just don't know where."

Maeve examines the jewelry shrewdly, flipping it over to inspect the inscription on the back.

If eyes could scoff . . .

"Probably came from a trinket shop on the boardwalk," she says. "I wouldn't waste time trying to fix it."

I must look disappointed, because she adds, "But if it's important to you, I'll find someone to repair it." She places it on a small tray on her desk. I almost protest—I don't want to leave my necklace behind—but a high-pitched beeping noise interrupts us.

Maeve looks up, annoyed. "That's my medication alarm. Dr. Hill prescribed new medicine I have to take four times a day. *Four times.* Who can be bothered?" She heads to her bureau to get her pills. She has five different pill bottles lined up in a row.

"Fetch me some water from the tap, will you, Jade? It's filtered." Maeve hands me a glass, and I dutifully go to her private bath. I still can't get over how obnoxiously ostentatious it is—marble everything, gold fixtures everywhere.

When I return, she's fumbling with the cap, unable to open it.

"Enough with these childproof caps already. Who do they think is going to get into my heart medicine?"

"Here, let me," I offer as I place the glass on her bedside table.

It's humbling. I struggle to get the cover off, too. I feel genuinely sorry for Maeve. Someone should be organizing her pills, putting them into those cases with the days and times. It's too easy to get confused when you take so many medications. I worry Maeve will need full-time nursing soon, but I'm glad that's not part of my job description.

I'm still struggling with this ridiculous cap when all of a sudden it pops off and pills go everywhere—and I do mean *everywhere*. At least they're blue and the carpeting is a pinky-beige, so they're relatively easy to spot.

"Oh shit." The swearword slips out as I get down on my hands and knees to retrieve the tiny tablets. They're under the bed, under the dresser, inside Maeve's slippers, and she is none too pleased.

"I'm so sorry. I'll get them all, I promise." It takes a while, but I'm fairly certain I've collected every last pill. To be sure, I check with Maeve. "Do you know how many there should be?"

"I haven't taken a dose yet, so there should be a hundred and twenty capsules. Count them all. I don't want a single pill vacuumed up."

I may have fallen back out of Maeve's good graces, but I carry the handful of pills to the dresser, where I placed the bottle.

I count and recount like a banker—all hundred and twenty pills are there. As I drop each one back into the bottle, I notice something else. I don't remember the exact names of the medications I overheard Conrad and Dr. Hill discussing, but this one doesn't sound famliliar. I sneak a peek at the other four bottles, and I don't recognize those either.

Were Dr. Hill and Conrad discussing a different patient? If so, who?

Either way, Maeve doesn't look well to me at all. She sprawls out on her chaise, feet up, back of her hand pressed to her forehead as if she's suddenly spiked a fever. "Take a break, Jade," she orders. "I'm going to rest for a while."

I check the time. Normally at this hour, Maeve would be getting ready for her daily swim. But not today. Her swimsuit is nowhere to be found. Sadness washes over me as I wonder if she'll have the strength and vitality to dive into the salty waters of her beloved ocean ever again.

Chapter 37

Holly

Shortly after lunchtime, Holly arrived at a small but neat doctor's office. Gail's influence was remarkable. Even though Holly had no prior relationship with Dr. Vernon Hill, a single phone call from the real estate maven was enough to get her an appointment that very afternoon. It was fortunate—her headache was worsening by the minute. It had passed the knocking-to-get-in stage. Now it was downright pounding.

The doctor's office was close to Allen Spellman's legal practice. The proximity reminded her to follow up with Shae. Since she was a fraud examiner, Holly had asked her to dig into those mysterious transfers from the house account to two unknown recipients. But she hadn't given any updates yet. Either way, Holly could handle that when she was feeling better.

The office was unlike any medical facility she had visited before. The waiting area featured a collection of antique leather chairs and ornate wooden tables. The floor was covered with uneven wide pine planks. An intricately carved walnut grandfather clock, tucked into a corner, displayed the current time, though it looked like it was from the past. Nearby stood a freestanding coatrack, unusual in this era of wall-mounted hooks. The artwork on display consisted of framed advertisements for old-fashioned medicines from the 1940s and earlier, including products like Carter's Little Liver Pills, Geritol, and Phillips' Milk of Magnesia.

While the place gave off vibes of a bygone era, it operated with modern efficiency. Five minutes after check-in, a nurse led Holly to an examination room in the back. The flat, stainless steel exam table—upholstered in a pretty seafoam green—creaked as Holly climbed onto it. There were no levers or hydraulics to adjust for her comfort. A thin paper sheet crinkled under her weight. Even the wall-mounted instruments looked slightly yellowed with age. The familiar antiseptic smell carried a faint, musty undertone.

The nurse who escorted her took her vitals. Dr. Hill arrived shortly afterward. Holly was glad no one had made her change into one of those flimsy johnnies that would expose her backside.

Dr. Hill glanced at his clipboard—no digital tablet for him—which held her intake information. "So, Holly, what brings you in today?" he asked with an affable smile, his big, bushy mustache offering a salutation of its own.

Holly didn't particularly love doctors. She didn't go as often as she should and couldn't say what her triglyceride levels were—or what that even meant—but she immediately liked this man. His friendly nature put her at ease, and she appreciated how he dressed—dapper, with a paisley tie and wide, button-on suspenders attached to his high-waisted trousers.

She described her headaches, explaining how they had been progressively getting worse. He didn't seem surprised when she talked about the zigzag lines and flashes of light—what she called an aura—that preceded the most intense pain.

"Those visual disturbances can be associated with migraines. Nothing to be alarmed about. Any idea what triggers them? Bright lights? Loud noises? Stress?" He shone a penlight into her eyes.

Holly flinched as if she'd peered into the sun. "No, not really." How could she admit that proximity to a handyman with a personal connection to her sister's potential killer might bring them on? She wanted headache pills, not psychiatric meds.

Dr. Hill asked her to look up, down, left, and right. "Looks good," he said. Using a handheld scope, he examined the back of her eyes.

When that checked out, he palpated her head, neck, and shoulders, checking for muscle tenderness, which was absent. Her blood pressure was good, and her reflexes were normal. Overall, she received a clean bill of health, but Dr. Hill had his prescription pad at the ready.

"I'll write you two prescriptions—one for a painkiller with a little codeine, another for a high-dose ibuprofen. If the headaches continue, just come back to see me so we can increase the dosage or try new medications."

The outcome surprised Holly, who didn't expect to leave with a permission slip for controlled substances. She needed to stay alert and focused to write, not be dazed and confused, but she gratefully accepted the prescriptions. It seemed Dr. Hill lived up to his reputation as the Candy Man, making it even more likely that he knew about lesser-known pharmaceuticals as well. She could look up the medication online, of course, but right now she had an expert in front of her. She opened her phone to remind herself of the name of the drug listed on the evidence inventory sheet.

"May I ask if you've ever heard of a medication called Lypotrel?"

Dr. Hill squinted as if squeezing out a memory. "Lypotrel . . . Lypotrel." His blue eyes brightened. "Oh yeah, that's an older weight-loss drug," he said. "But it got pulled from the market, maybe ten or fifteen years ago. I never prescribed it, so it wasn't on my radar, but why is it on yours? Looking at your chart, you have a perfectly healthy weight and great blood pressure."

How sad that she took his observation as a major compliment. She really needed to get out more.

"It's just something I stumbled across," she said, hopping down from the table. "Thanks again for fitting me in—I really appreciate it."

Holly returned home to find Ethan replacing the hinges on the screen door off the porch. Funny—she didn't remember that being on the to-do list.

"The door was really loud, so I took the liberty of getting you a new set of hinges. It's a supercheap fix, so don't even worry about it."

He stood tall, smiling, moving the door back and forth several times to demonstrate how quietly it opened and closed. "Keep it locked, though," he said, "because now someone could get in without you hearing them."

Holly nodded. She half expected her headache to get worse when their eyes met, but no—she wasn't feeling any additional pain, probably because she had taken two high-potency ibuprofen. She hadn't bothered filling the codeine prescription; she didn't want addiction to accompany her writer's block.

Ethan began packing up his tools. The sun was getting low, and she figured he'd had a long day as well.

She considered confronting him about his relationship with Conrad but didn't want to put Ethan on the defensive. She opted for a softer approach.

"Any chance you have time for a cup of tea or lemonade before you go? I wish I had beer to offer you, but I'm not much of a drinker."

The corners of Ethan's mouth lifted into a smile. "At my age, I can get a hangover just looking at a bottle of beer." He chuckled. "Lemonade sounds great."

Holly poked her head into the refrigerator, emerging a moment later with a grimace. "What about a nice tall glass of ice water?" she offered sheepishly. "I forgot I have a roommate with a sweet tooth. Jade drank all the lemonade."

"Water would be fine," said Ethan.

They sat down at her rickety old kitchen table with two mismatched glasses between them.

"So, what's happening in your writing world these days?" Ethan asked, looking at her with an intensity that made Holly feel shy.

But Holly reminded herself this wasn't just a friendly chat. She was on a mission to try to get some facts—without spilling the whole can of her sad, sorry beans. The last thing she wanted was to burst into tears talking about Anna. Next, Ethan would be consoling her, and then he'd have his arms around her, and then . . .

Maybe that wasn't such a bad idea after all. But no. It was far too much—too personal. *Keep it vague, just enough to tease out Handsome Handy.*

Holly sighed in frustration. "I've been trying to work on a new book, but it's not going great. Honestly, I'm a little stuck." *A little stuck, as in I may need the Jaws of Life to extract me.*

"Guess I'm lucky," Ethan said. "I don't get a handyman block."

She found his cute comment endearing. *God, I'd make the worst spy ever.*

"Writer's block is just an excuse for not writing, and if plumbers and such tried the same line, they'd quickly go out of business."

"You make a fair point, but I'm not starting from a blank page. How do you get over something like that?" he asked.

Holly shrugged. "I'm not sure. I've never had it this bad before. Pathetically, I've resorted to reading a self-help book about a Zen cat."

Ethan brightened. "You're reading *Meow Mindfulness*?"

"Oh no, not you, too." Holly narrowed her eyes. She kept talking, hoping to stop him from listing all the reasons he loved the book, which Holly would immediately interpret as flaws in her own writing.

"I'm trying a different genre this time," she said. "It's a little more rooted in nonfiction, but still dramatized." This was as much as she could share without being too revealing. Holly's mind screamed at her: *That's not how you do intimacy. You tell the whole, unvarnished truth.* But the pattern was set: If she didn't pick an unavailable man, *she* became the unavailable one. Her subconscious sabotaged every chance it got, never believing she was worthy of love. Guilt was like a cancer that way. It spread throughout her life, attacking in unexpected ways.

"Your new direction sounds intriguing," Ethan said. "Can you tell me more, or is it top secret until the book comes out? I have no idea how these things work."

Holly laughed. "It's not as exciting as it might seem. Most of this job is grunt work. We live by the axiom: Writing is rewriting, and a little research when necessary. That's actually where I'm stuck. I need more information about a crime—or a possible crime—that happened in Beauport almost twenty years ago."

Ethan's body visibly tensed. "Here? There's hardly any crime in this town."

"I know. This was highly unusual. Someone died in a suspicious fire." *Someone like my sister*, but Holly didn't need to say that because the look in Ethan's eyes told her he already knew. But why hadn't he said anything to her about it before, and why not say anything right now when the door was wide open?

The answer came as quickly as the question arose. She hadn't invited him inside her inner world. She gave off so many signals for Ethan *not* to pry that he would naturally respect her boundaries.

"Nobody has ever written about the fire at the Carmichael estate, and I have a connection to the town, so I thought it would be good material for a book."

Ethan pulled away, sitting back in his chair. He started to say something but stopped. "I remember that fire. Almost everyone in town knows about it."

He paused—maybe just a beat too long. "From what I remember, they said it was probably a gas leak. Is there really a story there?"

"Could be. That's actually one of the places where I've hit a wall. I got to look at the evidence box at the police station, and the report from the gas company might be counterfeit. And that's not all. The inventory sheet listed a prescription bottle recovered from the scene, but it wasn't with the other evidence. And good luck getting answers from the local yokel cops."

Ethan sank into thought, his brow furrowed. "Can't help with that pill bottle, but around here all gas service is from East Coast Gas and Propane. I happen to know a guy pretty high up in the company. I'm not sure how far back their records go, but if there's something to find, he'll get it for me. I helped rebuild his house after that nor'easter back in March of '18. He's still grateful I didn't jack up my prices like other contractors were doing, and we've become good friends."

And there was that pesky little voice again. *Just like you and Conrad are good friends? Interesting that your family benefited from their fancy fundraisers. Why didn't you mention* that *when we spoke about the Carmichaels?*

Holly kept those thoughts to herself. She could use his help getting the missing gas report, which would likely benefit her more than slinging accusations.

Ethan finished his water and got up to go.

"It's getting late. I should head home." He paused.

Holly tensed. She knew that delay—the way his gaze drifted to his feet, a sudden shift of his weight from one foot to the other—like a man in the midst of personal conflict. Was he feeling guilty about something?

The answer surprised her.

"Holly—I know this is unprofessional, but I really like you. I enjoy your company. I was wondering . . . um, if you'd like to have more than ice water with me?"

Despite her doubts, Holly smiled. "Like that promised lemonade?" she said.

Ethan smiled back with newfound confidence. "I was thinking more like dinner. Maybe tomorrow?"

Holly spoke without thinking. "I'd love that," she answered, and meant it.

Ethan cleared his throat. His mission was over. Now he had to depart, as gracefully as possible. "I'll be back in the morning to do the shingles on the outside," he said.

There was awkward silence as they both stood close, acting as unsure as middle schoolers. Ethan made the first move, leaning toward her. He gave Holly a quick hug. Somehow he got it just right—not too friendly, but not too distant—almost perfect. And she liked how he smelled—woody, masculine.

Could it be that the headaches she experienced around him, her worries about Ethan's link to Conrad and to the mangled book she received, and her concern about his reputation around town as a womanizer were all just a cover-up for her deeper emotional barriers?

Ethan said goodbye, then loaded his tools into his truck. Holly noticed he'd left his phone on the table. She picked it up, intending to bring it to him, when it buzzed in her hand.

She glanced down to see a text message pop up on his lock screen from a woman named Colleen. The message was short and sweet.

See you tonight! Pick me up at six? Followed by two heart emojis.

Ethan came back inside, realizing his oversight. He smiled appreciatively as Holly handed him his phone. "I'll see you tomorrow—already looking forward to our dinner," he said, beaming.

Holly returned a strained smile. "Yeah. See you tomorrow."

Gail had warned her. Why hadn't she listened?

Holly trudged upstairs, still in a daze. She needed to lie down. The headache struck as soon as she saw the text message and those telling heart emojis. Now her skull felt like it was cracking. So did her heart.

She told herself that Ethan did her a favor, or maybe the gods had, or maybe it was Anna's spirit. Whatever the source, it was freeing, and it was better for her to know now rather than later. She didn't need the distraction, especially not from a smooth-talking two-timer. She'd use his skills with tools and his connections to the gas company and send him on his way.

But her writing needed to stay on course; the time had come. She had to take the book seriously. And it had to be *this* book—the story of her sister. It was perfect. She'd come full circle. She was ready to stare down the dragon: do the research, get the facts, knock on doors, knock down walls if she had to. The disappointment over Ethan was just the kick in the ass she needed to take her work seriously.

Holly reached for the box beside her bed. She picked it up as if it weighed nothing. It took her a moment to realize why. She opened the lid, peering disbelievingly into the cavernous space within. She had moved on from the laptop where she had stored the book long ago. There were no backups. There was one—and only one—copy of *Beach Thriller,* and it was gone.

Chapter 38

Jade

Sunset is almost here.

I've been camped out near the garage for hours since I left work at five o'clock. I made a big to-do, loudly saying goodbye to Sid to make sure Conrad heard me leave. I walked all the way to the gate and then carefully stalked back, ducking for cover along the way. Thank God I remembered to store an apple and a soda in my bag.

This sleuthing business is *not* glamorous. Even after five, the sun is strong, and the air thick and oppressive. That's summer for you, even by the ocean. I'm hidden behind three trash barrels that are set out for the waste company to pick up in the morning. All I can say is, *ewwww.* But I do have a clear view of the main house, so I hang tight, waiting and waiting . . . but for what?

I'm stiff, achy, and have to pee like a motherfucker, but I'm not about to give up. Just when I think my bladder is going to burst, I hear it: music. It's faint, far away, but I'm sure I'm not imagining it. A side door to the house opens, and Sid emerges. He holds the door open, and what I see next nearly makes me gasp in shock.

Conrad pushes a fragile woman in a wheelchair outside. She's wrapped in a soft blanket and supported by pillows. It's difficult to tell her age—she's so thin it looks like she's wasting away. However, I can see she's much younger than Maeve. Who is this stranger? Where did she come from?

Sid closes the door with a quick nod to Conrad, who continues toward the path that hugs the ocean along the bluff. I do my best to creep behind at a safe distance, using the shrubbery to stay out of sight.

The sun hovers above the horizon, turning the sky into deep purples with brushstrokes of orange and red. The image of Conrad and this very sick woman in front of a dramatic backdrop is jarring.

He finally stops, locking the wheelchair in place. He gently—tenderly?—wraps the woman in his arms and lifts her out of the chair. He tries to set her on her feet, allowing her to lean on him for support, but she's unsteady and too weak to stand. So he cradles her as if she were a child, and together they watch the last drops of daylight seep into the earth, saying a sad farewell.

Chapter 39

Holly

Jade arrived home later than usual, plunking herself on the sofa, looking exhausted. Her eyes were heavy, her shoulders sagging forward. Chester was there for emotional support—for himself, not Jade, but that was a cat for you.

Holly approached with tea for two and an important question for her housemate. She took a seat across from the coffee table and poured hot water into their mugs.

"Jade, I'm not mad, but I'm wondering if you went against my wishes and borrowed *Beach Thriller* to help with the writing. Did you go into my room and take the pages out of the box?" Her voice rose with a dash of hopefulness.

Jade blinked. "Um, no," she said, sinking deeper into the couch, arms folded, on the defensive.

Holly bristled. She had to be lying. "Please, Jade, now isn't the time for games. I need a straight answer."

Jade looked confused. "I didn't take anything from you—certainly not your book."

Her conviction was undeniable, but there was a look in Jade's eyes—a hint of deception? She may not have taken the book, but Jade was hiding something, Holly had no doubt.

"I don't understand. It's missing. What could have happened to it? The pages didn't get up and walk away on their own."

Jade leaned forward. She peered at Holly as though she were being dim. "And books don't often take matches to themselves and write warnings telling you to get out of town." She fell back against the couch cushion, satisfied, and drank from her mug. "Good tea," she said, looking pleased with herself.

Holly reared back. She didn't want to consider this possibility—it was too fraught. Her voice was an anxious whisper. "You think . . . whoever sent me that book broke in and took my novel?"

Jade raised her eyebrows, tilting her head slightly, basically saying: *Come on. Don't be stupid.*

Holly looked around the room as if the intruder might still be hiding in a shadowy corner. "Fuck," she said, crossing her arms. "That is so damn scary."

Jade rested her elbows on her knees, fixing Holly with an intense, unwavering stare. "Don't you see, Holly? We *have* to get answers, and you *have* to finish the book. That's the only way to make any of this stop."

"It's gone. That's the only copy."

Jade shook off the objection. "The beginning doesn't matter. You can write that part of your story over and over again if you have to. It's the end that counts."

Holly awoke early from a fitful sleep. For a moment, she wasn't sure if she was in New York, Beauport, or somewhere else entirely. The dissociation made her feel nearly as unsettled as last night's dream.

The images were obscured, but the intensity of emotion carried into the morning as Holly poured herself coffee, feeling a rush of cortisol as though she were actively being chased. In her nightmare, she had been. Someone was after her—had been in her home—and Holly had run outside and sped toward the beach, desperate to escape. But the presence—was it even human?—followed her down the path and onto the sand that swallowed her footsteps, making her progress excruciatingly slow.

The edges of her dream were unclear, as if they had a vignette filter. Still, Holly remembered her frantic effort, heart in her throat, as she stumbled toward the water, crashing into the waves, each one getting progressively larger and more powerful until she went under. She tried to swim, but her limbs were heavy and weak. Then she felt someone grasp her ankle, pulling her deeper, until she woke up, gasping for air.

Holly shook it off, gulping her coffee like medicine. She settled onto the couch with a blanket. She was up earlier than usual, and the house was quiet. Jade was still asleep—and still hiding something. Holly was sure of it, but Jade wasn't opening up. She'd told Holly that she'd be extra busy helping Maeve with last-minute preparations for her fundraiser and might have to work late again. But Holly knew there was more to that story, too. Something was up at the Carmichael estate, and she couldn't shake the feeling it was connected to her missing novel.

Chester, her ever-faithful companion, jumped on her lap, purring loudly.

Holly's eyes closed, Chester's purr working like melatonin. But then flashes of the nightmare returned. Who was chasing her onto the beach? The presence had been familiar, someone she had trusted, allowed into her home. Was it Ethan?

Holly dismissed the idea. Just because Ethan was probably a womanizer didn't mean he was dangerous.

Whether her dream should be taken as a warning or not, Holly knew what she had to do.

Easy come, easy go, she told herself as she took out her phone and sent a message, hoping to catch Ethan before he left for the day:

Sorry, my headache is back. I have to cancel dinner and let's wait on the repairs. I need some quiet time today. Thanks.

She hit send.

Holly reread her text. *Thanks*? Why did she feel the need to be polite even when she seriously questioned this man's character? She was sure the answer went back to her childhood and gender roles in society, but that was more than she could tackle this morning. All she could manage was more coffee.

After her second cup and some snuggles with Chester, Holly felt better able to face the day. She made a plan. She needed a friend to talk to—a female she could trust. Holly got in the shower and prepared to head to the boardwalk.

Beach Thriller

vi

Princesses cry over boys. It comes with the territory. The arc of a princess story is to bring the characters close to their happy ending, then cruelly rip the proverbial rug out from underneath them.

Ariel was all blubber when she thought Prince Eric picked a girl without gills. Belle and Jasmine both cried rivers when they erroneously believed their respective true loves had perished. And Cinderella was a helluva hot mess thinking her prince would never come.

In later years, princesses got tougher and cried a whole lot less (looking at you, Pocahontas, Tiana, Mulan, etc.). But that's not reality, either. Love hurts. Loss stings. And Anna felt every bit of her sadness as she sobbed into Conrad's shoulder. It was evening, before sunset, and they had met in the guesthouse as had become their routine. He had brought dinner and candles, expecting a romantic meal; instead, he got an earful of bad news.

"It's okay. I'll talk to her, I promise," he whispered, rubbing her back.

"No, don't," Anna said, pushing him away. "I'm done working here. Your mother and Elizabeth treat me like garbage. And your future father-in-law sees one use for me, and it's not on my knees to clean."

"Baxter is a pig. The stories I could tell you would make you sick. And don't let Mother or Elizabeth rattle your cage."

"It's not them I'm most disgusted with. It's me. I'm the other woman who has to keep reminding you of your promise to stand up to them. I feel like the stereotypical weak-ass female from every outdated story ever told. I can't stand being that person and I won't do it anymore."

Conrad looked away, unsure what to say. He poured them both a glass of wine, but Anna refused.

"That's the last thing I need after your fiancée accused me of drinking on the job. It's unreal. You know I didn't take those diamond earrings, right? If anybody stole them it was Krystal. But don't tell your mother I said that. That poor girl lives on the edge, and I don't want to be the one to push her over." Anna knew she must look pathetic, with her red, swollen eyes, and puffy face, but that only made her feel more righteous.

"Anna, of course I know you didn't take them." Conrad stroked her cheek, gazing lovingly into her eyes. "And this is the last straw for me and Elizabeth. I promise. I don't care how she or my family react." He dropped his hand, his voice beginning to shake in anger. "I'll fix everything. Fuck them both."

His eyes darkened. The change came on so quickly, Anna took a step back, afraid of what he might do. She had seen his temper spark before, but this time it looked like he was about to erupt.

Anna parked herself on the window seat far from him, hanging her head in defeat. Her sorrowful state sucked the air out of Conrad's rage, softening him back into the sweet, caring man she had mistakenly fallen in love with.

The problem was, she *still loved him*. She loved *them*.

Conrad went to the stove in the kitchen and filled the kettle. "Here, I'll make us some tea. We can talk. Come up with a plan."

Anna sighed. "Tea won't fix this. Besides, you know that the stove is touchy. I wouldn't even try to use it."

"I know this is all my fault. But I don't know what to do. I'm . . . so lost." He sat beside her, his shoulders drooping. Tentatively, he took her hand as though she might refuse him. Then, unexpectedly, his expression brightened as if struck by a grand idea.

"Let's leave," he said, eyes wide with hope. "We can do it, Anna. Just go. Start over somewhere new—together. I don't know how much money I'll have if I piss my mother off this much, but we'll make it work."

Anna surprised herself when she burst out laughing. She laughed until she could scarcely catch her breath.

Conrad stared at her, bemused. "What? What's so damn funny?"

Anna looked up, wiping her eyes. Finally her tears didn't come from sadness. "This is all because of a penny. One stupid, worthless penny—and now you're going to run off with me, leave all this, all the money, all the comforts behind, and we're going to live some fairy-tale life where I'm a schoolteacher and you're selling houses, and we've got a couple of kids and a big fat mortgage. Is that it?"

Conrad leaned in close, their lips almost touching. "That penny wasn't worthless, it was priceless, because it brought us together. And yeah . . . selling houses for a living, a couple of kids, and a mortgage—it sounds like a beautiful life to me. What about you? Would you love me without all this?" He gestured around at not only the guesthouse but the grounds outside, the view, all of Miramar.

Anna paused as though thinking it over, but she knew her answer. "Absolutely," she said, kissing him, her eyes welling up again. "There's nothing I want more."

It was late when Anna slipped out the door, moonlight bathing the path back to her cottage. A chill hung in the air, the ocean breeze raising goose bumps on her skin despite the late-summer warmth. It felt refreshing—cleansing, even.

Anna buzzed with giddiness. She was going home to pack. In a few days, they would leave, start a new life. She wasn't sure where they would go or how she would tell her mother and Holly, but Anna and Conrad would work it all out—together.

With his love and support, she felt she could do anything. She flitted along the path, stars in her eyes and daydreams filling her head.

A noise in the dark caught her attention. She stopped. *What was that?*

She heard a twig snap, and a shadow passed in front of her. Anna didn't dare move. She wasn't alone. She saw a figure dart off into the distance, long hair flowing in the breeze. Was that Elizabeth? Had she been spying on them at the guesthouse? What did she see? How much did she know?

Anna retraced her steps. She had to tell Conrad that their dream life had quite possibly turned into a nightmare.

Chapter 40

Holly

The muffins at the Bean There Café smelled extraordinary.

She had bought one and mindlessly taken two bites before it was pretty much gone, so she bought two more.

The duo working the register had frowns that nearly scraped the floor. Holly knew why. Outside, the busker crooned like a dying animal. She thought he might be playing "Brown Eyed Girl," but who could tell when one song blended into the next? He might be industrious, but one could say the same about a parasite.

"I'm so sorry you have to deal with that," Holly said, tipping extra on her way out the door.

The girl with the heavy eyeliner and loads of piercings thanked her, while her coworker—equally bejeweled—blinked repeatedly as though trying to send Holly a cry for help in Morse code.

She considered grabbing a muffin for Jade, but she'd already left for work and wouldn't be home until late. Were the extra hours Jade was putting in *only* for the fundraiser? Holly had her doubts. It better not be connected to Anna. Asking questions could be dangerous for Jade, who, Holly knew, had a natural disregard for rules.

Although she was worried about her young friend, Jade had shown herself to be resourceful, persistent, and hardworking—good signs for her future. Would Holly be part of Jade's next life chapter? Would they stay close? Crazily, she hoped so.

Obviously, the young girl needed a positive role model, given the way her parents treated her. Those two were absolutely horrifying.

Holly would add them to her growing collection of characters bound for deadly mishaps. But Jade's life wasn't fiction. She was on the brink of adulthood and would carve her own path forward. It would mean a lot to Holly if she could be a grounding, guiding force as she progressed.

Holly exited the coffee shop, hoping to avoid eye contact with the busker—but no luck. He locked onto her the moment she stepped outside.

She tried to scoot past, lose herself in the crowd, but just as she thought she was in the clear, the busker called to her.

"Holly," he sneered. "You're still here?"

A chill ensnared her. How did he know her name?

"Haven't you learned?" The busker eyed her up and down.

Her skin crawled. She whirled to face him. "Why do you care? If you have something to tell me, just say it. I'm done with your stupid games." Holly stood tall and firm—well, as tall as her petite stature would allow.

"I've already told you. Be careful in this town. You can't trust anyone." His voice dropped half an octave. "That lawyer you saw—yeah, I know what you've been up to—do you know what he did before he passed the bar?"

Holly shook her head, dumbfounded.

"Ever heard of an evidence custodian?"

Again, she shook her head.

"You should find out what that means. And then ask who bankrolled your lawyer's law degree. Follow the money. People don't do big favors without expecting something just as big in return."

Without another word, the busker, in his scally cap and sweat-stained white button-down, picked up his guitar and started strumming his sad songs.

When Holly arrived at Serena's, her hands were sweaty and shaking. The busker's comments clung to her, just like her unsettling dream. *Evidence custodian.* Allen Spellman—her lawyer? It appeared the busker knew a lot more about Holly's life than she realized. She hadn't seen Spellman's name on the chain-of-custody tag plastered to the side of the evidence box, but that could be because his role was behind the scenes.

The bells on the door chimed as Holly entered. Once again, the soothing scents of sage and chamomile hit her. She found Serena seated in a green-brocade-upholstered chair, her hands resting in her lap, palms up.

Her eyes gently opened. "Ahh, Holly, I thought I might see you today." She smiled widely, stretching her arms overhead. "Perfect timing. Just finishing my morning meditation—have to keep the third eye open—and I don't have an appointment until ten. Have a seat."

"I brought you breakfast." Holly lifted the bag of goodies. "It's not the healthiest, but I needed a little comfort food."

She gave Serena a quick hug. Sunlight streamed in through the bay window, where Holly caught glimpses of Serena's stunning ocean view.

"You look exhausted, sweetheart. Are you sleeping all right? I've been worried about you."

"At this point, I'm worried about me, too," Holly admitted, crumpling into her chair. She rested her head in her hands.

Serena's caring eyes assessed her. "I'll help any way I can. Let's start with some tea. Herbal, okay? It's better for your nerves." A tea station was conveniently located behind the desk where she rang up purchases.

As Serena bustled about preparing their drinks, Holly looked around again at the beautiful decor of the psychic parlor. She loved all the warm, textured fabrics; the subtle scent of incense; the light refracting off crystals and glass orbs. Whatever opinions she held about the occult and psychics in general, this place made her want to believe.

Serena set two cups of tea on a small table between them.

Holly launched into it. "I went to the police station the other day. I had to see the evidence for myself—from the fire. Now that I'm back in Beauport, I can't ignore all the unanswered questions. I figured you know everyone in this town. Maybe you could give me some insight, psychically or otherwise. I'm not sure who to trust." She was horrified to feel her eyes fill with warm, salty tears.

"If there's one thing this town has in abundance, it's secrets."

"That's not surprising. I'm worried even my lawyer is hiding something from me," Holly said. "Have you ever heard of an evidence custodian? I'm not sure what that is, but—"

Serena reached for her phone. "I don't have to use my third eye for everything," she joked.

Holly allowed her friend to do the research, and she took a bite of the buttery blueberry muffin. It melted in her mouth, the sweetness spiking her serotonin. Damn, she needed this—a good friend, a warm cup of tea, some simple comforts. It worked wonders. She relaxed in her chair, muscles finally unclenching.

Holly wondered what Serena charged for her crystals. Some were said to offer health benefits, while others provided protection from dark forces. Maybe that would be helpful—a necklace with a protective gem. Even if it was a placebo effect, Holly would take it. Perhaps it would purge her nightmares.

She reached for a nearby stone hanging on a silver chain, embedded in a silver backing. She mindlessly held the jewelry in her hand, barely registering how the light reflected a color prism back at her. She was lost in thought, all the questions she had for Serena swirling through her brain. *What's Ethan Greene's story? And what about Conrad? What has the Carmichael family been up to for all these years? And how do Tommy Boy and Allen Spellman factor into all of this?*

Holly was jarringly brought back to the here and now. Serena had found something—but so had Holly.

This chain, this necklace. It was just like Jade's. The inscription on the back read *Beauport, MA*—in the exact same font—and the shape of the silver backing was identical to the one Jade had found in her parents' dresser drawer. The only difference was the type of stone—this one being an amethyst. All this time, she and Jade had only considered jewelry stores, never thinking the piece in question could have come from a psychic shop. Was that why Serena reacted so strangely to the necklace when she was over for dinner?

As Serena stated, Beauport was full of secrets, and evidently the local psychic was harboring one of them.

Chapter 41

Jade

There's a stack of last-minute party invitations to address, all new additions to the guest list. Maeve's criticizing my efforts. Meanwhile, the party is tomorrow and she's still inviting new guests. I can't believe the suggested amount written on the donation form. Clearly there's money in this sleepy little town.

Of course, all of these new invitations will have to be hand-delivered by the overworked (unappreciated) party planner. If I had a car, I'd be driving around like a postal worker.

Maeve picks up an envelope I've addressed, holding it between two fingers as though my flawed penmanship has contaminated the paper.

"Don't they teach you cursive in school?" she snipes. "Your *K*s look like *H*s, and your *D*s look like *O*s. Do it again, please. If you're going to print, at least go slower and be more careful." She issues her orders in the clipped tone of a military sergeant.

"Yes, ma'am," I say, snapping to attention like a good soldier. The guest list is nearby, with all the names of people who received invitations crossed off. There's one for the Realtor, Gail Provost; Ethan made the cut, as did Serena and Holly's lawyer, Allen Spellman. Tom Walker has been hired for security, so he won't receive one, but he'll still be at the big event.

Oddly, the attendees line up nicely with my suspect list.

I begin the invite re-dos, paying extra attention to the *D*s and *K*s. However, my thoughts are elsewhere. Before I can filter myself, a question pops out.

"What's in the tower, Maeve?" Impulse control isn't a strength of mine.

I shrink from Maeve's harsh stare.

"Why are you asking?" Her face darkens.

I try to act nonchalant, which also isn't my forte.

"Oh, I dunno—I've just heard music coming from up there, a piano song. It plays on repeat." My pulse quickens. It's not salsa-beat fast, but it's pretty darn close.

Maeve turns her head to peer out onto the balcony of her bedroom. "That's Conrad's private quarters. He's the man of the house now, and his business is just that—his business." She says this with a degree of disgust, which I can appreciate. She can't live here and not have a clue that her son carries a sickly woman up and down the tower stairs for twice-daily outings like she's his pet.

"I don't go up there. Not sure my tired old legs could carry me if I wanted to."

Maeve rises from her seat, her knotted fingers curling into fists. She walks to the window, her feet sinking into the plush carpet. I can't tell whether Conrad's personal life offends her or if my question puts her on edge. I get the sense she's unhappy about the mystery occupant—but for reasons unknown, she's unable to confront her perfect, can-do-no-wrong son about it. Or maybe, like me, she's seen Conrad's darker side and knows to proceed with caution.

"If I were you, Jade, I'd be careful making such inquiries." Her tone is soft. She isn't issuing a threat—it's more like a warning.

"Keep your focus on the party details and let Conrad manage his affairs without interference. My son has a temper. I suggest you don't trigger it." Maeve keeps her back to me, her gaze settled on the expertly manicured lawn, and the shimmering, yearning sea beyond.

"This party has to be perfect. It's likely the last one I'll ever have."

After I finish addressing the envelopes, I'm allowed a break. Trucks are arriving with supplies. Groundskeepers are trimming the lawn, tending the garden, and raking Maeve's private beach of every last strand of seaweed. In no time, the biggest event in Beauport will be underway.

I should be helping—there's plenty to do—but my focus is elsewhere.

I don't believe there's any truth to the old saying *Curiosity killed the cat.* It's cars, chocolate, and household plants like lilies you have to be mindful of. But curiosity *will* kill me if I don't find out what's going on up in the tower. Could it be connected to Holly's story?

Maeve is in a meeting with the caterer (I wasn't invited, whew!), and Conrad has gone into town, leaving only Old Sid—and he's busy in the kitchen now that Rose is gone.

Poor guy needs a better retirement plan.

My fingers brush against the brass keys in my pocket. The metal pokes into my skin as if prodding me on. First, I check if the teak door to the tower is locked. I turn the seashell-shaped doorknob, pull, and sure enough, it won't budge. But that poor woman is up there—I'm certain of it. With my ear close to the keyhole, I can hear the hypnotic melody of that plinking piano song. Is he holding her captive and torturing her with constant, repetitive music?

After double-checking that the coast is clear, I slip the key into the lock. It turns easily, and the door opens silently on well-oiled hinges.

I peer into a gloomy, twisting spiral stairwell. To my surprise, the stone steps go both up and down. I've not been shown the basement, but evidently, this is one way to access it. It's totally creepy in here—dank and poorly lit by a series of low-wattage sconces set into the wall. I'm glad I'm going up because my mind immediately conjures an image of what lies below: a rat-infested cellar with low-ceilinged rooms secured by metal bars, the stone floor covered only in loose straw—a dungeon from medieval times.

My first step inside is tentative, but I brave another. My muscles tense, my gut twists, but I've come too far to back out now. I close the door behind me, plunging myself into deeper darkness.

The stairs are narrow and small. It would be easy to lose your footing and tumble down. Cautiously, I ascend, the music growing louder with each step. I keep my sweat-slick hand pressed against the rough stone wall to maintain my balance. I'm already slightly winded from the climb and can't imagine carrying someone up and down these stairs without falling—but Conrad appears to do it repeatedly.

At the top of the stairs, I pause, unable to advance into the upper chamber. There's no door. Nothing blocks my way except my own fear. The music surrounds me, echoing off the stone walls. It's like a lullaby—it *should* be relaxing, but instead, I'm full of dread. It's now or never. I brave that last step.

The stairwell opens directly into a large, round room. Small windows are set high and evenly spaced throughout, like a fortress. I picture archers shooting arrows through the slim openings, which allow only small sips of light to enter, creating shadows that gather in the corners like shapeless monsters.

A large four-poster bed occupies the center of the room, across from a mahogany dresser. A worn, intricately woven area rug covers the cold stone floor. The bed is piled high with blankets. My first thought is that the room is empty, but then I see the pile of bedding move. From underneath comes a faint groan.

"Rose? Is that you? Conrad . . . is it time already?" The woman's voice is so weak, so faint, I can barely understand her. Even though someone is in her living quarters, she makes no effort to open her eyes. Given her frail condition, perhaps she lacks the strength.

"Um, no. I'm sorry. I'm . . . Jade," I say, making my way toward her bed. "Conrad sent me to check on you." The lie comes easily—they always do. But the sight before me leaves me at a loss for words.

Beside the bed is an old rocking chair. The varnish is worn, raw wood peeking through in places. The colors of the floral design painted onto the top have faded, as though the flowers themselves are dying. Nearby is a nightstand littered with pill bottles. A tall glass of water stands next to a pitcher, but I doubt this woman is strong enough to fill her own glass.

On the floor sits a Bluetooth speaker, playing the piano song that may haunt my dreams for a lifetime. The smell of mildew is pervasive, which can't be healthy—but it beats the odor of sickness that has saturated these stones.

The woman stranded in bed is like a castaway on a desert island.

Her long hair is lifeless, the color of faded straw, and just as coarse. Dark rings circle her shuttered eyes, but her face has very few wrinkles, perhaps because she so seldom sees the sun. It's fitting, given that she reminds me of a vampire's victim—drained of color, her life force dimmed to a waxy pallor.

She struggles to prop herself up on her pillows, determined to see who I am. When her eyes flutter open, I'm stunned. They glow like two of the clearest blue pools imaginable, set against strikingly pale skin. For a moment I can't look away. Her feet, which poke out from beneath the covers, are encased in thin gray hospital socks.

I take a seat in the rocking chair, which creaks faintly as I settle in.

"Jade?" she whispers as if my name is actually familiar to her. Has Conrad spoken of me? Has Rose?

"Yes, I work here at the house. And . . . what's your name?" My voice shakes. Perspiration beads on my forehead. The air is hot and stale, but that's not why I'm sweating. My anxiety is kicking like a horse.

She gathers her breath. Her voice leaks out in a slow whisper. "My name . . . it doesn't matter anymore."

My heart breaks. I thought *I* was lost and forgotten, but she's got my sadness beat by miles.

I'm not sure what to say or do, but I can't just stand around like an idiot. I ask a logical question: "Can I get you anything?" *Like, 911?* But all I add is, "Are you all right? Maybe you need a doctor?"

She sits up a little straighter. "No, the doctor checks in all the time. I'm not well, but there's nothing anyone can do. I just need my pills." She gestures to the nightstand.

"Which ones do you need?" I ask, taking the opportunity to read the labels. They're prescribed to Elizabeth Ward Carmichael. I recall the names of the medications I overheard when Dr. Hill was talking to Conrad—and many of them are here.

So wait, is this Conrad's wife? I remember in *Beach Thriller* that his fiancée was named Elizabeth. It hits me all at once. I never made the Baxter connection before. Probably because I wasn't sure how much of *Beach Thriller* was real and how much was fiction. But now all the dots are connecting.

Seeing Elizabeth's last name, Ward, on the pill bottles, makes me realize that Maeve's second husband, Baxter Ward, must be Elizabeth's father. Which means, Maeve married her daughter-in-law's dad. *Super cringe and totally incestuous.* And now they're keeping her up here like a drugged, dystopian Disney princess. Am I the rescuer in this story, or a mouse about to get caught in a trap?

All I know is that I don't get paid nearly enough for this shit. It feels like I'm putting together a bizarre puzzle, but the pieces are all misshapen and keep multiplying.

First things first. This lady is hankering for her fix, though I'm not about to oblige. I'm not a medical professional. What if I give her the wrong thing, and it kills her?

"I don't think I should give you anything," I say.

Elizabeth doesn't move, but her brow furrows. She's not too pleased with my response. She stays perfectly still as if trying to process my words, but her brain isn't firing correctly.

Kneeling beside her bed, I try for a better look at those mesmerizing eyes. I've seen my fair share of high people. The pupils are always dilated—and hers come at me like a pair of bowling balls.

Forget the drugs. What this lady needs is a way out of here.

Finally she speaks. "Please. I need my pain pills. My back is killing me."

Next to the prescriptions is a bottle of Advil. That should be relatively safe—at least I *hope* so. I dump two tablets into my hand and give her a glass of water. It's heartbreaking to see her hands tremble, just trying to bring the drink to her lips.

"Thank you," Elizabeth says, falling back onto the pillows, exhausted.

"Why are you up here? I have so many questions about this family and all their secrets."

"Oh, you aren't going to ask me about her, too, are you? I don't remember. I wish I knew, but it's all so fuzzy . . ." Elizabeth trails off, yawning, her head lolling to one side.

"About who?" I ask.

Elizabeth's eyes lock onto mine. I'm startled to see them look so alive. A fog has lifted, ushering in a sudden burst of lucidity. In a weak voice, she answers: "She worked here, like you . . . but she left, like most of the others . . . Nobody stays at Miramar for long, except for me, and I don't matter anymore. I've done too many bad things."

Her voice grows softer, like a toy running out of battery power. Her eyes drift shut. Next, I hear the soft inhale and exhale of each slow breath. Elizabeth has fallen back into a restful slumber. It's probably the only peace she gets.

I pull the blankets up to her chin and say a silent prayer that somehow, someway, she'll be okay.

I fear I've been here too long, that I've pushed my luck, and Conrad will return before I can safely escape the tower. I whisper a goodbye—not that Elizabeth hears me. I can't imagine what her world must be like—every second lost in a haze of delirium and confusion, with Conrad offering her moments of reprieve like sips of life through a straw.

Before I go, I use my new phone to snap pictures of all of Elizabeth's prescriptions.

It seems Elizabeth never left him at all. I text her: *I think I know what happened to Conrad's wife, Elizabeth.*

Before I can attach the pictures of the prescription bottles and explain a little bit more, a noise makes my heart race into my throat.

Footsteps, coming up the stairs.

Chapter 42

Holly

Holly didn't have an appointment with Allen Spellman, but she had plenty of questions for her lawyer. The glorious weather contrasted sharply with her sour mood. Sun bathed the cloudless sky, casting rays that promised a perfect beach day, but she had no intention of spending her afternoon on a beach chair trying to write.

If what the busker had said was true, everything had changed. Working backward and considering Allen's age and lengthy career as a lawyer, Holly concluded there was a good chance Spellman had worked for the police department when key evidence went missing from Anna's investigation. Did he take it? Was Spellman offered law school tuition in exchange for a favor? More important, who covered the bill? Follow the money, the busker had said. Holly intended to do just that.

Her determined steps carried her up a flight of stairs to Spellman's second-floor office. She'd have liked Serena to accompany her, but Holly now had reservations about her psychic friend. Why didn't she tell Jade that she sold necklaces just like the one that had lured her to Beauport? Holly didn't want to confront Serena before she had a chance to talk to Jade. But first: Spellman.

She balled her hand into a tight fist, rapping her knuckles against the door, only half caring that she might be interrupting a meeting. This couldn't wait, and some conversations had to happen face-to-face.

There was no answer, so Holly knocked again, this time much harder, allowing some of her anger to escape. Again, her forceful knocking resulted in silence.

Apprehension coiled at the nape of her neck. Glancing at her phone, Holly checked the time. Spellman might be out to lunch, but a faint inner voice told her something was wrong. Then it struck her—a faint odor she couldn't quite identify. It was moderately sharp, biting, and distinct. It unsettled her enough that she knocked a third time, knowing no one would answer. She tested the doorknob, almost hoping it would be locked. It turned easily in her hand.

She pushed open the door, entering the waiting room. Everything was as it had been when she'd visited last. The lights were on. The blinds were open, letting in large pools of sunshine.

He must be here, Holly thought. The coffee maker had half a pot brewed with the warming light still on. But the coffee smelled stale, and that scent of *other* clung to the air—the indistinguishable odor that unsettled her.

"Allen?" Holly's voice echoed. She called his name again and stepped toward his office, her movements hesitant. If he was in a meeting, it wasn't private. The door was wide open. Yet everything was eerily silent.

Her chest tightened. She peered through the doorway. For a moment, she couldn't process what she was seeing, but then her limbs turned to lead as she stared at Allen, slumped lifelessly over his desk. A strange sensation overtook her—almost like being pulled out of her body, drifting away for a moment—only to be rudely slammed back into awareness when the pungent stench of blood hit her nostrils.

Blood spatter covered his desk. It dripped onto the carpet, creating an abstract painting in various shades of burgundy. Near his lifeless hand lay a small, snub-nosed pistol—undoubtedly the weapon fired into Allen's skull—leaving half his head a bloodstained, shattered mess. Flecks of white were scattered among the crimson pools.

Holly found her scream. It tore from her throat, bouncing off the walls and ricocheting like a hail of bullets.

Life may pass unnoticed, but judging by the crowds gathered outside Spellman's office, death was a spectacle.

People stood shoulder to shoulder on the sidewalk, gawkers drawn by macabre curiosity. Holly found an empty park bench to rest on while waiting to give her statement to the police. Crime tape cordoned off the area. The whole scene reminded Holly of the last time she'd seen so many emergency vehicles—only this time it was Allen Spellman, not her sister, who would be wheeled into the awaiting ambulance.

Police and medical personnel swarmed in and out of Spellman's office with the industriousness of ants, taking photos and gathering evidence.

Holly shivered as Spellman's shrouded body rolled past her. A haunting vision of Anna took hold. She was back again, as if teleported, rushing alongside her mother through the open gates of Miramar.

Together, they waited anxiously for news. Deep down, Holly knew. Her mother must have known too because she burst into tears when rescuers announced they'd pulled a body from the rubble. Her mother's cries turned into wracking sobs when they saw, poking out from beneath the white sheet, charred and partially melted Nike Air sneakers.

Anna.

Who was the police officer who spoke to her mother that day? His face felt familiar, but his identity was lost to time. Same with the firefighter who had held Holly as she cried. Cried? No—more like wailed—in his arms. Thank God he'd stopped everything to help her. At that moment, she felt the pain might kill her, that her heart would explode in her chest.

The firefighter's embrace became her breath, his touch her heartbeat. He held on until her sobs abated, all while whispering how sorry he was. Eventually, a social worker took over, and he vanished into the chaos. Holly never got a chance to thank him. She didn't even know his name.

Finn, the cop from the evidence room, approached. He handed Holly a plastic bottle of water and placed a reassuring hand on her shoulder, his eyes weighty.

"How are you holding up?" he asked, taking a seat beside her. "If you need, we can take you to the hospital, or we have a counselor here you can talk to. But we do have some questions for you, if you're up to answering them."

Holly's mind drifted elsewhere. "It's not the same," she replied in a muffled voice, unable to meet Finn's compassionate gaze.

"What isn't?"

"Death. It's not the same in real life as it is in books. Words don't do it justice. I could write and write, but I'd never capture the horror of what I saw today."

Finn patted her arm. "My wife has read your novels, and she's one tough critic. You might be selling yourself short. Death is always traumatizing. And I'm sorry you had to go through that. Even as a cop, you don't get used to it." He paused. Holly wondered if he was reliving his worst days on the job.

Holly took a sip of water. "What happened in there?" she asked. She knew the what and the how, but not the why. Given the stench of blood that somehow, mercilessly, followed her outside, the when couldn't have been long before she arrived.

"Why don't you tell me what you remember and we'll go from there," Finn suggested.

Holly deepened her breathing, but that didn't calm her shaking limbs. "Allen is—was—my lawyer. I came to meet with him. We didn't have an appointment, but I wanted to ask him some questions, so I stopped by on a whim."

"Questions about what?" Finn asked.

The cop knew about the missing prescription bottle, but was he around when Allen worked as the evidence custodian? She quickly filled him in.

"You think Spellman took items from the investigation when he was working for the PD?" Finn sounded incredulous.

Before Holly could answer, a booming voice drew their attention. "Looks like a clear-cut case of suicide."

Of course: Tommy Boy.

The big man pressed his meaty paws against the back of the bench, leaning his oppressive girth over them, casting a tall shadow like an eclipse. "We still need an official report from the medical examiner, but I'd say you're in the clear, Holly."

Holly gasped. "Me? What are you talking about?"

"Knock it off, Tom," said Finn, annoyed.

Tommy Boy walked around the bench to stand in front of Holly, his thumbs hooked into his belt loops. "Just doing her a solid," he said. "I'd want to know if I was gonna face a murder rap."

Holly stammered, craning her neck to stare him down. "I came here to talk to my lawyer and found him dead. I'm the one who called you. Why would you—"

Finn cut her short. "Jesus, Tom, you're a real piece of work, do you know that?"

Tommy Boy shrugged. "Just being a thorough cop, *Boss*."

Holly's anger surged. "Are you trying to intimidate me?" she asked. "You get off on that, don't you? Another Sinclair girl to push around, just like you did my sister."

Did Tom Walker flinch? It was possible.

"I know about you, Tommy," she continued. "You use your authority to take advantage of frightened women. Well, guess what? I'm not scared of you. If you did anything to my sister, I swear I will not rest until I get justice."

Holly's speech bounced right off him. "Feisty, aren't we?" Walker said. "For the record, I saved your sister from spending a night in jail. I could have arrested her, but I talked Maeve Carmichael out of it. And as a show of goodwill, I'll let you in on a little secret about your lawyer. He probably offed himself because the FBI was closing in. Anybody might crack under that pressure."

"Wait, what?" Holly said. "The FBI was going after Allen? Why?"

Finn cleared his throat. "We probably shouldn't tell you all this, because it's still under investigation." He glared at Tommy Boy before continuing. "However, it appears Allen Spellman was up to no good. He's been stealing money from his clients, using it to pay off gambling debts, take vacations, and essentially fund a lifestyle he couldn't afford. Basically, he's been running a Ponzi scheme for a long time, and we've been working with the FBI to get to the bottom of it. Tom is right. He was probably facing arrest in the next couple of days. I guess someone tipped him off."

Holly's world tilted. She clutched the park bench for support. "He's been managing my family's money for years."

Tommy Boy whistled, low and long. "Yeah, that's probably not going to work out in your favor. Allen would make up stories about properties getting stuck in probate, then he'd hand out loans from his personal account to make it seem like he was a good guy and everything was going to be fixed in no time. He kept moving money around to avoid getting caught. Meanwhile, he was draining client accounts faster than my iPhone runs out of battery."

Holly went numb. "That's exactly what happened to me," she said. She didn't need Shae's forensic accounting expertise to tell her that her house fund was probably drained of every nickel.

Chapter 43

Jade

The footsteps echo louder as they ascend the stairwell. Fear surges through me. I don't have Big Sally from Baby Jail to bail me out this time. I've got no place to go, nowhere to run.

Spinning in a circle, I foolishly search for an escape route, thinking one will magically appear. This tower has only one way in and one way out. At least I see something useful: The bed is raised high enough for me to crawl under, and the bedding goes all the way to the floor, so I'll be well-concealed.

I slither on my belly across the cold stone floor until I'm hidden beneath the bed. It's like being in a cave. I'm sure no one can see me, but even so, the slightest sound could give me away. The noise of the party preparations helps to conceal me, along with the eerie piano melody.

In the dark, every sound becomes sharper. The footsteps are heavy—it can't be Maeve. It's someone bigger, but whoever has arrived isn't breathing hard, so I doubt it's Old Sid. It must be Conrad.

"You've heard enough of this song for today, Elizabeth," Conrad says, confirming my suspicion. Above me, Elizabeth groans in displeasure.

"More," she begs, her voice weak and croaking.

"Let's try something other than 'Clair de Lune.'"

Ah, so that's the song! The dreamy piano piece, which evokes the soft glow of moonlight, suddenly comes to an end. Conrad then switches to a different classical composition, this time with violins.

"Noooo," Elizabeth moans. "The moon . . . I want the moon. Please . . ."

The ache in her voice crimps my heart. Her words come back to me: "I don't matter anymore." But this song, for whatever reason, does.

Conrad sighs. A moment later, the music begins again, the first lonely notes calling out like a whisper of solitude.

Outside, it's anything but quiet. Landscapers are busy mowing the lawn and trimming the hedges before the party. For a moment, the persistent thrum of a loud gas lawn mower almost drowns out the music. I hear Maeve's sharp voice issuing orders to the rental company responsible for setting up the tent. I'm sure they can't get out of this crazy place fast enough.

I can relate.

My breath catches when Conrad approaches the bed. His proximity sucks the air right out of my lungs. A sudden rush of panic grips me. My phone might betray me—even a vibration from a text, Holly replying to my inquiry about Elizabeth, could do me in. I want to shut it off, but I hesitate to move a muscle.

The song gets louder, and Elizabeth hums along like she and the melody are one. The bed creaks above me as Conrad likely takes a seat on the mattress. He shushes her tenderly.

"You can't see well. Your hair is in your eyes," he says.

I imagine him brushing the strands away from her face. Is he looking at her lovingly, with care in his eyes, like when he wheeled her to the edge of the cliff to watch the sunset? What kind of guy is this? Does her incapacitation turn him on? She might not be tied up, but all those drugs she's taking could be just as debilitating. All I know is that I'm living a nightmare. I close my eyes, praying that it'll all be over soon.

"I'm so tired," says Elizabeth, who indeed sounds world-weary. "I don't care about my hair. I've done terrible things."

The mattress sags above me as Conrad repositions himself. "We've all done terrible things, Elizabeth."

"But I have blood on my hands," she says.

"We *both* have blood on our hands. You need to forgive yourself."

I bite my knuckles to suppress a gasp. Anna? Has Conrad all but admitted he killed her? Or did he and Elizabeth plan it together? They could have set the house on fire to cover their tracks.

"She's here," Elizabeth says.

My body turns cold and clammy. *No. Don't you dare . . .*

"Who is here?" says Conrad. "Are you talking about Rose? She moved on. She quit. I told you that, remember?"

"Not Rose," Elizabeth says slowly.

I offer a silent prayer to the universe. *Please, please, don't say my name.*

"Jade," she finishes as my stomach clenches.

Conrad inhales sharply. "What did you say?" The anger in his voice shrouds me.

"Jade . . . she came to see me."

"No. You're imagining things." His rumble deepens.

"She's . . . here."

My throat closes. Fear swallows my breath. The bed shifts as a heavy weight lifts. He's up and moving. I hear his footsteps. I close my eyes. A silent prayer loops in my head. The steps move toward the stairs. From the sound of it, he might be leaving. At last the tightness in my chest eases. He's going to look for me. But he won't find me—I'll sneak downstairs, run from this house, and never return. Maeve can have her party without me. But I'll make sure the police show up with a search warrant instead of an invitation.

I wait, listening. There's background noise outside, but what I don't hear offers relief. No more footsteps. Still, I need to wait a little longer. I start a silent countdown. I make it all the way to ten—when a pair of hands clamps around my ankles.

I scream in terror as strong arms drag me out from underneath the bed.

Chapter 44

Holly

Gail pushed the tiny plastic ball toward Chester. It rolled across the hardwood floor, the little bell inside tinkling like a delicate fairy. The cat pounced, swallowing the toy into his mouth, whipping his head side to side to break his prey's neck, then spitting it out and pawing at it until the thing was as good as dead.

So cute.

Gail rolled it again, and once more Chester attacked. Holly watched the game from across the room, thankful for this brief moment of normalcy.

She had been home for over an hour but couldn't stop smelling blood or seeing Spellman's lifeless body splayed across his desk.

Gail was a welcome distraction. For once, she wasn't talking about selling the house out from under her. Of course, the bank might do it anyway if she couldn't pay the tax bill.

"He took everything?" Gail asked, incredulous, referring to Spellman.

Holly could only shrug. "I don't know. My friend's a bank auditor. She's already looking into some oddities with the account. I'll have to tell her about Spellman's criminal activity as well."

"What a little shit."

"More like a gigantic turd, but I shouldn't speak ill of the dead," Holly said. "It's just hard to accept that he stole my family's money, and now I'll never know if he also stole evidence related to my sister's death."

Holly wished she could turn to Serena as well, but her psychic friend might not be trustworthy—and she wasn't in the mood for a confrontation. The day had drained her, and Holly's recent text exchange with Jade made matters worse.

In hindsight, she could have responded better to Jade's message about Elizabeth Ward. The poor kid was just trying to help, but Holly's nerves were frayed, her temper short, and her anger had spiked.

She thought she had been clear—the Carmichaels were off-limits, no investigating allowed. It wasn't safe. But instead of listening, Jade had asked about Conrad's wife—or ex-wife, Holly wasn't sure.

Find the answers . . . finish your novel. Holly kept hearing that jeering paper puppet calling out to her. She was finally listening, and the last thing she needed was for someone else she cared about to get hurt—or worse—before she could get her answers.

Jade should be a kid—working a simple job, making some money, and keeping her nose out of trouble—and Holly should be the adult. This was her mess to untangle. And whoever was trying to intimidate her into walking away was achieving the opposite.

Elizabeth Ward was part of the story, which was exactly why Jade *shouldn't* be asking about her. Holly's reply hadn't been gentle: *I told you very clearly that investigating my sister's death was off-limits.*

As a novelist, Holly didn't use text speech. She wrote books with real grammar and proper spelling, and her texts followed suit. Jade would get the point—loud and clear—without shortcuts.

If you can't honor that, this living arrangement will not work. Please don't put me in that position.

When she sent the message, she'd been full of anger and anxiety. But Jade hadn't responded—not to that message or to Holly's later apology—and now she worried her young roommate had gotten in over her head. Holly already had enough guilt for one lifetime.

She kept checking her phone while Gail absent-mindedly flipped through Holly's copy of *Meow Mindfulness*. Having tired of the ball game, Chester had slunk off to another room.

"Do you know what happened to Conrad's wife—Elizabeth Ward?" Holly asked.

Gail had her face buried in the book. "Did you know people believe the frequency of a cat's purr has healing qualities?" She peeked over the top of the cover. "I'm sorry, did you say something?"

"Elizabeth Ward, Conrad's wife. Do you know what happened to her?"

Gail was terminally perky, so seeing a shadow cross her face was unusual.

"Oh, Elizabeth. Yeah, Conrad's ex . . . there was some shit there." She returned to her reading.

Holly's worry for Jade deepened.

Gail kept talking with her nose in the book. "She worked for Ward Pharmaceuticals way back when—she was a lawyer, pretty high up in Daddy's company. Not saying it was nepotism." Gail turned to Holly and mouthed, *It was nepotism,* which made Holly smile.

"According to what you told me, it was also incestuous," Holly said, cringing.

The gossip lit Gail's eyes. "Mother-in-law becomes the stepmother. Oh yeah, that was the town talk for ages, but then came the even bigger scandal—I mentioned that when we were talking about the Carmichaels with Ethan, but we never got to finish the conversation."

"What was the big scandal?"

"Lypotrel," said Gail, as if Holly should know.

Holly's skin tingled. A quiet alarm went off inside her. "Lypotrel? That was the name on the missing prescription bottle in the evidence box."

"Interesting, but not entirely surprising. A lot of Maeve's money came from the Ward family and that drug specifically. I was actually working for Baxter Ward when the shit hit the fan."

"Wait, you worked for Ward Pharmaceuticals?"

Gail brushed it off. "I did some real estate deals for the company back in the day—found them a commercial plot, twenty thousand square feet of glorious commission." She grinned like a fisherman nostalgic for a big catch. "That's what initially brought me to Beauport. After scoping out properties for Baxter, I fell in love with the area and stayed. But they stopped looking for real estate when the company found itself plastered all over the news, and not for a good reason, so I started my own business. Funny how fate works."

But none of this was funny to Holly. She had no clue about the Lypotrel scandal. She hadn't realized there was more to know other than it was a weight-loss drug.

"So how did Lypotrel get them into trouble?"

Gail went stock-still. "It was a great drug—you dropped tons of weight on it, and it was really popular for a while. The problem was that some people thought more pills would mean more weight loss. Instead, it got you sent to the morgue. A high dose of that stuff was genuinely lethal. Ward Pharmaceuticals insisted the drug had passed all the FDA requirements, but an independent investigation brought on by a lawsuit revealed those documents had been tampered with."

"Tampered with?" Holly was appalled. "Someone knowingly put people's lives at risk?"

"Not just someone—Elizabeth Ward. She was working in the legal department at the time, so she had access to all the materials. She doctored the research and made the drug seem far safer than it was to get FDA approval, all while keeping Daddy in the dark."

"Oh yeah, I remember that story now. It was years ago," Holly said. "But I didn't pay much attention—and I certainly didn't realize it was connected to the Carmichael family. What happened to Elizabeth and the company?"

"Ward Pharma did all right. Baxter paid some hefty fines, but he could afford it—especially since they found Elizabeth was largely to blame, and she was fired. There was a plea bargain. Somehow she avoided jail time. It pays to be rich. But she faced her own punishment. According to the Beauport gossip mill, she had a mental breakdown from all the stress. She ended up hospitalized. I'm not sure what happened to her after that. I think she took off on Conrad and her father. Pretty sad story overall."

Holly felt her phone vibrate. Was it Jade finally texting back?

She looked—it wasn't Jade. It was Ethan.

Hope you're feeling better. And I have some explaining to do. Can we talk?

Usually, Holly's heart would skip a beat at a message from Ethan. But right now, all she felt was a deep, pervasive sense of dread.

Chapter 45

The Watcher

You've really escalated things, Holly. But I knew that would happen. You lit the fire under the pot, and it's boiling over. Someone was bound to get hurt, but did you think they'd end up dead? What was that like for you, seeing Allen Spellman splattered all over his desk? I can only imagine the shock you experienced. Death is ugly business, at least until the mortician gets involved and pretties everything up. But nobody was there to close Allen's eyes or repair the hole in his head. You had to see the entire bloody aftermath unfiltered, in its most raw and visceral form.

Trust me when I say you'll never dream the same way again. Instead of your refuge, sleep will become your battlefield. I've personally seen things, done things that I can never forget, let alone forgive.

Sadly, I'm more afraid of living than I am of dying. But that's the crazy thing about life—it can beat you up, tear you apart; it can take and take until you're nothing but an empty shell, until all you have left to carry you from one moment to the next is the air in your lungs. Yet it's so hard to let go.

Even with all my pain, my suffering, the hurt I've caused, all the terrible things I've done, I still sprout from the soil like a lone blade of grass in a desecrated field, hoping for redemption. But there's also the monster within. I often wonder if I'll ever be free of myself. Perhaps death won't even provide that release. So for now I'm here, and I fight, and I will continue to do all I can to protect myself, whether I deserve it or not.

Chapter 46

Jade

Explain yourself."

Conrad is hovering over me, so close I can feel his wet breath on my skin. We're standing in his spacious office on the first floor after he basically dragged me down the stairs from the tower. *Dragged* might be overly dramatic—but that's how it felt when he took my arm and marched me here like a child being sent to her room.

The low light of dusk seeps through a crack in the heavy drapes, illuminating his plum-colored face. His eyes are fierce and cutting.

"What were my explicit rules, Jade? They were simple: Stay away from the tower and only be here during designated hours. Is that too much to ask? After all I've done for you—all the help I've given—is this how you repay me? Maybe it's my fault for hiring a thief."

He spits out the word with disgust. Under any other circumstance, that might have stung. But not anymore. I stand firm, squaring off with him.

"Maybe get off your high horse, Conrad . . . Mr. I Keep My Wife Drugged and Locked in a Tower." Okay, not as punchy as I'd hoped—but I've stated my case. And I'm fired up. Seeing Elizabeth so frail, barely able to speak, a prisoner in her own home—I won't let this guy bully me. I just wish I had my knife.

Conrad looks ready for a fight, too. He rolls up his shirtsleeves, like he's about to jump into the ring. I catch a glint of light bouncing off the reflective surface of his fancy-ass black dial watch with the gold band. This guy is as full of himself as he is his status symbols.

"You are an ignorant child. You're speaking of things you don't understand. You think I'm *hurting* Elizabeth? I *love* Elizabeth. I've been taking care of her for years."

"Yeah?" I scoff. "If I'm lost at sea and *you're* my savior, I think I'll wait for the next boat."

Conrad slams his hand against the desk. "Do not mock me."

I'd seen his anger before, but this is different—raw and primal, like it could consume him.

Maeve's words of warning come back to me, and my bravado flickers. Fear rushes in—but I can't afford to show it. "If you're such a loving, caring husband, why don't we get the police over here? Maybe some medical help. Let them see the sorry state of your wife. Explain to them why you keep her under lock and key."

Conrad steps forward, the muscles visibly bulging beneath his button-down shirt. I don't stand a chance against him.

But the phone is mightier than the sword. I pull mine out, holding it like a grenade.

"Go ahead. Call whoever you want," Conrad says, meeting my gaze. "Dr. Hill is here regularly. Her medications are all prescribed to treat her mental and physical ailments. I don't care who checks on her—but it won't be you."

I'm pretty sure he's winding up for the punch line: *You're fired.*

But then his phone alarm goes off. He silences it, turns back to me.

"Elizabeth needs her medication," he says. "Stay put. I'll be back in five minutes. If you're so set on calling the police, we'll do it together. I have nothing to hide."

He rushes out the door—and I'm going to do the same. I'm not sticking around this loony bin. First order of business: Call the cops. ASAP.

I open my phone and see that Holly has texted back. *Shit.* She's pissed, too. For a second, I'm torn—call her or call the police?

That one second is all it takes.

I don't hear footsteps. I don't see the shadow sneaking up behind me. A hand clamps over my mouth.

My scream is muffled. I'm yanked backward, feet lifted off the ground. My phone slips from my grasp as I'm thrown over a shoulder.

He spins me fast—like I'm on a tilt-a-whirl. One second I'm airborne, the next, my head hits the doorframe. Hard. My vision blurs.

It's like getting slammed with a two-by-four—which I guess is pretty close to what happened. I'm upside down. Twisted images pass by. I'm woozy, fading, but aware enough to know I'm being carried down a flight of stairs. I try to ask where he's taking me, but my voice is a ghost, miles away. The ringing in my ears is deafening.

I feel sick. Disoriented. I can't hold on. The last thing I see before everything goes black is the glinting metal of Conrad's expensive watch as he carries me into oblivion.

Chapter 47

Holly

The sky was ablaze with glorious washes of yellow, pink, and lavender, but Holly hardly noticed the sunset. It was dinnertime, and still no word from Jade. She hadn't responded to her apology, so Holly followed up with a plea:

I'm sure you're upset with me. I know I could have been kinder. Please get in touch so I know you're okay. I'm worried about you.

She considered adding *X*s and *O*s—but were they at that stage? Holly felt like they were. Or at least *she* was. She fretted over Jade the way a mother would.

That kind of caring was probably foreign to her. Jade's parents were arguably the most wretched people Holly had ever encountered. To survive in that environment, you'd have to be supremely well-defended.

But would Jade lower her guard enough to accept Holly's apology and respond?

What if she didn't return at all? Even though Jade didn't have many alternatives, she had the wits and resourcefulness to survive anywhere.

Have I driven her away?

Holly felt sick at the thought. She hoped that Jade was simply giving her the silent treatment. But she couldn't shake the nagging feeling in her gut that something else was wrong. She tried to quiet her unease by focusing on the task at hand.

Holly studied her writing notebook, where she had jotted down suspects with columns for Motive, Opportunity, and Method written beside each one. She'd never crafted a detective story, but perhaps the bones of one were staring her right in the face.

- Tom Walker: police officer, alleged history of sexual coercion. Anna was potentially one of his victims when she narrowly escaped arrest. Tommy Boy had access to evidence and was present the night of the explosion.
- Conrad Carmichael: Anna's lover. It's always the boyfriend . . . She was with him that night with the intent to break it off. Did he get angry, take revenge?
- Elizabeth Ward: the scorned woman, maybe also a femme fatale? She'd killed before, albeit indirectly by doctoring the Lypotrel research to hide its deadly overdose risk. Could she have taken a more active role in Anna's death?
- Maeve Carmichael: fired Anna and pressed charges. Was she upset when charges were dropped? Maeve was also at home the night Anna died. Did she seek a more violent and final revenge?
- Allen Spellman: tricky. He had access to the evidence and had likely tampered with it. He was a criminal as well. But he had no apparent connection to Anna.

Holly left the Motive column blank. But what if he was part of a bigger plot—a cover-up involving Anna's death—and his suicide was actually a hit in disguise?

- Ethan Greene: Aka, Hot Handy. Shit. Too bad . . . but he either withheld or strategically omitted having a connection to Conrad Carmichael, outside of being the family's occasional handyman. Read *Beyond Horizons*, the same book that showed up mutilated with a scrawled threat. Motive, Method, Opportunity all unknown. But . . . the headaches?

Sadly, Holly added:

- <u>Serena</u>: Motive and Opportunity undetermined. Method unknown.

Clearly, she was hiding something related to the necklace, but perhaps unrelated to Anna's death. Holly kept her on the list anyway.

She jotted down other loose threads: Lypotrel, doctored gas report, her stolen copy of *Beach Thriller*, weird busker with his odd warnings, mysterious transactions from the house account to . . . where? Could those transfers have been Spellman siphoning money from the account over time?

Maybe the transactions were one thread she could tie into a knot. Holly tried Shae via FaceTime. She answered quickly, her beaming face oozing California effervescence. Given Holly's agitated state of mind, it was almost too much to bear.

"Darling, tell me good news only," said Shae cheerily. "Tristen has eczema because he's stressed over a history test. His hands and feet look like they've been savaged by red ants."

Holly didn't skip a beat. "I found a dead guy who blew out his brains with a handgun, and he's embezzled all my money." She forced a smile while Shae's face went slack. What Holly needed for this call was a little wine or whiskey—or better still, ayahuasca. Thanks to Ethan, at least the water was filtered.

By the end of Holly's recounting of the day's horrific events, Shae's usually sunshiny smile had turned into a stormy squall. Holly left out some details to spare her friend unnecessary worry—like the threats she'd received, the missing evidence, and her stolen novel. However, Jade wasn't a minor detail she could omit.

Shae shook her head in a slow sweep of disapproval. "That is a direct violation of the Sisterly Bond Laws: *Thou shalt not keep any wandering waifs sleeping under your roof a secret from your oldest, dearest friend.*"

Holly rebutted, "She's tiny but could definitely take me in a fight, so I don't think I'm in violation. But the next home intruder I let live with me, you'll be the first to know."

"Thank you," said Shae, sitting upright, satisfied.

"I wasn't just calling to tell you about dead people and teen runaways. I was hoping you'd have an update on my account. And not to add to your caseload, but maybe you can help me battle through some red tape so I can figure out if I have any money left. Pretty soon, Jade and I will both be squatters."

"You're not going to be homeless—that's not an option," said Shae. "And to answer your question, no, not really. Those transactions go to two private bank accounts, and I need a police warrant to get the details. Now that we have a crime, I might be able to help you get one, but it'll take more time.

"As for the rest of your funds, let me see what we can do. Hopefully, there'll be enough left for your basics. Either way, I'm not letting you starve. There's this thing called being a patron of the arts."

Holly's forehead creased. "I'm not interested in charity. I've made my own way in this world for forty years. I'll figure something out."

"'If he was beholden to pride, he would never have braved his many failures, thereby achieving great success.'"

"Are you quoting Chaucer to me?" asked Holly.

"No, *Meow Mindfulness*, page 172—a passage about King Fluff, the great mouse hunter."

Holly exhaled a sigh. "Maybe there's a way Chester can make me millions like King Fluff."

Eight thirty had come and gone. Enough was enough. There had been no word from Jade. Every call and text Holly had sent went unanswered. She couldn't sit on her ass and wait. She grabbed her car keys and drove her Kia up the windy road to the bluff.

Flashbacks hit her hard and fast. Holly's headlights reflected off the trees, bursts of light reminiscent of emergency vehicles from long ago. The air carried a familiar scent—the smell of summer by the ocean, dry earth mixed with salt water. But the last time she was on foot, her breath ragged, her panicked mother trying to keep pace.

She expected a headache to strike, but it blessedly stayed dormant.

Was she starting to be less fearful of her past, or were the headaches only an Ethan thing?

Holly gripped the steering wheel, trying to steady her body and mind. For Jade, she could face the Carmichaels again. She eased her speed. The tall iron gate of Miramar loomed ahead, its imposing spikes warding off would-be intruders. Holly's headlights illuminated the intercom. She pressed the buzzer and waited. A moment later, a croaky old voice answered.

"A bit late to be selling Girl Scout cookies, isn't it?"

"I'm Holly Sinclair—I live down the road. My friend Jade Jensen works here. I hope she's still on the premises, because she's not answering her phone."

"I see. One moment, please," the low voice drawled.

She heard a buzzing sound, then a click as the gate unlocked. It swung open slowly. Holly's vision blurred as she maneuvered her car down a driveway that she'd sworn she would never travel on again.

The home was as she remembered, as she had described in her book—the turreted tower, windows like dark eyes peering out from behind thick stone walls. She drove her car around the grand fountain in the middle of the circular driveway, parking in front of a large set of wooden doors. The fountain was off for the night. The man and woman, cast in bronze, held a tipped water jug, but tonight, nothing spilled out. Tomorrow would be different—the fountain would flow and glow. Crowds would gather under a large white tent assembled on Maeve's private beach.

She wasn't here for a trip down memory lane, but she found herself trapped in a time warp. There he was, silhouetted in the doorframe, poised and confident, Conrad Carmichael in the flesh. He had a sense of ease about him, as if no crisis were afoot.

He stood at the top of the stairs, looking down at Holly as he always did. She credited him for his sense of style: He was well-dressed in a nice polo and crisp slacks. He kept his hair neat and avoided late-night snacks; his waistline had changed little, and his jawline remained strong. They could have cast his handsome face in bronze and placed it in the fountain.

Yet Holly shivered at the sight of him. After all these years, she could hardly meet his gaze.

"Holly Sinclair," he said, coming down the stairs to greet her. "I can't believe it's you. It's been so long. How are you? You look great." He paused for a moment, appearing confused. "But the party is tomorrow. You got the invitation, right? I'm sure it was a surprise. We knew you were back in town, and—well, we wanted to reach out somehow."

Holly wasn't buying his horseshit charm. She launched right in. "I'm not here for the party," she said, clenching her teeth. "Jade Jensen lives with me. She didn't come home after work, and she's not answering her phone. I'm hoping she's still here."

Conrad's demeanor shifted. He pulled back, shoulders tightening, eyes darting around like a man looking for a way out.

"Jade lives with you?" His voice rose. "She never said."

"Where is she?" Holly asked. "I need to see her right away."

Conrad appeared nonplussed. "I apologize, Holly." A slight lilt suggested he was crafting a story on the spot. "Jade left hours ago. I'm afraid I can't help you. But if I hear from her, I'll get in touch. I do hope you'll make it to the party. We'd love to have you." He flashed her a stiff, toothy grin.

Holly recognized the look. She had described it many times in her novels—always when a character was lying.

Chapter 48

Jade

My eyes blink open, but I can't see well. A grimy, scratchy film coats my eyeballs. My head is pounding, a stampede beating against my skull.

What happened?

I have no idea where I am. For a moment, I am weightless, adrift in space and time. Apart from my throbbing headache, I have only a faint awareness of my existence. But it's enough to know I'm alive, so I take that as a win.

I come to my senses. I'm lying on my back, a dusty stone floor beneath me. The stones are cold against my neck. I move my limbs to shake them awake. They're stiff and achy.

With a grunt and groan, I roll to my side, pressing up to hands and knees. My stomach roils. I battle back a wave of nausea. Grit from the stone floor digs into my palms. I lean into the sensation. It helps clear my cloud of confusion.

I blink several times until my vision clears, but what I see makes little sense: colorful glass bottles in various hues stacked in rows, one on top of the other. It takes a moment for my eyes and brain to sync, and then I get it—wine bottles in a rack.

Okay, I'm in a wine cellar. But where?

The masonry work is familiar. I recognize the shape of the stones and the fine gray mortar holding them together. The wall curves around me like I'm inside a barrel. Am I beneath the tower? Either way, I'm still in Castle Carmichael. I never knew they had a wine cellar, but I wouldn't tell a teenager where we kept the booze, either.

Thick stone walls hold in the cool air and keep the light dim. A lone window sits high in the wall, almost touching the ceiling. It's ten feet off the ground and set into the stone, creating a sill that's about a foot deep.

A decorative metal grate covers the opening to the window. The wine must be valuable. Even if someone broke the window from outside, they couldn't get into this vault. The grate is made of sturdy wrought iron, with intricate scrollwork and sharp pointed spikes on both ends.

The glow of daylight slipping through is a cruel reminder of freedom that's frustratingly out of reach. The light is low and faint. Is it close to dawn? My body aches like I've been here forever.

As I take in my surroundings, memories rush back. Elizabeth. Her pills. The music. Conrad pulling me out from under the bed. Our verbal altercation in his office. Then . . . ? Conrad grabbing me from behind. His expensive watch was the last thing I saw before I woke up in this wine cellar turned prison cell.

Wherever I am, it doesn't look like anyone has been in this room for a long time. The bottles are covered in a fine coating of dust and old cobwebs. The dust is likely the reason for my itchy, swollen eyes.

Using a nearby wine rack as support, I pull myself up to standing, but I'm wobbly. My legs are like Jell-O. My mouth is painfully dry, my throat raw. A powerful thirst weakens me further.

The damp air settles into my bones. Slowly I release my grip on the wine rack, wrapping my arms around my chest for warmth. It's a good thing my legs don't buckle.

Across from the window is an arched wooden door. Its surface shows deep grain lines, darkened by age. The door appears sturdy. Large nails secure rusty iron hinges into the ancient wood. I pray it's not locked—but something tells me God isn't listening right now.

I stagger a few steps until my body slams against the door. I fumble for the metal handle, gripping it to keep myself upright. Pressing down the lever, I hope to release the door latch. It moves without any resistance, but I don't hear a click. I pull on the handle, not surprised when the door won't budge. I pull harder this time, but the results are the same. When I press my eye against the keyhole, I confirm my suspicions. Diffuse lighting illuminates a small stone landing outside the door, and beyond that are the tower stairs sloping upward out of view.

I'm down in the bowels of Miramar—maybe twelve feet underground, with a lone barricaded window high above me.

Patting my pockets for my phone, I remember I dropped it when Conrad abducted me. The key ring I always keep in my pocket—and that I hoped might hold the key to this door—is gone. Rage and panic build in my chest, the pressure so intense it feels like a bomb about to explode. I'm back in lockup, but my instincts tell me this is much worse.

I turn my attention back to the window. I've never felt so trapped, so hopeless, so alone.

I make a noise I didn't know was possible. It's like the call of a wild animal or the scream of a banshee. The wail explodes from my lips, but no one, not a soul, is around to hear it.

Chapter 49

Holly

Holly sat on the beach, watching the sun rise over the ocean, light reflecting off the surf, which was especially rough today. Maybe there was a storm brewing out at sea. The wild, crashing waves against the shore felt like a prelude to disaster.

"Not Jade," she whispered. "Not Jade."

She had been awake all night worrying, and still no word. Her call to the police was even less helpful than she expected. At least she spoke to Finn, not Tommy Boy. Holly gave him Jade's name, her useless parents' phone number, and explained how the missing girl had disappeared again.

"We'll look for her, I'll put the word out there. Just know runaway teens are notoriously hard to locate when they don't want to be found."

"But I have reason to believe she's in danger—that maybe this time, she didn't run."

"From my experience, the best predictor of future behavior is past behavior. Holly, I understand you don't trust the Carmichaels, but you have no real reason to believe Jade is in any trouble. Now, I know you've been through a hellish week—looking at the evidence from your sister's case, finding the lawyer's body—I'm sure there's a lot of trauma coming up."

Holly had felt crestfallen. Even Finn didn't take her seriously. How condescending to blame all her worry on past trauma. Jade *was* in danger, she knew it, and Finn was treating Holly like a dramatic child.

"I promise we'll do our jobs," he continued, as if that settled matters. "I'll file that report—I just want you to have reasonable expectations. But my honest advice? Call a friend, get some support, and trust that we'll do our job."

A friend? Holly wasn't sure who she could lean on for help. She wished Shae wasn't thousands of miles away.

Serena came to mind. Maybe she should put more faith in the psychic's abilities. Perhaps if she focused hard enough, she could intuit Jade's whereabouts. But the necklace and her reaction to it—what did all that mean? The best approach would be to ask her directly. What could it hurt?

Just as Holly crested the bluff from the beach, she saw a figure standing on her front step.

Maybe Serena really was psychic because there she was, knocking on Holly's front door. Holly hurried across the street, greeting Serena with a hug. Her hair was messy, and her long-sleeved T-shirt was slightly wrinkled. It appeared she had just rolled out of bed, but she was carrying a tray with two coffees from the Bean There Café.

"Serena, are—are you okay?"

"I'm sorry to show up early like this, but I couldn't sleep. Is Jade here? I had the worst dream about her. I'm afraid it was a premonition."

Holly gulped, opening the door for Serena to come inside. "And I'm afraid you might be right."

Hours later, Holly's mind was still reeling from all Serena had shared. In her dream, a strong wind had knocked Jade off a cliffside walking path. She fell into a dense fog and landed in an underground cavern.

"The cavern represents primal ground, where both growth and rot set in. The fog symbolizes unknown influences—a loss of control, same as the wind pushing her off her path," Serena said.

"What's it all mean?" Holly wanted to know.

"If it's a premonition, and I believe it is, then it means someone has taken her, and they're holding her against her will. I believe she's alive, but she's not safe."

Holly's intuition told her who had taken Jade. She had no doubt. The Carmichaels were behind her disappearance, just like they were to blame for Anna's death. As fate would have it, Holly had the perfect excuse to go looking around Miramar.

Initially, she had no interest in attending Maeve's show-off beach soiree, but once she realized it offered the ideal opportunity to search for Jade, Holly sprang into action. She spent the afternoon shopping and preparing. She splurged on a floral-patterned beach dress with some of her dwindling funds—no time for bargain shopping. She also purchased a pair of flats to wear while canvassing the creepy gothic estate.

After all Serena had shared, Holly felt she could trust her. But she needed more help if she was going to pull this off. She needed a team. Holly called Gail, who would be at the party—no way would her friend miss a social (read: gossip-filled) event like this, where she could also find potential high-end real estate clients. But would she agree to help?

Upon hearing her plan, Gail gasped. "That all sounds *very* dangerous. Maybe it's best to let the police do their thing."

"Their thing? Like neglecting cases and leaving murderers wandering the streets? I can't do that. Jade needs me, and I am *not* going to let her down."

Gail sighed, reluctantly accepting Holly's declaration. "Okay, I'll be there, and I'm glad that you trust me enough to let me in on your half-baked scheme. I'll help in any way I can."

"Thank you. Thank you so much. I'll see you at the party." Tears of gratitude welled in her eyes, but Holly wouldn't let herself cry. If she started, she might not stop. And she had far too much to do.

When she hung up, she noticed another text from Ethan. It was the second message he'd sent that day.

Hey, just hoping we can chat. Got done with work early today. Give me a call.

Holly didn't call. She had to keep her mind laser-focused, and talking to Ethan would do nothing but throw her off-balance.

It was nearing six o'clock. The party would start at seven. Holly was too stressed to have an appetite, but she needed her strength, so she rifled through her refrigerator looking for anything that could pass for a well-rounded meal, or even partially well-rounded. *A semicircle would do*, Holly thought wryly. And that was about what she found.

She lamented her lack of skills in the kitchen, but even she could stir-fry a few vegetables and make some rice. She put a drizzle of olive oil in the pan to heat, adding some coarsely chopped onions and peppers. Luckily, she had instant rice available, so the meal wouldn't take long.

As dinner cooked, she turned her attention to Chester, who was meowing at her feet. His meal required significantly less preparation. She plopped the contents of a small can of cat food into his dish, cringing at the smell, and was about to return to the stove when she heard a knock at the door.

Jesus, this is the last thing I need, Holly fumed. God help the Jehovah's Witnesses, if that's who was on the other side. With her anxiety maxed out, she might explode at the slightest provocation.

Holly opened the door with more force than intended, and it practically flew off its hinges.

"Careful, or I'll have more work to do," joked Ethan, who stood in front of her with a half smile, the evening light dancing in his eyes.

Holly's frustration and fear ebbed for a moment. Ethan took her breath away. He was usually dressed in his work clothes, but tonight he had on khaki-colored drawstring beach pants and a soft coral linen shirt over a white cotton tee.

He must have realized she was at a loss for words. "But seriously, sorry for just showing up like this. You didn't answer my messages, and I think I know what happened the other day. I'd really like a chance to explain."

Before Ethan could say another word, a blaring, piercing sound filled their ears.

Oh, shit! The smoke detector.

Ethan rushed past Holly, seeing the source of the smoke immediately—the dinner Holly had neglected on the stove. Thinking quickly, he reached into the cabinet under the counter, grabbing the fire extinguisher Holly didn't even know she had.

He removed the lock and pressed the nozzle, the spray covering her dinner, her stove, and much of her countertop. Smoke permeated the kitchen, everything coated in a haze as the alarm continued to blare. Holly stood stock-still. In the low light, Ethan looked like a blurry silhouette by her stove, extinguishing the blaze with the efficiency of a pro.

Holly's vision dimmed. She felt woozy, unsteady on her feet. Images began to flash in front of her. The crowd. The commotion. The heat, the flames. Fear and a deep knowing gnawing in the pit of her stomach. And Ethan. It was Ethan, coming out of those flames, covered in soot and sweat. Ethan, into whose arms she had crumpled.

Once again, his arms caught her—the same arms, but almost twenty years older.

Holly leaned against him. "It was *you* . . . You were the one who comforted me the night my sister died. My headaches. It was my memories, trying to break through. Why didn't you tell me?"

Holly steadied herself. Ethan gently released his hold to hit the button on the smoke detector, silencing the alarm. The emergency was over.

He wrapped his arms around her once more, this time tighter, pulling her into a bear hug.

"I didn't want to say anything that would trigger you. You obviously didn't recognize me when I came to the house, but I've never forgotten you. I've carried that night with me—still do. I thought you'd remember eventually, when you were ready."

He buried his face in her hair. Holly finally let the tears come. She allowed herself to feel everything: the loss, the fear, the deep pain, but also the love. She had lost so much, yet the pain was proof that love made life worth living. She felt it right here, right now, in Ethan's arms.

Drying her eyes, Holly pulled out of the hug. "I need a glass of water—and a little fresh air."

They opened the windows, letting in a breeze, the tang of salt air pushing aside the smoky residue.

"At least you know the new smoke detectors work." Ethan chuckled.

"That's right, thanks to my handyman, and what—part-time firefighter, who had the foresight to buy a fire extinguisher?" Holly was puzzled.

"Yeah, that's right. Beauport has an all-volunteer fire department, and I've been on it since my twenties. Believe me, plenty of people regret not making that simple purchase. I wasn't going to let you be one of them. My dad was a firefighter, too, so the lessons are ingrained in my DNA. Which reminds me—one of the reasons I came by tonight was to show you this report."

Holly took a big swig of water as Ethan removed a folded piece of paper from his back pocket. "My friend at the gas company came through. You definitely need to see this."

Holly opened the paper slowly. What she read chilled her heart.

Right there, in black and white—with no signs of Wite-Out, erasures, or any other changes—the report stated: *Markings near valve indicate possibility of tampering.*

Chapter 50

Jade

The thirst is killing me.

It's like the worst itch imaginable, one you can't scratch. There's not a drop of moisture in my mouth. My tongue feels thick and swollen, as if it barely fits between my teeth. Every breath scrapes my throat, which is raw, gritty as sandpaper. A headache pounds behind my eyes. I can't tell whether I'm thirsty or if I have a concussion. A welt has appeared on the side of my head where I hit the doorframe of Conrad's office as he was carrying me down to this prison.

Dehydration makes my thoughts cloudy. Every move I make feels slow, as if I'm moving through molasses. I try to swallow, but there's nothing—just my dry scratchy throat, a deep ache in my bones, and the urgent need for water.

Nobody has answered my screams, but that doesn't keep me from trying.

"Help, somebody. Please . . . I'm so thirsty," I say, in what has to be one of the lamest pleas ever uttered. It has all the force of a chirping baby chick. I suck down a breath, letting the fear ratchet up, hoping it'll fuel my resolve.

I try again, this time with far more authority. "Help! Somebody, please help! I'm locked inside."

My words echo back to me strangely, low and hollow, bouncing off the stone and the glass bottles, lingering briefly before fading into silence. I don't know how far the sound travels down here, or if it can reach the main house where Old Sid or Maeve might hear it. Regardless, they may be too old and hard of hearing to notice my desperate cries.

I wait and listen. Silence never sounded so loud.

Conrad. This is all because I found out what he's been doing to Elizabeth. She's his prisoner and the police would have arrested him if I had made that call.

I need to sit down. The room is spinning, and so are my thoughts. Would Maeve even help me if she could? There's no sure answer. It's quite possible she's involved in this house of horrors. She must know about Elizabeth, too. Is she protecting her son? That seems likely. Maybe she has been protecting him all along. Does she realize he probably killed Anna? Will she do anything to keep her perfect boy, her great legacy, out of prison, even if it means killing me?

When the answer hits me, I stop calling for help.

Tears fill my eyes. If only I could drink them.

I coach myself like I did in Baby Jail when some of the girls threatened to gut me like a fish, or when my father went into one of his drunken rages that sent my mother cowering in the closet.

You are Jade Jensen. You take no shit. You are a fighter. You are a survivor.

No. You are a crier.

Because that's what I'm doing, down on the floor, head between my knees—sobbing uncontrollably.

I've realized something. There's a reason nobody has brought me any food, water, or even a blanket to ward off the constant chill. It's because I'm just like Elizabeth—she's up there, and I'm down here. Her words and mine could be the same: I don't matter. And like her, I probably won't be an inconvenience for much longer.

My ragged breathing comes to a sputtering stop. I will myself to not think about water. Sure enough, the ache in my throat lessens some. I have to get the fuck out of here. No one is coming for me, so I have to rescue myself. But how?

I look up at the grate. If I can dislodge it from the wall, I could break the glass and wiggle my way through.

But first, I have to reach the damn thing. It's far over my head. I try jumping, but my legs don't have much spring. If I stretch my arms as high as I can, I still can't reach above the bottom spikes.

There's no way to tell if I can pull it off unless I can climb up there.

Before I can plot my next move, I'm caught off guard by a loud and powerful sneeze. The force scratches my raw, parched throat, but it also makes me think of Holly—how we first met because of my dust allergy.

I want to get back to her. Not just to warn her that Conrad is dangerous, but because . . . well, I guess because she's the closest thing to family that I have.

I'm struck with a deep feeling of sorrow. I don't open up easily. I don't let anyone in. Closeness is pain. Caring is an illusion. That's what I've learned about life. That's the greatest lesson my parents taught me. But then . . . there's Holly.

I guess you don't realize how alone you've been until someone comes along and treats you with kindness.

Chapter 51

Holly

Ethan, do you understand what this means? Someone set that fire. It's proof that Anna was killed." Holly's voice trembled. "I need to find a safe place to hide this. Someone may have broken into my house—I'll tell you about that later. My point is, I don't know where to keep this."

"Don't worry, I put in a request to have the gas company resubmit their report. They've already sent it to the Beauport PD. I'll hold on to this one—I can't think of a safer place." Ethan folded it up and slipped the paper into his wallet.

"Thank you for everything you've done. I feel like I might actually be able to get answers, after all these years." Holly was awash with both relief and anticipation. "I don't know how I can ever repay you."

"You don't need to repay me. That's what . . . friends do," Ethan said uncertainly.

Holly suddenly stilled, trepidation sinking back in. She took a deep breath and said, "But some things don't add up. I still don't think you've been completely honest with me. You asked me out—on a date, it seemed—but I'm not the only woman in your life, am I?"

Ethan couldn't meet Holly's eyes. She feared the silence that followed her question spoke volumes.

"No, you're not," he whispered.

Holly's throat constricted. She had hoped, really hoped, he would answer differently.

"There's something I haven't told you. I don't know how you'll feel about it, but you should know the truth. I have a daughter." Ethan's eyes met hers with emotion and vulnerability.

"I know that might scare you off. It's a big responsibility. She keeps me on my toes, and it's not easy getting involved with someone who already has a family. But she's the light of my life." He smiled with such pride and love that Holly's heart overflowed.

"A daughter? Ethan, I thought you had a wife or a girlfriend or, well, God knows what. A daughter is wonderful. I'd love to hear about her. Is she the one who texted? And I wasn't snooping. I just picked up your phone as a message from a woman named Colleen came through with a couple heart emojis."

Ethan hung his head, as though ashamed of what Holly must have thought of him. He took her hand in his, her reservations washing away.

"I was worried you saw that text message and got the wrong idea. My daughter is eight, she texts from her mom's iPad. She's the sweetest kid you could ever meet. Looks a lot like Colleen—we're divorced, by the way, no secret woman at home." He laughed. "We share custody. My daughter's name is Scarlet. It fits her vibrant personality, like the name was meant to be." Ethan was grinning ear to ear.

But panic hit Holly. She glanced at her phone. It was after seven. *Shit, Jade.* She was on a mission, and she couldn't be off schedule.

Ethan noticed her distraction. "Are you upset? About Scarlet?"

"No, not at all. She sounds wonderful. But I have a problem."

Holly let go of all her lingering doubt about Ethan's character and filled him in on Jade's disappearance, her suspicions about the Carmichaels, and her risky plan for the evening.

"Well, I was hoping you'd be my date tonight anyway. That's why I showed up dressed and ready for the beach ball." He motioned to his summery, beachy attire. "We should go together. After all the work I've done at the estate, I know the Carmichael home inside and out. Go get ready. And trust me, if Jade is there, we'll find her."

Chapter 52

Jade

I bite my lip trying to hold back tears. It takes a minute, but I center myself. I'm not going to let these fuckers beat me. I'm determined to get to that window.

The tall wine rack suddenly looks a lot like a ladder. I start pulling wine bottles out of their slots, one by one, until the rack is mostly empty.

The structure is tall and bulky, curved like the room. I tried to push it to get it closer to the window, but it's secured to the wall. I'm breathless from trying, but I'm not about to give up.

I slip my foot into the bottom opening of the rack, hoisting myself off the ground. I pull back to test if the wine rack will hold my weight without tipping over. It does, so I start climbing higher—left foot, right foot, one hand, then the other—until my shoulders are level with the grate.

I let go with one hand, leaning out as far as I can. My arms and legs are tired and shaky. But no matter how far I reach, my fingertips don't even touch the metal.

There's only one option remaining. Summoning all my courage, I push myself off the rack and leap into the air. In flight, I manage to grab two looping sections of the scroll-like design a millisecond before I would have fallen to the floor. My fingers latch onto the metal loops, and I hold on, but that's all I can do. With my feet suspended off the ground and my arms fully extended, I hang there like a piece of wall art. Rust causes brittle flakes of metal to break off under my grip and jab into my skin like painful cactus needles.

From up here, I can see outside. I'm looking out at a stretch of lawn that fades into a dense patch of trees and shrubs. The window is on the side of the house, not the front, so there's less chance of someone walking past it.

I pull on the barricade, hoping to free it from the wall, but I have no leverage. Even if I did, I realize it's securely attached to the stone with rusted bolts and brackets.

My muscles burn from hanging on so long. I have to let go. When I drop, my knees hit the floor—*hard*. I scramble back to my feet. Everything aches, blood pooling on my palms where the rust broke the skin. If I weren't close to death, I'd worry about tetanus. I pace the room, picking rust flakes out of my bleeding hands, feeling helpless like a caged tiger, and just as angry.

Out of pure spite, I reach down and grab the nearest wine bottle. I don't care about the vintage or the year. Mostly, I'm thinking about my aim. I cock my arm back, then whip it forward with velocity like I'm throwing a knife.

The bottle sails from my grasp, spinning end over end, streaking through the air and hitting the grate in a perfect bull's-eye. It shatters on impact with a loud explosion of glass. The crack is deafening in this confined space. A cloud of red liquid hovers in the air for a split second before splashing onto the floor. The red pool on the stones resembles a prelude to my murder. The air smells sickly sweet.

I don't know what I thought would happen. I guess I wasn't thinking much at all. But something in the middle of the puddle of wine catches my eye—it's the top of the broken bottle I just threw. The neck forms a perfect handle. The bottom is jagged like a shark's teeth.

I grasp it in my hands. It has weight and feels like a knife. I turn toward the door. My eyes narrow. Grinding my teeth, I tighten my grip on the makeshift weapon. I may not get out of here alive, but I'm not going down without a fight.

Chapter 53

The Watcher

This was what I worried about from the start. My worst fears have come true. I tried, I really did. But you couldn't—wouldn't—stop. Now it's too late. People *will* get hurt. There's no other way.

It all comes back to you, Holly. You wouldn't make the smart choice to pack up and leave. You're the same way at your job. You stubbornly write book after book, work through word after word, and despite no bestsellers to your name, you keep going.

That kind of determination is admirable in your career, but it's unsafe here. What did you expect would happen? The girl adores you, Holly. Can't you see that? She's searching for answers that need to stay hidden. And now that she's found a lead, I can't just keep watching. She knows too much. The girl is just like you—stubborn, persistent, and very intelligent. In short, she's a threat. And threats will be handled.

I was once a watcher. Now I need to be something else—something I haven't been in a long, long time. I recall the measures I took in the past to protect myself. The shame still burns. I prepare to become that person once again. I say a prayer for myself. Selfish, I know, because I'm not the one suffering. But I'll need forgiveness.

I don't know how the evening will unfold, but I am certain of one thing: Not everyone at the party will make it through the night.

Chapter 54

Holly

Holly experienced the most intense déjà vu of her life as she took in the scene before her. *The more things change, the more they stay the same.* This could have easily been a Carmichael party from when she was in her twenties—the setup was almost identical.

Tonight, the fountain flowed vigorously, underwater lights casting a serene blue glow on the bronze figures. It was into this pool that Anna had tossed her penny, the course of her life changing irreversibly.

Ethan maneuvered the truck around the circular drive. Despite the constant thrumming from the generators powering the party, Holly could hear the jazz band playing on the beach far below. A red carpet stretched across the lush lawn, guiding people to the stairs they needed to descend to reach the Barefoot Beach Ball. What a royal pain in the ass. A normal person would host this shindig on the large, beautiful open lawn, but not Maeve. She had to stand out.

The bluffs looked stunning at any time of day, but especially when sunset painted the sky with shades of pink and orange. Soon night would fall. By then, guests would be too absorbed in music, dancing, and drinks to notice much beyond their immediate surroundings—the partner in their arms, the cocktails in hand.

No sooner had Ethan cut the engine than a pair of valets, dressed in white shirts and black pants, approached. He handed over his keys along with some cash, though given the makes and models of the luxury cars pulling in behind them, it was unlikely he'd be giving the best tip of the night.

Ethan reached out his hand to help Holly step down from the cab. She thanked him while fixing the neckline of her floral dress.

"You look beautiful," he said.

The compliment coaxed a smile from her, one that quickly faded. They weren't here for a good time.

Holly watched one beleaguered server after another carry tray after tray of hors d'oeuvres to the stairs before they disappeared into the deepening twilight. They were like ants on the march, no different from the servers she and Anna had once been. And like before, their sweat equity would go as unappreciated as the air everyone breathed.

Several guests moved in and out of the house, probably using the two bathrooms on the first floor—no way would Maeve allow porta-potties to mar the beauty of her event.

"Should we split up? I need to find Serena and Gail." Anxiety flitted across Holly's skin. She couldn't fail Jade, and both women were vital parts of her big plan—which, in hindsight, felt more like a vague idea than a solid strategy.

"Let's head to the beach and get a feel for the party first. We'll probably find your friends down there. And don't skip eating—you need your energy, especially after your veggies turned into inedible flambé."

Holly allowed herself a moment of lightness. "Very funny. Maybe I invented a culinary masterpiece, but we'll never know, seeing as you doused it in chemicals." She gave him a side smile.

Ethan gently took her hand. A small jolt of electricity made her feel like a kid again. Together they descended the winding stairs built into the side of the cliff.

"I wish my folks were able to come to this party," Ethan said wistfully. "But with Mom's bad hearing and Dad's bum knees, it's just not like it was."

"Were they regulars at the Beach Ball?" Holly gulped. She hadn't asked Ethan yet about his family connection to the Carmichaels.

"They never missed one of Maeve's charity events," he said. "Even if she could be a snob, Maeve was always very generous to the causes my mom championed."

As their feet finally hit the sand, a rush of embarrassment compelled

Holly to fess up. "I saw a picture of you and your mother receiving a check from Maeve. It was in my sister's evidence box, on the back of a newspaper clipping about the fire. Conrad was in the photo, too. It made me wonder if you and he were closer than you said."

Ethan chuckled dryly. "You thought I was a philandering cad who also had a secret bromance with your number-one suspect?"

Holly grimaced. "That was the other reason I didn't text you back," she explained with a shrug.

"Trust me, Conrad and I never ran in the same circles."

With relief, she looped her arm through his and pulled him closer. What a strange feeling to be happy around this man, yet also filled with a deep sense of dread. Where was Jade?

The party buzzed around them. On the beach, a large white tent stood decorated with string lights, beneath which a long buffet table was stocked with tropical-themed dishes: tuna tartare, crab cakes, fruit skewers, and grilled shrimp, in addition to what the servers were passing around. The table also held a large crystal punch bowl that reflected the party lights like a disco ball.

At the far end of the tent was the jazz band, crammed onto a makeshift stage. People danced and swayed to the music in their party dresses, shorts the color of summer fruit, chino pants, and Hawaiian shirts, having the time of their lives, all with no shoes on their feet.

The servers did their best to keep up with orders, but there was also a lone bar—a thatched hut with a roof made of palm fronds, lit by tiki torches.

It was fortunate the tide was low enough to leave plenty of space for the barefoot ballers to mingle around the tent. The beach looked pristine; Maeve must have had landscapers clear the sand of every last scrap of seaweed.

With the shoreline glowing brightly, it was a magical sight, something Holly could appreciate more now that she was a guest. While many people were taking pictures of the moonlight rippling over the ocean waves, at least two professional photographers were also there to capture the festivities for the media.

After leaving their shoes at the shoe check station, Holly and Ethan worked the party, looking for Serena and Gail. The guests, especially those trying to dance, burst into laughter as they kicked up sand or stumbled on the uneven surface.

Holly scanned the crowd, also hoping to spot Jade, knowing deep down she probably wouldn't. But it didn't take long for her to see Conrad, who was holding court near the thatched-roof bar.

He was dressed in a relaxed linen blazer with palm patterns, worn over a crisp button-down shirt and white khakis. He was holding a cocktail served in a fresh pineapple.

She watched him from a distance. Her anger surged, but she kept it under control. Losing her temper wouldn't help Jade. She needed to be careful and strategic. Based on Conrad's suspicious behavior the night before, she was sure he was hiding something—most likely her missing friend.

To a casual observer, Conrad appeared to be his usual self, playing up to a group of women, one in a revealing top, who were splashing drinks and fawning over him as if he were a rock star or the second coming of JFK. However, Conrad wasn't entirely enjoying the spotlight. His eyes darted around, and his weight shifted from foot to foot in the sand. He paid scant attention to his fan club.

She doubted it was the heat from the tiki torches causing a light sheen of sweat to build on his brow. Something was making him nervous, which was understandable if he was holding a young woman prisoner. "Let's grab drinks," Holly suggested to Ethan. "Try to blend in."

Cool sand slipped between her toes as they moved through the crowd to the outdoor bar. Ethan ordered a coconut water martini from the bartender while Holly continued to scan the crowd for a glimpse of her team. "Tonight is worthy of something a little stronger than water. What would you like?"

The bartender, wearing a bright Hawaiian shirt, had his back to Holly as he prepared Ethan's cocktail, but something about him felt oddly familiar. When he turned around, Holly gasped. It was the busker. His pinched face made her flinch. What was he doing here? His lips curled into a twisted grin. "What will it be, ma'am?" His beady eyes lingered a beat too long. "Nothing," Holly stammered, backing away. "I'm not thirsty."

Ethan looked at her, puzzled. "A drink was your idea," he said.

"I changed my mind." Holly moved away from the bar before Ethan could question her more.

The busker called after her. "Did you follow the money like I suggested, Holly?" His voice carried a mocking tone. "Do it. It keeps taking you higher and higher, right up the Beauport money chain, if you know what I mean."

Holly slipped away into the dark.

Ethan caught up with her. "What was that all about?" he asked, martini in hand.

"I have no idea. That guy freaks me out," Holly said. She refocused her attention and scanned the crowd again.

Maeve was talking with Dr. Hill. She looked sophisticated in a high-neck, long-line maxi dress, white with a smattering of deep blue flowers. On her tall frame, the dress made Holly think of an elegant porcelain vase turned into a party outfit. Her earrings sparkled in the torchlight, and her arms were adorned with several glittering bracelets, no doubt real diamonds, which explained the armed security Holly noticed by the stairs. Unfortunately, one of the two police officers present was Tommy Boy. This was a private local party, but you'd think the president of the United States was there given the way Tommy stood puffed up and self-important.

Maeve carefully sipped her martini while Dr. Hill filled his glass from the punch bowl. The doctor seemed to enjoy the festivities, swaying to the beat of an up-tempo swing tune. Maeve remained still, radiating gentility, which Holly knew could quickly turn into a browbeating if someone failed to meet her high standards.

Except for her hair, which had changed from platinum to gray, Maeve appeared nearly ageless. If Jade were here, she most likely knew nothing about it. Maeve seemed far too composed to be carrying such a weighty secret.

The party dragged on. Locals who knew Ethan kept grabbing his attention, while all Holly wanted to do was look for Jade. But she needed her friends to keep an eye on Conrad while she and Ethan searched Miramar. Finally, Ethan spotted Serena talking with Gail and waved them over. Leave it to Serena to arrive in a bohemian evening dress—a sleeveless turquoise A-line gown embroidered with shimmering silver thread. Gail, meanwhile, looked like a middle-aged Barbie in a pink midi dress with flutter sleeves. Her bright lipstick, cotton candy nails, and signature perfume highlighted a look that matched her vibrant personality.

Gail lit up when she saw Holly and Ethan standing close. "Look at you two. If you're not the cutest, I don't know who is."

The joyful reunion proved short-lived. "We need you both to keep Conrad occupied while Ethan and I look for Jade."

Holly directed her friends' attention to their host, who had freed himself from his fan club and now stood alone near the edge of the dance area, craning his neck as if searching for someone. He wouldn't be by himself for long.

"Go start a conversation. Keep him busy," Holly said.

Gail snapped to attention. "If there's anything I'm good at, it's keeping people talking," she said.

"Where are you going to be?" Serena asked.

Holly turned toward the stairs. "Up there," she said, pointing to the top of the bluff. "Jade is inside that house—I just know it—and I'm going to find her."

Serena shivered. "Be careful," she said. "I'm sure my premonition was a warning not just for Jade, but for you as well."

Chapter 55

Jade

I'm the unlikely delinquent who did her science homework, so I know alcohol won't quench my thirst—it will only dehydrate me. But my thirst got so bad I couldn't resist having something to drink.

Necessity truly is the mother of invention. I turned a shard of glass into a makeshift knife that I used to remove the cork from a bottle of red wine.

I'm sure whoever bottled this baby in 1990 could never have imagined this scene: an underage girl held prisoner in a wine cellar beneath a stone tower using a broken glass shard to get a drink. Damn, I can't believe it either.

The first splash of liquid eases the burn in my throat. I'm sure my brain believes I'm giving my body what it needs. My thirst lessens as the gulps go down, and it stays that way for a little while. The wine sits sour in my empty stomach, but I can't stop drinking. It's only when half the bottle is gone that I realize I'm making a terrible mistake. Not only am I speeding up my dehydration, but I'm also zapping my wits in the process. I won't be at my best when I need it most.

I try to stand, but the floor feels like a trampoline, throwing off my balance—like I'm already drunk. I slump to the ground, doing what I've been doing for hours—a whole lotta nothing. Most of the day has passed, and the light outside the small window is starting to fade. The hardest part has been keeping my eyes open. It's like I have weights on my eyelashes, pulling my lids shut.

My cell smells like urine. Wine made it impossible to hold my bladder. I'm not proud, but I am human. As the sun begins to set, I wonder if I'll be left here to rot. Is Conrad going to starve me to death? But that's not right. It's water, not food, that I need. I can go a long time without eating, but dying of thirst could happen in days.

I make a promise to myself: I will get out of here somehow. I'll be free again. Reflexively, I reach for the jagged bottle top—my makeshift knife. If someone comes to finish me off, I'll be ready.

Meanwhile, the world outside continues to turn. The sun casts a pale glow across the distant sky.

I've seen shadows pass by the window, and there's been a lot of noise outside. The landscapers ran lawn mowers and leaf blowers all day. But that's not nearly as loud as the generators rumbling to supply power to the beach party at the base of the bluff. I knew we'd have generators on the property—that was included in the arrangements I made with the party planner, at Maeve's direction. She wanted the lights to be as plentiful as stars, she'd said. Now her big vision is muffling my screams as I slowly die of thirst.

I've thrown more than a few bottles at the barricaded window, but all I've managed to do is fill the space with sharp glass that makes it difficult to move around safely, not to mention the pools of pungent-smelling wine that have collected on the floor.

For a moment, I wonder if Maeve is pissed that I didn't show up for work. Then again, she might know exactly where I am. I call out for help once more, but my voice is weak and raspy.

My last hope fades as the loud noise of a powerful portable generator starts up right outside the window. The engine sounds like a jet rumbling overhead.

Despair is sinking me fast. The fierce girl is suddenly questioning the promises she made to herself. I muster the strength to stand up. Someone has to be nearby to start the generator. Naturally, my first thought is to bang on the grate, but it's too high for me to reach. Throwing the bottles hasn't helped—but damn it, I try again.

Another bottle. Another perfect strike. And another mess.

But this time, something actually happens. The window opens a crack.

My heart leaps into my throat. I shout with everything I have. "Here! I'm down here! Help me! I'm trapped!"

I go to the window and start jumping up and down, waving like a castaway trying to get the attention of a passing ship. The window is partly open now. Finally, I have some fresh air—and some hope.

I see a hand reaching in through the window. Thank God. I won't be here much longer. I keep screaming for help, even though help has technically arrived.

But something feels off. It's not a hand—it's a hose. I'm looking into the opening of a flexible ribbed aluminum tube, kind of like a tinfoil condom, pressed against the grate. The window opening is just wide enough for the tube to fit through. What the hell?

I scream again. "Hey, what the fuck? Let me out of here!" Nobody answers. Has the roar of the generator swallowed my screams? No, whoever is outside is only a few feet away. With the window partially open, they *must* hear me.

A shadow blocks the light. It's not cast by a person; it's square and boxy. Someone moved the generator, so it now blocks the window. The engine is roaring so loudly, it feels like it's in the room with me. The metal hose stays firmly against the grate.

I have a flash of understanding. I know a lot about cars. I know that engines produce gases that need to be vented. I feel paralyzed. Terror rips through every part of my body.

I'm staring at an *exhaust* pipe. And I know exactly what it's doing. It's slowly filling my cell with deadly carbon monoxide.

Chapter 56

Holly

A strange feeling washed over Holly the moment she set foot in the grand foyer. How was it possible nothing had changed in all these years? She remembered the many portraits encased in gold frames gracing the high walls, and the plush, velvet-covered furniture that harkened back to a gilded age, but she barely gave any of it a moment's notice.

She and Ethan entered Miramar through the front door wearing slippers. Maeve had set out a bin of disposable spa-style foot coverings near the entrance, which all guests were instructed to wear upon entering. However, the slippers weren't preventing beach sand from getting inside, as small grains were scattered across the flagstone floor. Guests came and went to use the two bathrooms off the main hall. Freestanding signs indicated their locations.

Elegant gold and silver helium balloons hovered near the front door, while gorgeous bouquets of cut flowers added splashes of color that sucked some of the dreariness from the air.

"Armed security only on the beach, but none inside? Guess it's more important to show off to the guests than protect their home," Ethan observed. "Hopefully, that'll work out in our favor. I'll check upstairs." He pointed Holly toward the wide staircase that wound its way to the second level. "Why don't you cover the first floor, and we'll meet back here in five?"

Holly nodded, and he was off in a flash.

She wasn't sure where to start. Besides the bathrooms, the rooms on this floor were blocked off with velvet ropes hanging between gold-plated stanchions. Holly remembered the layout. In front of her was the pantry entrance that led to the large gourmet kitchen. To her left was an office and a study, while the doors to the library, drawing room, and dining room were to her right.

Before she could begin her exploration in earnest, a low, measured, and deliberate voice—a ragged baritone full of dust and years—asked, "You seem lost. Should I have put the bathroom signs in neon?"

Holly turned around, surprised to see Sidney, the longtime butler, approaching with shuffling steps, pointing to the well-marked signs.

It was remarkable that he was still alive, let alone working at the estate.

"Actually, I'm looking for someone who works here," Holly said. She hoped she wasn't being careless. She didn't want Conrad to know she was snooping around, and it was possible Sid would tell him. But it would be foolish to pass up an opportunity to question the man who managed the entire household.

Holding her phone, she showed him Jade's picture. Recognition lit up his eyes. "Ah, I assume you're the young woman who showed up here last night. You still haven't found Miss Jensen?" he asked in a neutral tone.

"No, I haven't," said Holly, her worry impossible to hide.

Sid's expression remained inscrutable. "As I believe you were informed, she came here yesterday for work and left in the afternoon. I haven't seen her since."

Holly studied Sid's eyes for any hidden meaning, a subtle warning, or a hint that he was withholding crucial information, but no, they were as vacant as Holly's bank account. "And perhaps you'd also be well-advised to ask my son," he added in a quiet, almost conspiratorial tone. "He's on the grounds, bartending tonight."

Holly blinked in surprise. "Wait—the busker is your son?"

Sid stood tall with pride. "He knows more about the people in Beauport than I do. He's always around town, playing his guitar—*watching*. If anybody has seen Ms. Jade, it would likely be him."

Holly thanked him before slipping into the bathroom to make it seem like that was the reason she came inside the house. It was still the nicest place she'd ever peed. The toilet was like a throne with a crystal-beaded pull chain. Unbelievable.

She returned to the foyer and quietly maneuvered behind the velvet ropes blocking off the dining room. It was unlikely that Jade was here, but she had to check. Inside, a large dining table sat beneath a stunning crystal chandelier. The tall wingback chairs were all pushed in. A long, shiny buffet reflected Holly's image, as did the elegant mirror above it.

The storage closet was full of supplies, but there was no missing girl. She wasn't surprised. There were probably much better hiding spots elsewhere in this creepy house. Still, Holly felt compelled to check the closets in the drawing room and library before sneaking into Conrad's office.

She had never been inside Conrad's sanctuary, but found it to be well-furnished, if a little stuffy—heavy on the wood, with a dark area rug covering much of the floor, along with a leather couch and chairs, a freestanding bar, and an antique globe. If there was ever a place that practically shouted, *Drink bourbon!* this was it.

She scanned the tall built-in bookshelves and noticed they were roughly the size of the curtained windows. Maybe one of those books, if pulled out, could reveal a secret passage where she might find Jade hidden—but Holly didn't have time to test that unlikely theory.

Inside a closet, she discovered a folded wheelchair, which she assumed belonged to Maeve. But that was odd, considering Maeve appeared poised and steady on her feet at the beach.

Holly switched her focus to Conrad's large mahogany desk. Perhaps she'd find useful secrets among his paperwork. He had a computer. She moved the mouse, not surprised when the password field appeared.

Before she could investigate further, a startling noise echoed in the hall. It sounded as if it was right outside the office door. Quickly ducking under the desk, she waited in hiding, filled with fear. She heard the noise again, but realized it was just scuffling footsteps (oh, those silly slippers), which, fortunately, kept going. She peeked up, knowing she didn't have much time.

The desk drawers didn't contain anything of real importance—just some bills, loose papers, a flash drive, a small stapler, that sort of thing. She moved over to a nearby wooden filing cabinet. The key was still in the lock, and the drawer opened. Conrad's oversight had become her opportunity. In the top drawer, she found something that might be significant—a file labeled MEDICAL.

Holly reprimanded herself for not insisting that Jade find a different job. The first page in the folder was a revealing note from Dr. Vernon Hill about Conrad Carmichael.

It was a referral for psychiatric treatment. The medical code on the form read: *F43.12, Post-Traumatic Stress Disorder (PTSD), Chronic*. Below that was another code indicating the potential for violent behavior. From her quick read, clearly annotated by Dr. Hill, it was evident that Conrad not only suffered from PTSD, but he was a walking time bomb.

Inside the cabinet drawer, something else caught her eye: an opaque brown prescription bottle with a glass vial inside. Holly assumed it contained medication to help Conrad manage his chronic condition. But to her surprise, the prescription was old, long expired, and in Maeve Carmichael's name.

Holly read the label: *Lypotrel*. She wondered how large a dose would be needed for it to be lethal.

Chapter 57

Jade

I'm not ready to leave this crazy world yet, but I might not have a choice. Eventually my body will fill with enough gas to put me to sleep for good. I miss the time when thirst was my biggest concern.

I wonder how it will feel. Will I get dizzy, tired, and then just close my eyes for an endless nap? I think that's how it goes with this sort of thing, but I'm not certain. I haven't died before.

Conrad—straight-up psycho . . .

I already feel a little lightheaded. Spots dance in front of my eyes. There's an ocean rumbling in my ears, or maybe it's just the generator humming as it releases death into my cell. My breath comes short and quick. Am I hyperventilating?

My thoughts are scrambled, and my limbs tremble. But somehow I find a way to harness my fear. The hose . . . that's my only hope. I need to feed the tube that's going to kill me back out the window.

I gather my strength and climb up the empty wine rack, my whole body heavy and sore. I reach the highest point and wrap the fabric of my sweatshirt around my right hand. My head is still spinning, but I take a deep breath and jump.

For a moment, I think I might not make it. My legs don't have much strength, but I stretch my arm just enough—and oh my god, I've got it. I'm hanging on with one hand, swinging pendulum-like against the wall. Luckily, the sweatshirt protects my skin from the rusted metal that flakes off the grate.

With a desperate grunt, I swing my other arm up, grasping some of the dangling fabric of my hoodie so I can hold on with both hands. My fingers are close enough to touch the tube but not much else. I don't have enough leverage to push it back through the window.

The roar of the generator's powerful motor vibrates the metal, threatening my grip. Up here, the air tastes sour, tinged with gasoline. It burns my throat and causes tears to come to my eyes. But there's also another taste—freedom. I feel a slight breeze on my face, and a faint whiff of fresh-cut grass cuts through the gasoline smell. I'm inhaling both salvation and death at the same time.

I call out hoping someone will hear me, but with the music and the generator, I can barely hear myself. I'm not getting out of this that easily.

My one-hundred-pound frame has never felt so heavy. I'm hanging uselessly, pain in my hands and arms, tendons beginning to strain beyond their limits. It's no use. I feel my grip slipping.

But I have a sudden flash of inspiration. I can't push the tube out, but maybe I can stuff something in, like my hoodie—plug the opening and slow the gas that's filling this small space. It won't save me, but it'll buy me some time.

With my last shred of energy, I press my feet against the stone, which helps me to hold the grate with one hand, and with the other, I start feeding the fabric between the bars of the barrier and into the tube.

I'm at the point of complete muscle fatigue, but I steadily push more fabric through the opening until I've blocked it as much as possible. Still, it's not entirely sealed; there are gaps, and the sleeve of my hoodie hangs like a limp flag.

I can't make it perfect, but I can't hold on any longer. I have to do it—I have to let go.

I tumble to the floor, landing hard and shielding my head with my hands. I hear a horrible sound—a sickening crack—followed immediately by a jolt of pain that tells me that sound was my wrist breaking.

With a cry of agony, I roll to one side, cradling my useless limp limb with my other arm. The stabbing pain is so intense that I fear I might pass out. But I manage to scoot away from the window, huddling by the door on the other side of the room. I rest my injured arm on my thigh, trying to keep it still and supported. With my functional right hand, I reach for the broken bottle that doubles as my makeshift knife. I sit there, waiting and forcing myself to keep my eyes open.

Someone will come to make sure the job is done, but now it's going to take longer than expected. And when they arrive, I plan to give them one hell of a surprise.

Chapter 58

The Watcher

All these people make me queasy. It wasn't my idea to do this at the party, but the girl forced my hand.

I scan the crowd, put on a charming smile, and try to stay in character, but my eyes dart around. I need to ensure everything goes according to plan, and for that, I have to know exactly where all the players in my chess game are positioned.

I can be a loner these days. Trauma does that to a person. You learn to keep people at a distance, letting only a few into your circle, and even then, they don't really know the true you.

But tonight it's good to see an old friend, if I can use that term loosely. And it's perfect timing, as I'm handed exactly what I need to finish this once and for all.

I open the tower door, quiet as a mouse, closing it silently behind me. It's dark as night in here, but I know every stone in this house. I could descend the staircase into the depths blindfolded. Even so, I move slowly, one careful step at a time. She won't hear me coming, but there's a good chance she can't hear anything at all.

Chapter 59

Holly

Holly left the office and saw Ethan coming down the stairs looking crestfallen, and for good reason—no Jade.

When he reached the bottom step, she showed him a picture of Conrad's referral form.

He took one look and gulped. "Jesus—this guy sounds unhinged." Ethan's eyes flared. "We *have* to find her. Maybe we have to shake Conrad's tree a little harder. Let's get back to Gail and Serena and regroup."

They didn't have to go far. Both women were hovering on the steps near the front entrance of Miramar. From up above the party lights cast an ominous glow as though the beach were on fire.

"Gail, Serena, what are you doing up here?" Holly hissed, noticing that both women had left their drinks and their posts. "Where is Conrad?"

Her friends exchanged worried looks.

Gail spoke for the team. "Holly, we tried, we really did. We were hanging around the tiki bar—having a nice conversation—when an alarm went off on his phone, and he just took off—didn't even excuse himself—and rushed up the stairs. We followed, even though we were worried he might notice, but that guy was on a mission."

Serena chimed in. "We thought he was coming after you, but he disappeared through a door in the hall. We tried the door, but it was locked. Totally creepy." Both women winced.

So did Ethan. "I have a good idea where Conrad went," he said, his eyes darkening. He guided them into the foyer, and pointed to the teak door with a seashell doorknob—the entrance to the tower. "That's the one place I was never allowed to go. That door is *always* locked."

Holly had thought they'd checked everywhere on the first floor, but they'd blown right past this one, partially obscured by balloons and directional signs for the bathroom.

"How the hell are we going to get in there?" Holly felt stress building in her chest.

Ethan cracked a smile and pulled a multi-tool from his pants pocket. "You leave that to me. I'm cheaper than a locksmith. I've had to open my fair share of old lockboxes and car doors. The older the lock, the easier it is to open. An ancient castle door shouldn't be a problem."

"Gail, Serena, I need you both to provide some cover—try to keep people from seeing what we're doing," Holly said.

"What exactly are you going to do?" asked Gail.

Holly stood tall. "We're getting into that tower—and we're getting Jade the fuck out of here."

Chapter 60

Jade

My head lolls forward, straining my neck. Every sensation and sound feels distant, as if I'm having an out-of-body experience. The gas generator hums along, but it could be in another state for all I can tell. My senses aren't completely dulled; I'm acutely aware of the foul smell of wine, urine, gasoline, and mildew all mixed together. My vision dims, but the broken bottle I'm wielding as a weapon remains sharp and clear.

My busted wrist burns as if I had put it on the stove. Waiting is the hardest part. It's a different kind of torture than physical pain—a strain in my gut that won't let go, twisting my insides every which way. And what am I waiting for? A chance at freedom, not knowing if I'll die before I get my shot.

What I can't do is cry. The tears are gone, all dried up. But a bottomless pool of regret swims inside me. I've spent so much of my life angry, pissed at my parents, my misfortune. Now all I want is to live. To be part of a family.

Holly. Her name gives me hope. She's the first person to make me feel like I belong, like I matter. I'm gutted at the prospect of exiting this world like Elizabeth Ward—helpless, alone, irrelevant.

I don't matter anymore. Funny how this happens just when I start to believe I could be important to someone else. But that's how things always go for me.

Do I pray? I don't think I know how. Still, I send up a plea to the heavens. *God, give me one chance, one last shot.* I envision using the broken bottle to kill my would-be murderer. My lips move, whispering the words: *One shot . . . one shot . . . please.*

I'm leaning against the door when I hear it—a prayer answered. A click in the lock. Is it just my imagination? No, the door shifts, pressing into my back. I'm so weak, so exhausted, but this is my only chance.

I slide to my left. Whoever enters will see an empty room until they turn in my direction—then I'll be there, ready to pounce. But I can't stand up. I try, but it's no use. My muscles have no strength left. I'm running out of time. The door swings open. The room blurs into a haze. My eyes aren't ready for the low light from the hallway that fills my cell.

I'm still on the ground as a shadowy figure enters. It's Conrad, I'm sure, but with my blurry vision, he looks smaller and weaker. Am I just giving myself false hope?

Fear saws into my bones. The figure halts abruptly, facing the window. Conrad looks confused; he glances around but doesn't see me hidden in the shadows. I summon a burst of strength, pushing my feet into the ground as I ready my weapon.

One shot. One chance. Live . . . I want to live.

The figure turns, finally seeing me. I focus on the eyes of my target, wide with surprise, the whites expanding like an explosion. I don't hesitate—not for a second. Spitting out a disjointed war cry, uttered from a place of deep fear, I hurl myself forward, the glass bottle aiming for the throat. I imagine the bottle is glued to my hand. I won't let go. It's sharp as a razor blade, good enough to maim and, hopefully, to kill. I must be quite the sight—wild, frantic, radiating fury. Nothing is scarier than someone out of her mind with desperation.

I feel it immediately, the horrifying sensation of my weapon sinking deep into flesh. A wave of nausea roils through me, but I stab again and again. I don't know what part of his body I've struck. Throat? Shoulder? Arm? I'm blind from the rush of adrenaline. Warm blood oozes onto my hand and down my arm.

The figure grabs hold of me, a bloody arm wraps tightly around my chest, knocking the air out of me. I feel my attacker's strength and determination, just as I fear mine is fading away.

"I've got you now," a voice says before everything goes black.

Chapter 61

Holly

Gail and Serena stood near the front door, directing guests to the first-floor bathrooms and away from Ethan, who was working the lock.

Standing close to the door, Holly heard something she hadn't before—the notes of an evocative, dreamy piano sonata she instantly recognized as "Clair de Lune" by Claude Debussy.

Ethan stood up and turned to Holly. "Finally," he said. "We're in." He turned the knob and the door opened easily. A burst of cooler air bathed Holly's face. The stairs led up and down, but Holly heard a commotion above, so they hurried, moving quickly over the uneven stone steps as fast as they could.

Ethan took the lead, his body disappearing around the first bend in the stairwell, then reappearing before vanishing again. Up, up, up they went—the stone walls echoed with the sound of their quick footsteps. The piano music was audible even over the roar of what sounded like a fight.

They burst into a dimly lit room. Holly paused in the doorway, stunned by the sight before her.

Conrad was in the middle of a wrestling match with Dr. Vernon Hill. From the looks of it, Conrad wasn't winning. The front of his white dress shirt was soaked in blood. Holly could see he was bleeding from a cut in his neck—not a fatal wound, but definitely a messy one.

And he was hardly down for the count. In his bloodstained right hand, Conrad clutched a syringe, its needle hovering inches from Dr. Hill. Nearby, a frail, exhausted woman, swallowed up inside a large bed, gazed blankly at the ceiling as if she were catatonic.

"He's trying to kill her," Dr. Hill screamed as Conrad lunged at him with the needle. Shifting his weight, Dr. Hill dodged the strike in the nick of time.

Before Holly had a chance to intervene, Ethan pounced. He wrapped Conrad in a tight bear hug, lifting him off the ground from behind. In one violent motion, he pulled both Conrad and the needle away from Dr. Hill.

"Let me go!" Conrad demanded. "I'm going to fucking kill him." His legs bicycled uselessly in the air.

Ethan's biceps strained, but his vise grip held.

Conrad's eyes burned like the sun. His skin turned a deep, dark shade of crimson. The veins on his neck and arms pulsed, venom flowing through every part of his body. His muscles were coiled, vibrating—ready to snap.

Gone was the calm, composed, debonair host of the party. In his place stood a savage beast. A deep, guttural growl rose from his throat—more animal than human.

Dr. Hill's medical note came back to Holly: *PTSD . . . with potential for violent behavior.* That might have been a wild understatement.

The woman in the bed moaned as if she were in pain, but Holly went to help Ethan instead. Conrad's hand was close enough to Ethan's leg to deliver what could be a deadly strike. Who knew what was in that syringe?

Holly moved deftly. With a quick upward thrust, she seized Conrad's wrist with one hand. With the other, she dug her fingernails into his flesh. She pressed harder and harder until she felt blood. The coppery smell from Conrad's multiple wounds—the one to his neck and now to his hand—turned her stomach.

He yelped like a wounded pup, loosening his hold on the syringe. It fell to the floor with a clatter that Holly could hear over the music, the same song starting again. Maybe it was set to repeat.

Maddening, she thought.

She let go of Conrad, hoping he would give in now that he was unarmed, but instead he snapped his head backward, head-butting Ethan.

Incensed, Ethan spun Conrad around to face a stone wall. He opened his arms. For a moment, Conrad was free, but Ethan wasn't finished with him yet. He delivered a hard shove to Conrad's back, which sent him crashing into the wall. He hit his head hard enough to leave a smear of blood on one of the jagged stones. His legs buckled, but Ethan didn't give him a chance to fall. Coming up from behind, he wrenched Conrad's arm behind his back and then led him to the staircase.

Navigating down the narrow stairs was tough enough. Managing with someone else was nearly impossible. Ethan's grip loosened, and as it did, Conrad twisted at the waist, delivering an elbow strike to Ethan's temple that snapped his head back, and he fell quickly. On impulse, Holly threw herself behind Ethan to cushion his fall. His weight pinned her to the ground, trapping her for a moment.

"Dr. Hill—help, you have to stop him," Holly cried out.

Vernon Hill sprang into action, stumbling into Holly and Ethan as he raced down the stairs after Conrad.

Amazingly, Ethan wasn't far behind. He bounced up as if he were made of rubber. Holly was slower to get to her feet.

"Are you all right?" she shouted to Ethan's back, but he was too busy running down the stairs to respond.

Holly left the bedridden woman, taking a million questions with her. Was that Elizabeth Ward under the covers? What was Conrad planning to do to her? More important, how did Jade fit into all this? Did she see something she shouldn't have?

Holly stormed down the stairs, her back aching, heart pumping, and lungs sucking in air, in time to see Ethan chasing Conrad out the front door. She followed because Conrad held the key to locating Jade. She could barely keep up. They galloped at the speed of horses. From the corner of her eye, she saw Serena and Gail, just outside the entrance, mouths agape, but she didn't pause to explain. Piano music spilled out of the open tower door, clashing with the sound of jazz emanating from the beach below.

Plunging ahead, Holly descended the outside steps as if she were flying.

Conrad was sprinting full speed, Ethan close behind. To Holly's surprise, Conrad wasn't heading away from the estate or toward a car to escape. Instead, he ran down the red carpet toward the staircase leading to the party. Confused, Holly kept chasing after them as quickly as she could.

She reached the staircase. Stopping for a moment to catch her breath, she saw Ethan slip on the uneven steps and tumble down a flight. Ahead of him, Conrad vaulted over the railing near the bottom of the stairs, landing in the soft sand.

Where was he headed? Down the beach? Into the ocean? Nothing made sense.

Holly hurried down the stairs, being mindful of her footing. Below her, Ethan clambered to his feet before jumping the railing as Conrad had done. Sand flew up behind him as he continued his pursuit. For the first time, Holly wished for help from the Beauport police, but the officers had left their post by the stairs and disappeared into the crowd, all of whom were staring in disbelief at the ongoing chase.

It looked like Conrad was slipping away until he glanced back and stumbled, his feet catching in the loose sand. Ethan closed in. Before Conrad could regain his footing, Ethan leapt through the air, arms outstretched, tackling him just outside the party tent. They collided with the buffet table, then slid over the top like a pair of intertwined figure skaters, knocking off fruit skewers and spilling plates of shrimp before crashing into the punch bowl and landing hard on the sand.

Guests shrieked in astonishment.

Ethan landed on top of Conrad, pushing his face into the sand.

Tommy Boy appeared out of the dark. He lumbered over, reaching the mayhem at about the same time as Holly.

Dr. Hill brought up the rear. He was breathing harder than anybody. "He tried to kill Elizabeth," Hill told Tommy Boy, with his hands on his knees, wheezing out the words.

The cop sprang into action, grabbing his cuffs and reaching for Conrad. At last, it seemed, Tommy Boy was good for something.

The jazz music had stopped. The party guests were stunned into tense silence. Everyone was uncertain what to do and couldn't look away from the scene before them. Only the flickering tiki torches and gentle sound of ocean waves proved that time was still moving forward.

Conrad was handcuffed and dazed, propped up against the leg of the buffet table, his bruised face dotted with a five o'clock shadow made entirely of sand. His shirt was dyed red from the fruit punch, which intermingled with the very real blood from his neck wound.

Dr. Hill applied a gauze bandage to Conrad's injury—he had retrieved a first-aid kit from behind the bar, and it lay open at his feet. It was heartening to see the doctor care for the person who just moments ago had tried to kill him.

Little by little, an uneasy chatter filled the air. Holly wanted to grill Conrad for information about Jade's whereabouts, but Tommy Boy used his impressive girth to block her way. "Give the fella a second to catch his breath, will ya?" he said.

Holly got in his face—or his chest, he was that much taller. "Jade might be in danger. He knows where she is. Let me talk to him."

"Right now he needs medical attention. If there are questions to ask, leave it to us."

"I don't think you understand me. He knows about Jade. I need to talk to him now." She tried to push past him again, but Tommy Boy wasn't budging.

"You might have questions for Conrad, but I've got some for you. What the hell happened? Big author brings big chaos?"

Holly pressed her hands to her eyes, her head pounding, but she tried to answer him as succinctly as she could. "Conrad attacked Dr. Hill, I saw it all—and he's been keeping his wife—at least I think it's his wife—locked up in the tower, heavily medicated." She'd read crazy stories of people being held in captivity, sometimes for years, but never thought she'd be involved in one. "Whoever is up there, you need to check on her right away, make sure she's okay. And he may have taken my friend, Jade Jensen, but I don't know where."

Tommy Boy looked disapproving. "Still on that, are we? I thought I made it clear—runaways *run*. But I'll send someone to check on the woman in the tower." He waved to the second officer working the party, a young woman, possibly new to the force. He briefed her, told her to go check out the scene, and report back as soon as possible.

Before Holly could make another plea to Tommy about Jade, the busker sauntered toward them. He approached from the direction of the stairs, carrying two bags full of ice. Holly released an audible groan. He had on his tattered scally cap, which clashed terribly with his Hawaiian shirt, but Maeve wasn't around to scold him for his attire.

He came to a stop beside Holly, setting the bags in the sand.

"What about you?" asked Tommy Boy. "See anything unusual up there?"

The busker stared down his pinched nose at Holly and the cop before pointing toward the house. "Only thing weird I've seen up there is a generator."

Holly rolled her eyes. Could this guy ever give a straight answer? "There are a bunch of generators powering the party," Holly said. "You can't have all the lights down here without them. Nothing strange about that."

"I'm telling you, this one was strange. See, I went to the kitchen to get some ice. It's faster to walk out the back door and around the tower than to go through the house. So that's what I was doing and I notice this generator running, but nothing is plugged into it.

"Now, I've been a musician a long time . . . "

Holly bit her tongue, recalling the beleaguered staff at the Bean There Café desperate to muffle his sound.

"And I've played a lotta gigs, worked a lotta parties, and usually you plug something into a generator—an extension cord, an amp, you know? But there's nothing plugged into that machine other than a metal tube venting through a small window into the basement."

There's a basement? Holly's entire body thrummed with adrenaline. Then she remembered the tower stairs that went up—*and* down.

Her heart dropped. She whirled, shoving the busker aside brusquely, eliciting a cry of surprise and annoyance. She didn't pause to apologize. She increased her pace, long strides pushing through the sand, propelling her up the stairs, until Miramar was back in view. She sprinted toward the house.

Ethan was right behind her.

Chapter 62

Jade

A warm light appears before me. It's as bright as a star, but I feel no pain. I can look directly at it without wincing. I have a vague sense that I should be afraid, that I should run from this light. But honestly, I want it to take me. From it, I feel an overwhelming sense of . . . love, a love unlike anything I've ever experienced before.

The light intensifies. It's blinding, but where is it coming from? Nothing makes sense.

Then I hear a voice. My mind struggles to make meaning of the garbled words.

"Jade . . . are you down here? Jade?"

I'm here, I want to say, though I can't actually speak. But more important . . . who is Jade?

No sooner do I think of the question than I realize Jade is me. I am the girl who runs—who has been running her whole life until I got here . . . to Beauport . . . and to Holly. And that's who's calling my name. Holly. I recognize her voice.

I want to stop running and go to her. But the light. It's calling me—me and someone else, another person nearby. I'm not alone in here. A new memory strikes—my weapon, the glass bottle, sinking into flesh, blood leaking out.

Yes, my attacker—my would-be killer who came to finish the job—I got you first, and now we're both going into the light. I can feel their life force slipping away, same as mine is fading. We are now one—the kidnapper and the victim, fused into a single consciousness.

I can't explain it, but I hear their voice in my head as they lie dying beside me, talking to me telepathically, repeating the same phrase over and over.

I'm sorry . . . I'm sorry . . . I'm sorry . . .

Too late, I say back to them using my mind, not my mouth.

It's too late for sorry. The light has come for us both.

We must go to it. We must go. Our time here is done.

Chapter 63

Holly

Jade? Are you down here?"

Holly had never moved so quickly in her life. The girl who once got a C in gym class—which takes real effort—was somehow faster than Ethan now, her adrenaline peaking. The busker's words echoed in her mind: *Nothing was plugged into that machine except a metal tube venting through a small window . . .*

Time was her enemy. Every second could mean the difference between life and death.

She rushed into Miramar and down the uneven tower steps. The scent of mold was strong—musty and earthy, dank like wet, decaying leaves. Dampness sank into her skin. It felt like venturing into a crypt.

Ethan yelled to her breathlessly from above, "Holly, wait up—it might be dangerous!"

But his warning only made her descend faster, skipping steps, almost flying down the stairs. At the bottom, she lost her footing and stumbled into the opening, her knees colliding with the rough-hewn floor.

She righted herself as though nothing had happened; she couldn't allow herself to feel pain.

She called Jade's name again.

No response. All she heard was the muffled roar of the generator running outside. Was it a mistake to rush into the basement before turning it off? Nothing she could do now.

Holly had stumbled into a dank, gloomy landing—part of the neglected underworld of Miramar. An imposing wooden door stood directly in front of her, left slightly ajar with a key still in the keyhole. Holly tried to hold her breath, but it was impossible. The air didn't taste poisonous, but carbon monoxide was a silent killer.

She opened the door and stepped into the room without hesitation, aware that her safety was at risk. Ethan came up behind her, hunched over, hands on his knees, desperate to catch his breath. A faint smell of urine coated the air. Slowly her eyes adjusted to the dark as she took in the scene. Shards of broken glass littered the floor, scattered over pools of sour-smelling wine.

Outside the window on the other side of the room, the generator shuddered and roared, a tube extending from it pressed against a metal grate. A sweatshirt stuffed into the opening of the tube hopefully prevented a fatality—or two, as there were not just one, but two bodies lying on the floor.

One was unquestionably Jade. Was she moving? Was she alive? Holly couldn't say. She lay peacefully on her side, as though asleep. A second figure, female, with long, dark hair, had her back to the door. She huddled behind Jade, pressed up against her inert body, one arm draped across her waist. She was bleeding heavily.

Ethan didn't hesitate. He went straight for Jade, hoisting her off the floor like she weighed nothing. He heaved her over his shoulder while backing into the landing. "Drag the other woman out," he yelled to Holly. "I'll be right back to help."

As if in a dream, Holly reached for the second victim, grabbing under her arms and trying to avoid the raw wound on the woman's shoulder.

When she turned the woman over, Holly's world came to a stop.

Until that moment, she believed she had words for everything. She had built her life around words. But now Holly found herself both speechless and numb, as though she had dissociated from her body.

It's the trauma. The gas. I'm hallucinating.

The face before her was so familiar, so deeply carved into her memory, so very much . . . like her own.

Anna.

Chapter 64

Jade

I'm certain I'm floating—up, up, up I go. I'm weightless. But I'm not going into the light. Instead, I'm bouncing up and down, almost like I'm riding on a carousel.

As if by magic I'm suddenly outside. And then it hits me—oxygen, real, pure, glorious oxygen. I'm bathed in the stuff. Swimming in an ocean of it. I inhale so deeply, with such desperation, it's as if I'm sucking the entire night down. My lungs fill too fast. I gag, coughing so violently I fear my ribs might shatter.

I hear a man's voice telling me it's going to be okay—I will live.

Yes, I would like that very much. In fact, I want nothing more in this entire universe than one more day of life. Walking, breathing, being me. All of me—gangly, badass, book-loving, messed-up, utterly crazy me.

So many things hit me in this one moment—first my parents, may I never see them again: the drunk and the coward, yelling at me because they've grown tired of screaming at each other. Days when there was nothing but stale bread and vodka in the cabinets. Christmases with a tree so brittle it would have made Charlie Brown cry, and hardly anything wrapped underneath.

The moments that brought me here stitch together like a tapestry—the car I stole, Big Sally in Baby Jail, the necklace that set me off on my mission, the lies I told along the way . . . and the friends I made, too—especially the one I want to see most of all. Who took me into her home, sheltered me under her wing, and made me feel like I belonged somewhere.

Chapter 65

Holly

There was no time to think or process the shock. *Shock? No, it's more than that. You're a writer, Hol. Find a better word: stupefied? astounded?* She paused for a moment, but nothing seemed big enough—nothing fit the enormity of the moment.

Anna.

Holly got her hands under her sister's arms and pulled with all her might. It wasn't nearly as taxing as she thought it would be to drag her out of the room. She used her foot to close the door on the noxious fumes still filling the wine cellar.

Thankfully, Ethan reappeared, his arrival perfectly timed. There was no way for Holly to carry Anna up and out, and she didn't have the strength or the voice to tell Ethan who he was slinging over his shoulder.

"Jade is alive," he called out while rushing up the stairs. "I don't know how bad off she is, but I sent a cop to find Dr. Hill and we've called for an ambulance."

Holly kept pace behind him, still reeling. Was it all in her mind, a hallucination like the one she'd had with the woman on the boardwalk?

It wasn't long before they reached the safety of fresh air. There Holly found Jade, sprawled out on the lawn, moving slightly, which was a wonderful sign.

"Stay still, Jade," Ethan instructed. "Your body needs to conserve oxygen right now."

A small crowd of partygoers dressed in their beachy attire had gathered around, gawking but offering no real help.

Ethan gently laid Anna on the grass beside Jade. Holly approached cautiously, unsure and unsteady, half expecting the fresh air to have shattered the illusion. When Ethan stepped aside, Holly had a clearer view of the face looking up at the night sky. There was no doubt who this was—Anna's face was forever imprinted on Holly's mind. Time couldn't erase it.

For Holly, writing was painting with words. The page was her canvas, her prose her brushstrokes. The end result was a story that made sense. But right now nothing was making sense. Holly felt trapped inside a dream.

Kneeling beside her sister, Holly grasped Anna's hand, which felt cool to the touch. She was still unconscious and couldn't speak. Blood seeped from the cut on her shoulder.

Dr. Hill hurried across the lawn. He carried a first-aid kit, which would be useful for treating Anna's wound, but what she and Jade needed most was supplemental oxygen. With Ethan tending to Jade—he was a volunteer firefighter, after all—Dr. Hill triaged Anna. Holly stepped aside to let them work. She became an observer like the others. A profound helplessness overwhelmed her. The two people who mattered to her most might be on the precipice of death, and she could do nothing more.

Eventually a pair of ambulances arrived. A team of medics administered oxygen to Jade while splinting her broken wrist, cleaning her cuts, and checking her vitals.

With Jade in the hands of professionals, Ethan moved to Anna's side and checked her pulse. The past replayed before Holly's eyes. But this time, there was no gurney, no sheet, no death. Today there was life, even though Anna had lost a significant amount of blood. Still, her pulse was strong, Ethan reported. Her heart rate was approaching normal, and her lungs were clearing out the toxic air she and Jade had been breathing.

When Anna was stable enough, Holly returned to her sister's side. She stroked her cheek. It was warm to the touch. It was strange to see time pass so quickly—as Anna went from twenty-four to her forties, like turning a page in a book. She was as Holly remembered, except she had dyed her wavy, gorgeous auburn hair a less lustrous brown. Her heart-shaped face was fuller with age, and her hazel eyes retained the same color and depth Holly remembered.

"I don't understand how you're here. I have so many questions," Holly stammered. The tears finally flowed, racing down her cheeks like rivers heading to the sea. Her chest was heavy with sadness, relief, and profound confusion, leaving Holly breathless.

"I know you do," Anna whispered, her words choking out through her tears. She gave Holly's hand a weak squeeze. "Jade . . . is she—?"

"She's alive. She's going to be fine," Holly said. "Ethan got her out just in time."

She used his name as if Anna would know him, as if she'd remember Holly in his arms, sobbing while her sister was wheeled away. But no, it couldn't have been Anna. *There had been a dead body under that sheet, hadn't there?*

If it hadn't been Anna, then who had died that night?

"How?" Holly asked, her voice trembling, her whole body shaking as the initial shock began to fade. "Where have you been? How is this possible? How are you alive? And why were you in the cellar with Jade?"

Anna smiled faintly, light dancing briefly in her eyes as Holly's questions lingered in the air. Anna's smile widened as she held Holly's hand, their fingers entwined.

"I needed to keep you safe. I knew where to find her, and you," Anna said softly, her voice gentle as the night breeze blowing through their hair. "Because I've been watching. I've always been watching."

Chapter 66

Jade

Easy, easy," says a disembodied voice. A woman's face peers down at me, eyes filled with concern. An angelic glow surrounds her. Is this heaven? No. My head is pounding too hard, too real for it to be the afterlife. I think she's a medic of some sort.

As my senses sharpen, I become aware of my surroundings. I'm outside on a stretcher that's parked on the grass in front of the Carmichaels' house. I still feel untethered from my body, but a tube in my nose is delivering healthy air that's helping to revitalize me.

Blurry figures fuss over me like I'm some VIP. They check my vitals: pulse, blood pressure, and temperature. Evidently I'm stable enough, but my wrist feels like it's on fire. I realize it's been splinted. I tell someone it's still killing me, and before I know it, I'm on an IV drip delivering pain medication.

Holly. Where is Holly? And Conrad? *I stabbed him, right? Is he dead? Did he bleed out?*

I can't take a deep, full breath. My limbs weigh a thousand pounds. But at least the anxiety has finally left me. I am here, I am safe. I am finally out of my prison. I can relax, if only a little.

Someone touches my shoulder tenderly. I turn my head—finally, a familiar face.

Dr. Hill smiles down at me. "Jade, I need to look in your eyes with my penlight. Is that okay?"

I nod because I can't speak. Light fills my vision. I wince as though it pricked me. It's not like the ethereal light I saw before—this one hurts. He does it again in the other eye.

"Good, good," Dr. Hill says. "You're doing great, Jade."

But I'm not great. I'm actually trembling with fear because to my left, I see a big, burly cop settling Conrad into a folding chair. The guy looks like he's had better days. I guess my attack wasn't deadly, but at least he's where he belongs—in handcuffs. The cop comes lumbering over to me.

"Can you tell us what happened?" he asks.

Dr. Hill doesn't take kindly to the intrusion. "Officer Walker, she's recovering. Please, questions can wait."

Ah, so this is Tommy Boy.

A new person arrives. I only see them from the back—slender shoulders, hair in a bun, in uniform—a female cop, I guess. "We have medical personnel looking after the woman in the tower. But I found a pair of bloody scissors upstairs, under the bed. Someone got stabbed—badly, by the looks of it, but it's not the woman. She doesn't have a mark on her."

"Let me see those," Tommy demands.

I turn to look and there it is, a bloody pair of scissors, sharp as can be, stuffed inside a clear plastic evidence bag, the blades soiled with someone's bodily fluid.

"Who got stabbed?" asks the female cop.

"Probably Conrad," says Tommy. "He's got a neck wound like a viper's bite. Could have been the scissors."

"No," I say weakly. "I stabbed that asshole with a bottle, not scissors."

Tommy perks up. "Yeah? I don't think so. We have two stabbing victims. Seems like the woman was cut by some pretty sharp glass. Are you admitting to injuring her? Maybe trying to kill her?"

A woman? None of this makes sense. I'm so confused, my head aches even more.

"This young girl is in no shape to speak with the police right now," Dr. Hill interjects, placing himself between me and Officer Asshat. "Please hold off on your questions until she's medically cleared at the hospital."

Dr. Hill looks pleased with himself as the cop gives him a defiant stare, but then saunters off obediently in the other direction when the doctor doesn't back down.

"Sorry about that," Dr. Hill says. "Some people have their priorities all wrong. How are you feeling, Jade?" For a moment, the warmth in his voice comforts me. He rolls up his sleeves and reaches to check my IV.

In an instant, my body and mind separate again. Suddenly I'm thrust back in time to when Conrad grabbed me from behind, whipped me over his shoulder, and smashed my head into the doorframe before carrying me down the tower stairs to my wine cellar prison. What I remember most about the attacker was his watch—and I'm seeing that watch again, right here, right now—deep black face under domed crystal, slim gold minute hands, a band with tightly woven links.

I lift my gaze to meet the eyes of the person wearing it. *Dr. Hill.*

It all comes back to me now in a great rush—Baxter's closet, how he kept multiples of the things he loved, and Dr. Hill was into vintage everything. Maeve even let him have the run of the closet before I got involved. Could I have had my attacker all wrong?

He smiles down at me. My eyes flicker back to his watch, then up to him, and something in my expression must change because I see his face fall.

I twitch, reflexively pulling away from his touch. "Was it you?" I ask.

Awareness blossoms in his eyes, and then something new—fear.

"It *was* you," I say.

He backs away from the stretcher.

I lift myself onto my elbows. My chest expands as I breathe in as much air as possible. Then my voice pierces the night, erupting from me like a burst of lava. I shout as loud as I can: "It's him—Dr. Hill. He's the one who took me!"

I point at my attacker.

Dr. Hill doesn't hesitate, not for a second. He takes off running.

I can't move. All I can do is keep screaming as the night swallows him whole.

Chapter 67

Holly

Holly heard Jade's screams, but for a moment, an irrational fear kept her rooted in place. She worried that if she left her sister, even for a second, Anna might vanish and never be seen again.

But it was Anna who encouraged Holly. "Go! Go!" she urged. "Protect Jade. And here, take this." Anna pulled a cold steel blade from her pocket and pressed it into Holly's hand.

Holly gripped the handle hard. She sprang to her feet, turning toward Jade's scream.

"Dr. Hill—he's getting away."

Following Jade's finger, Holly turned just in time to see Dr. Hill heading toward the driveway, where the fountain kept spewing water as if this were just a normal party.

She chased after him. Her legs ached. Shock and stress drained her strength, but Jade's cries fueled her resolve.

Anna's plea did the same. "Protect Jade," she called again.

Holly pieced it together. Dr. Hill had been Jade's abductor, not Conrad. How Jade made the connection didn't matter; she couldn't let him escape. Holly replayed the scuffle in the tower from a different perspective. Had Conrad truly lost it? Was Dr. Hill Elizabeth's hero or her would-be assassin?

The answer was fifty feet away, and the gap was widening. Holly ran awkwardly after him, yelling for anyone's help, for someone to block Hill, slow him down, but crowds that had come up from the beach to observe the commotion froze like deer in headlights.

Mustering every bit of power she had, Holly pushed herself forward, but it was useless. He was too fast. Her lungs burned as her leg muscles tightened. With surprising grace, Holly hurdled a folding chair, wove around a table that Maeve had set out for gift bags, and zigzagged between guests as if they were posts to dodge. Still, the few yards between them felt like miles.

Dr. Hill was almost to the circular driveway. Police and fire trucks took up most of the available parking, but there was room for a fancy antique sports car that appeared to be his chosen destination.

Holly's lungs struggled for air. Her pace slowed. *Damn it.* He was escaping. She cramped at the worst possible moment, her leg seizing up. She couldn't go on. The pain was overwhelming. Her leg buckled beneath her.

The cops didn't understand, didn't know they had to catch him.

In her peripheral vision, Holly saw a figure darting out of the darkness. Conrad. He ran hunched over, hands cuffed behind his back, his head tilted like a battering ram. Was he escaping as well? *Great.* Men were always getting away with something.

But instead of running into the woods, Conrad turned toward Dr. Hill and charged. The angle wasn't ideal, but Conrad's speed was impressive given his injuries. A few seconds before Dr. Hill reached the waiting car in the driveway, Conrad threw himself on the ground in front of his feet.

Dr. Hill's foot caught Conrad in the ribs, and he tumbled over, yelping as he extended his hands to break his fall. He skidded face-first across the driveway's small stones.

Holly caught her second wind. Her leg was still cramping, she couldn't move quickly, but she ignored the pain and pushed herself forward. Conrad had bought her just enough time.

Dr. Hill was just getting back on his feet when she slammed into him from behind. Momentum carried them both over the edge of the fountain. They hit the water together like a cannonball. A geyser of water shot high into the air, turning dark red as Holly drove the blade into his leg.

He took Jade.

He tried to kill her.

My Jade.

Holly lifted the knife. The first time, she'd only wounded him. But this time—

"Holly, no!" It was Conrad's voice, calling her back to her senses.

She paused, her grip on the knife trembling, before forcing herself to release the blade. This wouldn't help Jade or Anna. The steel hit the ground with a clatter, bouncing off the cobblestones around the fountain. Holly slipped sideways into the water.

Dr. Hill flipped over, gasping for breath, and pressed his hands against his bloodied leg. Tommy Boy ran up—finally—huffing and puffing. He grabbed Hill by the shirt, pulled him out of the fountain, and threw him to the ground with authority. Wrenching his arms behind his back, he cuffed him with a zip tie.

"Vernon Hill," he said, still breathing hard. "You are under arrest for kidnapping. You have the right to remain silent . . ."

Holly plopped out of the fountain as Tom Walker finished reading Dr. Hill his rights, and medical personnel—who were certainly being kept busy tonight—came to tend to his wound.

She lay on the smooth stones, soaking wet, her chest heaving as she took in the air and the stars shimmering above.

Conrad, still cuffed, struggled to his feet and slowly made his way back toward the lawn, as if in a daze. He found Anna, collapsing beside her as if he might never move again.

"Anna," he said, resting his head on her shoulder, tears pouring from his eyes. "Anna."

He couldn't say another word, not with the sobs tearing through his trembling body.

The chaos continued to unfold.

The guests who weren't driven by morbid curiosity slipped out of the party one by one. The busker was giving a statement to the police. He seemed to revel in the attention. At last people wanted to hear from him. Tom Walker wanted statements from everyone involved—

especially Maeve, the party's hostess. When Holly heard him asking for her, she realized she hadn't seen Maeve since she observed her talking to Dr. Hill on the beach.

Her son had been stabbed, beaten, and put in handcuffs; her daughter-in-law had been taken from the tower and was receiving medical treatment. Jade and Anna were being loaded into nearby ambulances, though both were stable and out of danger. But where was Maeve? If ever there was a time for a control freak to show up, now would be it.

Holly's eyes darted around, but she didn't see the matriarch anywhere in the crowd. She was about to call out to Ethan when she noticed a tall figure step into the doorway at the top of the stairs leading into Miramar. Light spilled out from inside, outlining the imposing shape. It wasn't Maeve. Sid stood there, as if frozen in place, holding a white envelope in his right hand. Holly hurried over to him. Maeve's most loyal and trusted employee should know where she was.

Ethan joined her at the top of the stairs. Sid appeared to be in shock; his eyes, usually opaque, were even harder to read.

He presented Holly with the envelope. On the outside was written a single word, in black ink, penned in perfect cursive: *Finis.* Attached, where a stamp would usually go, was a sticky note with the same neat handwriting: *Sid, I've gone swimming. Please ensure this letter is delivered appropriately.*

"I also found this on the bed next to the envelope." He handed Holly an empty prescription bottle. The glass vial inside it was empty. She read the label. It was the prescription in Maeve's name for Lypotrel.

Ethan, Holly, and Sid stood together on Maeve's private beach, staring out at the dark sea which appeared to have fused with the night sky.

Gentle waves brushed the shoreline, but the beach itself was a mess. Sand-covered food became a late-night snack for opportunistic birds. The stage had been cleared, but trash was scattered about, and nobody had bothered to right the tipped-over chairs.

The three scanned the darkness for signs of a swimmer, but saw nothing. The only sound was the tide hitting the sand as it came in. Ethan called the Coast Guard on his mobile.

"She loved the ocean," said Sid, his stoic face crumpling. "And this house—oh, how she loved this house."

"They'll find her," said Ethan, who didn't sound hopeful, and Holly knew what he really meant. Eventually the currents would bring her body ashore.

"She's lived a rich, full life," said Sid, his voice melancholy. "It's the sort of life people read about. But now they'll do so in the tabloids."

Holly grasped the envelope Sid had given her, sensing something inside. She could feel its shape with her fingers—a pendant-like form clearly part of a necklace. She read the front again, a single word, *Finis*—Latin for "the end." In eighteenth- and nineteenth-century literature, that word usually ended a novel. Did it also signal an ending to a life?

The ocean waves lapped the shore, the water dark and vast, stretching out before her. Somewhere in its depths was Maeve, who had gone for her final swim.

Chapter 68

From the Desk of Maeve Carmichael Ward

I am of sound mind, but my body is failing. I'm simply hurrying it along. Before I go, I must unburden myself. I don't deserve it, but I hope my family will someday be able to forgive me. It was for them that I made the choices I've come to regret.

Many years ago, to protect my family's wealth and well-being, I decided to get rid of the woman who was interfering with Conrad's marriage to Elizabeth. After my first husband squandered all our money, the Ward fortune was the only thing that would save us. If I had only known that years later, I'd marry Baxter, none of this would have been necessary.

Conrad was misguided, thinking money wasn't as important as love. He didn't understand how hard life could be without it, having always had what he needed at his fingertips.

Firing Anna and banning her from the house didn't keep her from seeing my son. Then I heard the news from Dr. Hill, a loyal family friend, who treated Anna for nausea and determined she was pregnant. I knew my son would never leave her under those circumstances. Which is why I sent Anna a note, inviting her to the guesthouse.

I could mimic my son's handwriting, and I was aware of their lovers' hideaway. Not much happened at Miramar without my knowledge. I set out chocolates and wine to make it look like a romantic evening.

The chocolates were poisoned using a high dose of Lypotrel. The correct amount was easy to determine. Its lethality was just starting to make headlines. And I wasn't concerned about cleaning up the crime scene. Money can make a lot of problems disappear, including an inconvenient body.

Just as I finished injecting the chocolates with the drug, I heard someone at the door. I assumed Anna had arrived early, so I rushed out the back. In my haste, I carelessly left behind the vial of Lypotrel and the prescription bottle it came in.

I don't know how the fire started, but it proved useful, providing the perfect cover for my crime. The gas lines in the guesthouse were old and not up to code. But the gas company report suggested someone might have tampered with the lines—a big red flag for the police that would have merited more investigation. And there was the small matter of the medication containers I had inadvertently left at the scene.

I bribed Allen Spellman, the evidence custodian for the Beauport police department. He removed one of the bottles, which was badly damaged—the other was not recovered. Then he altered the gas company report. The cause of the fire became undetermined. The case went cold.

Our lives continued forward. In his grief, Conrad resigned himself to his loveless marriage. I thought his sadness would fade and he would come to appreciate the wealth and privilege it provided.

But that's not what happened, and I owe a profound apology to Elizabeth Ward as well as to Conrad. She saved my family's legacy and my home, but she did so at a grave cost.

Elizabeth worked in the legal department at Ward Pharma. It was right around the time the controversy over Lypotrel began. She started looking into it and learned about the drug's dangers and the company's cover-up. She also learned the signs of overdose. That's when she had a shocking realization: Her mother had died from the drug her father produced, and he had known all along.

Elizabeth confronted Baxter and planned to blow the whistle on him and the company if he didn't come clean. Baxter never intended to use his daughter as a scapegoat. But when she made threats, he had to take drastic steps to protect himself and his company.

He wouldn't go so far as to kill his daughter, but he would do whatever else it took to silence her. Dr. Hill's license and reputation were also in danger, as he had consulted for Ward Pharma and it was he who altered the manipulated studies at Baxter's request.

This made him eager to help with the cover-up. Together, they drugged

Elizabeth. Chemical restraints were just as effective at silencing her as physical means would have been.

Conrad was fed a steady stream of lies from me, Baxter, and Dr. Hill. He believed what Baxter told him—that Elizabeth had falsified the company documents for profit. That *she* was the architect of the cover-up, and that the stress of the discovery had exacerbated an underlying mental health condition. She had a sudden psychotic episode, a schizophrenic break, the doctor had called it.

For the next fifteen years, Dr. Hill kept Elizabeth in a state of permanent drug-induced delirium, and she took the blame for the company's lethal deceit. By this point Baxter and I were in a relationship—I condoned everything we did to my poor daughter-in-law.

Conrad dedicated himself to caring for Elizabeth, thinking it was the best he could do. He believed our lies. My sweet boy thought he was doing the right thing, not realizing what had been orchestrated behind his back by the people he trusted.

I lived with this guilt for many years. I would have taken my secrets to the grave to protect the Carmichael legacy, had it not been for recent events. You reach an age when you start to see things differently. Back then, I focused on family wealth and status. I still care about those things, but I have come to value my descendants more. A legacy continues through more than just property and bank accounts; it lives on through DNA.

With Elizabeth's poor health and Conrad's grief, I had no grandchildren. Our family name and history would end. I felt partly to blame. And I didn't foresee how this lack of grandchildren would affect me as I neared eighty with a heart condition, facing my own mortality.

I planned this party, a grand fundraiser that would remind the town of the Carmichael status before my heart gave out for good.

But then I learned one final thing . . . and decided this party would serve as my last farewell. *Finis.*

I do not deserve forgiveness for what I have done. But I do ask a favor.

Whoever finds my note, please return the enclosed necklace to my granddaughter, along with my deepest apologies.

Yours in death,

Maeve Carmichael

Chapter 69

Anna

I'm so used to watching, lurking, listening . . . but here I am, trying to be part of life again. After all this time, I get another chance to be connected and authentic, if I can figure out where to start.

I spent years keeping an eye on Holly and my mom. But I always stayed a safe distance away. I braved going to one book talk, but Holly seemed to notice me in the small gathering, and I took off, worried that my dyed hair and hood might not have disguised me well enough.

Life was really rough then. I was practically homeless, floating from one place to the next, living off a small sum my mother transferred to me every month. I squandered most of it on alcohol and drugs. Anything that would dull the pain, help me forget. I wasn't going to burden Holly with all that. Not when she seemed to have moved on, become so successful. I would only have brought her down. Just like I did my mother . . .

Carol's decline was my fault. The stress of everything I put her through caused her to break. We were going to tell my sister everything, but when my mother started failing, I couldn't make the choice on my own. The longer I waited, the more impossible it seemed. Holly was starting to heal. Who was I to needle that wound?

After countless lonely years on the run, I hit rock bottom. It was pure luck that my junkie buddy carried Narcan. My mother didn't sacrifice everything just to have her daughter OD on the street. I'd had enough. The blackouts, the bad relationships—if you can call fucking your dealer a relationship . . . I got cleaned up, got myself to AA, NA, every meeting I could. Eventually I took classes, became a certified nursing assistant. That was the best choice I ever made.

I got a job at the memory care facility where Mom lived. Some days, I know she recognized me. I'd sit with her, stroke her hair, tell her stories like Holly used to do for me when we were young. I was the older sister, but Holly was the storyteller, and her stories soothed me during the ups and downs of childhood. I hoped it did the same for my mom in her last months.

I kept an eye on Holly after Mom died. I knew she was hurting, but she had been for so long. I hoped she would finally move forward, without the burden of my mother's illness and the constant reminders of the past.

But then Holly moved to Beauport, and I knew the danger she was putting herself in.

I did my best, watching from a distance, making sure she didn't do anything that would put her in jeopardy. And then the girl arrived . . . *my Jade.* When I saw the necklace she carried with her everywhere, all the shops she took it to, trying to get it repaired, I knew. I knew the way only a mother knows. And I had to watch over them both.

Now here I sit, with Holly at Crescent Beach. The waves dance on the shoreline, the seagulls caw in the distance. We're sitting up, our legs stretched out on beach towels, a cooler between us, just like when we were kids. But we aren't eating, drinking, or even talking . . . Neither of us knows where to begin.

I glance at my beautiful sister. So many things have changed. Holly has creases around her eyes, same as I do. My hair is still auburn, but I muted the color with cheap dye from a pharmacy so I wouldn't stand out. I'm not the skinny, gangly girl of my youth. I've filled out in my forties, softer curves covering what was once a bony frame. Middle age seems to suit Holly. She's poised, even sitting here on a beach blanket. She carries herself with a confidence and wisdom that only time and experience provide.

The sun is strong, tanning my arms. Maybe it will hide the old track marks, but it will never cover my shame. If Holly has noticed them, she's kind enough not to ask.

What do I tell her? I guess that's what I hope to figure out today. We're sitting in a comfortable silence, letting the waves provide the soundtrack to our day.

It's Holly who speaks first.

"If I remember correctly, the last time we were together on this beach, Conrad invited us for an ice cream."

I surprise myself, laughing out loud at the memory, at how innocent I'd been that day. It's a wry laugh, but Holly brightens. She understands that our lives would have been completely different if we had picked another beach or gone at another time. She touches my arm as if she can't believe that I'm real.

"He did invite us to have an ice cream, didn't he?" I say. My memory of that day is vague, but so many others are painfully clear. The things I did to myself after I left Beauport. How can I ever be whole?

But each minute I spend with Holly takes me farther from my past: the men I knew, the streets, the bars, the addicts I ran with, the highs I chased. These all slowly evaporate as I embrace my new reality. I'm not that person anymore—sleeping in cars, doing things for a fix that make me feel filthy inside and out: unclean, unworthy, unlovable.

Poor Conrad. He didn't understand why I couldn't talk to him—and it's not because his mother wanted me dead. It's because he wants so much from me. He's trying to connect, to process all that's happened. But how can I give him anything when I've already given so much of myself away?

"Do you remember that Ned was working the Dairy Dip that day?" I remind Holly.

"Yeah, I do in fact. And I can't believe I didn't recognize that the busker was that weird kid from the ice-cream shop. And he's Sid's son? Crazy. Beauport really is a small town." Holly shakes her head.

"He was always a little creepy, but he saved me twice, you know."

Holly removes her sunglasses, squinting in confusion. "What do you mean? More than spotting the generator?"

I steady myself. I guess this is it. No more secrets. No more lies.

"When he wasn't at the Dairy Dip, Ned picked up odd jobs at the Carmichaels'—usually landscaping, gardening, that sort of thing," I begin. “He was on the grounds the day that Maeve called the cops on me about the diamond earrings that Krystal stole.”

“Oh yeah, Krystal,” Holly said. “Remember when she wanted to live with us because she got kicked out of her apartment for not paying rent?”

I turn my head away. Hearing her name sends a searing pain through me. But I center myself.

“Tom Walker showed up, took me aside—wanted to talk it over, he said, but he brought me to a secluded spot on the property to conduct his *interview* . . . I should have known better. Ned didn’t trust the cops—didn’t trust anybody who had authority—and I guess he followed us. When he came out of the bushes, Walker had his pants unbuttoned, and—well, you can imagine what he wanted in exchange for the charges being dropped.”

Tears spill down my cheeks. It was so long ago, but telling the story out loud brings all the fear and shame back like it happened yesterday.

Holly looks at me with such compassion I could crack. I deserve nothing from her for what I’ve done.

“Ned saved me. It’s that simple. He begged me to report Walker. He was obsessed with the idea of corruption in law enforcement, and this was a chance to call it out. But I couldn’t tell anyone. Not you, not Mom or Conrad. It was too much. Ned didn’t understand why I stayed silent. He knew that the Beauport PD was protecting Walker, blue covering for blue, and he wanted the truth to come to light. Just like with Conrad. He knew Conrad was lying to me, and he outed him.”

Holly again appeared confused. “What do you mean?” she asked.

So many layers to peel away . . . How Holly will react, I can’t venture to guess.

“Conrad was lying to me from the start. Ned told me so because he had a crush on me and hoped we’d break up.”

“What did he say?”

“The night of Conrad’s engagement party, when we met, Conrad wasn’t just engaged to Elizabeth Ward—he was already married to her.”

Holly gasps. I can’t blame her. I’ve sat with that betrayal for years, and it still feels fresh. “I guess Ned got the inside scoop on the secret wedding from his father, Sidney. The Barefoot Beach Ball engagement party, all that wedding planning? It was just for show. The paperwork had already been signed. It was a done deal. Some financial arrangement between the families. And I found that out the same day I went to see Dr. Hill about my other problem."

I keep it vague. Jade deserves to know the details of her story before anyone else. I owe her that. Thankfully we're sisters. Holly gets me. Instinctively, she doesn't press for more.

"I don't blame Conrad for getting married," I continue. "Maeve was a force of nature. And apparently the pressure was on because they were broke. Ned told me *everything*. Her first husband, Geoffrey, was a gambler who left the Carmichaels house-poor. Their life was an illusion—ritzy on the outside, shambles within."

"Just like Miramar itself," Holly says.

"Elizabeth was the ticket out. She was Conrad's high school sweetheart with a big bank account, daddy issues, and a whole lotta insecurity. Maeve preyed on her. Everything was transactional with her. She could deliver Conrad to Elizabeth, and in exchange, Elizabeth would keep the family afloat. Maeve made her pitch. Conrad didn't stand a chance. Some sons have no power when it comes to their mothers, even with a prenup like the one he signed. No Elizabeth, no money. The mortgage wouldn't wait for a wedding. So they had a quiet civil service—with Maeve's 'blessing,' of course."

"Then you came along," Holly says.

"Yeah, love at first sight," I say sarcastically. "Great until someone wants you dead."

"I still don't understand what happened that night," Holly says, her voice cracking. "I saw your body—I saw you being wheeled away on a gurney with a sheet over your head."

"You saw what I needed everyone to see."

Images from that night at the guesthouse hit me hard and fast. I can't tell her more yet. The tears resurface, overwhelming me. The number of people I've hurt, all to save myself, is staggering.

I see Holly crying, too. Tentatively, I place an arm over her shoulders.

"I'm so, so sorry," I manage to whisper.

“Me too,” she chokes out through her sobs.

“You? What could you possibly be sorry for?”

“It’s my fault,” says Holly, biting her lip, but she can’t stop crying. She takes off her sunglasses to wipe her eyes. “I should have been with you that night like you asked. If I’d only shown up when I said I would, none of this would have happened.”

“No—no, you can’t blame yourself. Believe me when I say the best thing that happened that night is that you *didn’t* show up. Your whole world would have been different if you had. I’m not exaggerating when I say it might have been over. If I could take it back, I would, but you have to understand, Holly. I hated myself for what I had to do to escape.”

Holly looks me in the eyes. Hers are red, filled with tears. “I don’t judge you—I don’t hate you. I just . . .” She can’t get the words out. Her chest is heaving. Every breath is a struggle. But she pushes through the discomfort to find her voice. “I just need my big sister again.”

And that does it. My dam breaks. Tears streak down my face. I wrap my arms around her, holding on like I’ll never let go, a single word tumbling through my head: *home*. This is home . . . this is my place . . . with her . . . my family. My precious sister.

“Will you forgive me? Please, please forgive me.” My throat closes up. I barely get out the words.

“Only if you’ll forgive me,” she says.

And there we are, with our feet in the sand, clutching each other and crying as if it’s a final goodbye.

Eventually we break apart and walk toward the shoreline. I understand something now that I didn’t before. It wasn’t Holly I needed forgiveness from—I needed it from myself. I believe she feels the same. And now we’ve given each other permission to do just that.

“I have something for you,” Holly says, reaching into her pocket. She takes my hand, placing my long-lost claddagh ring into my palm. The gold glints in the sunshine.

“I never thought I’d see this again.” My voice catches as I slide the warm metal onto my ring finger. I can’t believe it still fits—and feels like it belongs—just as it always did.

Holly smiles as we both wipe tears from our sun-kissed cheeks.

It's a perfect afternoon. The summer sun grips the sky as if it will never let go. A scattering of sailboats dots the horizon, moving swiftly thanks to a steady, warm, and pleasing breeze.

"What now?" I ask.

"I want to finish my story," she says. "Will you help me?"

I squeeze her hand. My love for her feels eternal. "Of course I'll help," I say. "I'll tell you everything."

Chapter 70

Holly

New York City, three months later

"True crime? For real, Holly?" Dan scratched his head.

Holly hovered in her agent's posh office on East 51st Street, taking in the view of the Manhattan skyline through the window behind his desk. "You said to try a new genre. So I took your advice. And it's not too far afield from where I've been. There's no apple orchard, but there are tortured sisters, a dark family legacy, and a real-life crime that went unsolved for almost two decades."

Car horns blared outside his window, angry taxi or Uber drivers.

She'd expected to miss it more. Manhattan had colorful umbrellas, same as at the beach, but underneath them, determined food vendors sold roasted peanuts and boiled hot dogs. New York had no shortage of buskers either, but none played as discordantly as Sid's son—the accidental hero of the story. After a few days in New York, catching up with old friends and now meeting with Dan, Holly found herself missing the cottage, the ocean waves, her friends and family in Beauport. The quaint seaside town felt like home again.

"I don't know how you managed to get a completed manuscript to me so quickly. Maybe ocean living has been good for you," he said from his brown leather desk chair.

"My return to Beauport has been nothing short of life-changing. And it's all documented—right here in this book."

Holly held up a stack of white pages she believed was the best thing she'd ever written. She had opted to hand-deliver the manuscript, even though she could have emailed it. But this book was too personal, too important to blast it off into the ether. She wanted to see Dan's reaction. He had promised to read the first few chapters while she sat in his office.

Reading is rarely a spectator sport, but five pages in and Holly could tell he was hooked. She watched him read for a while until it was obvious he wasn't going to be stopping anytime soon, so she went to grab some tea in the building's cafe. When she returned a couple hours later, he was just finishing up, and she could tell he hadn't left his chair once. He glanced up from the pages with a smile on his face as wide as a canyon. "This is all true?"

Holly nodded. "I started it ages ago as a thriller novel, but I was closer to the truth than I realized. Honestly, I've never written anything this fast or easily. The words just poured out of me—and thanks to Officer Finn McNeil from the Beauport PD, I can assure you that I got the procedural parts correct."

Dan's expression turned gloomy. "Do we have permission for this, Holly? The legal ramifications could be immense. A publisher is going to need assurances."

"I got permission from all the parties involved to tell the story using their real names. They're all happy to sign releases too."

How quickly the dark clouds covering Dan's face parted.

"I think the result is a suspenseful, true-to-life page-turner," Holly said.

Dan agreed. He picked up the phone and started calling publishers.

Beach Thriller

vii

Today would be Anna's last day alive, but she didn't know it yet. She had no idea her life was in grave danger.

She had accepted that her sister was a no-show. Holly was unreliable on a good day, but there was no time to dwell. Anna had to end things with Conrad, and it had to happen tonight.

Anna replayed the events in her mind as she trudged up the winding road to Miramar. She had a note in her hand, sent by Conrad, inviting her for a romantic rendezvous at the guesthouse. God, how she wished Holly were with her. She wanted nothing more than to fall into Conrad's arms, to believe all his beautiful lies and promises about their future. But she had to stay strong. She wouldn't give him the chance to draw her in again. She would end it. She wouldn't be the other woman. Especially not now. Being pregnant made her decision seem even more urgent—she wanted to raise her child in a clean, honest life.

She held the stone pendant Conrad had given her as a symbol of his love.

"The jade stone has power. It'll help protect our love."

But it carried extra meaning because of what it wasn't. The necklace wasn't showy; it likely hadn't cost a fortune, and that was the whole point. With one gift, he was telling her their love would be authentic—down-to-earth and real. The sentiment was what gave it value.

Now, as she approached the gate to Miramar, she wondered if anything Conrad had told her was true.

She entered the code Conrad had given her and slipped through the gate, taking a roundabout path to the guesthouse with its breathtaking ocean views. As she crossed the cool grass, she kept repeating her mantra silently: You can do this, you can do this. It was late August, and the sun was beginning to set a little earlier. The air was starting to shift, a crispness setting in, reminding her that autumn was just around the corner.

The guesthouse stood before her, warm light shining from the windows, tempting her with memories of the love and passion she had felt inside. How naive she had been. Tears welled in her eyes as she began to mourn a relationship that hadn't yet ended.

She approached, took a deep breath, and slowly turned the door handle. As she stepped inside, she picked up a strong scent of cinnamon. Conrad had set up their usual candles, which flickered brightly in a corner near the kitchen. On the counter, she noticed an open bottle of wine, two crystal wineglasses, and an assortment of her favorite chocolates. He was expecting a romantic evening and had no idea what she had come here to do.

Anna gently closed the door behind her and took off her light summer jacket, hanging it by the door. She moved around the corner, expecting to see Conrad waiting for her. But what she saw froze her in place.

She felt her knees weaken. She opened her mouth, but no sound came out. Blinking, she tried to clear her vision. The scene in front of her seemed impossible. On the floor, sprawled next to the counter where the wine and chocolates awaited her, was a figure she thought she recognized. She called out quietly, nervously, "Hello . . . Krystal? Krystal, are you okay?"

Krystal didn't move.

Anna stepped closer, peering down at the lifeless figure lying on the kitchen floor. She could see the dead woman's eyes bulging open, gazing up at the ceiling, two glassy windows staring into a void.

Shock and fear erupted in Anna's gut. A scream rose in her throat, but she clamped her hand over her mouth. Krystal, her former coworker had yellow, rotten-smelling foam covering her mouth.

Anna hadn't spoken to Krystal since the day Anna lost her job. She didn't know much about the girl other than that she was now dead. She didn't need to be a nurse to make that determination. But she still forced herself to check for a pulse just in case, cringing as she placed her fingers on the cool, dead skin covering Krystal's carotid artery. Nothing. Anna's world tilted.

What had happened to her? Anna remembered reading somewhere that victims of poisoning often foamed at the mouth. Then she saw it, next to Krystal's hand, on the cold kitchen floor—a half-eaten chocolate.

Anna got up, legs weak, and examined the candies on the tray. They had been arranged in neat rows on a nice platter, but several pieces were missing. Her hands shook violently as she picked up one of the chocolates, using a napkin out of an abundance of caution. She refused to look down, unable to meet Krystal's lifeless eyes again.

Holding a chocolate truffle with a decorative swirl up to her eyes, Anna examined it like a gemstone through a jeweler's loupe. She turned it in her fingers until she saw a tiny pinprick on one side. She gasped.

Anna checked the clock on the gas stove, which was often on the fritz. Conrad should have been here by now. But he wasn't coming. She was sure of it. He was counting on her to get bored, restless—and then hungry. To pop one, two, maybe three chocolates into her mouth while waiting for him. And then she'd be the one on the ground, not Krystal, with rancid froth coating her mouth.

Poor girl. Anna's heart broke for her. It had been about a week since she and Conrad had met at the guesthouse. Had Krystal begun staying here? She remembered how she'd asked Holly for a place to crash. The girl was perpetually living on the edge. Perhaps she'd been fired as well and was broke, homeless, and had nowhere else to go. Hiding in the guesthouse on the Carmichael property would seem like a perfect solution to her troubles. Instead, it was the end of all her problems forever.

Anna used a knife to cut open one of the chocolates. Besides the creamy filling, out spilled a viscous opaque goo. She dropped the blade. When she bent to retrieve it, something shiny caught her eye. A glass vial. The guesthouse wasn't perfectly level, and the small glass container had rolled into a corner of the room. The label was full of small print, mostly indecipherable, but one word stood out to her: *Lypotrel.*

Anna didn't know what Lypotrel was, but she was certain that it must be deadly. She was equally certain the poisoned chocolates had not been intended for Krystal, but for her. Had Conrad lured her here, deciding he'd had enough of her and she'd become inconvenient? Or perhaps Elizabeth, in a jealous rage, had orchestrated this entire scenario, planning to rid herself of Anna once and for all.

Regardless of which Carmichael had done this, Anna knew her life was in danger.

Panicked, she raced back down the long road, leaving Krystal's body untouched, the vial of Lypotrel back where she found it.

Breathless, she reached the beach cottage and snuck inside quietly, waking her mother with urgency. Her face streaked with tears, she told Carol, a nurse, what she had found. They left the house in a rush, Holly, sleeping peacefully, unaware they'd departed, Anna filling her mother in on the details as they raced back to the Miramar. No secrets went untold.

When they arrived at the guesthouse, Carol Sinclair showed little reaction. She had worked in emergency rooms for years and had seen the results of horrible illnesses, accidents, and even violence. Her professionalism kicked into gear, but her grim expression conveyed her dispiriting conclusion.

"We need to call the police," Anna said, but her mother shook her head.

"Someone in this family wants you dead," Carol said. "If they don't kill you, they'll certainly frame you for this girl's murder. Your prints are all over this place, I'm sure."

Anna was stunned. "But I don't have a motive."

"Isn't this the same girl who was stealing from the Carmichaels? And you took the fall for it?"

"That's hardly a motive for murder," Anna said, horrified.

"It doesn't matter how probable a motive is—it just needs to be possible—and with the Carmichaels' money, their power, it will be enough. This was cold, calculating murder. They won't stop until they get you. They'll either send you to jail or finish the job—silencing you for good."

"But what are we going to do?" asked Anna.

Carol thought quickly.

"Will you trust me?" Carol said, gazing deeply into her daughter's eyes. Her voice was confident and calm. "You need to do exactly as I tell you. It won't be easy. It will be the hardest thing you've ever done. But you'll be safe—I promise."

Anna didn't hesitate. "I'll do anything."

Carol gave her daughter's hands a firm squeeze. "Take off your clothes."

Epilogue

Jade

The following summer

Bright sunshine fills the newly constructed patio in the back of the beach cottage. Holly, Anna, Chester, and I have all been living here for the past year. We winterized the screened-in porch and used it as an extra bedroom. Gail's vision for an outside living space was pretty awesome. Ethan did the construction himself—leveling the ground, laying the brick, doing all the edging and plantings. I helped a little. I would have done it for free, but Ethan insisted on paying me.

"Mom, if you're going to the kitchen, could you bring us some lemonade?" I ask.

I'm sitting under the umbrella at a big picnic table with Ethan's daughter, Scarlet, who is the cutest nine-year-old on the planet. Fine, maybe that's an exaggeration, but she's full-on adorable, with her big ponytail, cherubic face, and expressive blue eyes. We have drawing paper and colored pencils. Scarlet loves animals and she's been sketching Chester, who's become her shadow.

Anna, passing by with an empty platter she used to bring Ethan burgers and hot dogs for grilling, gives me a surprised smile. Her eyes well with emotion.

"What?" I ask. "We're thirsty."

"That's the first time you've called me Mom." Her voice catches.

My smile slips out. I shrug, but inside, I'm melting. "Do you like the sound of it? Should I try it out some more? Mom, could you get me a hot dog, too?"

Scarlet joins in. Her voice is tiny but bright. "Mom, could I have one, too?"

We all laugh.

"Could you both say please?" Anna says, her face glowing. She rests her hand gently on my shoulder.

My heart swells at her touch. I often think about what she went through—giving birth to me up in the attic, the same attic that became my hideaway many years later. My grandmother, Carol, acted as her midwife. Carol used her job as a traveling nurse to move between her house—where she and Holly lived—and the beach cottage, secretly caring for her pregnant daughter. And then saying goodbye to me for what she assumed was forever.

After I was born, Grandma Carol took me to the fire station in a nearby town and left me in a Safe Haven baby box like I was a package for UPS. Her only request was that they pass on the necklace Conrad had given my mother as a keepsake, and that whoever adopted me kept my birth name, Jade. My adoptive parents couldn't even do that right. They gave me the name, but not the necklace.

I asked my mother why she insisted I have a necklace that came from the guy she thought tried to kill her. She told me that the jade stone represented protection, and she believed it had kept her safe the night of the fire. That made the story even cooler in my mind. But then I got a little teary when she said it was important to her that part of my origin story—her fairy tale—be with me always.

As for Serena, who suspected my necklace was the same one Conrad had purchased years ago, she had to check her sales records and consult her spirit guides before revealing this sensitive information to Holly. Evidently, those spirit guides don't always respond quickly. I came here because of the necklace, but I didn't tell Holly I was hoping it would lead me to my biological parents. I knew it was part of my history, and I wondered what I'd learn if I traced its origin. Plenty, it turned out.

Thanks to Holly and now my birth mom, I've never felt this open, this connected, this *loved.* And I don't hold a grudge about my adoption.

Adoption is a wonderful way to build a family. I just drew the short stick in the parent pool. It's just luck—for better or worse. Some parents are simply shitty, adoptive or not.

Maeve also knew about the necklace. Conrad told me that his mother had discovered the gift before he gave it to Anna, along with the note he'd written—a promise that they'd always stay together.

Conrad didn't know Anna was pregnant, but Maeve did—and that was the proverbial straw that broke the camel's back and compelled her to commit murder. Never mind the wicked stepmother—Sinister Granny deserves her own movie.

And poor Krystal. Living on the edge. We can only speculate that she was using the guesthouse on Miramar as a temporary residence. What isn't up for debate is that she ate the poisoned chocolates before my mother had the chance. Wrong place, wrong time, tragic ending.

Maeve must have figured out her plan had gone awry the moment I showed her my necklace. She put it together quickly. In addition to recognizing that pendant, it turns out I have eyes like Conrad's. Maeve didn't know who died in that fire, but she must have guessed Anna and I had survived.

I would have perished years later in the wine cellar if my mom hadn't found me. According to the doctors, when Anna opened that door, it provided just enough ventilation to buy me the minutes I needed until Holly showed up.

Anna had been at the Barefoot Beach Ball in disguise. She knew I had disappeared, and fear for my safety finally gave her the courage to confront Maeve and ask about my whereabouts. Dr. Hill had just told Maeve what he had done to me, expecting her to be relieved I was out of commission and no longer a threat. Instead, in a final gesture of redemption, she told my mother where I was and gave her the keys to the wine cellar to save me. I don't think anyone saw her after that. She wrote her letter and took her final swim.

Dr. Hill is trying to cut a deal to save his sorry ass. He confessed to panicking when he overheard my threats to call the police about Elizabeth. Once he took me, he knew he had to get rid of me. He couldn't risk his misdeeds regarding Lypotrel and his drugging of Elizabeth to surface. He'd lose his license and likely go to prison. But he couldn't bring himself to get his hands dirty, so he came up with the less messy idea of using the generator to do me in. He hoped to make it look like an accident—that I locked myself in getting wine for the party and a nearby generator malfunctioned, causing a "tragedy." Takes diabolical to a whole new level. Dr. Death and Sinister Granny—what a pair.

We still can't answer all the questions. We're pretty sure it was Maeve who made the cash offer on the beach cottage. It would make sense that she didn't want the past living so close by, and she certainly had the means. As for the mutilated book, we've reason to believe it was Tommy Boy. Officer Finn has some incriminating surveillance footage of Walker near the house the night the parcel appeared on our doorstep.

Walker is no longer on the force. He's awaiting trial for charges of sexual coercion and rape. After Anna came forward with her story, other victims felt empowered to do the same. There's a long list of charges spanning more than two decades. Some are outside the statute of limitations in Massachusetts, but not all. Walker will likely end up behind bars for a very long time.

And luckily, I kept Rose's business card. Rose had bought the story Dr. Hill was selling about Elizabeth's mental health, so she never found herself in the danger that I did when I threatened to go to the cops.

Holly called the family and we were able to connect the dots: Krystal was Rose's missing sister. After the murder, Anna hadn't known how to reach Krystal's mom, but Carol was able to locate them and set up a monthly bank transaction from the house fund that Spellman had been pilfering from. It was the only thing she could think to do as reparation for hiding Krystal's death. The money was delivered anonymously and untraceably, which explained one set of odd transactions on the account. The other had gone to Anna, so Carol could help support her daughter while she was on the run. When Rose finally learned the truth about what happened to her sister, she and her family were amazingly compassionate. Anna faced charges for improper disposal of a body. Nobody wanted to see that case in court, including the DA, but the law is the law. My mother got probation—three years or something like that—and Krystal's family supported the ruling. Rose finally found closure, as did her ailing mother. It was after her mother had received a cancer diagnosis that she sent Rose to Miramar in a final attempt to learn what happened to her missing daughter. She got the truth shortly before she passed. She blamed Maeve Carmichael far more than Anna, who was a victim in her own right. And she understood that Carol did what most mothers would do—sacrifice everything to protect her child.

Despite their forgiveness, I know my mother will never be completely free from guilt. But carrying shame helps no one.

The most heartbreaking story of all is Elizabeth's. She knew nothing of Maeve's plot. Like everyone else, she believed Anna had died in the explosion. With her rival gone, her life with Conrad moved forward. But then she found herself scapegoated for the Lypotrel scandal.

Elizabeth's guilt—*the blood on her hands*—stemmed from a false belief that she was responsible for the deaths of the Lypotrel victims. Her drug-affected mind was vulnerable to the ongoing gaslighting by Baxter Ward and Dr. Hill, until she accepted their story and blamed herself for her father's wrongdoings. Now that she's off all the medications, her thoughts and memories are clearer. It will be a long journey, but she's on her way to some form of recovery.

And then there's Conrad . . . my father. He wasn't in the tower trying to kill Elizabeth like Holly and Ethan believed—he was trying to save her from Dr. Hill. He became suspicious of the doctor after the sudden increase in Elizabeth's medications, along with my accusations. And he was right. With Baxter dead, Maeve and Dr. Hill decided it was time to get rid of their Elizabeth problem for good.

I grip the stone pendant I've been wearing constantly since I got it back, good as new, from the jeweler. Sometimes I have flashbacks to those frightening hours in the wine cellar.

I should be angry, but honestly, I just feel sad for everyone involved.

Conrad comes over. He overheard me when I finally called Anna "Mom" for the first time.

"You know, I could be Dad," he says hopefully, his dark eyes smiling.

Onyx eyes. I can't believe I didn't notice it before. But in other ways, we have little in common. I'm in ripped jeans and a baggy T-shirt, and he's wearing a polo shirt and khaki pants. But it's what's on his wrist that makes me cringe.

"Let's just stick with Conrad for now. I can't call you Dad until you get rid of that watch." I roll my eyes in that way only teenagers can pull off.

His face gets red. "Oh yeah, for sure," he says. "Sorry about that."

He removes the watch and stuffs it into his pocket. Maeve had allowed Dr. Hill—a collector of vintage items—to take whatever he wanted from Baxter's closet before the items were given away. And given Baxter's habit of owning multiples of things he liked, both Dr. Hill and Conrad ended up with identical watches. It was this odd quirk of Baxter's that allowed me to identify my kidnapper.

Anna arrives with two glasses of lemonade. She brushes Conrad's arm affectionately before heading back into the kitchen, not wanting to interrupt.

"Speaking of Dr. Hill, any word about his trial?" I ask.

Conrad shakes his head. "These things take time. Hill has good lawyers—but trust me, no lawyer or plea deal is keeping him out of prison. You have nothing to worry about." But Conrad doesn't appear to be at ease.

"What is it?"

He grimaces. "One of the things that bothers me most is how it was all so worthless. It was all for money. I should never have married Elizabeth, but I felt so guilty and responsible for taking care of my mother and keeping the Carmichael estate. I should have walked away from everyone except your mom. I loved Anna. I never recovered after I thought she died. I guess . . . I guess I just blame myself for what happened to you."

He doesn't realize he's talking to Jade Jensen 2.0, the new and improved model. This version comes with a lot more wisdom and understanding.

"You were traumatized," I say. "That made you susceptible to all the bullshit that Dr. Hill, Baxter, and Maeve piled on. You believed you were doing the right thing—caring for Elizabeth, following doctor's orders. I don't blame you at all."

Conrad's gaze travels up to the sky. He tilts his head back, probably to keep the tears from spilling out.

"She's nearly made a full recovery, you know. I'm sure the investigators of this Lypotrel nightmare will want to talk to me, and I have to deal with the divorce settlement, too. I just want Elizabeth to be happy—and healthy—again. I'll give her everything I have if it'll give her a fresh start."

"Good for you," I say. "Money is just money. It's people who give our life meaning. You'll find a way to make it all work."

I don't share that Elizabeth and I are in touch. She told me "Clair de Lune" was the song they used for their wedding processional. So much loss. I just hope she'll be able to move forward eventually.

I'm glad to know she's living with relatives in Connecticut while she gets her health and her life back on track. She and Conrad have a complicated dynamic to work through, and the same goes for Conrad and me. He's a good guy who got caught up in some terrible circumstances. And yes, he shouldn't have had an affair, shouldn't have lied to Anna about being married. But I shouldn't have stolen a car, among my other crimes. We all deserve a shot at redemption—except maybe Maeve and Dr. Hill.

Gail bursts onto the patio. She's got her killer red business suit on. She's been hunting. I can see it in her eyes.

"Guess what just sold for *well* above asking," she says in a lilting, singsong voice.

"The house?" Conrad sounds hopeful.

"Sold. It's going to be quite a windfall for you."

She and Conrad share an embrace.

"I'm so excited. I'm ready for a new start. Goodbye to Miramar and good riddance, especially after all that happened there." Conrad shudders.

He and my mom have been reconnecting. They have many years and a lot of pain between them, but I'm hoping they'll eventually find their way back to each other. Conrad wants to stay in Beauport, even after he's out of the mansion, and I believe that's because of me, but also because of my mother.

Serena passes by, her face buried in a copy of *Woof-Woof Well-Being*, the latest smash publication from the author of *Meow Mindfulness*. She peeks over the cover. "I'll tell you what I'm going to do for my own windfall. How about *Canine Consciousness* or *Connect With Your Pet Psychically*?"

"You may need a catchier title," I suggest, and we all laugh.

Holly and Ethan come over, arms wrapped around each other. Scarlet notices, and from her smile, I can tell what she's wishing for.

"You two lovebirds are in luck as well. That cute little three-bed I told you about? The owners will be putting it on the market soon. So get your checkbooks ready."

"Thank goodness for *Beach Thriller*," says Holly.

We're all excited. The publisher's advance was much bigger than any of us expected. The advance reader copies should arrive soon, and there's already movie interest, too. I wonder who will play me? She needs to be a total badass, that's all I can say.

Speaking of badass, I'm in the acknowledgments section of *Beach Thriller*. And not just for being another victim in the story, but for helping solve the case and for editing Holly's second draft. I'm obsessed with writing. I've signed up to take the GED exam, and I plan to study creative writing. But for now, I'm learning from one of the best and connecting with family at the same time. That's the most important part.

After lunch, we all find ourselves on the beach, but Scarlet is the only one playing in the sand. Aunt Holly's phone warbles. Yeah. She's been Aunt Holly since I found out. It's her friend Shae, calling from California.

"Let's take a group photo," Holly tells her. "I'll hold up my phone so you can be in it as well."

Shae has been helping Holly recover the money that Spellman stole. The good news is that Spellman kept various bank accounts, so Holly should get some of it back.

We gather for the photo with the ocean as our backdrop. Aunt Holly puts her arm around me. I rest my head on her shoulder while

Ethan hands his phone to a kind man who volunteers to take our picture.

"I love you," she whispers, squeezing me tight against her.

"I love you, too," I say, and I mean it.

We break apart, and I wander to the shoreline, looking out over the water. It's a beautiful beach day, but I shiver. Maeve Carmichael's body has never been found. Maybe the currents carried her away. But it feels strange. I can feel eyes burning at the back of my neck. I turn around, and no one's there. I've had that feeling a lot lately. Like someone's hiding in the shadows, waiting.

And watching.

Acknowledgments

With everything I do, it's a team effort—and that team starts with my partner in work and in life, Kathleen Miller. She's part of the story from before there are any words on the page to the hard-fought ending, and with it through the final edits to after publication, when we're promoting the work. Without her incredible contributions, Jamie Day would be something else entirely, and for that I'm eternally grateful.

Others have infused their talents into these pages, most notably Clair Lamb, my longtime wordsmith guide, who praises only what is earned, and whose endorsement of this book in its near-final form is a testament to the power of collaboration. Her instincts and talent serve not only the reader, but also this humble writer. Thank you, Clair, always.

Also at the top of my couldn't/wouldn't want to do it without you list is my longtime editor, Jen Enderlin, who believed in Jamie Day from the start, supports my creativity in every way, is patient, kind, but also profoundly creative herself, and deeply perceptive. If you enjoy these books, please send Jen some gratitude, because her brilliance shaped every page.

My supportive agents have been remarkable stewards of my career, and I thank Meg and Rebecca for insights and suggestions that I took to heart, worked into the manuscript, and got a much-improved story as a result.

There were a number of critical readers along the way, whose feedback I value, but none more so than Colleen Rowe-Joyce, Judy Palmer (aka my mom! Go Mom!), Sue Miller, and Greta, our book-loving

Chiweenie, who you can follow on Instagram (@jamiedaybooks) and see her hot takes on what makes a novel work.

But if you've read this far, you should know it really takes a village, and that includes my amazing team of marketers, Brant and Erica especially, the production team at St. Martin's Press who gets the work into stores (thank you, Christina!), and all the sales and design professionals who lend their talent to this work of fiction.

It's a magical thing to create a world from our imagination, but what makes it special, fun, and so worthwhile is doing it with amazing people, and connecting with you, my readers—so from the bottom of my heart, thank you for coming along for the ride.

I literally couldn't do it without you.

Always in gratitude,

Jamie

About the Author

Jamie Day lives in one of those picture-perfect coastal New England towns you see in the movies. And just like the movies, Jamie has two children and an adorable dog to fawn over. When not writing or reading, Jamie enjoys yoga, the ocean, cooking, and long walks on the beach with the dog or the kids, or sometimes both.